Praise for
A Table by the Window

"Food writer Juliette D'Alisa adores her temperamental, trilingual family of restaurateurs, but she could do without their bossy skepticism of her online love interest who's so unlike them. Rainy, windy Portland has never felt quite as warm as it does when Juliette navigates long-distance romance, career decisions, and a genealogical mystery. A delectable tale from Hillary Manton Lodge, *A Table by the Window* includes recipes that are like a warm welcome to the D'Alisa family table."

—MEG MOSELEY, author of *Gone South* and *When Sparrows Fall*

"Warm, witty, and a culinary delight! Hillary Manton Lodge's crisp writing reminds me of a vintage romantic comedy but with contemporary appeal as the story unfolds with perfect pacing and recipes to make you drool. More than once I found myself wishing I had a pastry chef in my own kitchen. Wonderfully romantic in all the best ways!"

—CARLA STEWART, award-winning author of *Chasing Lilacs*
and *Sweet Dreams*

"Not since *Under the Tuscan Sun* have I read a book that I both tasted and felt to such an enchanting degree. Author Hillary Manton Lodge has woven a captivating tale of one woman's quest to discover not only herself, but the truths behind an old-world family legacy. With a touch of whimsy, the perfect helping of romance, and a hearty sprinkle of laugh-out-loud humor, *A Table by the Window* is a delight."

—JOANNE BISCHOF, award-winning author of the Cadence
of Grace series

"An endearing, smart, must-read novel! *A Table by the Window* is a delicious tale that had me slowing down so I could savor it longer. Major props to Hillary

Manton Lodge for not only taking me on a beautiful journey alongside Juliette, but for making a non-foodie like myself want to take up a new hobby."

—KATIE GANSHERT, award-winning author of *Wildflowers from Winter* and *Wishing on Willows*

"Hillary Manton Lodge combines a perfect voice, endearing characters, and delectable recipes into a heart-winning story. *A Table by the Window* hooked me from the first page to the very last word. Bravo, Hillary!"

—LESLIE GOULD, best-selling and Christy Award–winning author

A TABLE *by the* WINDOW

A Novel
of Family Secrets
and Heirloom Recipes

HILLARY MANTON LODGE

WATERBROOK
PRESS

A Table by the Window
Published by WaterBrook Press
12265 Oracle Boulevard, Suite 200
Colorado Springs, Colorado 80921

The Scripture quotation is taken from the King James Version.

The characters and events in this book are fictional, and any resemblance to actual persons or events is coincidental.

Trade Paperback ISBN 978-0-307-73175-3
eBook ISBN 978-0-307-73176-0

Cover design and photography by Kelly L. Howard

Published in the United States by WaterBrook Multnomah, an imprint of the Crown Publishing Group, a division of Random House LLC, New York, a Penguin Random House Company.

WaterBrook and its deer colophon are registered trademarks of Random House LLC.

Library of Congress Cataloging-in-Publication Data
    Lodge, Hillary Manton.
    A table by the window : a novel of family secrets and heirloom recipes / Hillary Manton Lodge.
        pages cm. — (Two blue doors)
    ISBN 978-0-307-73175-3 (pbk.) — ISBN 978-0-307-73176-0 1. Families—Fiction. I. Title.
    PS3612.O335T33 2014
    813'.6—dc23

                                                    2013044117

Printed in the United States of America
2014—First Edition

10 9 8 7 6 5 4 3 2 1

For Danny—I'm glad we clicked.

Life is a combination of magic and pasta.

—FEDERICO FELLINI

I can't believe she left you the prep table," my brother Nico groused as he and my oldest brother, Alex, carried the piece up the stairs to my apartment. "That's a solid French oak cutting service. And that wood inlay? It's unbelievable work. Nice and tall too. Don't have to stoop. I hate that—chopping vegetables and getting a crick in my back. Too young for that. Great storage for knives and tools beneath. They don't make them like this anymore."

"Have you noticed that Nico hasn't said anything about the cameo and pearls?" I asked Alex with a wink.

Alex winked back, adjusting his grip on the table to keep it level.

"Really, Juliette"—Nico fixed me with his sincerest expression—"I'd buy it from you. I'm serious."

"I'm serious about keeping it," I said, keeping my voice light. My second-oldest brother was nothing if not stubborn. "Be careful around that corner."

One last step. "But it's the perfect prep table!"

"I know it's the perfect prep table." I held the door open while my brothers carried the piece inside. "That's why I want to keep it. Watch the back left corner; it's awfully close to the railing."

I breathed a sigh of relief once the table touched down in my kitchen without injuries.

"But I'm a chef!" my brother beseeched, splaying his hands in old-school

Italian style. "I was nominated for a James Beard award—I chop more than you do!"

"First," I began, wishing for a moment that I wasn't dealing with the piquant blend that was our father's Italian persistence and our French mother's stubbornness, "I don't think anyone's going to forget about your nomination anytime soon. Second, I'm not going to argue with you about who chops more," I said, trying to keep my frustration at bay. "I like the table. *Grand-mère* willed me the table. I'm not going to argue with our grandmother's last wishes. *C'est la vie.*"

Nico muttered something unflattering in Italian. Alex and I exchanged glances.

I breathed deep to keep my emotions in check. "I have homemade ice cream in my freezer," I said. "I used my Tahitian vanilla beans. And I still have the lavender caramel sauce I made last week."

As I suspected, my more tempestuous brother thawed by the time I served up the ice cream, complete with caramel sauce and a shortbread cookie for kicks.

My brothers are notoriously easy to placate.

"I'm sorry I was…insensitive about the table," Nico said around a bite of cookie. "I like the table. But you should have it. You were Grand-mère's favorite anyway."

"No, I wasn't," I protested, then took a bite of ice cream myself. "I just saw her more because I worked the register at the patisserie all through high school."

"You were also the one she taught her pastry secrets to," Alex pointed out. "But that's all right."

I shook my head. "She loved all of us. I know she did. I can't…I can't believe she's gone."

Nico lifted his spoon. "This is her ice cream recipe, isn't it?"

"Of course."

"She'd like that." He flipped the spoon over, consumed the contents, and held out the empty utensil. *"Salute!"*

"*Salute,*" Alex and I echoed, clinking spoons together out of respect for ice cream and ice cream makers, past and present.

I gave the prep table a more thorough inspection after my brothers left. It had been in Grand-mère's kitchen for as long as I could remember; I used to perch beneath it as a child.

Having it in my own kitchen was bittersweet and unsettling all at once. I could be jocular with my brothers about it, but on the inside I was still heartsick from the loss. Two months had passed since she had succumbed to a stroke. Most of the grief had subsided, but a familiar ache had taken residence in my heart.

While Grand-mère had certainly been getting on in years, her death took my family by surprise. Though her estate had always been well organized legally, none of us were emotionally prepared to deal with what she had left behind: a small but profitable bakery, the apartment above, and an extraordinarily fluffy bichon frise named Gigi.

The bakery had closed and its employees quickly hired elsewhere—no one trained pastry chefs like Grand-mère. Gigi now resided with my parents, and the prep table resided with me. I redirected my focus to the table. The cutting board was four inches thick, with a spacious three-by-four-foot work surface. Half of it was oak, the other half an inset slab of marble, perfect for making pastry or candy.

After our *grand-père* passed away in 1976, Grand-mère left France and moved to Portland to be near my parents—they had, after all, created Sophie, the first grandchild. But rather than live out her golden years wrapped up in the lives of her offspring, Grand-mère opened a bakery—La Petite Chouquette—in an old house on the edge of Portland's Pearl District. The name of the bakery roughly translated to "The Little Pastry Puff," in reference to the small, round pastries that were used in profiteroles and croquembouches.

I knew the prep table was one of the pieces Grand-mère had brought from France. She'd used it in her apartment kitchen—I remembered her rolling out slab after slab of pâte brisée over its surface.

There were two drawers beneath the cutting board on either side of the table; strong legs curved into a flat base with two more deep drawers. Casters on the bottom allowed the table to roll, though it took effort. The piece was very, very heavy.

For a moment, I felt guilty for keeping the table. After all, I was the sibling who went to culinary school, got scared off by the realities of a commercial kitchen where I wasn't related to half of the staff, and hightailed it into restaurant management before migrating into food writing. I certainly spent a fair amount of time in the kitchen, but Nico was right—he cooked more.

But I remembered Grand-mère teaching me to use a chef's knife, how many turns to give croissant dough for maximum flakiness, how to pipe a crème anglaise filling into a *chouquette*. No, there were too many memories, too many afternoons spent bent over that table for me to be able to part with it.

Besides, Nico had inherited Grand-mère's Alsatian earthenware, as well as her copper cookware.

I pulled my thoughts away from my brother and back toward the table. The drawers were still full; inside, I found an egg timer shaped like the Arc de Triomphe, a wooden-handled French herb chopper, an assortment of keys, embroidered tea towels, cheesecloths, and a set of seven linen napkins, yellowed but intact.

So many memories.

The last drawer, however, stuck when I tried to pull it open, no matter how hard I tugged at the faceted glass knob. Curiosity got the better of me, so I reached for my metal spatula and wedged it with care into the crevices around the drawer, loosening whatever age and dust held it in place. With another sharp yank, the drawer released instantly, nearly clattering to the floor.

Inside there was a thin blue cookbook, written in French, and thirty or so recipe cards scattered at the bottom of the drawer.

The book I instantly recognized as Grand-mère's favorite—the one she referred to when she couldn't remember an ingredient or measurement from a classic recipe. I cast a longing glance at the cards. There wasn't time to look at them, not really. Not with the two articles for the newspaper I had due.

The recipes would wait. Lunch break over, I gathered my things and readied myself to get back to work, grabbing at the last moment the choker-length strand of Grand-mère's pearls from my dresser.

With her table in my kitchen and pearls against my skin, she felt just a little bit closer than before.

Marti's phone call woke me up the next morning. She was wondering if I could bring in some bagel samples from the new bakery that opened in the Hawthorne District.

I lived thirty minutes and a bridge crossing from Portland's trendy Hawthorne neighborhood in the southeast, but the fact that I'd be at least an hour late to the office would matter less than the necessary job of bagel testing. The fact that one of the other staff writers, Sam, lived much closer likely hadn't occurred to Marti, but I wasn't about to attempt negotiations.

Marti was my editor. She kept spices in her desk—some of them under lock and key—and a full-sized fridge in her office. Every restaurant manager within the Portland metro area knew what she looked like and how she liked her steak cooked. At five feet one, one hundred and ten pounds, she was the sort of force people went out of their way to please.

Working in the food department meant that every day was a Marti party—if the woman wanted bagels, bagels she would have. If she wanted to do a full-page spread on Ethiopian cuisine, we would learn everything about it, as fast as we could. Life at the paper, under Marti, could be fun. It could also be a little dizzying, if not frustrating. But for every one writer on staff, there were another twenty freelancers and journalism interns vying for one of the positions in the Food and Dining section. More than that, I owed Marti for seeking me out and giving me a direction when I couldn't find a place within my beloved restaurant business.

She was the one who'd followed my food blog and suggested a column, which had later turned into a staff writing position with just enough benefits and vacation time to earn the title. She was the one who had passed on a cookbook ghostwriting job, which had turned into a somewhat reliable part-time job. Against the odds, I'd carved a strange little niche for myself, and leaving it all behind wasn't in my immediate future.

Restaurants may have been my first love, but that didn't mean we were meant to be.

Marti chased out my mental wanderings when I arrived at work. "Bagels!" She clapped her hands together as if I'd just brought her a surprise. "What was the shop like?"

"Like a bakery in the Hawthorne District—handcrafted goods, upcycled furniture and décor, filled with people far more hip than me."

She lifted a bagel from the bag and sniffed it. "Thoughts on staying power?"

"Judging from the bagels alone, two years. The ciabatta looked good—"

"Nobody's cared about ciabatta for five years."

"True. The place was nice, but maybe not as special as I'd hoped for. It didn't take me by surprise."

"I hear that. Let me try a bagel." She picked one out of the bag and sniffed it, then closed her eyes and took a bite. She chewed for a brief moment before her eyes widened and then narrowed. "What was that?"

"The bakery special."

"Well, the bakery special's especially...spirited. I need a drink." She shivered. "Nasty. What else have you got in there? I need to whitewash my palate."

"Orange poppy seed and sweet potato."

"Give them to me," she said, holding out her hand. "There's nowhere to go but up. Speaking of, about your molasses article—I need more schmaltz. I want Grandma's kitchen with a hint of mothball nostalgia." She checked her watch. "Can you get the piece to me in a couple hours?"

"Of course," I said, as I tried to reconcile mothballs and molasses in my head.

"And Tenth Street Bistro just changed chefs."

"I heard. Lunch tomorrow?"

"I'm meeting with the higher-ups, but you and Linn can make a trip of it. Where are you with the organic farming piece?"

"Almost ready. One more interview should fill it out."

"Until then, make me hungry!"

My mind continued to work over the mothball and molasses issue. Over the years, I'd become skilled at giving Marti whatever spin she wanted, even if it wasn't my own vision for the piece. As I walked back to my desk, I reminded myself that I had a paying job as a food writer, a position about as difficult to land as prima ballerina in a paying dance company. I swallowed my pride and conjured up all the fuzzy joy I could from a white-sugar by-product. Gingerbread? Maybe gingerbread was key—everybody loves the idea of it, even if they don't actually eat it.

After my day had finished and I'd satisfied Marti's schmaltz craving, I packed up my things and left for home. Winds from the gorge pounded rain against my windshield. Portland, Oregon, was not famous for its good weather. Even with the spring equinox technically around the corner, there was no weather-related hope in sight.

A week before, local scientists had been wringing their hands over the season's lack of rainfall. But in my twenty-eight years in Portland, I knew my city was plenty capable of producing enough precipitation to make up for lost time.

As much as I craved a giant pot of tea in my apartment, I stopped by my mailbox first. Inside I found the usual suspects—catalogs, bills, promotions. A reminder that my lease would be up in two months. A coupon from Sur La

Table. I thumbed a suspicious square envelope made of heavy linen paper tucked among them.

Safe in my kitchen, I opened the envelope.

I shouldn't have felt bullied by the piece of paper on my table, but there it was. A save-the-date card from an old college friend. A glance at the calendar told me I was free.

Dang.

I didn't mean that. Not really. Of course I wanted to celebrate my friend's happiness. Just like I celebrated the happiness of so many others—including my sisters, Sophie and Caterina. At two years shy of thirty, I was old hat at celebrating other people's happiness.

Before she passed, my grandmother would pat my hand and tell me that someday I would meet the right young man and that I should hold on to him with my whole heart. She'd always said it like that, from the time I worked her register with my pink and yellow braces until I was an adult at Caterina's wedding. My whole heart. For years I waited, believing that my grandmother's prediction would prove true, and for a little while, I thought it might. I was still young—barely twenty-three at the time. Nico had his own restaurant, and I was bursting with ideas for him about marketing and décor and menu. Nico, five years older, had no intention of listening to his baby sister, even if I'd successfully rebranded and revitalized three other restaurants belonging to family friends. Instead, he wanted me to keep quiet and manage the front of the house.

Nico's sous-chef and best friend, Éric, however, had listened. Originally from Morocco and seven years my senior, Éric was too old for me at the time, but I didn't care. He was handsome and talented, spoke beautiful French, and liked what I had to say about his food.

He took me to restaurants all over Portland, delighting in introducing me to all kinds of foreign cuisine. We ate pho and curry, octopus and tagine, sashimi and sopaipillas. I gained five pounds, and I'd never been happier.

Of course it couldn't last.

No man I'd met since Éric had ever measured up, whether it was to Éric himself or my memory of him. Our relationship ended four winters ago, but its echoes still resonated in my personal life.

Or lack of a personal life—echoes are the loudest in empty spaces.

I tucked the save-the-date card away and with it my own feelings of regret. Instead, I busied myself with dinner preparations. In one pot, I set the red pepper sauce to reheat gently. I filled a second pot with water, threw in some sea salt, and had just placed it on the burner when my cell phone rang.

"Etta, ya got a minute?"

I wedged the phone between my shoulder and ear while opening my pantry to look for pasta. "For you, Nico, I might even have two. What's going on?"

"Are you home?"

"Yes…"

"Can I come over?"

"Are you going to explain why you're being evasive?"

"Tell you in a minute," Nico said, just as my doorbell rang.

~ RED PEPPER PASTA ~

1 lb pasta of choice (I like campanelle and farfalle at the moment)
4 red peppers
1 large shallot
2 to 3 cloves garlic
Crème fraîche
Heavy cream (optional)
Red pepper flakes
Some sugar
Some salt

Some milk

Grated parmesan cheese (pecorino works too)

Fresh arugula, for garnish

Note: This recipe is not particularly...precise. But we're not baking here. It's okay to make things the way you want them in a sauce like this.

Roast the peppers. This can take a bit, so have handy a book or your phone or your child or something. You can use an oven, placing the peppers on a baking sheet covered with foil and placing them under the broiler, top rack of the oven. A hot grill works too. Once the tops get nice and blackened, turn the peppers and repeat until they're completely black and blistered. Using tongs, place the peppers in a Ziploc bag and let them sweat for a while. You can alternatively place them in a bowl and cover the bowl with plastic wrap.

While the peppers are sweating, chop the shallot and garlic. In a medium saucepan, heat some olive oil over medium heat. Add the shallot and garlic. Throw in a pinch or two of red pepper flakes—if you like things spicier, use more. Sauté until the shallot is golden but not dry. Remove from heat.

Pull out your blender. Slip the blackened skins off the peppers and scoop out the seeds; don't worry about having little tiny bits of charred pepper skin in there—it's good for flavor. Stick your finished peppers in your blender. Add the shallot and garlic mixture and purée.

When the mixture is quite smooth, transfer it back to the saucepan. To get every bit of sauce from the blender, add about ¼ cup of milk to the blender, swirl it around, and pour the liquid into the pot. Add a couple of dollops of crème fraîche. Add some heavy cream (or don't, if you prefer). Stir, and bring sauce to a gentle simmer.

Taste it. At this point, I added some salt and about $1/2$ teaspoon or so of sugar to bring out the sweetness of the peppers. Maybe even a whole teaspoon. Not a lot, but enough.

Let it sit on the burner on low while you cook the pasta.

Rinse and drain the pasta, and add to the red pepper sauce. Stir to combine. Serve with grated cheese and snipped arugula over the top. You could also put some extra crème fraîche on the top, if you're not afraid of the extra calories.

Serves 6

All you need is love. But a little chocolate now and
then doesn't hurt.

—CHARLES M. SCHULZ

The sound of the doorbell resonated inside my apartment.

I massaged the bridge of my nose. "Please don't tell me you're
outside."

"I'm outside" came the answer, both from the phone and from the other
side of my door.

Oh brother, my brother. "If you're thinking you dodged the family's flair
for drama," I said, as I opened the door, "think again."

"I would never suggest such a thing," he said, standing in my doorway
with a briefcase in one hand and a brown paper bag in the other, which he
handed to me. "For you. For your collection."

I reached inside the bag. It was a small jar of grayish-red crystals. "Is
this…"

"I had a friend pick it up for me in New York."

"Come in. I want to take a closer look at this stuff."

I made a beeline for the kitchen, and Nico followed behind. Under the
bright kitchen lights, I examined the contents of the jar. Inside there was
Amethyst Bamboo Salt, one of the rarest, most expensive salts in the world.
The crystals were shaped irregularly and smelled both sweet and smoky, like a
campfire for s'mores.

"Thank you," I said, still poking at the salt with my fingers. "But my birthday isn't for a while longer. What's this about?"

"Can we sit down?"

I hesitated. "I've got pasta water on the stove. Do you mind standing in the kitchen?"

"Don't use your new salt in your pasta water."

I moved the jar protectively away from him. "I'm not going to dignify that with a response."

He took a seat on one of the kitchen stools. I added campanelle pasta to the boiling water and gave it an absent stir.

"I've been thinking," he began, leaning forward.

With Nico, that could mean anything. "What have you been thinking about?"

"It's been a while since L'uccello Blu closed."

I put the spoon down. "If a while means four years, then yes," I said, trying to tamp back the stinging sensation of old guilt.

"I wish it hadn't ended the way it did, with Éric leaving like that. He was more than a sous-chef; he was a good friend."

"I know." After Éric left the restaurant, the kitchen never regained its balance. Nico's dishes were brilliant, but his support staff lost their footing. Service became uneven, and the business suffered. While some less expensive eateries can survive being a hit-and-miss experience, L'uccello Blu was haute cuisine. The restaurant could only comp so many plates of cold, late food. Online reviews ranged from nostalgia over the restaurant's former glory, while others chronicled the many ways they'd been disappointed by their dining experience.

Discouraged, Nico closed the doors of L'uccello Blu four months later.

"I've learned a lot since then," Nico continued. "Working with Dad at D'Alisa & Elle was a good experience, even if it wasn't what I wanted at the time. And then there's the James Beard award."

"Really?" I teased him. "I hadn't heard." The nomination had come about after Nico had taken on an executive chef position. Dad had, I think, been both proud and a little jealous, but masked the latter well. After all, with Dad, Nico had learned to balance his extravagant tastes with good sense.

And yet, if Éric had stayed at L'uccello Blu, maybe Nico still would have learned those lessons in his own kitchen. We'd never know.

"I want to open a new restaurant," Nico said, his voice quieter but resolute. "I've learned a lot. I'm ready."

"That's great, Nico. I'm really happy for you. You want me to smooth it over with Mom and Dad? After the nomination, they're probably expecting it."

"We haven't talked about it directly."

"But you've talked about it indirectly?" I teased with faux innocence. "What did you say? 'So, Dad, how would you feel about it if, hypothetically speaking of course, I left Elle and opened a new restaurant?'"

"Would you shut up a second?"

I smirked and elbowed my brother in the ribs. "Sorry—got carried away in the fun there."

"What I wanted to know is if you would go in on it with me."

"I don't think I heard you correctly. Would you mind rephrasing?"

"I want you to manage the front-of-the-house operations, like before. Except, this time I would listen to you."

My mouth dropped open as my mind tried to comprehend the idea. "How long have you been thinking about this?"

"A while."

"Oh." After so many years, the chance to work at a restaurant again was tempting. I would be lying if I said I wasn't interested. "You've got to know I'm useless to you as an investor."

"As an investor, yes. But you have contacts. People love you and they trust you. And if you opened a restaurant, they would trust that restaurant."

"So...I'm Queen Elizabeth, the figurehead—and you're Parliament?"

"No. I just know the food. You know the business."

"You grew up in the business too. And you actually had one."

"But this was your thing, remember? And you were good at it," Nico pointed out. "And with your work at the newspaper, you know even better what elements matter to diners, beyond the menu."

I didn't let my face betray my thoughts. I thought I was done with the restaurant business forever. Now the tables had turned in a way I'd never expected. I waved a hand, trying to stay casual. "I write about restaurants, but the business—it's been a while, Nico."

"You were always intuitive about what would work and what wouldn't. That hasn't changed. You can tell which restaurants have staying power and which ones will go under. That last place...what was it?"

"Bando."

Nico nodded encouragingly. "You said they wouldn't make it a year, and they closed in eight months."

"Too much overhead, too much money spent on monogrammed everything, and mediocre food." I shrugged. "It didn't take a genius."

"Maybe not, but you knew better than they did."

"It was an educated guess." I moved from the stove.

"Where are you going?"

"Colander. You're awfully twitchy—keep talking."

He shrugged. "You know what a restaurant should look like, what makes a good server, and how not to waste money where it doesn't belong."

"Brand-new kitchen equipment and an overgrown wine list."

"See?"

"So..." I carried the pasta pot to the sink and dumped the boiling contents into the colander. "Explain to me how all of this will come to fruition. None of this is cheap, you know."

"After the nominations were released, I got a call from Frank Burrows."

My eyebrows flew upward. "Really?" I had met Frank a few times—he owned and invested in several of the more successful restaurants around town. "What did he say?"

"He said that he'd be willing to invest if I decided to strike out on my own again."

"Awards are magical things."

"I told him yes." Nico cleared his throat. "But on the condition that you would manage."

I set the colander down harder than anticipated. "I could manage it? You told him that?"

"Well..."

"Nico!"

"What?" His fingers splayed defensively in front of him. "My apologies. But he seemed to get really excited about it."

"In your perfect little world, the one you presented to Frank Burrows, what am I doing?"

"You're managing the restaurant."

"No, I mean..." I exhaled hard. Nico's skull could be so thick sometimes. "Am I still working at the paper? Am I still a critic? Have I been having problems with potential conflicts of interest? Am I using my talents to put together our PR materials?"

"Good idea."

"Nico!"

"What? You like working at the paper?"

My mouth opened and closed a few times. "You were ready to change my career without consulting me?"

He shrugged. "It's not the career you're supposed to have, and we both know it. And I knew that if you didn't want to, you wouldn't be afraid to tell me off."

That was true, at least. "How much thought have you put into this?"

"I think we could do this," he said, his voice sincere. "I think it could be grand."

I ran a hand over my face. "I'm not going to jump in blind. I'm going to have to spend some time in thought. And prayer, Nico. Lots of prayer."

"I have projections and ideas," he said, diving into his briefcase.

"Fine. Just leave them on the coffee table."

"Enjoy your salt," he said.

I waved good-bye, my heart too overwhelmed for speech.

I couldn't sleep and it was Nico's fault.

And mine.

Honestly, opening a restaurant was up there with the "Hey, there's an empty barn so let's put on a show!" mentality. It may have worked for Mickey Rooney and Judy Garland, but we were grownups, Nico and I. At least I was. The economy was difficult, the stakes high. Putting an existing newspaper career at risk was crazy.

It wasn't as though I *loved* my job. I liked it fine. But I knew in my heart that running a restaurant had always been my dream. When I was little, I didn't play house with my friends—we played restaurant. I liked food writing. But love? Deep love? Writing for print wasn't a walk in the park, despite the illusions of some. There were deadlines and edits and a lot of combined right- and left-brain function, and the inevitable hurt feelings when I had to write a less than glowing review.

Like the rest of my siblings, I'd grown up at the restaurant, washing dishes, busing tables, hostessing, waitressing. I idolized my mother, my grandmother, and my sister Caterina and the food they created. But all it took was my first internship during culinary school to teach me that cooking outside my father's kitchen was a completely different experience. Outside his kitchen, I discovered what a real working kitchen was like and what it was like to be the one everyone picked on.

Some people thrive on that kind of pressure, but I discovered quickly that I wasn't one of them.

Discouraged but still trying to stay within the industry, I decided to study business at the University of Oregon. After graduation, I helped my father keep the books, freshened up the restaurant's logo, and focused the branding. His friend, another restaurant owner, hired me on to do the same for his place. I was cheap labor, fresh from school, but I had good ideas that tended to be received well. One job led to another, and when Nico offered me a position at his new restaurant, I accepted gladly.

The idea seemed exciting at the time, until I realized Nico wasn't ready to listen to his kid sister.

And then after Éric and the closing of L'uccello Blu, I backed away from the more creative work, sticking to paying suppliers and staff. I was both heartbroken and bored, but the bookkeeping paid my bills. In the evenings, I continued to experiment with food the way I had with Éric. I ate, and then I blogged. And because of my ties to the industry, I snagged the attention of Marti.

The rest was its own kind of history.

Was I restless, or was it time for me to go back to the business? And was it fair to want change when food-writing jobs were so difficult to come by?

Either way, it wasn't helping me sleep, not that I'd slept well of late.

What would Grand-mère have thought? Writing for the paper hadn't made a lot of sense to her—though she understood it more than blogging. Would she be glad to see me going back to restaurant work?

I glanced at the clock: 1:26 a.m. I'd been sleeping poorly since Grand-mère passed, but this new dilemma was only making it worse. I thumped my head deeper into my feather pillow, balled my fists, and threw an entirely ineffective tantrum.

Rather than lie in bed feeling sorry for myself, I threw back the covers, planted my feet on the floor, and did what I did most nights—headed for the kitchen.

Some nights I cooked. Others I baked. Tonight, I saw my new salt on the countertop and decided to put it away, so I opened up my pantry to examine the untidiness within.

It didn't disappoint.

The truth was, some people collected antiques; others, pig figurines. Me? I had a thing for dry goods.

Strangely shaped artisan pasta. Heirloom beans. Exotic rice varietals. Multi-colored salts. Spices from around the world. I was a sucker for all of it, and the stranger the better. And while the rest of my apartment was clean enough for polite society, my pantry looked like something from an episode of *Hoarders*.

I tried not to collect for collecting's sake, and I strove to use all the ingredients in a timely fashion. But I'd become so busy at work that my pantry had grown to resemble an elitist food bank. Even my family found it a little nuts. And civilians? I usually chose to draw a veil of discretion over that particular hobby.

Behind one oversized cupboard door, boxes of pasta were piled haphazardly in one section, crowding the spice rack. Farfalle, campanelle, rigatoni, cavatappi, linguine, gemelli, orecchiette. I had to wonder, at what point was it appropriate to step back and admit a pasta problem? Oh, and there was a bag of organic penne hiding in the back.

In another cupboard I kept my tidy packages of heirloom beans and rice varietals; some dried red corn cowered in the back corner. I pulled out the containers and began to alphabetize them, fully aware that I was taking the mess inside my pantry and making it much, much worse.

I organized the pastas from acini di pepe to gemelli before I closed the cupboard, backed away, and turned my attention to my grandmother's worktable.

My apartment kitchen could barely accommodate the addition, but I would have found a place for it even if it hadn't. Grand-mère had been gone for only a couple of months. And while we could tell ourselves that at ninety-six we couldn't expect her to stay with us forever, it felt as though after conquering nearly a hundred years on earth, shouldn't she be able to conquer another hundred?

But in the end, she was gone, and none of us were ready.

With a heart full of memories, I turned my attention back to the table and the contents of its drawers. I re-sorted the kitchen tools I'd examined previously, separating the ones I'd use from the ones I'd store elsewhere. Still full of energy, I moved on to the linen drawer.

I filled a large glass bowl with warm water and oxygen bleach and set the linens to soak, knowing they'd return to a truer white after an overnight bath and a spin in the washing machine.

I opened the last drawer and paused. With a deep breath, I scooped the recipe cards and cookbook out of their drawer and carried them on a tea tray to the living room.

Thinking Marti might like a series on family recipes, I sorted through the recipe cards, selecting the ones that our readers would be interested in— soufflés, tarts, *gougères,* galettes, crepes—things that would be accessible to my West Coast readers.

I skipped over the squab recipes. The angry letters from local ornithologists? I could do without them.

The cookbook was well used, with splatters of various sauces and broths marking the pages. There were notes in Grand-mère's tiny handwriting, all of them in very precise French, *naturellement.*

I looked at the clock.

Three thirty in the morning. With a frustrated sigh, I picked up the phone and called Nico.

He picked up. "It's late," he said, "or early. I'm not sure which. What's wrong?"

"I can't sleep," I said, sitting up in my armchair and crossing my legs. "Your restaurant idea. Your fault. So, tell me—what kind of restaurant were you thinking?"

"The kind where people sleep. It's innovative that way."

My head tilted in exasperated doubt. "You didn't have any specific plans?"

"Of course I have specific plans. I have too many plans—that's why I need you."

"There's market research to be done and menus to be designed. We'll have to hire a graphic designer and get a billion permits from the city. It's not just me hanging up curtains in the front and you whipping up a bunch of pasta in the back."

"Of course I know that. Stop being a brat."

"Sorry."

"So you're in?"

I squared my shoulders. "I'm thinking about it."

"Listen, stop worrying. We'll do all the market research your heart desires. Frank's got friends in city council; he's done this a half dozen times. We can hire a graphic designer, but Alex is handy with that kind of stuff these days."

I shook my head. "You can ask, but Alex has his hands full."

"I'll take that into consideration. Anyway, I figured that we'll probably do a bit more than pasta if we're doing a dinner place."

"What are you thinking?"

"Something intimate, with its own personality. Not as formal as L'uccello Blu. I have too many ideas, honestly, but that's something we can talk about. Would you agree to a meeting with me and Frank? We'll throw some ideas around."

"I don't know. It might be too soon to bring him into the planning process. Any planning process."

"But," Nico countered, "if he's in it from the ground up, he'll feel more involved and will stay interested."

"Do you remember when Sophie and Nelson were engaged? Sophie kept asking Nelson's opinions on the wedding planning to keep him involved. He told her she could have whatever she wanted, but that wasn't enough for Sophie—"

"And this relates how?" Nico interrupted.

"Hear me out. Sophie persisted until Nelson cracked, and lo and behold discovered that he didn't actually want to register for the Kate Spade dishes and wanted the wedding colors to be red and brown rather than red and yellow. They nearly came to blows. Or at least Sophie almost did. Nelson doesn't have the genetic predisposition for violence."

"Why don't I remember this?"

"No idea. But there's a moral to the story: don't ask for input unless you're willing to receive it."

"Point taken. I still think it's a good idea."

"Fine."

"Fine," said Nico, satisfied now that he'd gotten his way.

"I'm going to sleep now. Night!" I hit the End button on my phone and, just in case Nico was feeling vengeful, powered it off.

I decided to make a mug of warm vanilla milk. As I stirred the milk on the stove, my thoughts landed again on Grand-mère's cookbook.

I fingered through the pages while I sipped my milk, adding a couple more recipes to the ones I thought the paper would find useful. Satisfied that I had plenty of material, I slipped the dust jacket off so I could take the book to work without worrying about potential damage.

As I removed the fragile paper, something caught my eye.

There was a photo. An old, faded photo attached with paste, it seemed, to the inside of the dust jacket. It was a portrait of a man, ordinary enough, but his face, with its strong chin and dark brows, took me completely by surprise.

With a sharp knife, I carefully separated the photo from the dust jacket. Once it was free, I flipped the photo over to see if there were any dates or inscriptions on the back and found nothing.

The photo was old, no doubt about it. The book itself was dated 1936. It was my grandmother's cookbook—I knew that for sure. I had many memories of her referring to it when she was in the middle of making something throughout my childhood.

The man in the photo wasn't my grandfather—my grandfather was fair, whereas the man in the photo was dark. My mind swirled with confusion. Why had the photo been hidden in such a strange place?

He had to be significant, whoever he was. Because not only had Grand-mère kept his photo all these years, but the man in the photo looked exactly like my brother Nico.

After a good dinner, one can forgive anybody, even one's relatives.

—OSCAR WILDE

*T*hroughout my life, I'd faced many confusing situations, but nothing had prepared me for that photo. Obviously, it had to have held some sentimental value for my grandmother or she wouldn't have felt the need to keep it. From the light stains and gentle fraying around the edges, it had been handled often.

The fellow had to be family. The particular, difficult arch of Nico's eyebrow, the dimple on the right cheek—he and Nico couldn't *not* share genes.

I knew about my grandfather, but this man had obviously been a part of my grandmother's life as well.

Was he a great-uncle I'd never heard about? a second cousin? The resemblance to Nico was so striking I found myself studying the image for differences and found few. Maybe the hairline was a little different, but with Nico's shaggier hairstyle, it was hard to say.

Or perhaps...it could have been a very different relationship. He could have been a lover.

If that was true, there were two possibilities I could figure out. Either she met him before her marriage, which meant there was a chapter of her life that perhaps the rest of the family knew but had never shared with me, or Grandmère had been involved with him after her marriage, which meant she'd had an affair.

That wasn't an uncommon happening in France—or anywhere, for that matter—but that didn't make it easier to think about.

If this man was related to Nico, it meant he was related to me. And my mother.

And no matter who he was, there had to be a story in it somewhere.

The next morning, I called my second-oldest sister, Caterina, on my way to work.

When she wasn't chasing after her boys or maintaining a meaningful relationship with her husband, Damian, Caterina taught an Italian language and cuisine program that she'd built from the ground up. Her classes were in high demand among foodies in the Chicago area; heaven knew she was busy, but I knew she'd take my call if she could and call me back if she couldn't.

"Jules! I'm missing you terribly this morning," she said when she answered her cell phone. "And not just because the boys' nanny didn't show up and I am completely behind on work. I still have to review the curriculum for this month's series, never mind the menus."

"Sorry about that. I'd come and play hide-and-seek with the boys if I could get there in a reasonable amount of time. How's registration?"

"Always hopping, my dear. Always hopping. I'm glad I like my job, because otherwise I'd go crazy."

I couldn't help but grin. Cat's twin boys were three years old and high spirited in a way that surprised none of us—Cat's childhood high jinks were some of my mother's favorite stories during family gatherings.

"If you need someone to bounce ideas off of, I'm a phone call away," I told her. "Hey, listen—I found a photo inside Grand-mère's prep table."

"Oh, I forgot you got that table. If I had room for it, I'd consider stealing it from you."

"You'd have to get in line behind Nico. Anyway, I found this photo, and I was wondering who it might be. It's a man," I said, trying to choose my words carefully. "And he looks like family. Did she have a brother or something?"

"No brothers, as far as I know. I know Great-grandpa Bessette really wanted a son and there was a bit of trickiness for a while over who would inherit the château. What does the guy in the photo look like?"

I waited for a bicyclist to choose his path before driving through the intersection. "Honestly, Cat? He looks like an old-world version of Nico." I didn't tell her just how unnerving the resemblance felt to me.

"Oh, really?" Caterina paused and considered that tidbit. "That's interesting. Most of Grand-mère's family were pretty fair. I've always assumed the darker coloring that you, Nico, and I inherited came from Dad's side of the family. When in doubt, blame those swarthy Italians, you know?"

"I always think of the Provençal French being a bit darker, themselves."

"Usually, yes, but not Grand-mère's family. She told me once that her blond hair was one of the reasons she was considered a famous beauty."

"I remember that now," I said, as three skateboarders glided past my front fender.

"Not that she couldn't have a secret dark-haired brother. Look at us—Alex and Sophie are plenty blond. Sophie didn't have hair on her head until she was almost two. Her baby pictures are hysterical… Listen, I've got to jet, but good luck with the genealogy stuff."

"Thanks. And good luck with your curriculum."

"I'll get it figured out," Cat said. "I always do."

We both hung up, and after an admirable job parallel parking, I spent a moment envying my sister's life. It wasn't perfect—she and Damian had been through the wringer of fertility treatments before they conceived the boys. But they struggled forward, and they did it together. Damian supported Caterina's work one hundred percent, and I respected him for that.

Most of all, I admired the way Cat had decided what she wanted to do and pursued it, undaunted. Had I somehow missed that gene?

With the question of genetics and Nico's restaurant fighting for elbowroom in my thoughts, finding my own work groove required more mental discipline than usual.

My coworkers were not helping.

Whitney from Metro tracked me down moments after I arrived, panic in her eyes.

"Juliette, can I get your advice?"

I turned away from my computer. "What do you need?"

Whitney lowered herself to the extra chair in my cubicle, practically shaking. "I'm throwing a dinner party Saturday—haven't had one since my kid was born."

"I didn't know you had a little one."

"He's five."

Not so little anymore. "Okay. How many people?"

"Six, including myself and my husband."

I tapped my fingers on the desk. "Dietary restrictions?"

"Excuse me?"

"Anyone with food allergies? Any vegans or diabetics?"

"No—all carnivores and healthy, as far as I know."

"And how formal do you want everything to be?"

"Put together, but relaxed."

"Well, you can go lots of ways. Baked pasta—lasagna, baked ziti, that sort of thing—is easy to serve to a group. But if you serve pasta, you'll want to include a vegetable side dish—or two—and a bread, as well as a dessert. Something light. Enchiladas are good too, but you'll need to serve rice, beans, and salad. And you don't want to forget the condiments." I ticked them off on my fingertips. "Fresh salsa, guacamole, sour cream, that kind of thing."

I watched Whitney's face tighten with panic.

"Or really simple, just make up a big batch of chili," I said, trying to think of the simplest possible solution. "You can make it with or without meat, dress it up with a couple kinds of beans. I like using navy and black beans." Whitney's eyebrows began to unpinch, so I continued. "Throw in a chipotle pepper or ancho chili and add some cocoa powder to the traditional spices—"

The frown returned. "But I don't *have* to do that, do I?"

"Want me to write up a quick recipe for you?"

"Would you?"

"Sure." I pulled a three-by-five-inch card from my desk drawer and jotted down ingredients. "The best thing about chili is that it only needs to be accompanied by corn bread."

"Really?"

"And if you make it in a slow cooker, you can start it before work and let it cook all day. You get home and it's done. Doesn't get much easier."

Whitney nodded. "Corn bread." She brightened. "I could use a mix!"

I nodded, secretly horrified but relieved to see her look so happy.

Whitney left, and I thought that was the end of it.

But it wasn't. On Thursday, Jake from Obits wandered to my desk, wondering what to cook to impress a dinner date. Later that morning, Sonia needed a killer chocolate dessert to offset her mother-in-law's menopausal behavior.

By eleven thirty, Marti called me into her office.

"You've been popular lately."

"Yeah, sorry—I'll finish the Earthbound Organics piece by two, definitely."

"Don't worry about it; it just got me thinking. Whitney practically went all over the building singing your praises."

I smiled and felt myself relax. "Did she really?"

Marti leaned back in her chair. "You know, I think there's a renewed interest in event planning. I'm not thinking canapé events—just casual dinner parties. I think…I think there could be a market waiting for a 'keep-your-pants-on' approach to social gathering cuisine. Something approachable, by somebody who drinks a normal amount of coffee and recommends boxed corn bread."

I held up a hand. "For the record, I did *not* recommend boxed corn bread."

"I think there's serious potential here. The traffic at your desk has tripled."

"I also brought in a plate of *fleur de sel* caramels. That might account for some of it."

"Say we put your regular column on hiatus for a bit. Instead, what if we tried a series? You provide a complete dinner-party menu, all the shortcuts included. We'll try it for—I don't know—two to three weeks and see what happens."

"You know I don't do shortcuts, right?" If anything, I tended to annoy my friends with my recommendations to make tortillas by hand and spent a day per month making stock.

"Corn-bread mix isn't so bad."

I wanted to argue that some mixes had very metallic aftertastes from the rising agent, but clearly, Marti wasn't going to budge. "I'll give it a whirl," I conceded. I could make it work, couldn't I?

At five minutes past noon, a small wad of paper flew past my face and landed on my desk. I uncrinkled it and read the note, scrawled in pencil. *Lunch today?*

"I'm right here," I told Linn, not even bothering to raise my voice.

"Come on," she said, her voice barely muffled by the cubicle wall between us. "I've heard passing notes is a time-honored tradition; I just missed out on it when it was age appropriate."

"These days, I think the kids text."

We left for the food trucks moments later. There was a new Korean food cart I'd been wanting to try, and Linn was more than game. "Asian food is hard," she told me during the walk. "I'm always curious to see how a chef balances traditional tastes with Western palates."

She would know—Linn's mother was Chinese, her father Irish American. We'd met once I started on staff at the paper and instantly bonded over our love of food and diverse family cultures. Whereas I'd grown up steeped in traditional European foods and the gospel of Carême's four mother sauces, Linn learned Chinese cuisine from her mother and a fearless appetite from her father.

Linn inherited the best attributes from each parent—her mother's delicate Asian features and her father's long limbs. She wore her smooth ebony hair in a closely cropped pixie cut, which was both practical and chic in a way that made me rethink my own longer hair about once a week.

Linn's Intel-employed husband tended to occupy her evenings, but lunch was my territory. Our friendship thrived happily on discovering new and delicious places to share a midday meal.

"So what's the deal with this new column Marti's got you working on?" Linn asked as we walked through a light Portland drizzle.

I described the basic concept as we sidestepped puddles.

"It could be fine," Linn said, her voice neutral. "But I'm worried she's trying to turn you into some kind of semi-homemade Sandra Lee or Rachael Ray. They each have their own place in the world, but it's not really your thing."

"No. But it might be fine if it's mostly entertaining. I enjoy a good dinner party as much as the next person."

"Or more. But you're hard core when it comes to cooking from scratch. You make your own crème fraîche like a grandmother in the old country. I don't want to sound snotty, but I don't know how you find the time."

"It helps to be single," I answered ruefully. "And to be fair, I haven't slept well since Grand-mère passed. It's a good time to make tart crust."

"If you didn't use your powers for good rather than evil, we couldn't be friends," Linn pointed out. "I hope you know that."

"Oh yes."

"I hope you find a man soon. I'll feel better when you eat Trader Joe's freezer foods like the rest of us," Linn said as we waited for traffic to pass before crossing the street.

Three more seconds and we strode across. "I like their chicken marsala as much as the next girl."

"That's good news," Linn said with an approving nod. "So—men? What's stopping you?"

"I go out," I said, feeling the defensiveness creep into my voice. "But either they know what I do and they set out to impress me with their love of squid ink—"

"That would be off-putting," Linn agreed gamely as a bicyclist swerved around us. "Unless squid ink is your thing."

"Or they don't know, and they get really nervous, and we don't make it to date two. I've been set up, I've been speed dating...I don't know. I just haven't met someone really interesting, who thought I was interesting back."

"Does he have to be a food guy? Because some food guys are really fussy."

I grinned at her. "And we're not?"

"It's less attractive in a man."

"Well, if I could make it past three dates, I might be able to tell you."

"Fine. So what's this about you not sleeping?"

I shrugged. "You know. Things have been crazy."

Linn nodded; she was a good enough friend and a skilled enough journalist to read between the lines. "I understand. You'll call me if you need to?"

"Of course," I said, though I suspected I never would. Not because Linn wasn't great, but because the last thing I'd want to do at four o'clock in the morning was make someone else as sleepless as me. "Hey, look," I said, eager to shift the subject, "the line's not that long at the Korean cart!"

Linn clapped her hands, partly from the spring chill and partly out of excitement.

We ordered our *bibimbap* bowls full of vegetables, rice, egg, and beef and carried the paper bags close as we speed walked back to the office.

"Hey, everybody, I'm home!" I yelled as I opened the door to my parents' house on Sunday evening.

Gigi the bichon frise came running, but my twelve-year-old niece ran faster, wrapping her arms around me in an oxygen-depriving hug.

"Chloé, I need to breathe, darlin'," I said, patting my niece on the back. "Are your mom and dad here?"

She loosened her hold around my neck. "Sorry. I just haven't seen you in so long! Why haven't you visited lately?"

Direct and to the point, with a splash of guilt—something she'd learned at the feet of masters. I tried to loosen her grip a bit more, just enough to allow air. "Work. Sorry—it's been busy lately."

"We need to go have an aunt date. Aunt Cat's still in Chicago, so you're my only aunt, and my mom's been *totally* crazy lately. Oops," she said, covering her mouth. "I shouldn't have said that since she's your sister. They're not here yet, anyway. Grandma and I had kitchen lessons today."

"I see." I bent over to pet Gigi. "I was just talking to Caterina today—she asked after you, so know you're not forgotten. But we'll try to fit an aunt-niece day for the two of us sometime soon, okay?"

She shrugged. "Okay. Want to see my blog? I redesigned it."

"Sure." I allowed Chloé to pull me into the living room.

We passed my oldest brother in the hallway. "Hi, Alex!" I slung a quick arm around his shoulders.

"Hey," he answered, giving me a *thwack* on the back, smiling. "Been a while."

With Alex's divorce now six months in the past, his facial expressions had shifted from constantly wary to occasionally happy—I cherished that smile.

"*Giulietta? Giulietta* is here?" I could hear my father gaining on us.

I checked out the perimeter of the room. "Is Nico here yet?"

Alex snorted. "It's too quiet—can't you tell? Last time, I could hear him from my place," he pointed his thumb in the direction of his apartment over the garage.

"Good point." I turned my attention to Chloé, who had settled into a chaise near the fireplace with her laptop. "I like the layout! Very bohemian."

Chloé beamed. "Thank you. I totally made the background myself in Photoshop."

"You did a beautiful job." I looked over my shoulder. "Dad, what did Mom make for dinner?"

"*Gigot de sept heures,* and it smells like perfection... Do not tell your mother, but I may have added two more cloves when she was turned around."

"I won't say a word," I assured him, mainly because my mother might feel the need to start from scratch.

My dad threw his arm around my shoulder as we walked back down the hall. "When are you going to meet a nice man, Etta? Someone with the energy for the restaurant business. Someone like Nico."

Like that wouldn't be awkward. "I don't know, Dad," I said, mentally fumbling for an appropriate answer when the front door opened to reveal Nico, Sophie, and Nelson.

An accounts manager at Nike, Nelson seldom raised his voice, became emotional, or exhibited enthusiasm of any kind.

My own temperament was less fiery than Nico's or Caterina's, and Alex could be self-contained when he wanted to be, but Nelson was a whole other brand of stoic. We didn't much know what to do with him. I tried not to view their marriage as a cautionary tale, myself. But Sophie married him; he was family, whether he wanted to be or not.

Alex's marriage had run the opposite way—his ex-wife, Stephanie, had been tempestuous and hot tempered, leaving their marriage after four rocky years. The fact that my oldest two siblings had married at the opposite ends of the drama spectrum hadn't gone unnoticed. Of my married and formerly married siblings, Caterina seemed the happiest. Marriage, on the whole, remained an elusive mystery to me.

The clamor at the front door brought me back to the moment.

"I have the wine!" Nico announced, lifting the bottle in the air as if he'd just conquered the Western world.

I hoped for his sake he'd brought a Beaujolais instead of a Sangiovese.

Mom hadn't been happy when Sophie brought a Chianti to go with the cassoulet.

"How are you two?" I asked, greeting Sophie with a hug before giving Nelson one as well.

"Great," said Sophie. "We're buying a new car. A crossover SUV. More room."

"Sounds, um"—I seldom knew how to respond to Sophie—"fun. Nelson, are you excited about that extra room?"

"Yes. Sure." His head bobbed up and down.

"Are you just going to ignore me?" Nico demanded, pretending to be standoffish before picking me up in a hug. "Have you thought any more about my offer for the prep table?"

I looked at him blankly, once again struck by his resemblance to the man in the photo.

The photo itself practically burned a hole inside my bag; I half expected an errant family member to sift through my purse's contents and find it.

Maybe it wasn't an issue. Maybe it wouldn't rock anyone's world. But Grand-mère hadn't been gone very long. I didn't know the polite length of time to wait before asking the rest of the family if they knew of any excommunicated family members or former flames. For now, I would hold my tongue.

"The table?" Nico reminded me, bringing me back into the present.

"You're selling the prep table to Nico?" Sophie put her hands on her hips. "You should have told me. I would buy it from you; it's such a great statement piece." Gigi tried to greet her, but Sophie shooed her away with the wave of a hand. "I can't believe you didn't offer it to me too."

"I didn't offer it to anybody," I said, intent on staying composed. "Like I said before, Grand-mère willed me the table. I like the table. I'm keeping the table. End of story."

"You don't have to get upset about it," Sophie said huffily.

"I'm not upset!" I fired back, despite my attempts to retain my serenity.

Attempt failed.

"Alex?" my mother's voice cut through the bickering. *"Venez préparer la table. Est-ce que j'entends la voix de ma Juliette?"*

Sophie rolled her eyes. "English, Mom, please. Nelson is here."

My mother walked out of the kitchen looking more elegant than any woman holding a dishtowel had a right to. I noticed signs of stress—losing her mother had added new lines to her eyes and shadows in her face. For the first time, she almost looked her seventy-two years. Her expression revealed nothing, though she appeared a bit more tired than usual. "Sophie, I wasn't speaking to Nelson, was I? And he should learn French. Honestly. You've been married fifteen years. I learned English—"

"Maman!" I cut in before we could get into a linguistics disagreement.

Having a trilingual family can be high maintenance sometimes.

Or all the time.

"Juliette! Ma petite fille! Comment t'allez-vous?" She proceeded to kiss me on both cheeks, pat my hair, and go through the rounds of French motherly attentions, the better to make sure I was fed, groomed, and loved.

"Everyone!" she said, finally switching to English and addressing the crowd. "There is a creamy leek soup, a frisée and fennel salad with lime vinaigrette, *gigot de sept heures,* and a fig tart with crème fraîche for dessert. Someone go get Chloé—it's time to eat."

We all took our seats in the long, spacious dining room. Alex passed plates around, while my mother updated us on our sister Caterina's latest escapade in Chicago. As we dove into the hearty lamb stew, the conversation turned to Grand-mère.

"Have you decided what to do with the bakery?" Sophie asked, verbalizing the question none of us had dared to pose.

The chatter stilled.

My mother took a small bite of the lamb, chewed, and swallowed. "Your grand-mère willed it to your father and me, as you know. I have started to clean the apartment. The patisserie—I have not yet decided, but I will have to decide soon."

"You'd earn a fortune leasing it," Sophie noted.

I looked at her sharply, as did Alex and Nico.

"What? It's true," she protested, holding up her hands. "Don't look at me like that. You were all thinking it."

My father placed his hand over my mother's. "We will tell you all about our decision once we have made it. Until then, do not allow the business to distract you from your own affairs."

I pressed my lips together to suppress a smile. My father wasn't usually so diplomatic, but I had a suspicion he was as worried about my mother as I was.

I lifted my wineglass. "To La Petite Chouquette," I said. "No matter what the future brings."

We clinked glasses all around and returned to the familiar, easy dinner-table chatter. I watched as Nico asked Nelson about his thoughts on the euro, Sophie aired her concerns about triglycerides, Alex ribbed Chloé about a boy at school, and my father slipped a bit of lamb to the dog. I felt the familiar blanket of loneliness wrap around my unwilling shoulders, even as I heard the currents and eddies of conversation swirl around me.

Nonetheless, I straightened the napkin over my lap and continued to eat my dinner with a pasted-on smile.

After dinner I said my good-byes, then turned my Alfa in the direction of my apartment complex.

My temperamental Italian car often raised eyebrows from car aficionados. Granted, it wouldn't have been my first choice. But my father had a deep love for Alfa Romeos, and Alex enjoyed tinkering with the ones in the family's fleet. In a way, it was the perfect hobby, since each car required a reliable amount of tinkering. I'd inherited my own car from Cat when she moved to Chicago, keeping it over the years in an effort to avoid car payments.

The car made it home without incident. At my apartment complex, exterior lights cast a yellowish glow on the steps to my door. I slid the key into the lock and let myself in. This was my home, dark and silent.

I flipped a few lights on, my shoes off, and settled on the sofa with my laptop. I'd spent the last four years telling myself that maybe tomorrow was the day someone new would walk into my life. I was finally acknowledging that this person in my head—the person who wasn't intimidated by my job or family—wasn't going to appear in the life I'm living. Not like this.

I had two choices: I could sit at home, feeling sorry for myself, or I could do something about it. I could try yet another singles mixer. But I liked the little privacy I had, and the microcosmic nature of the restaurant industry didn't lend itself to the keeping of secrets. With online dating, however, at least I wouldn't necessarily have to use my real name. My family wouldn't have to know.

The old-world part of me had hoped for the moment when I'd see a man across a crowded room and *know* that he was someone special.

The truth was, Éric wasn't coming back, and after four years, I still hadn't had a proper rebound relationship, much less found a life partner.

When I was young and Grand-mère taught me to make croissants, I remember her telling me to find a man who could respect my mind and the things I could make with my hands.

I owed it to her to try.

~ SEVEN-HOUR LEG OF LAMB ~

For the lamb:

1 4-pound shank-end leg of lamb or a 4-pound piece of shoulder, trimmed

3 tablespoons extra-virgin olive oil

Kosher salt and freshly ground black pepper, to taste

1 bottle dry white wine

2 bulbs garlic, unpeeled and sliced in half through the widest part

10 sprigs each fresh rosemary, thyme, and savory

5 fresh or dried bay leaves

For the beans:

2 cups dried white beans, preferably cannellini, soaked overnight in water

5 cloves garlic, smashed

3 sprigs fresh thyme and parsley and a bay leaf tied together with kitchen twine

10 whole cloves

1 large onion, halved

Kosher salt and freshly ground black pepper, to taste

2 tablespoons extra-virgin olive oil

2 tablespoons crème fraîche

Preheat oven to 300°F. Dry the lamb with paper towels and rub with oil; season with plenty of salt and pepper. Heat a 6-quart dutch oven over medium-high heat. Add lamb and cook, turning occasionally, until browned on all sides, about 12 minutes. Transfer lamb to a plate. Add wine and 2 cups water to the dutch oven; scrape up browned bits from bottom of pot. Nestle garlic and herbs in a large oval casserole dish; place lamb on top of herbs; add wine mixture from dutch oven. Cover lamb with tinfoil; transfer to oven and roast, basting frequently, for $3^1/_2$ hours. Uncover, flip lamb (a pair of tongs and a wooden spatula is good for this), and continue to cook, basting frequently, until lamb is very tender, 3 to $3^1/_2$ more hours. Transfer to a rack and allow to rest for 20 minutes.

Meanwhile, prepare the beans. About $1^1/_2$ hours before the lamb is done, drain beans and transfer to a 4-quart saucepan along with 6 cups water, 4 cloves garlic, and the herb bundle. Insert the cloves into the onion and add to the pot. Bring to a boil, reduce heat to low, cover, and simmer until beans are tender, about 1 hour. Remove pot from heat. Season the beans with salt and pepper.

Discard herbs and strain beans, reserving cooking liquid. Transfer 2 cups beans, $^1/_4$ cup cooking liquid, oil, crème fraîche, and one of the garlic cloves to a blender and purée. Stir puréed bean mixture and about 1 cup of the cooking liquid back into pot and cover to keep warm until lamb is cooked. Check seasonings again, adding salt and pepper as necessary.

Serve the lamb sliced or torn into rough chunks, alongside the beans. Best when eaten in good company.

Serves 6 to 8.

4

There are two kinds of people in the world. Those who love chocolate, and communists.

—LESLIE MOAK MURRAY

*T*he conversation over dinner the previous night inspired me to invite Maman to lunch and light shopping the following Tuesday. I knew Maman tended to keep a busy social calendar, but was pleased when she agreed to meet me on Northwest Twenty-Third.

We were close, but not in the traditional American mother-and-daughter sense. I was aware, growing up, that my mother was different from my classmates' moms.

She worked, for one, and not as a nurse or a teacher or a bank teller, but as a pastry chef. In the mornings while she worked—she'd be at work at five—my sisters supervised my exodus to school. In the afternoons, Maman would be home and we'd have adventures. We attended museums, walked through gardens. She took me to nice restaurants, where I was expected to behave in a civilized fashion.

I was the baby of the family, which my siblings reminded me of constantly, Sophie in particular. "When I was your age," she'd say, "I took care of myself and I lived at the restaurant."

By the time I showed up, though, the restaurant had been a success for multiple years and life had become more stable. Maman had time to do things with us in the afternoons, rather than work in the pastry kitchen in the morning and manage the front of the house in the evenings.

Unlike my classmates' moms, my mother had style. She wore silk, good jewelry, and high heels. She'd sooner die than wear a themed sweater, unless the theme was "nautical stripe." She never complained about finding jeans that fit, partly because she had most of her clothes tailored anyway.

And if I hadn't already figured out that my mother was different, once or twice a month, she would excuse herself, sit out on the patio, and have long phone conversations in French with her cousin Sandrine, while smoking a single cigarette.

After the loss of Grand-mère, though, shadows had appeared beneath her eyes. The phone calls to Sandrine—recently sans the cigarette—had increased.

That Tuesday we met in front of LeLa's Bistro. "You are so sweet, *ma biche*," Maman said when she saw me. "You know how I love Vietnamese."

Maman ordered the pork meatball *bánh mì*, and I ordered the lemongrass chicken bánh mì, with an order of shrimp salad rolls to share.

"People forget about the French and the Vietnamese, sometimes," she told me as we waited. "The French brought their baguettes, and the Vietnamese used them to make bánh mì sandwiches. And then the French came home with a love for Vietnamese chicken soup deep in their souls."

"There are perks to imperialism," I noted. "How are things with Grand-mère's estate these days?"

Maman peered at me. "Are you worrying about me?"

I gave a small smile. "Maybe a little."

"You must stop that, you know. I am fine. I will die one day. Prepare yourself. I didn't, and look where it got me."

"I think grieving is normal," I said, dunking my salad roll into peanut sauce.

Maman lifted a shoulder. "I think I may visit a *psychologue*, just for a little while. But until then, everything is fine. Her estate was very neatly prepared. I sent some jewelry last week to your *tante* Margueritte. She sent me a nice note back." Maman gave an approving nod. "She was brought up well. And as for the patisserie, *je ne sais pas.* I hate to leave it there, but I hate to sell it or lease it to strangers."

My ears perked up. "Oh?"

"I hate to leave it empty, but it is difficult to clean out. *C'est la vie.* I cannot have it all."

"I'm happy to help with the cleaning."

We both leaned back as our sandwiches arrived. *"Ah, bon.* You are such a good girl," she said. "And these? These are very good sandwiches. We should give them our full attention." Maman patted my hand. "Death is a part of life, *ma fille.* Let us not worry overmuch."

A part of me had hoped that Marti would forget about my new column. But when I returned from lunch with my mother to find a half-dozen e-mails from her on the subject, I knew it wasn't meant to be. Marti's mind had set to work, and now she wanted my input.

From: Marti, sohelm@theoregonian.com
To: Juliette, dalisaj@theoregonian.com
Subject: Column

Thinking about your new column. What do you think for your first entry? Upscale southwestern cuisine? Or pull more from your French/Italian roots?

Discuss?

From: Marti, sohelm@theoregonian.com
To: Juliette, dalisaj@theoregonian.com
Subject: Column

Some updated French might be nice, especially in light of the renewed interest in Julia Child. Just a thought. Maybe a lighter, northwest take on French fare?

From: Marti, sohelm@theoregonian.com
To: Juliette, dalisaj@theoregonian.com
Subject: Column

Or is Julia Child too much of a cliché at this point? I'm going with yes.

From: Marti, sohelm@theoregonian.com
To: Juliette, dalisaj@theoregonian.com
Subject: Column

Waffling on the Julia issue. She did write an enduring cook-book, which is more than can be said of the "celebrity chefs" who populate the Food Network. I hate the Food Network.

I resisted the urge to smack my forehead against my monitor.

From: Marti, sohelm@theoregonian.com
To: Juliette, dalisaj@theoregonian.com
Subject: Column

Except Bobby Flay. He is kind of cute.

After reading the last e-mail, I took two minutes to breathe deeply and then hit the Reply button.

From: Juliette, dalisaj@theoregonian.com
To: Marti, sohelm@theoregonian.com

Subject: Re: Column

How about family comfort food? I found a collection of my grandmother's recipes in a table I inherited. How does a Saturday brunch menu sound—or instructions for a crepe party?

We could include a recipe for savory crepes, which are usually made from buckwheat. With the popularity of whole grains of late, might be a nice spin.

I hit Send and hoped that my suggestions would appeal to Marti. E-mail taken care of, I made myself a cup of MarketSpice tea in the test kitchen. I watched the tea steep—the water growing darker and darker—not realizing until the last moment that I really couldn't wait to be home, working on the restaurant that wasn't.

I spent the next few hours working as quickly and efficiently as possible. Once I'd accomplished all I'd set out to do, I shut down my computer, said my good-byes, and headed to the grocery store—my day was far from over.

"It's really great of you to do this, Etta," Nico said as he folded the cloth napkins into elaborate fan shapes and nestled them inside the wineglasses.

"One meeting," I answered, tightening my apron around my waist. "One meeting with Frank Burrows. That's all I'm committing to."

"You should have let me cook."

"You're not the only one who went to culinary school. Besides, I needed to test the recipes before handing in the piece to Marti."

"I never thought I'd say this, but there's too much food here. Are you sure you weren't stress cooking?"

"Me?" I arranged my features into their best imitation of serenity. "I'm not stressed. Not stressed at all. No stress here."

"That's good."

Perception has never been Nico's strong suit.

For the meeting, I'd laid out a wide variety of fillings and sauces on the table, with the sauces in my antique chafing dishes to stay warm. And it was true—there was a lot of food. I'd provided prosciutto, roasted red peppers, toasted walnuts, fig preserves, and a cheese sauce made with fontina. The savory ingredients were intended for the brown-butter buckwheat crepes.

For dessert, I'd provided sweet crepes made with my grandmother's recipe. Antique china bowls containing Nutella, sweetened mascarpone, lemon curd, and sliced fresh fruit fought for space on the table.

The crepe I was most proud of, though, was my stracciatella crepe. In a nod to the gelato flavor, I'd attacked the chocolate bar with my trusty Microplane zester and incorporated it as a last ingredient in my chilled crepe batter.

Nico reached for one of the stracciatella crepes and tore off a corner. "These are really good. Texture's perfect. Just the right amount of chocolate. You haven't lost your touch, you know."

"Thanks."

"I'm actually a little mad I didn't come up with them myself."

I shrugged. "You probably would have at some point."

"You should have been a chef. You're more creative than I am."

A dozen responses soared through my head. "It's not for me," I answered simply enough.

"Do you think you'd be able to leave the newspaper?"

"I don't know yet," I said, filling the crystal pitcher with ice water. "We'll see."

A knock sounded at the door. Nico stood up straighter. "You'll keep an open mind?"

"If you make me say 'I'm thinking about it' one more time, I'm going to go medieval on your copper cookware."

Nico winked at me but said nothing as he moved to open the door.

I untied my apron and smoothed my bangs, pasting a smile onto my face as Frank Burrows came into view.

"Juliette D'Alisa!" his voice boomed when he saw me. "Great to see you. How's Marti these days?"

"Well fed, as always," I answered, shaking his hand. "She's a great lady."

"That she is. Tough, but good. Did I see you last month at the winemaker's dinner with Jim Haberman?"

"I was there, so you must have. That was a wonderful night—I still think about those pinot truffles they served for dessert."

"Well, this," he said, eyes wide over the spread on the dining room table, "looks incredible."

"That's very generous of you. Please, take a plate. We'll be experimenting today, and the best compositions will go into my new column series."

Over the next few moments, I did what I did best—hostess. I explained the crepe ingredients and assembly, and made sure the bottles of Pinot Noir and Auxerrois were close at hand, as well as the water and espresso.

The crepes were assembled, various combinations attempted. We made small talk as I photographed the best results. When we were all full, we moved to the living room with our beverages.

"If we do decide to move forward with a restaurant," Frank said, "those stracciatella crepes have to be on the menu."

Nico nodded and sipped from his drink. "You're right. They had just the right amount of chocolate without being overwhelming."

Two compliments in one night? "Thank you," I said with a genuine smile. "So, Frank, you said it—if we do move forward with a restaurant. If we did, what's your vision for it?"

"I'm just the money guy. My job is to find people with vision, with a voice, who have something to say with their food. Obviously, the nomination for the James Beard award is great, but I was already mulling the offer when I had dinner last month at D'Alisa & Elle. Elle's a Portland fixture, of course. But exciting? Not always. But Nico's menu—a breath of fresh air."

If I didn't know better, I'd think Nico had grown three inches taller just listening.

"Now, Nico," Frank continued, "if there are some grand family plans for you to take over the restaurant from your dad, I don't want to get in the way of nepotism. But if you'd like to strike out again, I want to be your guy."

Nico nodded. "I'll be honest—I'd love to have my own place again, but I need a collaborator. At Elle, that's my dad. If we do this, I'd like Juliette to join me."

"Now, Juliette," Frank said, turning to me, "you orchestrated the update at La Taverna some six years ago, isn't that right?"

"You have a very long memory," I said, impressed. "I worked with Montage and Nonna's Table as well."

"I should have guessed Montage. Good work."

"Portland already has a selection of industrial, minimalist restaurants that have experienced certain amounts of success," Nico said, leaning forward and tenting his fingers. "To do another would be redundant. We grew up at D'Alisa & Elle, but we don't want to be in competition with it either. And let's face it, the economy is still in recovery. So I'm thinking something small, boutique…a bistro, a café, that sort of thing. Now, I have a hard time with small." Nico paused to laugh at himself. "It's not in my nature, you know? But as a business model, it's very wise. So, a small restaurant. French and Italian flavors—"

"It has to be special, though," I interjected without thinking. "Not gimmicky, but special. L'uccello Blu was more of a trattoria, so maybe we want to go in a different direction. Crepes are very French, but they're not huge sellers in the States at this point, so I think a crêperie is out of the question. Coffee should be served, obviously, but I don't think anyone's worrying about Portland suffering a café shortage anytime soon."

Nico examined his empty demitasse cup. "Speaking of, do you have any more of this espresso in the kitchen?"

"There's more. What about a date restaurant?"

"Interesting," Frank said approvingly.

Nico left for the kitchen, coffee cup in hand. "I'm listening."

"Something romantic, but not in the traditional restaurant sense. No table-cloths. Certainly no violins. I'm thinking warm, dark wood, leather uphol-stered chairs, corner booths, low light. A central hearth. Sophisticated. Sexy. Unfussy."

"Leather chairs—they are expensive for restaurant furniture," Nico argued upon his return.

"True," I conceded, "but comfortable seating encourages diners to linger and order more."

"I like it," Frank said. "If you want leather chairs, I can make it happen. And I think you're right—the leather would look expensive, set the tone for the dining room."

I did not gloat.

Not visibly, at least.

Nico held his grudge for all of thirty seconds before moving on and throw-ing out ideas for cuisine. "Sophisticated takes on familiar items. A perfectly roasted quarter chicken."

"Always a favorite," I agreed.

Nico nodded and continued. "A meat loaf with grass-fed beef and veal. A house ravioli. A selection of steaks served with pommes frites."

"How about an elegant ratatouille to satisfy the vegan crowd?" I suggested.

"Smart. I was thinking about another vegetarian pasta entrée, but a Thomas Keller–inspired ratatouille would make a lot of Portland people very happy."

"It's also gluten free, for people with dietary concerns."

"Elegant and approachable. I like it." Frank made a few notes in his legal pad. "What about location?" he asked, wiping a crumb from his mouth. "Is there an area you guys have thought about?"

"I was thinking...," Nico began.

I shifted in my seat, hoping he wasn't about to say what I thought he was about to say.

"Pearl District?" Nico asked me, an eyebrow lifted.

"That," I said, my voice firm, "is a discussion for another time."

After Frank left, I methodically began the process of returning my apartment to its original state. I didn't say a word. Nico stayed two steps behind me, following the motions of helping but really, I knew, waiting for me to say something.

I remained silent.

Nico shadowed me.

His Gallic impatience finally kicked in. "So?"

I turned, my eyes innocent. "So?"

"Seriously."

I crossed my arms. "What?"

"The patisserie space—it's perfect!"

"Of course it's perfect, Nico, but Grand-mère has hardly been gone a couple of months, and Mom's been to the building just long enough to leave the sign that the place has closed due to Grand-mère's passing. She lost her mom. Using the space isn't a conversation I'm ready to have with her."

"We would lease it. That way the space would stay in the family. You could live in the apartment—"

"That would depend on if I committed to the restaurant."

"So? Are you in or out?"

"I'm…I'm still thinking. It's a big deal."

"I know, Etta. I know."

I shrugged. "You hogged the impulsive genes—what can I say?"

"Is this about your commitment issues?"

My mouth dropped open. "What?"

"You've got commitment issues. It's why you're still single."

As soon as he said the words, Nico seemed to realize that, as far as things to say to make me want to agree to starting a restaurant, accusing me of commitment issues was probably far, far down the list.

Actually, it didn't make the list.

"I've, um, got to go." Nico looked away. "My shift starts soon."

He was out the door in a matter of seconds.

Angry at Nico, at my singleness, at my life, I continued to scrub my kitchen until my hands hurt. When I finished, my kitchen sparkled and I could barely take a full breath without inhaling a lungful of cleaning product.

Wearily, I sat down at my computer. I toyed with Pinterest and read articles on Salon.com while ignoring the thoughts in the back of my head.

Since I'd hardly eaten any of the food I'd made for the meeting, I made myself two crepes—one savory, one sweet—to nibble on as I navigated the various online matchmaking websites.

Did they work? I had no idea. But I was tired of being the single-girl punch line of the family.

I knew there were dozens of sites to choose from; I picked the one that I'd heard of that wouldn't cut too deeply into my cheese-buying fund. By dessert, I'd written a satisfactory profile that sounded a little flirtier, I hoped, than a job résumé.

I closed my laptop and stood, feeling empowered by the fact that I'd done something constructive for my love life. A moment passed and I hadn't stepped away. I lifted the laptop screen and checked my e-mail.

Nothing.

Too soon for a response.

Wasn't it?

I checked again.

When I didn't see a response—again—I closed the screen and walked away. There would be time to embarrass myself tomorrow.

~ Stracciatella Crepes ~

2 eggs
$3/4$ cup whole milk
$1/2$ cup water
1 cup flour
3 tablespoons unsalted butter, melted and cooled
    to room temperature
Pinch of salt
3 ounces bittersweet chocolate, grated and very
    cold
3 tablespoons clarified butter, for cooking

Mix the eggs, milk, water, flour, unsalted butter, and salt in blender; place batter (still in blender vessel) in refrigerator to chill. Batter should be slightly thicker in consistency than heavy cream.

Once cold, gently whisk in the chocolate shavings. Blend again; transfer batter into a mixing bowl (if you like), and allow to rest for 1 hour, or up to 24.

Heat crepe pan or small frying pan with a small amount of clarified butter over medium heat. Pour in $1/3$ cup batter or enough to leave a thin, even coat to the crepe pan.

When edges are crisp and the crepe seems willing to move, flip and cook on opposite side.

Transfer to plate. Can be stored in refrigerator or frozen longer term. Serve with chocolate ice cream, mascarpone, or whatever sounds delicious—be creative!

Note: Clarified butter is simply butter that's been heated and had the milk solids removed. Because the milk solids will brown and burn, clarified butter works better for sautéing things at higher heats. Sometimes it's sold as *ghee,* but sometimes ghee has other spices added to it, so read the label carefully unless you want kicky crepes (which could be interesting under the right circumstances).

To make your own, simply heat butter in a shallow pan until it melts and separates, and spoon off the milk solids that froth up at the top. Save the milk solids for soups, or spoon over oatmeal. If you want to be precise, strain the butter through a fine sieve and a cheesecloth. (If you don't, I won't tell.) Just be sure to use unsalted butter.

5

Foods, and the meals we make of them are our clocks,
our faithful calendars.

—SALLY SMITH BOOTH

I poked my head into Marti's cubicle first thing the next morning.
"I've got something that I think you might be interested in." I placed
Grand-mère's cookbook and recipes on her desk, flipping the book open to the
page with the recipe for *gâteau au chocolat,* which I thought would hold the
most appeal. "It was my grandmother's. I thought we might do a story on heirloom recipes, dishes handed down through the generations. She was the proprietress of La Petite Chouquette," I reminded Marti. "Her recipes are gold."

To my surprise, Marti didn't seem particularly enthralled. "Cool," she said,
closing the book and handing it back to me. "I think it's a good idea, but your
approachable entertaining theme is, I think, the best field for you right now."

Normally, I would have let it go, agreed with everything Marti had to say.

Not this time. "I appreciate those thoughts," I said, aiming for my most
respectful tone, "but I do think these recipes have a lot of merit. Vintage is big
right now, and my grandmother helped train some of the best pastry chefs in
Portland." When Marti didn't interrupt, I rushed ahead. "We could spin it as
a tribute to a great lady, profile her, and include a few of her most personal
recipes."

Marti studied my face, her face inscrutable. "I'll think on it," she said at
last. "A tribute piece could have a strong human-interest element. Focus on the
crepe party piece," she said, leaning back in her chair. "I'll get back to you."

"Sure," I said, hanging on to all the bravado I could sustain. "I'll have the crepe party piece ready for you by end of day today."

"Excellent. For the next installment, I was thinking about fondue."

"Oh, fun." I brightened. "I'll get right on that."

"You can cover how to throw a fondue party. They're trendy again and pretty straightforward, when you think about it."

"Right. I'll start working on that as soon as the crepes are turned in."

Marti gave me one of her awkward, overly enthusiastic thumbs-up signs— my signal that I'd been dismissed. I gathered up the cookbook and recipe cards and walked back to my desk.

I was pleased and amazed at how I'd fought for the piece about Grand-mère. How long would Marti take to decide? My idea was solid. Sure, I had plenty to work on in the meantime.

By the time I got back to my desk, I had formed a plan. If Marti didn't want to do a piece with the recipes, there were other local periodical publications that would. I could write the piece and sell it as a freelance article. And if no one bought it, I would post it on my blog.

I filled Linn in on my plan as we made a coffee run.

"It's a solid idea," Linn assured me as we speed walked down the sidewalk. "Marti will pick it up."

"You know," I said, "this isn't my usual thing. I write what she tells me, eat what she tells me, and I'm good at it."

"You are," Linn said. "I would tell you if you weren't."

I grinned. "Thanks. Anyway, this is the first time I've really wanted to chase a story."

"Got the bug, did you?" Linn asked, as we arrived at our favorite purveyor of Stumptown coffee and ducked inside.

"I guess," I said, sliding into line. "But it's more complicated than that." I filled her in on Nico's restaurant plans and how he'd offered me the opportunity to manage it.

Linn's eyes widened. "That's big, Etta. Frank Burrows is the real deal."

"Sh," I cautioned, looking around. "This isn't public information yet."

"Sorry. My ma wishes I were more discreet. But you managing a restaurant—that was your thing before you came here, right?"

"On a smaller scale, yes, but that was a long time ago."

"So would you leave the paper?" Linn asked, before turning to the barista. "Americano. Very hot, please."

"I'd have to. If I was lucky, I might have time to keep ghosting the cookbooks... Do you want to split a cinnamon roll?" When she nodded, I ordered it along with a café au lait.

"Good call on the roll," Linn said once she'd torn a piece off. "You can try with the ghosting, but restaurants take over your life. You know that better than anyone."

"Oh, I do."

"I like the cardamom in the rolls. Well, no matter what, we'll still see each other. Don't let the specter of missing me influence your decision."

I laughed. "I'll keep that in mind. You want to go get fondue with me next week?"

"To research your new assignment? I'm game. I like melted cheese as much as the next girl."

The barista called out our drinks, and we picked them up at the end of the bar. "To melted cheese," I said. We tapped our paper coffee cups together and laughed.

By the time I left work that day, I had five texts from Nico, each one a differently worded version of "Have you decided about the restaurant?"

I wished I had. And if wishes were fishes, I would have something to eat for dinner—my larder was otherwise empty.

Faced with an echoing refrigerator and a rumbling stomach, I picked up my purse and headed back out the door.

Garlic, onions, and herbs scented the air outside D'Alisa & Elle. I let my-self in the back door, greeting servers and staff as I made my way inside. When I saw the light on in the office, I knocked on the door. *"Coucou,"* I called, pok-ing my head inside. *"Bonjour, Maman!"*

"Ah!" Maman turned to face me, spinning her chair. *"Bonjour, ma fille.* How are you tonight?"

"Hungry. I thought I might try to snag a dish of pasta or something."

"Mais oui, certainement. The Bolognese sauce is very nice today. And some soup? When I was in the kitchen earlier, there seemed to be a lot of soup."

"That sounds perfect." I paused to take in my mother's appearance. Her hair was gently mussed, and she wasn't wearing any eye makeup. "What's wrong, Maman?"

"I'm not feeling well today. I'm just…tired," she said. But her eyes touched on mine only fleetingly.

"Oh," I said, not buying her answer at all. "I hope you feel better. When do you head home?"

"About an hour or so. You'll be at family dinner this week, yes?"

I'd actually considered skipping a week to get caught up on work, but something in her eyes made me rethink my plans. "Yeah, I'll be there."

"Bon. Go off and get your dinner now, *ma cheri.* Make Nico give you some bread too."

I said good-bye and closed the door, no less concerned but aware she was unlikely to elaborate.

In the kitchen I found Nico, working away, shouting orders. "Hey!" he said once he saw me. "Can you lend a hand? We're short a guy tonight, and we're just this side of the weeds."

"I was gonna come grab some dinner. If you feed me, I can stay for a little bit."

"Sold. Tie up your hair, grab a jacket, and scrub in. Do you mind working first and eating later?"

"Do you have a little bread hanging around?"

"The focaccia is very good today. Mario! Give my sister some bread."

"Yes, Chef! Heads up," Mario called back, and a wedge of focaccia flew toward my face.

I caught it, ate it quickly, and got myself ready to help. "How behind are you?"

"A ten-top came in. We're almost there, but it's slowing down everybody else. Enzo!" he called out. "How's that asparagus?"

"Thirty seconds, Chef!" Enzo shouted back.

"Where do you need me?"

"We went through a lot of chicken tonight, and I need more chicken breasts pounded. After that, I need you to prep more vegetables."

"Yes, Chef," I said, slipping easily into the role. I worked quickly, replenishing the supply of prepped chicken before moving on to the vegetables. Once those were done, I lent a hand at the roast station. Nico got the ten-top's appetizers sent out, followed shortly by the entrées. Slowly, the energy in the kitchen shifted from manic and harried to calm and efficient.

After an hour, Nico turned to me. "Things are slowing down. I should probably feed you."

"I'd be fine with that," I answered, wiping my forehead with a grin. "That was fun."

"Yeah? Fun enough that you've put more thought into my offer?" Nico asked as he handed me a bowl of pasta topped with Bolognese sauce.

"Mom was right—this is really good," I said after a bite. "She also suggested you send me home with soup."

"We can probably work something out."

"So…here's the thing," I said, leaning against the counter. "My job is tough, but I'm good at it. I don't know that I want to give it up. But I also really, really love restaurant work."

"It's in your blood."

"I know. What if we strike a compromise? I checked my ghostwriting schedule—I've got two books, but then I'm done for a while. I can help the restaurant get set up, and once it's off the ground, I can decide then if I want to stay or hire someone else to run it for you."

Nico studied the ceiling. "You won't reconsider?"

"Not tonight, no."

"You really think you can get the restaurant up and running while working at the paper?"

"I'm used to working all hours."

Nico shrugged. "I can't argue with that. All right, then. Shall we shake?"

"Sure," I said. "Just know that you've got tomato sauce on your hands."

Once I returned home, I found a surprise in my inbox. The e-mail was from OrangeYouGlad, a man with a good-looking photo whose family owned an orange grove in California.

I loved orange groves, always had. Reading the note, I entertained visions of walking hand in hand with a loved one in an orange grove, him plucking an orange off the tree and offering me a warm, sun-ripened wedge.

OrangeYouGlad, who confessed to be named Martin, asked if I was interested in having a phone conversation. If so, he included his phone number and a list of times when he would be available.

A phone conversation! I felt as though I'd graduated to the next step.

Twenty-four hours later, at the appointed time, I called Martin.

To my surprise, the throaty strains of "Someone Like You" filled my ear.

I liked Adele just as much as the next girl, but the song itself was…

Not masculine.

But maybe he was just really into British soul music.

Or something.

I noticed he had a nice voice when he answered. Maybe a little vague. "Glad you called," he said.

"You're, um, welcome." Silence. I cleared my throat. "How was your day?"

"Fine. Work is good."

"That's good," I said, at a loss. How was this supposed to work? He asked to speak with me, and so far I felt as though I'd interrupted him at a bad time. "So, tell me about the orange grove."

"The grove is fine. This time of year, it's mainly maintenance work, working the soil."

"Oh."

"What about your work?"

"Busy," I answered automatically. "My boss has me working on a new project that I'm not particularly in love with." At. All.

"That's too bad. Do you like what you do otherwise?"

"I do."

"Good. That's good."

I stifled a yawn and wondered if there was anything else I could do while I was on the line. Martin wasn't exactly requiring my full attention span.

To prove that point, he asked who the real Juliette was. I wandered around my apartment in search of my nail polish while reciting an off-the-cuff version of my online personal statement.

If he noticed, he didn't say.

"What are you up to this weekend?" I asked as I decided between taupe nail polish and pale pink, also contemplating an edgier gray.

"Buying a TV. My old one died."

"Ah."

Nowhere I could go with that. If he needed help choosing a dutch oven or a cheese grater, I'd have several tips to offer.

"So if you could play any position in football, what position would you play?"

I paused applying my nail polish, midswipe. "Pardon?"

He repeated the question.

I really had heard right the first time. Amazing. "Receiver, I suppose," I said after a moment's thought. "In a family full of quarterbacks, it was the sensible thing to do."

"Right on," he said.

Not that I had any idea what I was 'right on' about. "What made you decide to try online dating?"

"I was seeing this girl for a while, and everything was great. But then she moved to be closer to me—I can't leave the grove, you know—and she went crazy. Seriously, she went berserk. It was a really big deal. So we broke up—had to—because she went nuts. Decided to try the online thing. Found you, so that was cool."

"Cool," I repeated, wary. In my experience, what men attributed to insanity was really women doing something they didn't understand or agree with.

I chose not to share this thought with Martin.

"Tell me about your spiritual beliefs," I said, since he had checked the box that indicated a belief in Christianity.

"Gotcha," he said. "I would say that my faith in God is strong because my love for God is so strong. I read my Bible every day. I go to church every Sunday. Well, not last Sunday. Or this week, because I'll be out of town."

"It happens." I paused. "Well, I need to be going." I waved my freshly manicured hand in the air to encourage it to dry. "It's been nice getting to know you, Martin."

"Let's do it again soon," Martin said.

I made some noncommittal noise before hanging up.

Unsettled after my phone call with Martin, I retreated to the kitchen. I retrieved the farm-fresh apples I'd bought earlier in the day and began to peel them.

Maybe Martin wasn't the kind of guy who was very good at expressing himself with words. My cousin Letizia wasn't much for phone conversations or e-mails, but in person she was a lot of fun to be with. Martin could be similar.

I placed the peeled and chopped apples in a bowl and prepped the dry ingredients. It was important to remember, too, that Martin had grown up in the family's orange grove. The culture had to be very different. Less communicative.

And, I thought as I whipped the eggs, it was important not to make a snap decision based on a single conversation.

I finished with the cake steps, adding the melted butter and flour to the batter and pouring the whole thing into the springform pan.

Reality settled in the moment the pan hit the oven.

Martin was a moron.

There was no getting around it.

As the cake baked, I settled at my computer and looked over the men in my life.

I wasn't interested in any of them, not seriously. Maybe I was at the wrong matchmaking site. The man I wanted was clearly not here. In a moment of decisiveness, I clicked through my account options to remove my profile for good.

My finger clicked the final button, and my heart swelled with hope that I'd never have to speak to Martin again.

A split second later, silence fell and everything turned black in my apartment.

~ French Apple Cake with Almonds ~

I like a mix of apples, some firm and tangy, others soft and sweeter for a bit of variety. Whatever you do, do not spice the cake! Cinnamon and nutmeg do not belong in a French cake.

Serve with crème fraîche to be French, but freshly whipped cream or homemade ice cream won't taste bad either.

$^3/_4$ cup flour
$^3/_4$ teaspoon baking powder
Pinch of salt
4 large apples
2 eggs, at room temperature
$^3/_4$ cup sugar
$1^1/_2$ teaspoons vanilla extract
$^1/_2$ teaspoon almond extract
8 tablespoons butter, melted and cooled to room temperature
$^1/_3$ cup sliced almonds

Preheat oven to 350°F and place a rack at the center of the oven.

Generously butter an 8- or 9-inch springform pan, and place it on a baking sheet.

In a small bowl, whisk together the dry ingredients (minus the sugar).

Peel, core, slice, and chop the apples into 1-inch pieces.

In a large bowl or stand mixer, beat the eggs until frothy and pale. Add the sugar, vanilla, and almond extract.

Add the flour mixture and melted butter in stages—half of the flour, half of the butter, remaining flour, remaining butter.

Fold in the apple cubes, mixing until they're incorporated. Pour completed cake batter into the buttered springform pan, catching all the batter with a rubber spatula.

Bake for 45 minutes, remove, and sprinkle almonds across the top. Bake an additional 5 to 15 minutes or until a knife inserted into the center comes out clean and the almonds are just toasted.

Allow the cake to cool on a wire rack for 5 minutes. To remove from the springform, run a sharp knife around the edge to loosen the cake. Lift the base from the baking dish and slide the cake onto the serving plate, minding no apples are lost in the process.

Note: The cake will last up to 3 days when covered, but if it's still there 3 days later, invite a friend to help make it through the leftovers.

6

Comfort me with apples: for I am sick of love.

—SONG OF SOLOMON

*B*y the time the power came back on, I'd lit candles and spent ten whole minutes reading a paperback book. After my apartment flickered back to life, I checked on the apple cake, reset the oven, and tidied up the kitchen. Once the cake was ready, I sliced into it and continued my book, letting my laptop remain in repose for the rest of the night.

Marti called me into her office the next morning.

"Write the profile about your grandmother," she said. "I won't promise to run it, but I do want to read it."

"That's fine," I said, my heart beating faster as I thought about the piece, how I would write it, and which recipes I would include. "Thank you."

At lunchtime, Linn peeked over our shared cubicle wall, insisted that on this—the worst of Fridays—we needed to find something divine for lunch.

"What's going on?" I asked.

"My sources aren't calling me back, I misplaced my notes on the restaurant I'm covering, and my husband has to work late, even though we had a date planned for tonight."

"Ugh, I'm sorry. I'll see what I can do."

I picked up my phone and made a few calls, and after dropping my surname (a technique I tried to use only for the forces of good), I managed to snag two spots for tea service at the Heathman Hotel.

"Do you mind a late lunch?" I asked Linn, elbows propped on the cubicle wall. "The Heathman can't seat us until two, but if you want a lift, this will do it."

"Tea? You want to go to tea? I heard you talking to them, but I figured it was for you and your niece."

"Tea. You've never had tea at the Heathman?"

"I'm Asian. I know tea."

"But at the Heathman?"

"I'm not eight. Let's go to Bluehour instead."

"Oh come on. It'll be fun." Usually these conversations with Linn went the other way around, with her egging me to try something more daring. It was fun to reverse roles this once. "Eat a snack now," I said, "and meet me in the foyer at a quarter to two."

An hour and half later, I stopped by the ladies' room to freshen my lipstick and add a bit of grooming cream to my hair. Already wearing Grand-mère's pearls with my sweater, plaid skirt, and boots, I was glad I had accessorized for an afternoon out.

"I need to borrow some lipstick," Linn told me the moment she saw me in the foyer. "Next time I say we need something divine, read between the lines and understand I was referring to a food truck or one of the restaurants on the *Diner* list."

"Hush," I said, fishing in my purse until I found a lipstick for her. "You'll like it."

Linn squared her shoulders. "My mother made sure I knew how to perform a proper tea service by the time I was six. I'm not tea simple."

"I never said you were. You've been to English-style teas, though, haven't you?"

"My dad's Irish American," she replied dryly. "I don't even know how to answer that question."

"Fair enough. Just give it a whirl, okay? It'll be a tea party. Tea parties are cool."

"I'm going to make *Downton Abbey* references."

"Whatever floats your boat."

She swiped the lipstick onto her mouth, then smooshed her lips together. "I'm going to call you Violet."

"Lucky me. I'm a Maggie Smith fan. Let's go!"

Linn dragged her feet the entire way, but we still made it in time. Since I'd used my real name for the reservations, we received attentive service from the start.

"I'll have the Earl Grey," I told the waiter, not bothering to consult Linn. "She'll have the Citrus Nectar."

"I don't even get to choose my tea?" Linn complained, exasperated.

"You'll like it."

"I don't like herbal tea."

"What are you, four? You'll like this one."

"You're so bossy. Did Marti get back to you on the profile you wanted to write?"

I brightened. "She did! And she's letting me write it, though she said she wouldn't promise to print it."

"That sounds exciting, I think."

"I'm looking forward to it," I said, leaning backward as our tea arrived. "Grand-mère was a fascinating woman. Really ahead of her time. It'll make a great piece—I'm not worried."

"She seemed cool when I met her at the bakery that one time."

I nodded, remembering. "She liked you. She loved your hair—thought it was very chic."

"Your gran had good taste, then. What's your angle for the article?"

"A woman ahead of her time. She attended pastry school before she married my grandfather. Did I ever tell you that?"

"When was that, the forties?"

"Late thirties, I think." I poured Linn's tea into a cup for her and sweetened it with sugar. "Her father didn't want her to go, but the woman had a passion for baking. She was the favorite daughter, apparently, so he let her go. She was seeing my grandfather at the time, but they didn't get married for another few years."

"Shocking."

"It really was. They loved each other," I said, "but she gave up baking outside the home after they married. When he died, though, that's when she came to the States and opened the patisserie. How's your tea?"

"I don't hate it," she said, eying her empty cup. "Could you pass the teapot?"

"Of course. Ooh, look—there's the food!"

Linn sat up a little straighter when the first course arrived, smoked salmon profiteroles.

By the time we'd moved from the panini and tea sandwiches and on to the Parisian Opera Cake and devil's food teacakes, Linn had downed almost everything set in front of her, as well as an entire pot of tea.

"It's all so good!" she said, wiping her hands on her cloth napkin. "I love the tiny portions. And they just keep bringing food! I love this. We should do this every day."

"I completely agree."

"So do you think writing about your gran will be healing? Or difficult because she hasn't been gone very long?"

I leaned back in my chair. "Probably both. I picked up my phone to call her yesterday. I've always heard of people saying they did that after losing someone, but it never occurred to me I might do the same without thinking."

"I'm so sorry. I hope writing the article turns out to be a positive thing. Did you decide what to do about the restaurant?"

"Yes and no," I said with a sly smile. "I've decided to do both."

Linn's eyes widened. "How's that going to work?"

"Well, both, until the restaurant actually opens. And then I'll decide if I'll stay on or if I'll hire someone else to manage it."

"That sounds…both gutsy and indecisive. I like it." Linn lifted her teacup. "To success!"

"To success!" I echoed, grinning broadly as our teacups clinked.

Nico called two days later while I was looking in vain for my shoes. "I think we need to talk to Mom and Dad tonight," he said. "Before family dinner. Tell them about the restaurant. If I'm going to start asking around, looking for a sous-chef, I should probably tell them what we're up to first."

"That sounds very wise," I told him. "I would be there early, but my shoes have gone AWOL."

"And, Etta, I'm serious about the patisserie space."

I opened and closed the closet door before responding. "How are you planning on approaching that?"

"Simple—we'll offer to lease or buy it. The property stays in the family. Mom will like that."

"True. But Mom might also want to get market value for it. Have you looked at comparable properties?"

"I have."

"We can't afford them."

"Well…"

"You can certainly ask, Nico." I checked beneath my bed. "Just be prepared if she decides to be practical."

"So tonight, then?"

"I don't know. My shoes might not turn up."

"Then you'll just have to go barefoot," he said, chuckling as he hung up.

My shoes finally appeared—one beneath the couch, the other under a fallen throw pillow—and I set off for my parents' house. Nico waited for me beside his car, a black version of my own red Alfa.

"Have you been waiting long?" I asked, glad the morning's rain had cleared off.

"Nah, just got here. Are you ready?"

"I'm having a fit of nerves, to be honest." I forced a smile on my face. "It'll be good."

Nico clapped me on the back. "It'll be great. Keep your chin up, Etta."

The scent of cooking food greeted us even before our parents made it to the entryway.

"Ah! *Bonjour*," Maman said when she saw me. "I found another box of papers at the apartment. There were some photos as well. I brought it in our car, if you're interested for the article."

"I am. Thank you. How are you?" I asked.

Both of my parents looked wearier than usual. "*Comme ci, comme ça*," Maman replied, though her answer certainly clarified nothing. My father offered me a glass of water. I took a sip and tried not to worry.

Nico held out the platter he'd brought with him. "I have some focaccia," he said. "I thought we could sit down for a little while before dinner and chat."

My parents and I sat down at the table, while Nico pulled a small stack of plates out of the cupboard.

My brother does make serious focaccia. He tops them with figs, shallots, and blue cheese, or red-pepper bruschetta with feta—it's divine, every time.

I watched as my mother lifted a slice of focaccia to her plate and took the tiniest nibble.

Not good.

Nico sat down with a goofy smile on his face and proceeded to tell my parents all about his crippling heartbreak when L'uccello Blu closed its doors (as if they didn't know), his gratitude for the position at D'Alisa & Elle (a nice touch), and our new and brilliant plans to open another restaurant (the finale, for now).

My parents took it all in very calmly—even my father, from whom my brother inherited his flair for drama.

"It is very good," my father said, with a nod of approval. "Very good for you to make these plans. I knew you would not always be at this restaurant."

Nico's shoulders relaxed. "You are not upset?"

"My father wanted me to stay at the family restaurant. I didn't want to, so I left the country." Our father gave one of his patented shrugs. "I understand. I would prefer if you were able to open your own restaurant in this country, though."

Nico beamed. Having earned approval from the parental faction for the restaurant, he moved in to finish off his pitch.

"I was thinking about spaces," Nico said, casting a significant glance in my direction. "*We* were thinking—"

Thanks, Nico, I thought. *Thanks for unilaterally pulling me into this.*

"We'd love to use Grand-mère's patisserie space. Remodel it and bring it back to its former glory. Keep it in the family. We'd want to lease or buy it, of course," he said, holding up a hand, "but it has such wonderful memories. We think it would be perfect."

Obviously, if the restaurant failed, Nico could rely on a lucrative career in sales.

To my surprise, my mother nodded. "*Bon.* Maman would have liked that."

Nico grinned and clasped her hands, thanking her profusely and spinning tales of how wonderful the restaurant would be, laying on his gratitude as thick as French butter. Dad found a bottle of wine and poured glasses for each of us, and Nico proposed a toast to our new endeavor.

My mother took the tiniest sip from her glass.

I put mine down. "What's wrong?" I asked, looking from one parent to the other.

They exchanged glances.

"There are some things to talk about," Maman answered. "But they will wait for now."

"But—," I protested.

She shook her head firmly. "They will wait."

Sophie, Nelson, and Chloé arrived minutes later. "What's going on?" Sophie asked when she saw the wine poured and the half-eaten focaccia.

"I'm opening a new restaurant," Nico announced. He swept Sophie into a hug and then twirled a giggling Chloé around the room before returning to give Nelson a staid, manly handshake.

I smiled as I watched, but my eyes darted over to my mother. Something was wrong. Something was very, very wrong.

We sat down to dinner moments later, a meal of veal scaloppine that my father had prepared, paired with sautéed escarole and stuffed artichokes. My father prayed for the meal in Italian, the lyrical vowels and consonants soothing my nerves.

I prayed as we passed plates around, prayed that the ominous vibe I picked up was just the result of an overactive imagination.

My mother was quiet until we began to eat. "I feel so…so blessed," she began, "that you were all able to be here today. I know Caterina wanted to be here, but she is taking care of her own family.

"I saw my doctor," my mother continued, her voice small but steady. "It's cancer. Ovarian. They're sure."

I felt the whole of my breath leave my body.

"I have a treatment plan, which I plan on following," she continued. "The doctor has spoken about aggressive treatment."

"What stage?" I asked, feeling dizzy.

She reached across the table and squeezed my hand. "Three."

The rest of the dinner passed in a blur. We spoke awkwardly about chemotherapy, radiation, doctors' appointments, and the wig maker who made her friend Evelyne a divine Brigitte Bardot-esque wig.

At home, I picked up my phone to call Cat, put it down, then picked it up again.

"Hi, hon," she said when she answered the phone. Her voice sounded hoarse. "She told you?"

"Over dinner."

Cat cleared her throat. "I'll be flying out in two weeks, so I'll be there for her surgery. She told me not to, of course, but I'm doing it anyway."

"Oh," I said. "Are you bringing the boys?"

"They'll stay home and have Daddy time with Damian. I'll bring them out on another trip when it's not so...so fresh."

"That makes sense."

"Are you doing okay?"

"I'm hanging in there," I said, not knowing exactly what to say. I didn't want to add to my sister's stress—after all, it was her mother too. "Go to bed," I said. "It's late."

"I won't be able to sleep."

"Test recipes," I advised. "That's what I've been doing since Grand-mère died."

Caterina swore in Italian, then French, and then Italian again. "I'm glad Grand-mère is missing this, but I can't wrap my head around the fact that Mom's facing cancer so soon after losing Grand-mère. We worship a good God, but I am well and truly dismayed right now."

I could only murmur in agreement. I didn't know how to talk about it with her, not yet. "I hope you get a little sleep," I said at last. "Let me know if you want me to pick you up at the airport."

We said our good-byes, and I hung up. Still reeling, I opened my laptop and opened my web browser.

One e-mail in my inbox.

From a man. From the dating site.

How on earth could that have happened? I had canceled my subscription, hadn't I? Despite my confusion, I couldn't stop myself from opening the e-mail and reading it.

Dear BellaGrazie,

It seems strange to send a letter to someone whose name I don't actually know, but I suppose that's the nature of this beast. All of that said, I enjoyed reading your profile. You sound like a fascinating person to get to know. E-mail me back sometime—I'd like to hear from you.

Formula1Doc/Neil

Without really knowing what I was doing, I found myself typing a response with increasingly furious speed.

Dear Forumla1Doc/Neil,

I'm really not sure how I managed to receive your e-mail because I thought I canceled my subscription. But my power went out (I still don't know why), and here you are and here I am, so I guess it didn't work.

None of this is your fault—you sound really nice, truly. But you see, my life has become particularly complicated over the last 72 (or so?) hours. Very, very complicated, which is why I'm getting out of this online thing now.

How complicated, you ask?

Well, I might leave my job. I'm not sure. It feels wrong—it's the sort of job that loads of people would really like to have, but I can't decide if I love it or hate it. And I'm agreeing to open a restaurant with my brother, which might be an even bigger disaster because I accidentally scuttled the last restaurant. (My advice: Never date a coworker in general, your brother's sous-chef in particular. Just don't.) But on the other hand, it might be really great.

I really don't know. But I do know that my mother was just diagnosed with Stage III ovarian cancer. And I don't know how to handle that. Not at all.

Also, (and I can't believe there's an "also" on this list) my grandmother passed away. Which is awful enough, but I found a photo among my grandmother's belongings that is quite old and looks just like my brother. And not at all like my grandfather, whom I surmise, at this point, could very well not actually *be* my grandfather. Maybe he's a stray great-uncle or something. Who knows? But he meant something to my grandmother, and I don't know why.

So considering that my personal and professional life is in a state of upheaval (all very recent, mind you), I strongly suggest you find one of the other nice women on this site, the sort who have their lives together, have a better grasp on their personal genealogy, and enjoy, I don't know, softball. Or scrapbooking. Trust me, it's better for everyone this way.

Sincerely,

BellaGrazie/Whatever/Juliette

I sent the e-mail, clicked the Cancel Account button once again, closed the laptop lid, and went to bed in the hopes that tonight, of all nights, I might be able to find temporary oblivion in sleep.

~ Nico's Mini Focaccia ~

These make a wonderful light dinner with a salad or a perfect party appetizer if cut into wedges. Make sure they turn golden when you bake them—the flavor is in the color. They do take a while to make, but they're worth it!

For the sponge:

$1/2$ cup all-purpose flour

$1/2$ cup warm water (105–115°F)

1 teaspoon active dry yeast

For the dough:

$3^1/4$ to $3^3/4$ cups flour

1 cup warm water

2 teaspoons fine sea salt

1 tablespoon (or so) olive oil

To make the sponge, combine the flour and water in a large bowl with the yeast. Stir until smooth. Seal the bowl with plastic wrap and let stand for 2 to 8 hours at room temperature.

After the sponge has fermented, prepare the dough. Add the cup of warm water and salt. Add flour gradually, stopping when the dough begins to pull away from the sides of the bowl.

Prep a surface to knead on, such as a floured pastry cloth, with the remaining flour. Knead the dough on the pastry cloth, folding it, pressing it down with the heel of your hand, and folding again several times, working in just enough of the flour to produce a soft, stretchy dough—about 3 to 5 minutes. Remember—overworked dough is tough dough. Put the dough in a warm spot in the kitchen, and allow it to rise in a cloth-covered, oiled bowl until the dough doubles in size.

Line two baking sheets with parchment paper. Punch the dough down; ignore it for 10 minutes. With oiled hands, divide the dough into eight equal pieces with four pieces on each baking sheet. Press each piece into a 4-inch circle. Brush the tops with oil, then poke them with your fingers to create the indented surface. Cover with plastic and ignore for 30 minutes while the dough rests.

Heat oven to 400°F. Salt and pepper (freshly ground pepper, per usual) the tops. To parbake: bake 6 to 8 minutes, until the rounds have lost their doughiness but haven't browned. To fully bake: bake 14 to 17 minutes, until lightly golden. To bake par-baked rounds: bake for 7 to 11 minutes, until lightly golden. The joy of parbaked bread is that the bread can be saved—refrigerated or frozen—and baked fresh for another day. You can also wrap up the remaining dough and keep it to bake later, for up to 5 days.

The focaccia is very good plain—perfect for dipping in oil and vinegar—but if you want to put toppings on it, pull out the rounds at the 7-minute mark and finish the baking with the toppings.

For the toppings—sauté shallots in olive oil, add dried figs, a bit of honey, pine nuts, and thyme. Keep on the heat until the pine nuts toast—this doesn't have to be an exact science. Remove from heat; add some crumbled gorgonzola. Bake on top of rounds for the remaining time. After removing them from the oven, you can also add some slivers of prosciutto. (Don't bake with the prosciutto—it will turn tough and chewy under the heat.)

Or go another route and add roasted red peppers, feta, parsley, and pine nuts. Top either version with cracked black pepper.

Makes 8 servings.

7

Don't let love interfere with your appetite. It never does
with mine.

—ANTHONY TROLLOPE

*T*he next morning I awoke to the alarm on my phone, per usual. I
shut off the alarm and tapped to check my morning e-mails as I
awoke.

A sale at Anthropologie. I needed to renew my antivirus software. I had an
e-mail from Formula1Doc.

I sat up.

That couldn't be.

I wrapped myself in my terry-cloth robe, shoved my feet into slippers, and
marched—albeit sleepily—to my laptop.

Sure enough, when I lifted the lid, I found that my cancellation hadn't
been the done deal I'd assumed, and my computer screen waited patiently with
another set of questions to be answered before closing my account.

Who knew that quitting online dating would be more difficult than the
process itself?

Curiosity prodded me to open the e-mail from Formula1Doc.

Dear Juliette,

I'm so sorry to hear about your mother's diagnosis. A cancer
diagnosis at any stage can be extremely difficult; a stage III

result even more so. In my real, day-to-day life, I'm a physician. My specialty is immunology, not oncology, but if you have any questions, you can feel free to ask. I don't mind.

From everything you've told me, you have every right to feel overwhelmed. The restaurant sounds exciting, though. I have no familiarity in that field, but I think it sounds cool. What kind of restaurant? There's a place not too far from work that I eat at regularly. They make great macaroni and cheese, and the atmosphere is quirky and homey. When I'm there, it helps me to decompress from work. I admire the people—restaurateurs, I guess, is the right word—who have the insight to create a space and a menu and a place for people to eat and feel better. A different kind of healing than the one I've studied, but very effective.

Anyway, you've obviously got a lot going on, and I completely understand if you've decided not to pursue any romantic relationships for the time being. If you'd like a friend, though, you know how to reach me.

On second thought, if you do cancel your account, that might not be true. My personal e-mail is Neil.McLaren.F1@netmail.com.

All the best,

Neil

I read the e-mail three times before I remembered that I hadn't used the bathroom yet. After a trip to the lavatory and a hot shower, I read the e-mail a fourth time over a breakfast espresso.

He sounded nice. Really nice. And not the least bit intimidated.

Interesting.

I dressed for work, wishing it were a Saturday morning rather than a

Monday morning. My eyes still felt gritty, and my spirits were uneven. A second strong cup of espresso nudged my brain cells into action. As a preemptive pick-me-up, I stopped by the corner bakery for a *pain au chocolat* to have as a midmorning snack.

My phone rang minutes before I stepped inside the threshold of the newspaper. I tensed the moment I saw my mother's cell number. "Is everything all right?"

"Etta," she said, her voice gently exasperated, "I have cancer. Everything is not all right, but I still have a life to live and I don't need everybody thinking I'm at death's door every time I make a phone call." She paused. *"Je regrette.* Your father...and your brothers...and your sisters...everyone's been a little—"

"I get it, Mom. I'm sorry—you're right. What's up?"

"Your aunt and uncle are coming down for the weekend, and they'd like to have brunch with us next Saturday morning. Are you free?"

Henri and Margueritte didn't often make the trip down from Seattle; I sat up straighter. "I'll make time."

"Ten thirty. Your father's cooking."

"Want me to bring something?"

"You can ask your father." A thread of exasperation tinged her voice. "He won't let me plan anything."

"He loves you."

A sigh. "I know."

"I love you, Mom," I said, being careful not to let my voice catch.

I loved her. And she was sick, and there was nothing I could do about it.

Linn swung by my desk near noon. "I'm out for lunch. Want to come?"

"No, I'm going to be working through lunch." I offered a smile. "Thanks, though."

"Are you okay?" She tilted her head. "You look a little peaked."

"Thanks."

"Sorry. What's going on?"

"My…my mom is sick." I looked away and fiddled with some papers on my desk. "We all found out last night."

Linn's face turned from teasing to serious. "Oh, Juliette, I'm so sorry. Is there anything I can do? Want me to bring something back for you? Soup or something?"

"Sure," I said, trying to sound more normal than I felt. "Soup would be great."

"You'll tell me if you need anything, won't you?"

"I will," I promised, with a wan imitation of a smile. "Are you still up for fondue? How does tomorrow look?"

"I am if you are—are you sure?"

I shrugged. "Life goes on," I said, though at the moment I wasn't so sure.

I took my laptop out that night for a dinner date. I found a quiet nook at Palio and set myself up with a panino, salad, and one of their signature Mexican mochas. While I came with the intention of working, I found myself typing out a letter rather than an article.

Dear Neil,

I have to admit I did not expect to hear back from you. I admire your fortitude in the face of my typographical meltdown. I assure you that in real life I tend to be one of the most stable people I know.

This might be because I know a lot of Italians.

My closest work friend stopped by my desk this morning and asked how I was (I look a bit wretched today), and I could barely tell her. There was something about *talking* about it that seemed like it would make it more real. This is probably a phenomenon that you, as a doctor, have studied.

Since you seem to know everything about me, it's only fair for me to ask about you. How did you get into medicine? Do you have any Italians (or Frenchmen) in your family? And—I have to ask—what's your favorite food?

À bientôt—until later!

Juliette

I arrived at my parents' home Saturday morning with baguettes and Meyer lemons. The bread I brought for practicality—my *oncle* Henri was not an easy man to get along with. Younger than my mother by five years, Henri's temperament ran to the taciturn, his opinions fixed, his demeanor unyielding. A resident of Seattle since his college days, he reveled in pointing out the city's superiority to Portland.

His wife, Margueritte, chose not to speak very often, and I didn't blame her.

I figured the best I could do was bring some of the best bread the city offered, hoping that chewing might prevent arguing.

The lemons—they were an impulse purchase. Faced with three straight weeks of Portland's wind and rain, I was defenseless to their charms.

Everyone sat around my parents' huge oak table, passing around heaping plates of food. The scents of frittata, pain au chocolat, cut fruit, and carafes of steaming coffee wafted around the threads of conversation.

While everyone ate, I took the opportunity for some genetic reconnaissance. I'd spent an hour that morning looking at photos of my grandfather Gilles at several stages of life, and I could confirm without effort that Henri, at least, looked just like him. They shared the same fair coloring, the same hairline, the same nose, the same stubborn chin.

No paternity questions there. But I knew there were five years between my mother and her brother.

A lot could happen in five years.

While my mother did share Henri's eyes and cheekbones, they were admittedly the same as my grandmother Mireille's.

Different fathers? To the naked eye, it was entirely possible.

Nico, sitting at my left, interrupted my thoughts with his elbow. "I'm interviewing a potential sous-chef later. He looks great on paper—Kenny recommended him."

"Oh good," I said, though I had secretly hoped that our kitchen might be the only one that could function without a sous. I pushed thoughts of Éric from my head.

"Do you think it's a good idea," my uncle asked from across the table, "to open a restaurant in this economy? The market hasn't been kind to small businesses for quite some time."

I shrugged, holding on to my calm even as Nico looked ready to throw his forkful of frittata across the table.

Honestly, the last thing we needed at this gathering was an old-fashioned schoolyard food fight.

"A poor business model won't survive even in a good economy," I pointed out. "Our job is to come up with a strong concept, requiring a modest budget, and execute it deliciously." I turned to Nico. "Wouldn't you agree?" I asked my brother, though I focused on my uncle before Nico could open his mouth and get us both in trouble. "Everything that is beautiful and noble is the product of reason and calculation," I said, quoting Baudelaire.

Henri shrugged, his usual response to Baudelaire. "Just make sure there is enough reason and calculation," he said.

"Enough." Maman's tone did not invite further argument. "This is a family gathering, not a business meeting."

Henri opened his mouth to protest, but my mother merely held up her hand. "Not here."

The table chatter started back up moments later as everyone returned to their food and conversations.

"I can't believe we're related to him," Nico grumbled.

I gave his arm a blithe pat. "I wouldn't worry about it overmuch."

Once the guests had gone, the rest of us lingered longer over coffee. Maman carried three more boxes of my grandmother's papers and photos into the living room, boxes that had migrated from Grand-mère's apartment to my parents' home.

"I'm working on a story about Grand-mère for the paper," I told her. "How she was trained in pastry during the late thirties, giving up her career to raise a family but teaching her daughter pastry technique—it's a good human-interest story."

"She did not speak much of those days in France," my mother told me. "The days before the war, you know. And her life with my father..." A shrug.

I leaned forward. "Were they happy?"

"Happiness is transient," my mother replied.

"How so?" I asked, hugging my arms to myself.

"My father...well, Henri is not so different from him. He was a good man, but stubborn. They disagreed about things, the way married couples do. Maybe more so. My mother loved pastry and wanted to open a patisserie in the village. My father felt it would be shameful. Your grand-mère, she contented herself with baking for us and throwing parties with the very best food." She smiled. "That made him happy, and it made her the toast of the village."

"So that's why she opened the patisserie here after he died. I never put that together." I smiled. "Thanks for pulling these out for me."

Back home, I took a closer look at the boxes' contents. There were very few photos of my grandmother as a young woman, but cameras weren't household items at the time, especially in the South of France.

One photo showed her on her wedding day to my grandfather Gilles. Marked 1943, the portrait showed a very serious bride and groom. Grand-mère's dress was lovely, of course, but I searched her expression for any signs of joy and found none.

The more I looked at the photos, the less I thought of my grandmother as Grand-mère. When I looked at her, I saw Mireille Bessette, a woman near my age who happened to be living her life seventy years ago.

I knew wedded bliss to be a very modern concept, but Mireille looked awfully grim for a woman who just married of her own free will, with no goats used as inducement.

The photos I had were usually labeled with dates on the back, but the wedding photo had no such notation. At my desk, I took the photos of Mireille and lined them up in chronological order as best I could.

There was another man—I was sure of it. I didn't have any concrete evidence, but the more I looked at Mireille and Gilles, the more I believed that the man in the photo I found was my true grandfather.

My cell phone buzzed while I was still midthought; I picked it up absently.

"Jules! Guess who got tickets to hear Feist tonight at the Bing Lounge?" Linn practically yelled the question into my ear.

I sat up straighter. "Really?"

"Are you free?"

"Absolutely! What about your husband?"

"He's strictly a Decemberists kind of guy. Feist isn't his jam."

"Then I'll start getting ready now."

"That's all I could ever want."

We made plans to meet and drive over together, and for the first time in a week, I felt a little lighter in spirit.

8

Sharing food with another human being is an intimate
act that should not be indulged in lightly.

—M. F. K. FISHER

In preparation for the concert, I changed into a black jersey wrap
dress with long sleeves, black patterned tights, and black boots. I
added a vintage-looking silver collar necklace and a coat of soft pink lipstick to
keep the look from being too severe. When Linn arrived, I threw on my red
trench and Burberry-esque scarf.

Feist had just finished her first set when I felt my phone vibrate in my boot.
Fearing a family emergency, I glanced at the phone. A text message from Nico.
"Where are you?"

"Bing Lounge with Linn," I texted back.

My phone vibrated again a moment later. "Cool. See you soon."

I had no idea what that meant. Later in the evening? Later that week?
month? Who knew? While Feist and her band sang "My Moon, My Man," I
double-checked to see if I'd had an e-mail from Neil.

Still nothing.

Two songs later, I felt a tapping on my shoulder. I turned, curious, to find
my brother and a stranger standing just behind me.

"What are you doing here?" I asked, trying to walk that fine line between
being heard over the band and disturbing other people's experience.

Nico grinned; I knew he'd have a long story on the subject once the concert was over. Since he didn't seem to need anything but an acknowledgment

of his existence, I turned back to face the front and enjoyed the rest of the band's set.

Afterward, I asked him again how he'd managed to get in.

"I simply asked the nice young lady at the door," he said, wearing his European charm like a strong cologne.

I knew for a fact that more than a young lady stood between my brother and the interior of the venue. "It's an invitation-only event."

Another shrug. Linn looked impressed, but I wasn't. I knew my brother could charm the brass knuckles off a bouncer. And not only had he gotten himself in, but he'd smuggled the stranger in as well.

"I'm Adrian," the stranger said, rather obviously giving me a visual once-over as he proffered a hand and grinned.

"He's the one I was interviewing for the sous-chef position," Nico explained.

"Ah," I said, and found myself taking a defensive step back.

Adrian stood two inches taller than my brother and possessed the kind of long lashes and ringlets many women would envy. On some men, it would look effeminate, but on Adrian the opposite appeared true.

He was good looking, and with the show of friendliness turned my way, I suspected the feeling was mutual.

Not that it mattered. I'd fallen for a coworker once; never again. Adrian could flirt with me all he wanted, but I wasn't interested. Far from it—remembering how things had ended with Éric made me sick to my stomach.

"We were thinking of going out for a bit," Linn said, no doubt thinking she was performing a kindness by extending the evening. "You're welcome to join us."

"We'd love to," Adrian said, his grin somehow growing wider.

I narrowed my eyes. "How are either of you here? It's Saturday night, after all." Since it was the peak time for diners, almost no one in the restaurant industry had Saturday night off. At least not until midnight.

"Adrian is the sous-chef for the breakfast and lunch service at Mirrorage,"

Nico explained. "And since I'm going to leave Elle at some point, Dad wanted Manuel to get a few Saturday dinner services under his belt."

"Fair enough. Mirrorage is a great spot."

"So, food?" Linn slung her purse strap over her shoulder. "I'm hungry. I wish the Spicy Pickle were open later. I want their Parisian wrap."

"If French sounds good, Little Bird isn't more than a few blocks away," I pointed out.

"If by a few, you mean ten blocks, sure."

"I don't mind the walk, if you don't."

"We shall escort you both," Nico said gallantly. He offered an arm to Linn, who cackled at him before starting off on her own—a Southern belle, Linn wasn't.

Adrian stayed by my side as we walked. "Nico said you're to manage the restaurant's opening and possibly continue afterward."

"That's right," I said, keeping my voice businesslike. "I'm a food writer at the paper."

"I've read your stuff," he said. "You're tough."

I bristled.

"No—tough in a good way. Somebody has to be."

"Thanks," I said, though I still couldn't tell if I'd been paid a compliment or not. "How are things at Mirrorage?"

"It's a good place. The owner's a fair man."

I nodded. "He's friends with my dad."

"It's good work, but I'd prefer to move to a dinner service. That's where all the action is."

I shook my head. "I can't understand how you and Nico and the rest of you enjoy that kind of work pace, night after night."

"Every seating is an adventure, a race, but one where you have to be precise. It's like a competition against yourself."

"Like golf?"

"Sure, but with knives and fire."

I couldn't help myself—I chuckled, and Adrian's smile could have doubled as a flashlight.

But I didn't care how handsome or charming he was—I had learned my lesson with coworkers in general and sous-chefs in particular.

"I brought Adrian because I knew you had to meet him," Nico told me as we walked inside Little Bird.

For a brief moment I felt myself go pale. He *wanted* me to meet him? As in, a setup? Was my brother *trying* to sabotage the restaurant before it opened?

My circulation returned to normal when Nico began to recount the interview, Adrian's credentials, the many things he and Adrian shared in common, and their instant friendship. I nodded and listened intently.

There wasn't any need to panic. Sure, there was some kind of flirtatious vibe, for now. But if this was the guy Nico wanted to hire, fine. We would work out a professional rapport. There would be no weirdness. And if necessary, I could hire someone else to manage the place and be done with it.

Couldn't I?

I unrolled my silverware from my napkin, scooting my chair backward as I arranged the cloth onto my lap. A server arrived promptly, and I accepted my water glass with gratitude.

Adrian clutched his own glass with one hand, stretching the opposite arm over his chair back. "So, are you seeing anyone?"

I choked on my water.

Linn handed me an extra napkin. "Are you okay?"

"Fine," I gasped.

I wanted to say, "Yes, I am seeing someone, *thank you very much*." I wanted to say that my near spit-take was not indicative of any awkwardness.

But Neil and I were only writing letters. And owning up to online dating here, in front of Nico and Linn, was not something I'd prepared for.

"Not at the moment, no," I said.

Linn covered a chuckle with a cough around the time she kicked me under the table.

I kicked back.

"Good to hear," Adrian said. He leaned forward, his knee just barely touching my leg.

I tried to shift back, subtly, but my chair had stuck to the floor. Worse yet, my legs were crossed and I only had one foot connecting me to the earth. One wrong move and I could topple over. Why hadn't I listened to my mother when she told me to only ever cross my legs at the ankle?

"You review a lot of the restaurants around here, don't you?"

"I do, yes. So does Linn," I added, hoping to throw a bit of his attention her way.

Didn't work.

"How does it feel to be the one us kitchen guys sweat over?"

I parsed through his question, trying to decide if the double entendre had been intentional. But one look at his face—full-on man smolder—and I realized that it had.

Why were the men who flirted with me the brash, smarmy types? I avoided self-tanner and Lycra like the plague, and yet…here we were.

"I take my job seriously," I answered, sounding very much like Mary Poppins. "People choose restaurants to celebrate important moments in their lives, to find relief from the workday, to be taken care of. The best restaurants do those things, but add"—I paused, trying to find the right words—"an element of delight. Of surprise. And the worst restaurants do the opposite of that. So I want to guide people to the good ones."

"It's a social responsibility," Linn added. "There are so many restaurants in Portland, and the scene is so competitive, we try to direct people to the establishments that get it right."

I was grateful for Linn's interruption, though without it I would have tried to steer the subject to my stance on inter-kitchen dating. But Nico had gotten bored with the topic at hand and instead brought up the latest newsworthy pastry at New York's Dominique Ansel Bakery. Linn chimed in, and the three of them maintained an adult conversation without me.

Just as well.

Nico called me at home after we parted to discuss the evening. "What did you think of Adrian?"

I stuck my phone between my ear and my shoulder while I reached for my toothbrush. "Can we talk about this later? During daylight hours?"

"Come on, Jules. Just your first impression."

I squeezed a strip of toothpaste onto my brush. First impression? I had twenty. "I haven't eaten his food, so I can't say anything definitive. He seemed like a nice enough guy—probably a lot of fun to have in the kitchen. Do you think, though," I asked, phrasing my words carefully, "that the two of you might be *too* similar?"

"How do you mean?"

"I'm sure you already know this," I said, my voice dry, "but you're a lot of personality. Just you, by yourself. But two Nicos in the kitchen? That's a lot of Nicos. Think about when you and Caterina have tried to cook together."

"That's because Caterina is disorganized and bossy."

I did not comment.

Yes, Caterina was a bit disorganized, and sure, she was bossy—all of us had an authoritative streak. But she also ran a very successful cooking and language program. No, the trouble lay less with Caterina than with the fact that no kitchen in the world was large enough to contain the two of them. If they tried to cook together, half of the food would be burned on the outside and raw on the inside, overspiced and oversalted.

"You get along with Adrian very well *now*," I said at last, having brushed the teeth on the left. "But imagine after a long and busy weekend dinner service, when your customers are cranky and sending things back for no good reason and you're short two dishwashers and four waiters. Just think on that."

"I am the chef, you know. My word in the kitchen is law."

"I just want to make sure you're thinking everything over."

"I am. I am a very thoughtful man."

"Yes," I said dryly. "You're known throughout the land for being extraordinarily contemplative." I spat a mouthful of toothpaste into the sink, just as my phone buzzed. An e-mail? "Hey, it's been fun chatting, but it's late and I'm going to bed. Good night, Nico."

Truthfully, though, I hadn't intended on going straight to bed. Instead, I'd planned on sitting down to see if Neil had in fact written me back.

My hopes were not disappointed.

Dear Juliette,

I was very glad to see your e-mail in my inbox. In answer to your questions, no, I'm not related to any Frenchmen or Italians. My father's people were all Scots—loud, burly fellows with a penchant for grudges and kilts. (As they are my kin, I am not allowed to say "skirts." But it is a piece of fabric that looks like a skirt, so there you are.)

My mother's people are Danish and Swedish. I suspect your ancestors could out-cook my ancestors any day they chose, as neither the clansmen nor the Vikings are known for their culinary prowess.

From your profile it sounded as though food is a big part of your life. For me, food is a way for my body to gather the nutrients it needs to allow my cells to produce ATP (that's adenosine triphosphate). But my favorite ATP triggers probably include macaroni and cheese, mashed potatoes, fish sticks, and vanilla pudding.

Sorry. It's not pretty, but I like to be truthful.

I went into medicine because my parents always wanted me to be a doctor. What they really wanted was for me to be a surgeon, but I don't have the temperament for it. I'm not particularly competitive. I am good at research, though, and analysis. Working at a research hospital is a good fit.

This is not to say my colleagues aren't competitive. But on the whole, research isn't as cutthroat as surgery can be. Research requires patience and the willingness to do tedious things over and over.

There is a large medical research community here in Memphis, so there are a lot of transplants like me. I'm originally from North Carolina. It's a different style of barbecue here (another good way to trigger ATP—barbecue), but it's growing on me. I miss the ocean, but with the Mississippi I don't feel as landlocked.

I don't know why I'm rambling about the local landscape.

How's your restaurant coming? I have no idea about the time lines of that kind of project. Do you have a location? And something else I've always been curious about—who makes the menu?

These are probably stupid questions. If I were asking about antigen development, I would know exactly the questions to ask. But that's what makes getting to know other people interesting, right? Unlike some of my colleagues, I do believe there is more to life than antigens and antibodies.

Don't know what to say after that; everything I could think of sounded cheesy. Oh well. If you're reading this at night, sleep well (also—I'm guessing you're a night owl?). And if you're reading this in the morning, have a blessed Sunday.

All the best,

Neil

By the time I finished reading the e-mail, I realized I'd been holding my breath. It was a good letter, I thought, in a way that reminded me of a Jane Austen novel. He expressed himself well, even using a semi-colon accurately.

He seemed nice.

And smart.

Funny, but not too much.

You like him, said a rogue voice from somewhere deep within.

Before I could overanalyze my actions, I hit the Reply button.

And then opened another tab to research what I could about immunology. After a few minutes of reading, I began to type.

Dear Neil,

To be honest, I have no idea how much this e-mail will make sense. It's after midnight, and I have to wake up for church tomorrow—but what a crazy night!

I went to a concert with a friend (the one from work I think I mentioned in my earlier e-mail). We had a great time—Portland has an amazing music scene. Not only are there tons of great local bands, but it's a regular stop for most of the better bands.

Anyway, my friend got tickets to an invite-only event, which my brother managed to crash—he's skilled that way. He brought a friend of his, whom he's decided to hire as our sous-chef, and the four of us went to dinner afterward. It was a little awkward because he was...friendly...and I have (at this point in my life) a very strict do-not-date-coworkers-ever policy.

I've done it before, and it did not end well. At. All.

I expect that was all clear as mud. Sorry. To sum up, it was weird, but I have hopes that its recurrence can be prevented.

In other news, after brunch with my family, I came to the scientific conclusion that my uncle could possibly be my mother's half brother. Scientific, using the study of a) photographs and b) live subjects. No, no DNA was harmed (or examined, really) through the duration of the study. But the fact of the matter is, my uncle looks like my grandfather—a lot—and my mother doesn't. And neither do any of my siblings.

Scientific, right? I thought you'd be impressed.

The restaurant is coming along well. We're putting the staff together (hence the sous-chef episode). As far as location, there's a space my brother would like to use. I'm hoping it works out.

My brother and I will be working the menu out together; our investor will probably have some say in it as well.

Never worry about asking (perceived) silly questions about restaurants—at least as long as I'm permitted to ask stupid questions about immunology.

Everything I know about immunology I learned from Wikipedia. I'm not ashamed to admit it. In fact, I now know the difference between in vitro, in situ, and in vivo. Impressed? Thought not. What area of immunology do you specialize in? (When you tell me, feel free to send me links that might be more accurate than Wikipedia.)

I do have to agree on the state of Danish and Swedish food, for the most part. The Scottish, however, can make some mean shortbread.

Do you feel like you've settled in Memphis, at least for now? What's North Carolina like (other than the barbecue—I am, at least, educated in the geography of barbecue)?

Now for a very important question—what kind of music do you listen to? (Again, I'm from Portland. This is a very big deal.)

Have a wonderful night!

All the best,

Juliette

That night, I did sleep well, and with a tiny, insistent smile in my heart.

9

I did toy with the idea of doing a cook-book.... I think
a lot of people who hate literature but love fried eggs
would buy it if the price was right.

—GROUCHO MARX

I woke up at five Sunday morning with a single stray thought winding
through my head. I had no idea what Neil looked like.

Theoretically, his picture had been available, back when I'd subscribed to
the matchmaking service, before I'd impulsively canceled it.

What if he was really short?

What if he was too old?

What if he was ugly?

And when had I become so very shallow?

No amount of berating quieted the thoughts in my head. Despite the fact
that it was still oppressively dark outside, I struggled from bed, switched on my
bedside light, and shuffled awkwardly to my laptop's resting place in the living
room.

The bright screen burned my eyes. With sluggish fingers, I typed Neil's
name into my search engine.

Well, there was a Neil McLaren with a burgeoning music career and another from Illinois who was a sex offender. But I quickly located the Neil
McLaren, PhD, MD.

According to the photo on his doctor's profile, he was...handsome. Light
reddish-brown hair. A nice jaw. Kind eyes. Early thirties.

I could live with that, I decided, and made the trip back to bed.

The following week, on Saturday, I woke up bright and early. This was partly because I wanted to browse the farmers' market downtown. Also, I still wasn't sleeping well, so when morning came, I'd been ready for it for at least an hour or two.

I examined the bags under my eyes in the bathroom mirror. Either I needed to buy a new eye cream, or I needed to solve this sleep issue soon. I wanted to sleep, but once my head hit the pillow, the stillness allowed plenty of space for my thoughts to roam. I thought about my mother's diagnosis and ran variations of best- and worst-case scenarios through my head. I thought about Grand-mère, how much I missed her, and how much I wanted to ask her advice. I thought about the photo.

I thought about Neil—those were my least worrisome moments. And while I tried to pray in the darkness, asking the Lord for peace and sleep, rest only ever visited with reluctance.

But now, with my sleepless night behind me, I focused on the task ahead. The morning was bright and crisp, the ground damp with dew, the sky dotted with scant clouds. Basically, the perfect Portland spring morning. I threw my trench coat over my outfit, grabbed my canvas bag, and set off for the market.

The clear skies had half of Portland's residents out at the market. I wove through the crowds, enjoying the eclectic music and stall offerings. I found asparagus, rhubarb, sorrel, and some beautiful, earthy wild mushrooms.

After picking up the produce I'd set out for, I wandered through the stalls of prepared foods. There were artisan cheeses, sweet and savory tartlets, kettle corn. Other stalls boasted Nepalese cuisine, Polish cabbage rolls, and Greek gyros. The scents I followed, though, were the sweet ones. I spotted a booth full of pastry and headed right toward it. There was something about the shape of the *kouign amann* and the particular shade of the almond croissants that looked familiar.

Once I got closer to the booth, I understood why.

"Clementine!" I called out, waving like a madwoman.

The dark-haired woman looked up at me, her face brightening. "Juliette!"

I reached the table with a few long strides. "It's been ages!" I exclaimed, clasping her hand over the table. "How are you?"

"Terrific," she said, bangles clanging as she propped a hand on her hip. "And out of work."

"You're kidding! I thought you were at Vinery."

"I was, but I left for an opportunity at La Pastiche."

I grimaced. "Ooh."

The restaurant had risen quickly to great acclaim, but had been mismanaged and closed its doors after a year.

Clementine shrugged. "I've got my fans who visit me here every week, and I'm thinking of a food cart soon." She tucked a strand of hair behind a multipierced ear. "I saw in the paper that Mireille passed away. I'm so sorry."

"Thanks," I said simply. "She's missed."

"She was an institution. I learned so much from her. She made me make everything over until it came out the way she wanted. I was so mad at first— and then I tasted what she made."

"She was special."

"I got it all right, in the end. Everything but *canelé*—I could never get the centers as soft and the outsides as crisp." She shrugged. "The advantage to being in the States, though, is hardly anyone knows what good pastry is supposed to taste like."

"Not that it really changes anything."

"Nope. What are you up to these days?"

I filled her in on my work at the paper before segueing into the new restaurant. "We're planning on using the patisserie space," I said. "It'll need some remodeling, of course, but I think it'll be really nice in the end."

"Have you hired your pastry chef yet?"

"I know Nico's been talking to Mario Angioli, but nothing's final."

"You should hire me." Clementine restocked her tabletop pastry case with several swoon-worthy confections. "I can make a pâte à choux you'd swear was French. I'm great at candies and chocolate, and I make great ice cream."

I hugged my arms to myself, trying to contain the excitement blossoming in my chest. "That'd be great, wouldn't it? Grand-mère would have loved it."

"I think so. After telling me to use a gentler touch with my laminated doughs."

"Let me take your card. I'll talk to Nico and see what I can do."

"Absolutely not," Nico said as we sat inside La Petite Chouquette Sunday afternoon. "I've already settled it with Mario."

"But he hasn't left his job, and he's got a couple kids, doesn't he? I'd feel bad pulling him away from something stable to join a start-up. Clementine's between jobs as it is."

"That can't be a good sign."

"Her work received a good deal of acclaim at La Pastiche—the fact that the place was mismanaged by the owners was out of her hands."

Nico didn't respond, so I continued. "She interned under Grand-mère, so her work is flawless. Just consider it. I think she'd be an impressive feather in the restaurant's cap."

"I'll think about it. For now, let's take a look at the space."

"Keep thinking about it," I said. "I called Clementine and asked if she'd come and audition for us."

"Here?"

"She interned here, she's familiar with the kitchen—why not?"

Nico scowled.

"Look at it this way—it's free dessert."

"I took an economics class, Etta. There is no such thing as a free dessert."

"Please? For me?"

"Fine." Nico's frown didn't change, but we turned our attention to the inside of the patisserie. The truth was, it looked sad and lonely without custom-ers bustling about and Grand-mère behind the counter—like a walnut shell without the meat nestled inside. For the first time, I felt truly at peace about using the patisserie. It needed the scents of food being prepared and enjoyed, the movement of people coming together to share meals.

"We can put tables around here, like this," Nico said, his arms gesturing as he drew in the air. "Maybe put a bar here—"

I shook my head. "No bar. We don't want to be a sixty-forty place."

"A what?"

"Where sixty-year-old divorcés go to meet forty-year-old divorcées. Come on. Do you want a middle-aged man sitting up there, twirling his scotch and hitting on a woman while a jazz combo plays? I'm getting hives just saying it out loud."

"The bar will make money."

I had to concede the point, at least for the time being. "We'll talk about it later. Let's talk about what we're going to call this place."

Nico chuckled. "You know, I hadn't even thought about it."

"Really?" I walked outside, and he followed me. We stood together, taking in the building."

"My last place was L'uccello Blu," he said. "I liked that."

A smile curled on my lips. "You know, the two front doors here—we could paint them."

"I don't really care. That's up to you."

"I'm just saying, we could paint them blue. L'uccello Blu, Two Blue Doors—"

"Two Blue Doors." Nico rolled the words around in his mouth, testing them. "I like it." He clapped his hands together. "That was easy. Do you want to take a look at the apartment?"

Moving on, then. "Probably should," I said, wrapping my arms around myself. I hated the idea of being in Grand-mère's home without Grand-mère, but the apartment couldn't sit empty forever.

We had a couple of options—we could remodel and use it as extended seating. It did have a lovely little balcony, which would be nice during the summer dining season.

The renovations would, of course, take money. We'd have to knock out walls, remove bathtubs—pretty much gut the thing.

But as a living space, the apartment itself wasn't in terrible condition. It was clean, having been attended to weekly by a housekeeper. Spacious by Portland standards, the space boasted two bedrooms and two complete bathrooms.

All that living space, however, was buried under decades of bric-a-brac and tchotchke. I wished Maman would take me up on my offer to come in with her to parse through the rest of it. But I respected her grieving process. Maman knew how to get things done, and when she was ready, we'd take care of it soon enough.

The kitchen, though—I loved that kitchen. Always had. It boasted a deep farmhouse-style porcelain sink, with lovely old fixtures that read "hot" and "cold" in French. It had a south-facing window that overlooked the patio garden—a perfect little slice of Provence.

"What do you think?" Nico asked, ruffling his hair as he looked around.

"It'd be a shame to change too much, I think," I said slowly.

Nico turned, his gaze sweeping the interior. "You may be right," he said.

By the time we came downstairs, I could tell Nico had forgotten about Clementine Grey's dessert challenge.

But she, clearly, had not.

I'd left the soon-to-be-blue doors open, and Clementine had let herself in. As we entered the kitchen, I could see her putting the finishing touches on two bowls of something chocolaty.

"What is that?" I asked, taking a closer look.

Clementine finished her plating and stepped back. "Nutella mousse with hazelnut liqueur, served with chocolate-dipped hazelnut shortbread."

She was good; I had to give her that. Nico and I shared a deep, genetic affinity for the chocolate-hazelnut spread. Without hesitation, I picked up the spoon and dug in.

An intense, perfectly complex Nutella taste met my tongue. My eyes slid shut. "That is so good."

"Try it with the shortbread," Clementine instructed.

I dipped the chocolaty-end of the shortbread into the mousse. The crunch of the cookie set off the rich mousse like a dream. A chocolaty, hazelnutty, Nutella-y dream.

Dragging my attention away from dessert, I looked to Nico to see his reaction.

He stood staring at me, spoon in hand, mousse untouched.

I frowned at him. "What on earth are you waiting for? Eat!"

Nico scowled but dug his spoon into the mousse. He took a bite; his face froze.

"Seriously," I said, working two more spoonfuls, "I might lick the bowl."

Nico shrugged. "It's pretty good."

Clementine squared her shoulders. "Pretty good?"

"You want the job?"

"Yes, I do," she answered.

"I'll think about it," he told her, his expression guarded.

"Thank you," Clementine replied, unfazed.

I scooped another bite of mousse. "This shortbread? It's perfect."

"It's the French butter. I get it from your grandmother's supplier—he gives us, I mean, me, a good deal. I bake croissants for him. He imports French butter but can't bake. Isn't that sad?"

I nodded, nibbling at the shortbread. "The butter certainly imports a richness of flavor that's quite special."

"You should hire me." Clementine wiped down her work surface with brisk efficiency. "Your grandmother trained me. I'm CIA certified. Graduated at the top of my class, which is not"—she poked the air with her index finger—"common. At all. Pastry—real pastry—is a man's world. Cupcakes," she said, rolling her eyes, "don't count. My laminated pastries are flawless, and I have excellent chocolate technique. My macaroons taste French, and I'm excellent at custards—"

"You're good," Nico interrupted. "And you can have the job. I'll talk to Mario."

Clementine inclined her head. "Fair enough."

Nico turned to me. "She's bossy."

I patted his arm. "Think of the mousse, Nico. Just think of the mousse."

~ NUTELLA MOUSSE ~

$^1/_2$ cup Nutella
$^1/_4$ cup crème fraîche
$1^1/_2$ teaspoons hazelnut liqueur (optional)
$^1/_2$ cup cream
Chocolate curls, toasted hazelnuts, or chocolate-dipped hazelnut
     shortbread for serving.

Add the Nutella, crème fraîche, and liqueur in a medium bowl and beat with an electric mixer until smooth.

Whip cream in a separate, chilled bowl (metal is ideal).

Fold the whipped cream into the Nutella mixture until completely combined. Spoon the mousse into serving bowls and refrigerate for 20 minutes. Serve with a sprinkling of chocolate curls and hazelnuts, chocolate-dipped hazelnut shortbread on the side, or both. Admire how something so simple can taste so good.

CHOCOLATE-DIPPED HAZELNUT SHORTBREAD

1^1/$_3$ cups hazelnuts with skins removed, divided

1 cup all-purpose flour

^{1}/$_2$ teaspoon baking powder

^{1}/$_2$ teaspoon salt

8 tablespoons (1 stick) butter, room temperature

^{1}/$_3$ cup sugar

1 egg

1 teaspoon vanilla extract

4 ounces good-quality semisweet chocolate

Preheat oven to 350°F.

Bake hazelnuts on a parchment paper–lined cookie sheet until fragrant, about 10 to 15 minutes. Set aside and allow to cool.

Lower oven to 325°F. Chop 1 cup hazelnuts until fine or pulse in a food processor.

Mix dry ingredients together in a medium-sized bowl.

Beat butter and sugar until pale; add egg. Incorporate dry ingredients slowly, followed by the hazelnuts. Blend until nuts are evenly distributed throughout the dough.

Roll out shortbread to ^{1}/$_4$-inch thick; cut into desired shapes—long and rectangular, square, or heart-shaped—with a knife or cookie cutters.

Bake on parchment-papered baking sheet until very lightly golden, about 12 to 16 minutes. Watch them closely—overbake and they'll be dry, underbake and they'll have less flavor. Cool on wire racks.

Melt chocolate in a glass measuring cup in the microwave or in a double boiler over the stove. If you use the microwave, cook in short bursts, stirring in between. Once melted, dip one end of cooled cookies into the melted chocolate. Return cookies to baking sheet.

Rough chop remaining $1/3$ cup hazelnuts. Sprinkle nuts over chocolate-tipped cookies. Allow the chocolate to set.

Makes 1 to 2 dozen, depending on cookie size.

10

I think preparing food and feeding people brings nourishment not only to our bodies but to our spirits. Feeding people is a way of loving them, in the same way that feeding ourselves is a way of honoring our own createdness and fragility.

—Shauna Niequist

After coffee with Clementine, I couldn't fight the desire to take a more detailed look around Grand-mère's apartment. I stood in her living room and looked around for something, anything, that might illuminate Grand-mère's past in general, the photo in particular.

Not that I had any idea what I was looking for.

I'd already found the photo. A part of me saw the space but didn't *see* it— running it through the familiar filter of a hundred Monday afternoons. Mondays, because the patisserie was closed on Mondays. Grand-mère made us milky tea to drink with the pastries she'd baked fresh for us on her day off.

If I was going to find answers, though, I would have to look past my memories and see the space for what it was.

Relics of past relationships—what physical objects survived? Keepsakes if the romance ended sweetly, but what if things ended bitterly? In many ways, my relationship with Éric had defined the last half decade of my life, but I had very few items with ties to him; no one else would know their origins but the two of us. How could I glance around my grandmother's space and think I'd be able to unearth anything?

I sat down on the ivory velvet divan and mentally cataloged the things I had because of Éric. A cookbook, a silk wrap. A few photographs on my computer and phone, but nothing ever printed. A set of olive-wood salad tongs. Oh, and the slip of paper with his "fortune" on it that read: "Only love lets us see normal things in an extraordinary way." Sappy, yes. But he gave it to me after dinner at his favorite Chinese restaurant, Shandong, and I still kept it, half-crumpled, inside my coin purse.

Of these things, only a few notes in the cookbook might tip someone off, but that someone would have to know both of us well. No one would look at the silk wrap, in its shades of red and gold, and think of Éric.

No one but me.

Another strike against the modern age; I had no pressed flowers, no initialed handkerchief. No letters tied with a silk ribbon, not even a lock of hair.

As for Grand-mère, there might be photographs. There could be all sorts of things, but I wouldn't know unless I looked.

The closets seemed the best place to start. It felt so invasive, searching through a dead woman's belongings. Would she mind? Or would she want to keep her secrets to herself?

I had no idea. But my curiosity overrode my sensitivity.

In her bedroom, I found the old dresses my sisters and I had played with as children, and even more dresses in garment bags, with sachets of lavender on each hanger. She had a lovely shoe collection, including several pairs of Ferragamo flats all wrapped in silver tissue. There were handbags, of course. Tiny ones.

From a wardrobe perspective, she led a wonderful life. Wonderful and mysterious. There were party dresses and day dresses, cocktail dresses and holiday dresses—but who was she with when she wore them? Was she happy?

No voices jumped out to tell me one way or the other.

For the next hour I explored the apartment, wishing I knew what I was really looking for.

That Tuesday, I picked up my sister Caterina from the airport.

"Darling!" she cried when she saw me, her arms outstretched, fingers waggling.

People looked, as they always did. Caterina attracted plenty of attention, with her Nigella-meets-Giada good looks and her oversized personality.

We hugged and exchanged Continental-style kisses, which Cat had told me once we could get away with without being tacky, since we were clearly of European descent.

"How's Mom?" she asked as we strode purposefully out of the building. "I've chatted with her over the phone, but it's hard to get a read."

"She's Mom," I answered. "She looks worn and tired, but good luck getting her to slow down long enough to pry information out of her."

"All right, then. I'll admit that was partly why I wanted to come out for her appointment—I figured I had a better chance of finding something out if I happened to be in the same room as the doctor."

"You are very good at getting information out of people," I observed.

"HIPAA fears me."

"Just so you know, Sophie's coming to the appointment too."

"I figured. Even packed an extra air canister in case she sucked up all the air in the room." She made a face. "I'm sorry. That was mean."

I resisted the urge to laugh. "But possibly pragmatic. How were the boys when you left?"

"Growing again! It's unreal." Caterina looked over at me, smiled, and threw her arm around my shoulders. "Terrible circumstances, but I love getting to see you."

I rested my head against her shoulder. "I need to come out and visit you next, I know."

"Who said anything about visit? Say the word and I'll find you a job and a place to live. We'll even throw in one of those Edible Arrangements things."

"I do like fruit in pretty shapes, so that's a strong offer," I answered gamely. "But I couldn't leave, not now."

"Of course not. But someday. And I'm not just saying that because I could use the occasional bit of childcare."

"Of course not," I said, pointing ahead. "There's the car, to the right."

"I can't believe that car's still running. Alex is a wizard."

"He's an accomplished tinkerer," I agreed.

"How's he doing?"

"Pretty good. He works a lot—more than he used to, I think. But he's more relaxed now that Stephanie's moved on."

Caterina snorted in disgust. "I could kick her."

I couldn't disagree. "He's done an amazing job with the apartment over the garage. Did you see it when you were here last?"

"Didn't get a chance, but he was telling me about it."

"Lots of updates. His goal is to make it zero energy, totally self-sustaining. I suspect there are some psychological reasons for it, but he seems to be enjoying the work."

Cat shook her head. "I wish I could be here more. I miss you guys."

During the drive to our parents' house, Cat caught me up on her classes, the boys, and Damian's job as a caterer. I told her what I knew about Mom's cancer, which turned out to be the same as what she knew, with the exception of the fact that Mom thought her oncologist looked like an older Vanessa Paradis.

The entire family met together for dinner at D'Alisa & Elle. While there were plenty of patrons dining and milling, eating at the restaurant felt almost as familiar as eating at my parents' home. The tables, the art, even the carpet under my feet—I knew it all by heart.

We ate from huge platters, family style. Cat showed off pictures of her twin boys, and we marveled over Luca's death-defying antics and Christian's finger-painted artwork. We laughed and argued and stuffed ourselves full of food, none of us brave enough to speak of the appointment the following morning.

When Sophie had heard about the preop appointment, she'd invited herself; Cat had followed suit. Maman had asked me to join the party, and I rearranged my workday to accommodate the trip.

But when I arrived at the house to meet her on Wednesday, the sight of Sophie's car parked on the street made me wish I'd picked up a second cup of coffee.

"Oh good, you're here," Sophie said when she opened the door. "I wanted to get on the road soon. Traffic."

"I…um…sure." I looked at my watch. I was really, really early, because the traffic was so thin.

Mom stood behind Sophie, where she could shrug and shake her head without Sophie noticing.

"Hey!" Cat strolled down the hall, looking tousled, tired, and fashionable all at once. She was the only person I knew who could make jet lag chic. "Are we heading out? Which car are we taking?"

"Let's take mine," Sophie said decisively. "Safety rating, you know."

No, I didn't. I bit back a retort about a car being as safe as its driver, but when it came to Sophie, snipy comebacks never solved anything.

Sophie drove. Mom sat in the front seat. Cat and I sat in the back, with a pile of library books and a Trader Joe's bag full of Chloé's outgrown clothes shoved in the middle.

I flipped absently through one of the books while Sophie maintained a one-sided conversation with Mom about her diet in general and flaxseed and green tea in particular. Cat texted her husband for updates on the boys.

By the time we arrived at the hospital, I'd made it to the third chapter in a novel about a dystopian society. The society seemed easier to manage than my oldest sister.

Sophie tried to get Mom to let her carry her purse; Mom declined.

Cat retaliated by offering to carry Sophie's purse, as well as mine.

Out of self-defense, I stayed two paces behind the three of them. There were no good reasons for me to get caught in their cross hairs—Mom could fend for herself.

Sophie let the receptionist know we'd arrived; she tried to fill out the requisite paperwork, but Mom reclaimed (or wrenched—I couldn't tell) the clipboard away.

I exhaled in relief. Sophie could be fearsome with a clipboard.

Cat started to sift through the purse she held, ostensibly for prescription tranquilizers with Sophie's name on them.

We settled on a bench facing the bank of windows, and I had just started to flip through an outdated issue of *Sunset* when my phone beeped.

Sophie glared at me.

I ignored her. The e-mail icon appeared in my corner of my screen. Before I could pause to think about the ramifications, I paged to my inbox.

Neil. It was an e-mail from Neil.

Dear Juliette,

Sorry it's been a while. There was a weeklong immunology conference in Miami; I was on several panels, and I gave a couple lectures, and now I feel like I'm giving excuses.

I got busy, but here's the thing—I thought about you the whole time.

My face flushed—he was thinking about me? I felt fifteen all over again.

Took a tour through the Everglades. Saw some gators. A couple of them looked like coworkers.

I laughed.

Sophie leaned over my shoulder. "What is that? What are you laughing at?"

"Nothing." I felt my face flush a deeper red.

"Nothing?" Cat echoed.

"Nothing that would interest either of you." I tried to return to my reading casually.

"I doubt that," said Cat.

Sophie leaned closer.

I elbowed her in the ribs. "Seriously!"

"Ow!"

"Filles!" Mom cut in.

"Gabrielle?" the nurse called from the doorway.

I flushed deeper. How embarrassing, to be caught squabbling with my sister in the oncology waiting room.

Over an e-mail from a boy, no less.

Sophie didn't seem the least bit chastened.

Suddenly, I wanted to scream. All I could think about was how much I didn't want to go through my mother's closet, the way I was going through Grand-mère's. But here we were, at an appointment for cancer surgery. The cancer felt real, for the first time.

And for the first time, I was truly scared.

"Juliette, let's go!"

I looked up to see Mom following the nurse and Sophie waiting for me, exasperated.

"This is bad, Soph," I said, just out of Mom's earshot.

"Of course it's bad," she retorted, hiking her purse higher on her shoulder. "Why do you think we're here?"

The appointment went about as well as it could. Mom sat on the exam table, Sophie sat in the first chair, and Cat offered me the second. The nurse exclaimed over how small the room was before she strapped an ID bracelet onto my mother's tiny wrist and gave brusque instructions about fluids and fasting before the surgery. When the doctor asked if she had any questions, my mother demurred. Sophie, though, came with a list of questions she'd compiled with the help of WebMD. Cat made jokes and teased Sophie, trying to lighten the mood and further incensing Sophie in the process.

I wished I'd asked Neil for questions. Instead, I just sat quietly, feeling like the kid at the grownups' table. I clutched Maman's purse, holding it on my lap so it wouldn't have to sit on the floor.

Afterward, I returned home to my apartment, numb. A stack of work needed my attention, but I couldn't will myself to sit at my computer.

Without being fully aware of what I was doing, I flipped the lights on in my kitchen and began to measure out chicken stock and arborio rice.

The butternut squash in my pantry found itself quartered and set to roast in the oven. I plucked a few leaves of sage from my kitchen herb garden and minced them fine. Butter, shallots, rice, and herbs. Roasted squash and parmesan. The risotto took shape, its savory scent filling my apartment.

When it was done, I looked down at the work of my hands. Sure, I couldn't fix anything. Some things—okay a lot of things—had to remain in the hands of God. But food?

That I could take care of.

With steadier hands, I packed risotto into lidded glass containers and placed them in a foil-lined bag to take to my parents.

I didn't remember Neil's e-mail until I went to bed. In the dark, I reached for my phone and read the last few paragraphs.

There were just a few more lines about the conference, some notes on the food (because he knew I'd wonder), and sweet words at the end.

I'd told him I had too much going on, that my life was too complicated.

Somehow he'd snuck into my thoughts and my life, all without having met face to face.

He made me happy.

With my mother sick, I felt guilty taking that time to be happy.

I wanted to write him back, but I didn't know what to say. Instead, I put my phone away, rolled over, and tried not to think about how cold my feet felt.

The next two weeks sailed by. My mom made it through surgery without complications, other than a poor response to the anesthesia. Cat stayed on for three more days, and between the two of us, we filled the freezer with easy meals. I knew Cat was glad she'd come out, but I could read the strain on her face as she tried to keep up with her family in Chicago while helping tend to our mom. By the time Damian called to tell her about his most recent trip to the ER—Luca had had an unfortunate incident with a waffle iron—I could tell she was ready to break.

Still she pressed on, helping me sort through the back bedroom at Grand-mère's apartment.

I thought about Neil every night. Still couldn't figure out what to say.

Even as my family life demanded an increasing amount of thought and attention, my workload increased as well. I wrote about fondue—fondue and barbecues and taco bars—and continued to work on the piece about Grand-mère on the side.

Marti called me into her office a week after Maman's surgery. "Good news!" she said, eyes dancing. "I'm sure you've guessed from your reader feedback, but your new column has been very popular."

"Oh good," I said, both pleased and disappointed. If we'd had poor reader feedback, I might have been able to convince Marti to let me pursue other source material.

"I wanted you to know that we've been discussing syndication with other print and Internet news outlets. Also, *Portland Sunrise* is very interested in having you appear on the show."

My eyes widened. "Television?"

"I'll put you in touch with the producer, of course, but they're particularly interested in having you do a demo of the fondue party."

"But what's to demo?" I asked, trying and failing to picture it in my head. "Do people not know how to dip things in warm sauce anymore?"

Marti leveled her gaze at me. "How to set it up, how to keep temperatures stable. Just mime the existing piece—no need to reinvent it. Let me know once you're in touch with *Sunrise,* and put your thinking cap on for your next installment. I think this could be very successful, Juliette."

I nodded, thanked her, and walked back to my desk. Television? The idea frightened me. I wasn't Cat—I wasn't smooth and charming in front of people. In front of an audience, every ounce of poise I possessed tended to sweat itself out.

For twenty minutes, I sat at my desk, trying to wrap my head around the situation and think of solutions.

Twenty minutes later, I was no further than when I'd begun.

~ BUTTERNUT SQUASH RISOTTO ~

2 cups chicken stock

$1^1/_2$ to $2^1/_3$ cups water

1 cup dry white wine—sparkling is fine

3 tablespoons butter

1 clove garlic, minced fine

1 large shallot, minced fine

2 cups arborio rice

4 tablespoons minced fresh sage

1^1/$_2$ cups roasted butternut squash
^{1}/$_3$ cup freshly grated parmesan cheese
Cracked black pepper

Preheat oven to 425°F. Cut squash into quarters, place onto a foil-lined baking sheet, and roast for 35 to 45 minutes, until squash is soft and fork tender. Measure out 1^1/$_2$ cups and set aside.

Set the broth and water to boil in a medium saucepan. Reduce heat to a simmer.

Over medium heat, melt butter in large saucepan or enameled cast-iron dutch oven. Add shallots and cook until soft; add garlic. Once the garlic is soft, add the arborio rice. Stir mixture until rice begins to turn golden. Add sage.

Add the wine to the rice, stirring constantly until liquid is absorbed. Add chicken stock mixture ^{1}/$_2$ cup at a time, stirring until liquid is absorbed each time; continue until rice is al dente and mixture becomes creamy. Be patient!

Stir in squash and parmesan. If the risotto is too thick, add additional stock.

Serve hot with generous amounts of cracked black pepper, and enjoy with a green salad. Refrigerate leftovers.

Serves 4 to 6.

11

All great deeds and all great thoughts have a ridiculous beginning. Great works are often born on a street corner or in a restaurant's revolving door.

—ALBERT CAMUS

rue to their word, *Portland Sunrise* made contact within a few hours. The assistant producer e-mailed, I e-mailed back, and within a couple of hours, we'd nailed down a date for my appearance on the show. I entered the event on my calendar with a knot in my stomach.

"You look as white as a sheet," Linn commented, peering over the cubicle divide.

"I'm not charming on camera," I answered. "I can fake it through radio, but the camera doesn't lie."

"The camera lies sometimes—it can't be that bad."

"Oh, it is," I assured her. "My sister Caterina's wedding? Videographer decided to get up close and personal with the bridesmaids during the ceremony. I made a series of faces—entirely by accident—that became Cat's favorite part of the video."

"Not her favorite part, I'm sure."

"She told me it's the part she watches when she's depressed, because it gets a laugh every time."

"Oh." Linn reached over and patted my shoulder. "Well…morning TV should be better. Different. No one's getting married."

"Yes," I said drily. "I'm sure it'll help to be talking at 7 a.m. Because I'm so good at stringing sentences together that early."

"I've heard you talk at seven in the morning."

"Did it make any sense?"

Linn thought for a moment. "No, I don't think it did."

"That's all right. The show will either go fine, or it won't." I looked up at Linn with a straight face. "My next task is to figure out what part of the country to flee to if it goes poorly."

"Pick a place with sun and I'll come visit you."

"Noted," I said, and we each returned to work.

When I left the newsroom for the day, I stopped at Whole Foods for groceries before returning home. I knew my parents had enough prepared food to last for a month or two, but my own larder had grown empty. Once at home, I rolled up my sleeves, slipped an apron over my head, and got comfortable in the kitchen. There was something about the rhythm of chopping vegetables, of seasoning food, of watching it transform that helped me relax.

Maybe I was barely succeeding at work or as a daughter, but if I roasted asparagus for twenty minutes, it would become bright and toothsome. My world had become unpredictable, but at least I could rely on the goodness of the Lord and the consistency of green vegetables.

Once I had dinner on the table, I wrote a short note to Neil, apologizing for my lack of correspondence and bringing him up to date with my mom's surgery, Cat's visit, and my upcoming TV appearance.

Afterward, I drove to the patisserie and took measurements of the space before writing a list of updates. We needed to get bids on the remodeling, and that kind of follow-through just wasn't in Nico's wheelhouse.

I repeated the process—or some variation—over the next week, working, cooking, and driving back and forth between my apartment and the patisserie. Late Friday night, while the rest of Portland was just beginning to celebrate the weekend, I unlocked the upstairs apartment and took a look around.

It took me all of thirty seconds to make the decision.

"I need the apartment over the patisserie," I told Nico while he was on break at Elle later that night. "My job is only getting busier, and I can get more done if I'm only walking downstairs to get to the restaurant rather than driving three miles in inconsistent traffic."

Nico opened his mouth to speak, but I cut him off with a raised hand.

"You wanted me to do the restaurant; I'm doing the restaurant. This is my price. And no, we don't need the upstairs for seating just yet. Better to launch with the existing downstairs and expand from there." I gave a curt nod. "I think that's it. I've got to get back to work and finish my list of contractors to call in the morning." I paused, smiling. "I also thought I'd ask Clementine if she wanted to room with me."

Nico may have wanted to say something, but I didn't stick around to find out, striding instead for the door as quickly as my ballet flats could carry me.

But Nico was, in truth, smarter than I gave him credit for. He didn't even try to outrun me; he picked up his phone instead.

"Yes?" I said, feeling sheepish when I answered. I sat in my car, keys not yet in the ignition.

"I'm not moving that prep table again. Alex can help you move that table. I will give you money to hire movers to move the table. But me? Not happening. Not doing that again."

"Okay."

"Okay, then." He cleared his throat. "And Clementine's all right."

"I know. That's why we hired her."

He grunted his good-bye. I hung up with a smile. I smiled even larger when my phone beeped, announcing a new arrival in my inbox from Neil.

Dear Juliette,

Glad to hear your mom came through surgery fine, but sorry to hear your job's gotten more complicated. You'll have to let me know how the TV thing goes; that sounds interesting. I was happy to see a note from you in my inbox. I also won't pretend that I'm not glad I make you happy. To be honest, it kind of scares me too. Does that make us even?

My siblings—I've got a much older sister and a younger brother. We're not as much in one another's business as your siblings, but reading between the lines, it sounds as though your siblings win the gold cup when it comes to nosiness. My sister keeps to herself—she's an investment banker in Atlanta. My brother and I see each other more often. He's slogging his way through law school at Tulane. Medical school's not easy, but I'd sooner relive my residency than do what he's doing.

However, that might be because I'd rather be in a lab than a library, writing about decisions people made in Wyoming, twenty years ago. To each his own. My brother wants to go on to work for nonprofits; he's a cool guy.

As much as I enjoy hearing from you, you were honest from the beginning—you've got a lot going on in your life. If I don't hear from you, I assume you have other things to do than e-mail a stranger in Tennessee. Do me a favor, though? If you decide not to continue to write, let me know. I'm the kind of guy who likes to have everything out in the open. If I wanted to be playing awkward relationship games, I'd audition for *The Bachelorette*.

I hope you don't watch *The Bachelorette*. My sister watches it (although she pretends she doesn't), and it makes no sense to me.

Top Gear—that's a show I can get behind.

Neil

Dear Neil,

I may be flaky and distracted, but I promise I wouldn't stop e-mailing without some sort of communication first. I'm horrified you'd have to ask, but I can't pretend it's not justified.

What is *Top Gear*? I looked it up and found both an American and British version. Which do you enjoy? What's the appeal? I'm not much into cars, but my dad and oldest brother are obsessed with Alfa Romeos. In the long run, this works out for me—when mine breaks down, I usually have someone to fix it. I used to have a Jetta, but it was too reliable. What kind of car do you drive?

Well, it's official—I'm moving. It seemed like a good idea until I remembered how much I hate packing.

My grandmother had a patisserie (i.e., bakery, for the uninitiated) with an apartment above it. When she passed away, the building became my mother's. My brother and I are using the patisserie space for our restaurant, and I'm moving into the apartment. It makes a lot of practical sense on paper, but in reality, quite a few of her things are still there. I don't want to clear it out—there are a lot of memories there, you know? But I've spent too much time driving between the restaurant and my place, and life will become simpler when I can shorten one of my commutes.

My official moving date is Monday. Monday, because that's when the men in my family can get off work to help. It's worth taking the day off in order to get the manpower.

Agreed about *The Bachelorette.* I don't understand how people might imagine picking a spouse based on how well a diving-with-dolphins or dining-in-Spain date went. I'm not married (obviously), but I've always been under the impression that marriage involves, you know, work. And life. And not a great deal of glamour.

Those are my thoughts. Some of them, at least. Is it strange to say I miss you, when we haven't exactly met?

J

When my alarm chimed on Monday morning, my senses snapped to awareness in record time.

Moving day.

As I moved through my morning routine, I felt acutely aware of the fact that this was my last day in my apartment. The last time I'd accidentally clank the glass door in my shower, last time I'd brush my teeth at that sink, last time I'd make coffee in that kitchen—my sentimental Italian genes wouldn't shut up. I dressed for the day in jeans, a bright pink tee, and a gray cozy hoodie, then pulled my hair back into a ponytail. At the last minute, unable to deny my Italian heritage, I threw on a multistrand necklace.

Who says you can't accessorize when you're moving?

Light makeup, a swipe of lip gloss, and I felt ready to face the day.

Ready until I looked out my front window and saw the approaching figures below.

Nico. Alex.

And Adrian.

I ducked away from the window and wiped the gloss off with the back of my hand. Don't know why I bothered—I had a feeling Adrian would flirt with any woman, provided she was wearing a little mascara and was still breathing. Seconds later, one of the men knocked on the door.

Oh well. At least it was free labor, even if it was costly to my mental health.

"Are you ready?" Nico asked, hands on hips as he surveyed the packed and taped boxes stacked throughout my living room.

"As much as I'll ever be." I hugged Alex and turned to Adrian to wave hello. "Thanks for giving me a hand."

"Anytime," Adrian replied, giving me an appreciative once-over as he shrugged out of his leather jacket and rolled up his sleeves. "You look good."

"Hmm," I said, less than wittily.

Over the next several hours, we made countless trips up and down the steps, packing away my life into the moving van below. For once, the Portland skies opted to cooperate, the clouds gray but not damp.

Adrian—and his snug black tee—seemed to revel in the opportunity to show off his upper arms. He kept a running count of how many boxes he'd carried, egging Nico to keep his own tally.

Alex just rolled his eyes and carried my bronze floor lamp down the stairs. Later, Alex and Adrian moved the prep table. Without complaining.

Once the moving van and all the cars were full and my apartment wasn't, everyone piled into vehicles to make the trip to the patisserie, my new home.

Nico took the keys to my car. I slid into the passenger seat of my parents' truck, next to Alex. I watched as my car pulled out of the driveway. I had just buckled my seat belt when Adrian rapped against the window.

"Nico left without me," he said when I rolled down the window. "Can I catch a ride with you?"

"Of course," Alex said, before I could suggest that Adrian could hitch a ride on the trailer and keep my couch steady.

There was no help for it. I unbuckled and scooted over into the middle to make room for Adrian.

He winked.

I had sincere doubts about the series of events that led to Adrian being left behind, especially once the two of us had buckled our seat belts and found ourselves in a kind of awkward truck cuddle.

"Do you have enough room?" I asked Adrian, wide eyed, and scooted farther away, to the point that I was practically in my oldest brother's lap.

For all that, Adrian practically ignored me during the drive, instead asking Alex about his job managing Elle's catering business.

At the apartment, I busied myself with the kitchen supplies, getting stuff ready enough to have things to eat off for lunch. While Nico and Adrian continued to move everything in, Alex offered to make the trip to Elephants Deli to pick up lunch for everyone.

Maman had offered to have Alex take things to Goodwill, but I'd demurred for some reason or other that I made up on the spot. Really, I didn't want to accidentally donate something that might provide answers, even if it was just a sewing box.

I had my reasons, none of which lent to a seamless move. With every new box and chair, finding places for everything became increasingly difficult. Nico and Alex dismantled Grand-mère's bed while Adrian unloaded my own bed from the trailer.

"Where do you want that trunk to be once we're done?" Nico asked, pointing at Grand-mère's huge gray steamer trunk, the one that had always been at the foot of her bed.

"Right there," I told him.

"Are you sure? It's old."

"It's vintage," I clarified. "It can stay."

Once the space had been cleared, the difficulties only increased.

Nico squinted at the headboard as if it were a loaf of bread gone stale. "So...how does this go together?"

"Where's the hardware from when you disassembled it?" I asked.

Nico shrugged. "Alex did it."

Of course Alex wasn't there, having fled to the deli.

Coward.

Adrian eyed the pieces. "So there's, like, nails somewhere? Do you have a hammer?"

"Don't be stupid," Nico said, hands on his hips. "There are screws and bolts and washings and stuff."

"Washers," Adrian corrected.

"Whatever." Nico waved a hand. "I'm a chef, not a construction worker."

I patted his arm. "But you do make beautiful composed salads. Where are the tools, anyway?" I asked.

Nico frowned. "Alex had them last."

If I didn't know better, I'd think Alex had hidden them and fled the scene on purpose.

Rather than try to be helpful, I followed suit and retreated to the kitchen. Telling Nico to give up on the assembly would only make him more determined. I figured that as long as the tools were AWOL, the likelihood of my bed sustaining serious damage remained low.

I was halfway through the crudités prep when I heard it.

The electric screwdriver.

Darn it.

In the end, all the boxes and furniture made their way into the new apartment. And between the four us of, there wasn't a leftover from the deli to be found. Alex fixed my bed (he had to undo what the guys did in his absence), and all was right in the world. I hugged my brothers good-bye.

Adrian gave me a warm smile and a hand on my arm. "I'll see you later," he said, his eyes flickering over my face. His gaze rested on my lips before returning to my eyes. "Good night."

I stood frozen as he walked out the door.

Nico appeared not to have noticed, excusing himself to use the bathroom.

"I think Adrian may have a thing for you," Alex said dryly.

I sank onto the couch, my head in my hands. "Don't say it."

Alex chuckled. "Don't have to—he certainly wasn't hiding it—the guy's interested. It was impossible to miss."

"Unless you're Nico."

"True." Alex patted my shoulder. "Have fun with that."

12

No one who cooks, cooks alone. Even at her most solitary, a cook in the kitchen is surrounded by generations of cooks past, the advice and menus of cooks present, the wisdom of cookbook writers.

—LAURIE COLWIN

*N*eil e-mailed me the next morning.

Dear Juliette,

Where to begin? First, the only *Top Gear* worth watching is the British version. They really love the Alfa Romeos too. It's three middle-aged English guys driving some great cars and some not-so-great cars and getting into various kinds of trouble. I highly recommend, even if you're not into cars yourself. There's enough human comedy that the show is universally accessible.

But then, I'm a car guy. Who knows how trustworthy I am on that subject.

I hope your move went smoothly and better than expected. Were you able to get everything in the way you wanted? I hate moving myself, though when I was in medical school, I had a system that worked out pretty well. Did your siblings behave?

Work is a pain lately. Running lots of assays, having trouble
getting the data that I'm looking for. I feel confident in my
suppositions, but getting the science to cooperate is the hard
part. In the meantime, I run lab tests and hope that one of these
days I'll find out I really might be right, after all.

So here's a conversation starter—what brought you to online
dating?

Neil

I read the e-mail twice, my face turning pink without my permission, for
all the worst reasons.

He didn't say anything. He didn't answer my questions about missing
him.

I pressed my lips together and closed out of my e-mail window.

Had I completely, utterly, and literally misread him? Had I read him correctly, but he changed his mind?

My computer screen offered no answers.

Frustrated and not a little embarrassed, I closed my laptop, put away my
breakfast dishes, and redirected my attentions to Grand-mère's vintage
cookbook.

After work Tuesday, I returned to a home that needed a lot of work. I put on
my yoga pants and zipped a hoodie over my tee, setting Stacey Kent to play on
the stereo before I set to work. After making a call for the carpets to be sham-
pooed, I vacuumed as much carpet as I could reach with my machine. With a
soft cloth, I washed the pale blue walls, erasing years of fingerprints and scuffs.

The kitchen—I fit my things in where I could. The tile needed the love of
a good bleach pen, and mine had dried up.

In the bedroom, I moved Grand-mère's things out of the closet and into the spare room, temporarily. In reality, my mom and Sophie needed to go through and decide what to keep and what to donate. Until then, I made just enough space to be able to hang the things I needed to hang.

As the hours wore on, the last of the sun faded, but the work had kept me warm. I shed my hoodie and surveyed my progress.

My eyes fell on the steamer trunk by my bed. More of Grand-mère's treasures or attractive storage space for my own things? As much as I wanted to explore, I needed to stay on task, which meant getting cleaned up and going to City Market for groceries. My work had paid off, though. The apartment smelled of fresh air and cleaning products. I could see my kitchen table. Some of my own décor hung on the walls.

Grand-mère would have approved.

Dear Neil,

You asked an interesting question. Why did I try online dating?
I imagine the reason most people do—I was lonely.

And it wasn't for lack of people around me. There is a special
kind of loneliness for the single and the busy, people with friends
and jobs and family and the gnawing awareness that as I get
older and more responsible, I'm still alone.

Now, I know some career singles who don't mind. But I do, even
now that everything is busier and crazier than ever.

In the meantime, I'm in the market for a roomate. Looking,
mostly for the sake of being practical, but also for the company.
Do you have a roommate? I remember in college when living

alone seemed like an unattainable luxury, but now, I don't know. Maybe privacy is overrated.

(Not all privacy. Do you know how hard I have to work to keep my entire life from being common family knowledge? Very hard. And I only succeed part of the time.)

That's me. What about you?

J

On Wednesday, my father called and asked if I would come by D'Alisa & Elle in the morning, before opening. When it came to reasons, he was mysterious.

I showed up on my way to work, not knowing exactly what I was in for. When I arrived, he'd clearly been there for hours, greeting me with a warm hug and kisses on both cheeks.

"*Ciao, bella,*" he said, his hands grasping my shoulders. "I am so proud of you. This new restaurant? It is very exciting. I love my restaurant. I want you to love yours."

We turned to face the dining room, taking in the space that had supported our family for so many years.

It was ornate without being fussy, fancy without being cluttered or dated. The furniture had a lovely patina.

"I have been thinking," he said. "Your *nonno*'s ninetieth birthday is this summer. Your mother and I were going to go and celebrate with the rest of the family, you know, but with the surgery…"

"I'm sure they understand," I said.

His lip twitched. "Perhaps. But perhaps they will understand better if I send you to Italy in our stead."

"Me?"

"You haven't been in a while, and your aunts and uncles have been asking after you. We've canceled our own tickets and would like to pay for yours. Think about it."

My eyes widened. "You had me at 'send you to Italy'—of course I'd go!"

He grinned. "*Bene,* I am glad," he said, enfolding me in a familiar hug. "I hoped you'd agree—it is such beautiful land, and I want my family to know you better. There was one more thing, as well."

"Oh?"

He looked out onto the dining room. "I am thinking," he said, "of updating some of the tables and chairs. They've been here for many years and are starting to show their age."

"They're so lovely, though," I said, reaching out to stroke the back of one chair. "They're good quality pieces."

"Best not to keep things the same for too long," he said. "But some of the furniture, of course, could still find some use, especially with a little restoration."

I couldn't help but smile at the twinkle in his eyes.

"Well, if you're just getting rid of it," I said, "we could probably find a use for it."

"Oh?"

"If you don't mind."

He slung his arm around my shoulders. "Oh, not at all."

On Thursday morning, I called in a personal day. My immediate pieces were turned in, and I needed some time to myself. I decided to use the day to cook, rest, and get organized. I moved the last of Grand-mère's clothes carefully into the guest room, making a mental note to ask my mom to help me parse through them. Like a true Frenchwoman, she had very high quality clothes, many of them still fashionable.

For the thousandth time, I regretted that, at five feet eight, I was far too tall and large all over for Grand-mère's clothes. Not that I was huge by any means, but Grand-mère was not only petite but more devoted to her girdle than I could ever be. Sophie could probably wear some; Chloé others. Even her shoes were far too tiny.

Once I'd cleared the closet and hauled my own things inside, I moved on to the steamer trunk. It creaked as I opened the lid, as all good steamer trunks should. A vague memory passed through my mind—me sitting on the trunk and Grand-mère telling me about how she'd brought it from France. Though she'd come to America in the seventies, the trunk had to be far older.

I found linens folded inside—lace tablecloths, Provençal prints, high-thread-count sheets and pillowcases edged in tatted lace. Sachets of lavender preserved the contents. I sat back and sighed.

The contents were lovely, but ordinary. Where better to hide a good secret than a steamer trunk? I set the linens aside to launder with some oxygen bleach later.

I checked my e-mail. Nothing yet from Neil.

All of a sudden, I missed Éric with a pain that took my breath away. We probably weren't soul mates, he and I. But I always knew where I stood. I knew he would feed me and it would be delicious.

Maybe I wasn't cut out for online relationships, in any format but the casual Facebook kind.

I thought of the tagine Éric made for me while we were dating, full of aromatic spices and hearty lamb. I had lamb in my refrigerator, as well as plenty of carrots—I checked my watch. Eleven o'clock.

It would be a late dinner because of the marinating time, but delicious. And if I decided against cooking it up that night, I could always make it for lunch the following day. I grated ginger, chopped garlic, and measured out the remaining spices for the lamb marinade. When it was done, I set the lamb in the fridge and returned to my computer.

Still nothing from Neil.

Fine. The rumble in my stomach reminded me that while I'd been prepping food for over an hour, I hadn't actually eaten.

I was rummaging through my fridge when my phone rang.

"Etta? It's Sophie," my sister began, as if I couldn't recognize her voice. "Would you mind picking Chloé up from school today?"

"What's up, Soph?" I asked, stalling. How did she know I'd taken the day off?

"It's just that I have a doctor's appointment that just came up, and I thought I could make it work, but Chloé's school is getting out early, and I need to make this appointment."

The panic in her voice gave me pause. "Is everything okay?"

"Fine. Everything's fine," she said.

So, basically not, then.

"I can pick her up," I said. "When does she need me to be there?"

A brief pause. "Twenty minutes?"

I counted to fifteen twice, once in French, once in Italian. "I need to leave now, that's what you're saying."

"Yes?"

I rolled my eyes at the question that wasn't a question. "Fine. I'll be out in a moment. Have a good appointment."

Sophie was still thanking me when I hung up.

Oh well—less time organizing meant more time to see my niece. I hadn't seen enough of her lately anyway, and being out of the house meant I was less likely to check my e-mail. I shoved aside my collective resentment, gathered my keys and purse, and stepped out into the fragile Portland sunshine.

If I was very lucky, Chloé wouldn't mind stopping for lunch.

~ LAMB TAGINE FOR TWO ~

Don't be intimidated by the ingredient list! The scents coming from your kitchen will make the prep work worth it. Be sure to have all your ingredients measured out before starting. You can absolutely double or triple the recipe, if you want to enjoy it with friends.

For the marinade:

1 tablespoon olive oil

1 pound lamb, cut into large cubes

1 clove garlic

1 teaspoon paprika

$^1/_2$ teaspoon ground cinnamon

$^1/_2$ teaspoon sea salt

$^1/_4$ teaspoon cardamom

$^1/_4$ teaspoon fresh ginger, grated

$^1/_4$ teaspoon turmeric

$^1/_4$ teaspoon coriander

$^1/_4$ teaspoon cumin

Pinch of cloves

Pinch of cayenne

For the stew:

1 tablespoon oil

1 medium onion, cubed

3 medium carrots, peeled and cut into sticks

4 dried apricots, halved

2 cloves garlic, minced

$1^1/_2$ teaspoons freshly grated ginger

Zest of $^1/_2$ lemon

$^3/_4$ cup beef broth or stock

1 medium-large sundried tomato, minced very fine

$1^1/_2$ teaspoons honey

$^1/_4$ teaspoon ground caraway

$^1/_4$ teaspoon allspice

Pinch of saffron

Toasted sliced almonds, for garnish

Blend marinade spices and savories, from garlic to cayenne, in a quart-sized Ziploc bag. Dry lamb pieces, then toss with olive oil in a medium bowl. Add lamb to spice bag and coat the meat thoroughly. Allow lamb to marinate, refrigerated, for 8 hours or overnight.

Heat oil in stew pot, dutch oven, or proper tagine if you have one. Add onions and carrots; cook until onions begin to soften, about 5 minutes. Add garlic and ginger and cook until fragrant. Add lamb, followed by remaining ingredients. Bring liquid to a boil, reduce heat and cover, allowing to simmer for $1^1/_2$ to 2 hours. Stir occasionally; cook until lamb registers 145°F with a meat thermometer.

Serve hot over couscous, straight from the pot. Garnish with almonds and enjoy.

Note: If the tagine liquid is too thin, you can thicken it with a slurry of $1^1/_2$ teaspoons cornstarch and $1^1/_2$ teaspoons water and cook for a few moments longer. Just be careful not to overcook the lamb.

~ Pine Nut Couscous ~

1 cup chicken broth
$^3/_4$ cup couscous
$^1/_4$ cup toasted pine nuts
1 tablespoon minced fresh parsley
1 teaspoon lemon zest
Teeny pinch of saffron, if you're feeling generous

Bring broth and saffron to a boil in a small saucepan with a fitted lid. Turn off heat, add couscous, and stir the pot once before covering and allowing the couscous to absorb the liquid—about 5 minutes. Fluff the couscous with a fork and add the pine nuts, parsley, and zest. Serve hot with the tagine.

13

One cannot think well, love well, sleep well, if one has
not dined well.

—VIRGINIA WOOLF

*C*hloé came bounding toward my car when she saw me. "This is so
cool! Mom texted me to say you were coming. I like your car. Can we
go somewhere? I need to go somewhere for a school assignment, so could we go
together?"

"Ah—repeat that?"

"I have this creative writing assignment. My teacher wants us to go to a
secondhand store or antique shop, find an object, and write about the origins
of that object."

"That sounds like a good project."

"Everybody was complaining about it, but I thought it was kinda cool. So,
can we go?"

I checked my watch and then shifted my Alfa into gear. "Yes. I know just
the place. But first? I need lunch."

"If you hadn't gotten out early," I said as we pulled up to R. Spencer's in the
Sellwood District, "this might not have worked. As it is, they close at five, but
time shouldn't be an issue today."

Chloé nodded. "Have you been here before?"

"I have," I said, unbuckling my seat belt. "I have a soft spot for antique china and table linens."

"My mom hates antiques."

"True. What do you think?"

Chloé shrugged. "I don't know. Can we go in?"

"Sure."

We walked beneath the blue awning and entered the store. Chloé sniffed the air. "What's that smell?"

"Time," I said, winking at her. "Want to look around?"

A female store associate appeared from behind a mahogany highboy. "Anything I can help you with?"

I shook my head just as Chloé took off in the opposite direction. "Look at this! You have to see this—it looks just like Grand-mère Mimi's!"

Both the associate and I followed her enthusiasm. Chloé stood, pointing, right next to a steamer trunk that did look just like Grand-mère's.

"Oh," the associate said pleasantly, "you've got a wonderful eye. This isn't just any trunk either."

Chloé and I watched as the woman lifted the lid to reveal the beautiful interior.

"This trunk was made by Goyard—you can see the label here. E. Goyard Aîné—that's the name that Edmond Goyard gave to the business when he took over the company from his father. The distinctive red ribbons beneath the lid are one of their signature details, as well as the brass fittings. Goyard, the brand, is one of the oldest French makers of luxury luggage. They're a sought-after item as it is, but this one has some special details.

"Some trunks," she continued, "have secret places to store special belongings. The Victorians liked their secrets, especially. A lot of desks from that era have hidden areas, usually for private correspondence. In this trunk, there's a hidden panel behind the decorative painting—see?"

We watched as her fingers slid the painting to the side, revealing a small cubby.

"Cool," Chloé breathed. She looked up at me, eyes gleaming. "Is there a secret hiding place in Grand-mère's trunk? Have you looked?"

"I've looked inside," I said, choosing my words carefully. Just because one Goyard trunk had a special hiding place didn't mean Grand-mère's did as well. Except...

I had a gut feeling that, this time, I would find something. Something more than old clothes. I would look again, but the last thing I wanted was my niece looking over my shoulder, ready to tell Sophie everything.

"I'll tell you what," I said at last. "I've got to go home and get some work done, and you've got a project to work on. How about we take a look at it tomorrow night, when you come over with your parents for dinner?"

Chloé's dimples flashed. "Perfect!"

It was—as long as I made sure to check out the trunk first.

Sophie's car shaded the driveway when I pulled up to her house. Chloé unsnapped her belt. "Thanks so much for taking me to R. Spencer's. It was supercool—I can't wait to work on my project." She wrinkled her nose. "I'm such a geek."

"The best sorts of people are," I told her, unbuckling myself. "I'll walk you in."

Gigi greeted us at the door. "What are you doing here?" I asked, bending over to give her a pat.

"We're keeping her for now," Chloé said, shrugging out of her coat.

We found Sophie inside, paler and more worn than usual. Sophie greeted her daughter, planting a kiss on her forehead, smoothing her hair, and asking after her day before sending her down the hall to begin her homework.

"So—you're taking care of Gigi?" I asked, trying to make conversation.

"The dog required more energy than Maman could give her," Sophie answered before looking away.

I didn't get the feeling that Sophie would devote much more herself. Maybe Chloé would become a devoted dog walker. "Is everything okay? You seem more…tense than usual."

Sophie crumpled. "They ran tests at the doctor's!"

I took her arm and led her to the sofa. "Yes?"

Cancer. It had to be cancer. It made perfect sense—Mom got diagnosed, Sophie got scared, and sure enough the doctors found something.

"I made them check twice to be sure." She held her hands out. "I don't know what I'm going to do!"

"We'll figure it out," I said, clasping one of her hands. "What did the doctor say?"

Tears ran down Sophie's face. I hadn't seen her this upset since Todd Bianchi broke up with her right before her senior prom.

"The doctor said I'm allergic to *dairy*," she spat out. "Dairy! No milk, no cream, no butter, no cheese…" A sob escaped. "What am I going to do?"

"Aw," I said, relief flooding over me as I comforted my sister—my high-maintenance, high-strung, much-loved sister. "I'm sure we'll figure something out."

Back at home, I walked straight to Grand-mère's trunk.

Just to see. Just to find out.

I lifted the lid and examined the top panel, which did look just like the one at the shop. When it moved beneath my fingers, my heart stopped.

A hidden panel.

A hidden panel with a box tucked inside.

It was a small box, but then again, secrets didn't necessarily require much square footage.

My face flushed and my fingers shook, ever so slightly, as I opened the painted tin box.

A gentleman's handkerchief with the initials "GR" embroidered on the corner. A man's wristwatch. Gold cuff links, cleverly shaped like tiny pastry cutters. A lock of dark hair in a yellowed envelope. A narrow engagement ring with a row of tiny inset diamonds.

I fingered the ring.

I guessed the handkerchief—and the initials—belonged to the man in the photo. My grandfather Gilles's surname had been Durand—and he had been blond.

Did the hair belong to the mystery man? It seemed to have more curl than the man in the photo, but it was hard to tell.

The pastry-cutter cuff links were particularly clever. Was he a pastry chef? a craftsman of pastry tools? simply fond of pastry-related men's accessories? I suspected the first, but would remain open minded.

I looked at my finds.

There was no room to question whether Grand-mère had been involved with another man or not. I couldn't think of any other explanation—she had one sister, so it couldn't have been a brother's belongings. Most telling were the cuff links—her father hadn't been thrilled about her going to pastry school in the city, so they certainly weren't his.

And then there was the ring. Had she been married before Grand-père Durand?

My mind continued to process the secret in the trunk even as I began to prep the tagine in the kitchen.

Why would Grand-mère hide a previous marriage, if that's what it was? Had Grand-père Durand known? How could he not? How did the romance I grew up hearing about work into the story?

I ached to confide in someone. Since my last reply to Neil, I'd heard nothing. Sure, it had only been a couple of days, but as night fell and the silence stretched, I began to wonder how long our relationship would last.

Feeling maudlin, I set to work chopping carrots.

When my marinating lamb hit its eight-hour mark, I assembled the rest of the stew and set it to simmer on the stove, swimming in saffron-spiked beef stock and jewel-like carrots. The smell was already intoxicating, and soon that scent would fill the apartment.

Some girls would rather smell like sandalwood or jasmine than stewed lamb, but as long as it was really *good* lamb, I didn't mind one bit.

Since my dinner would be late, I made myself a plate of antipasti and poured a glass of Pinot Noir. I also checked my e-mail—nothing.

I bit my lip. Ego bruised, I took my food and drink into my new living room, built a fire in the fireplace to dispel the spring chill, and relaxed by looking at cookbooks and Grand-mère's recipe cards. Ingredients, edible chemistry—these things made sense to me, even if my life didn't.

A road map, anytime, Lord, I prayed.

As the tagine simmered away on the stove, my apartment smelled increasingly delicious. I couldn't help but think of Éric, the first time he'd made me tagine—which, not coincidentally, was also the night we shared our first kiss.

My first kiss.

When we dated, I daydreamed about marrying Éric, being half of a restaurant couple like my parents. They were the daydreams of a very young woman, but I'd enjoyed them. Everybody knew what a talented chef Éric was, and unlike the rest of my family, he was genuinely interested in my thoughts and input. He was the first man I'd ever met who wanted me to taste his food and listened to my comments.

In fact, Éric's trust in my palate was one of the reasons I had the confidence to move into food journalism.

I continued to page through recipes, marking ones I wanted to test and possibly write about on my blog. My stomach began to growl; the timer couldn't sound soon enough. When the lamb was nearly ready, I assembled the couscous.

To prep dessert, I peeled an orange, sliced it, and plated the slices. In a separate bowl, I mixed a bit of lemon juice with some sugar and cinnamon. When everything was finished and the lamb was done, I ladled the tagine over the couscous and carried my bowl to the couch. With my feet tucked under a blanket, I ate my dinner alone, contented.

Sometimes not having to share has its benefits.

After dinner, I washed my dishes, put away the leftovers, and wiped down my countertops. By the time I was done, my clock read just past midnight.

A late dinner, but worth it.

When the knock sounded at my door, I nearly dropped my bottle of Method spray. I placed it safely on the counter, tiptoed to my door, and looked through the viewfinder.

Nico.

I flung the door open. "Do you have any idea what time it is?"

"You're awake," he said, giving me a companionable hug.

"You didn't know that. I could have been in bed, sound asleep."

"Your lights were on." Nico stopped and sniffed the air. "That smells good. What is that? Is that tagine? That smells like…"

My stomach tightened as he thought.

"Like Éric's recipe," he finished. He followed his nose to my kitchen. "Did you make tagine? Do you have leftovers?"

"Do you have a reason for being here?" I countered. "I'm about to go to bed."

"I was thinking about the restaurant on my way home. Thought I'd drive by to see if you were awake."

"And the lights were on. Want some tea?"

"Sure," he said, perching on one of my kitchen stools.

I had some orange left over, so I put some on a plate and gave it to him with a fork. "What's on your mind?"

He chewed his bite of orange. "This really reminds me of Éric," he said. "You know he's opened a place in Seattle?"

"No," I said, my heart constricting. "I didn't."

"He was a good guy."

"Yes." I didn't trust myself to say anything else.

"I want to start drawing up some plans for how we want the layout to be remodeled. There's a restaurant auction on Tuesday—want to join me? I'm on the lookout for a range."

I wrestled with the thought in my hand. On the one hand, I didn't want to leave work again. On the other—I wasn't sure about sending Nico out on his own. "Okay," I said. The schedule would work out somehow. I made two mugs of tea and handed one to Nico. "I'm planning on getting some contractor bids for the remodel this week. While I'm doing that, both of us should be figuring out which suppliers to use." I sat down. "The other thing is that Mom and Dad are sending me to Nonno's birthday in July."

"You're going? I was wondering if Mom and Dad were going to continue with the trip."

I shook my head. "It's too much, what with Mom's treatments. She'll just be starting radiation around then."

"Want to do some wine tasting for the restaurant while you're there? I'd like six or seven Italian wines on the wine list."

"Where would I find a winery?" I asked, smirking. My uncle's home, where our nonno lived, was in Montalcino, in the heart of Tuscany. You could pretty much throw a rock in any direction and hit a grape.

I was about to tell Nico how I wanted a couple of French wines on the list as well when I felt a light bulb switch on in my brain.

Italy was next to France.

Grand-mère's sister, Cécile, still lived in the family château.

I thought of my own sisters—Grand-mère may have been able to hide things from her children, but her sister?

Sisters have a way of remembering secrets.

"That sounds like a good idea," I heard myself respond casually. "I could go to France too. There might be some wines and cheeses we'd be interested in.

And then there's the Bessette family château," I said, trying to sound offhand. "You know they make their own honey. We could incorporate that into some of the dishes. The lavender too."

Nico clapped his hands together. "*Bene!* You will enjoy the trip. It's been a while since you crossed the pond, hasn't it?"

"It's been a few years," I agreed. "And I haven't been to the château since I was a kid."

"Are you sure the tagine can't come out of storage?"

"I'm going to bed, and so should you. Besides," I said, "eating Moroccan food this late will only make you dream about Bob Hope or Bing Crosby."

"Not Dorothy Lamour?"

"Not usually."

He rubbed his mug handle with his thumb. "I would have liked to open a new place with Éric."

I gave a sad smile. "Some things just aren't meant to last."

~ Moroccan Oranges ~

1 orange, very sweet
1 tablespoon sugar
Juice of 1 lemon
$1/4$ rounded teaspoon cinnamon
2 to 3 mint leaves

Peel orange, using a sharp knife to remove as much of the outer pitch as possible. Slice the orange; quarter the slices, if you like. Arrange on a plate. In a separate bowl, whisk the sugar, lemon juice, and cinnamon. Pour the mixture over the orange slices. Garnish with mint leaves or sliced almonds and serve.

When we eat together, when we set out to do so deliberately, life is better, no matter what your circumstances.

—THOMAS KELLER

I woke up the next morning with heady beams of sunlight filling my room. My spirit still felt frayed around the edges. I reached for my phone and wrestled with my apathetic self, the one who didn't feel much like getting out of bed.

The mail icon on the screen gave me reason enough to lift my head just a little.

Just because I had sun *and* an e-mail did not make everything okay. And yet I opened the e-mail just the same.

Dear Juliette,

Sorry it's been a few days, but I didn't want to rush writing you back. In all honesty, I've written and rewritten this e-mail a few times.

In one of your last e-mails, you said, "Is it strange to say I miss you, when we haven't exactly met?" My answer is no; I don't think it's weird. My reasons might be different than yours.

A long time ago, you were very clear about not wanting a romantic relationship. I respected that and have enjoyed your correspondence in friendship.

Here's the thing—I'm going to be in Portland next month to meet with a colleague at Oregon Health and Science University. While I'm in town, I'd really like to meet you in person.

I know you're busy and there's a lot going on in your life. But if you've got time for me, I'll be in town from Wednesday the 14th to Sunday the 18th. If you're free, I'd like to see your face.

Neil

I put my phone down, stunned.

Meet.

Before I could lose my courage and talk myself out of it, I hit the Reply button.

Dear Neil,

Consider my calendar marked. I look forward to seeing you :-)

J

I typed quickly and hit Send before I lost my nerve. To my surprise, another e-mail arrived a short moment later.

I'm glad. May I take you out to dinner on the 15th? I know it's a Thursday, but to be honest I'm not sure I can wait until Friday.

Neil

I smiled and wrote a quick reply.

I like Thursdays :-)

J

My family came over for dinner that night to see how I was getting along in Grand-mère's apartment.

Sophie used it as her opportunity to share her news. Before we sat down to dinner, she told her tale of woe. "That's what my doctor said," she ended, with a tragic shrug of her delicate shoulders.

My father shook his head.

My mother crossed herself.

Nelson patted Sophie on the back.

Nico laughed out loud.

Sophie threw a pillow at him, and the moment was over. Blessedly over.

"Come on, Soph," Nico said. "There is more to life than cheese. At least you don't have to give up eggs—I can still make you pasta with olive oil and tiny tomatoes. I'm starved. Anybody else starved? Etta? Is dinner ready?"

"It is." I leaped from my seat and made a beeline to the kitchen, where the roasted chickens rested. After making sure the vegetables were sufficiently glazed and seasoned, I plated everything and carried it into my little dining room.

Every seating surface had been called in for duty. I would have been fine with a dinner eaten in the living room, but my parents had been traumatized enough for the evening. Each person sat cozily elbow to elbow, but no one complained. In truth, Nelson was likely the only one who would even notice. We settled in to eat, prayed for the meal, and passed plates around.

"Aunt Juliette?" Chloé asked as she handed me her plate. "Since we haven't looked inside the trunk yet, can we do it tonight?"

I froze.

I'd meant to move the contents of the secret compartment and replace them with something else for Chloé to find.

But I'd gotten distracted.

Whoops.

I cleared my throat. "Sure. Absolutely. Good memory there, Chloé."

"The trunk?" my mom asked. "What trunk?"

"The trunk," I said, aware of how strangled my voice sounded. "Grand-mère's trunk? In the bedroom. Who wants carrots?"

"It's supercool," Chloé continued, her eyes bright. "We saw one just like it at the antique store yesterday."

"Another old trunk?" Sophie tucked her napkin over her lap.

"It was *just* like Grand-mère Mimi's. The lady at the shop said it was a Goyard or something. But what was cool was that it had a secret compartment. It was totally hidden in the lid. Juliette and I are gonna look at Grand-mère Mimi's."

I had to say this for my niece—her factual recall was quite strong.

"Your grand-mère Mimi brought that trunk here from France," my mother said, taking a delicate bite of chicken. "It was quite old. I didn't know it was a Goyard, though."

"It'll wait until after dinner," Sophie said, handing Chloé's plate back to her. "Eat up."

At last, something Sophie and I agreed about.

"You think Gran had something secret stashed in there?" Nico asked Mom.

Mom lifted a shoulder. "Not that I know. But she was a very private lady. Very French."

I processed that information. One way or another, I had to get to my room and move the tin out of the secret compartment.

I served up everyone's dinner before retreating to the kitchen, removing my apron, and walking back out with a bottle of chilled white wine. "Chenin Blanc, anyone?"

Half of the group raised glasses, and I walked around the table to accommodate. By the time I reached for Nico's glass, he was midstory and gesticulating riotously, per usual. If I timed it just right…

I poured the wine into Nico's glass, positioning it in the line of fire. And sure enough, his hand hit the glass, sending a slosh of white wine over my blouse and jeans.

"Don't worry," my mother said. "It's white. It'll wash."

"It's so cold!" I said, in a tone I feared sounded too theatrical. "I'll let you finish your own glass, Nico. I'm going to change into something dry."

And just like that, I was out.

In the bedroom, I went straight to the trunk, removed the tin, and hid it in a shoebox before sliding the shoebox beneath my bed. In its place I put a few items of jewelry I'd found in the back of one of the bureau drawers, wrapped in a lacy handkerchief.

With the family scandal hidden away—for the time being—I shrugged out of my damp clothes and used the edge of my bathrobe to absorb the last bits of wine from my skin.

I shrieked when the knock sounded at my door.

"It's just me," said my mom's voice. "I just wanted to know if you needed any help setting your clothes to soak."

My eyes darted to the trunk. Closed.

She'd never know. At least not tonight. "I…um…" I pulled on a pair of dry jeans and a jersey Tracy Reese top before opening the door. "Sorry. I just had to get zipped up."

I received a blank look. Nudity for a Frenchwoman is less of a deal than nudity to an American. I could have opened the door stark naked and she'd never have batted an eyelid. "Do you think I can just throw the clothes in the wash? It was just white wine, after all."

"I suppose that's fine. What's your blouse made of?"

"Rayon."

A slight wrinkling of the nose. "Oh well, then, I suppose it's fine."

I smothered a smirk. My mother hated synthetic fibers. I doubted if a thread of poly had ever touched her skin.

"You've done a very nice job with the apartment," she said, taking in my bedroom. "I want you to make it your own."

"I'm not ready for that," I said plainly. "And besides, Grand-mère had very good taste."

"She did."

Maman cast a critical eye on my ensemble, squinted, and then handed me a bracelet from on top of my dresser. "There," she said, satisfied once it encircled my wrist.

"Thank you." I clasped her hand as we walked back to the dining room together.

After the meal, Chloé practically bounced from her seat. "Can we go look at the trunk now?"

"Oh, right," I said casually, as if I'd forgotten. I brought a cheese plate and a carafe of coffee to the table for the men, while Chloé, Sophie, and my mom followed me down the hallway.

"See?" Chloé said when she spied the trunk. "Just like the one at the shop! It's got the red and everything."

"You're right," I said as she lifted the lid with reverence.

"Be careful," Sophie told her, stepping forward to help.

My mom placed a gentle hand on Sophie's shoulder. "Let her open it," she murmured ever so softly.

If Chloé caught the exchange, she didn't show it. Her eyes glowed as she carefully slid the panel back and peered inside. "There's something in here!"

Sophie's eyebrows flew up in surprise. "Really?"

Chloé's hand disappeared inside and returned, holding the handkerchief gingerly. When she saw the necklace and earrings inside, she gasped.

"She must have tucked them inside for safekeeping and forgotten," Mom said.

"They're so pretty." Chloé held the necklace up to the light, examining the gold chain and enameled pendant.

"You should keep them," Mom said, taking the necklace from her hands and opening the clasp. "If you like."

Chloé nodded, wide-eyed.

Mom fastened the necklace around her granddaughter's neck and examined the effect. *"C'est belle."*

Chloé glanced up at her mom, still holding the earrings. "If I had pierced ears…," she said, her voice trailing off.

"Not until you're thirteen," Sophie reminded her firmly.

"You can save them," I suggested. "They'll keep."

Chloé beamed, and I basked in the happy family moment, trying not to think what might have happened if they knew the truth.

~ SIMPLE ROAST CHICKEN ~

3 to 4 pounds free-range chicken, giblets removed

1 lemon, halved

3 cloves garlic, crushed

5 sprigs fresh thyme

3 sprigs fresh rosemary

4 tablespoons butter, softened

3 tablespoons *herbes de Provence*

Coarse sea salt

Fresh cracked pepper

$1^1/_2$ cup mini carrots

$1^1/_2$ cup fingerling potatoes, skin pierced

1 sweet potato, peeled and cubed

3 shallots, quartered lengthwise

Allow chicken to sit out for 1 hour until room temperature.

Position oven rack to the lower position, remove upper racks, and place a cast-iron skillet or roasting pan onto the rack. Heat oven to 450°F.

Prep spices by placing them into small finger bowls.

Dry chicken thoroughly with paper towels.

Place lemon, garlic, and fresh herbs inside the bird's cavity and fasten the legs together with cotton twine.

With your fingers, coat the chicken with the softened butter, both on top of and beneath the skin. Be generous!

Sprinkle the herbes de Provence all over, followed by a generous amount of salt and pepper.

When the chicken is ready and the oven is hot, remove the skillet and place the chicken inside, breast side up.

Roast chicken for 45 minutes, remove from oven, and rotate chicken with a long fork and tongs until it's breast side down in the pan.

Baste chicken with the buttery pan drippings. Add veggies to pan, toss with pan juices, and sprinkle with salt and pepper. Continue to roast for another 20 to 25 minutes or until a meat thermometer registers 165°F.

Remove from oven; return chicken to breast-side-up position and allow bird to rest for 15 minutes. Serve with roasted vegetables and fresh crusty bread.

15

Let's face it, a nice creamy chocolate cake does a lot for
a lot of people; it does for me.

—AUDREY HEPBURN

Mireille's Chocolate Cake

When I was a little girl, my grandmother made chocolate cake.

It's a common enough occurrence; most French women have a chocolate cake in their repertoire. But this one was hers, which is what makes it special to me.

I love historical recipes. I love recipes with a past, with meaning. And as much as I love new flavors—whatever pomegranate/sweet potato/quinoa concoction we celebrate now—I love finding recipes that remind us where we've been.

Less concerned with fat, that's one thing, or antioxidants.

Whether we're healthier now than we were at another time…that's a discussion for another day. But what I love about old recipes is how unselfconscious they are. They're not trying to be hip, only tasty. I think that singular aim lends itself to more focused food—food without an identity crisis, food that knows its station in life.

This cake is just a chocolate cake. It's not a Mexican chocolate cake, not a salted caramel chocolate cake, not a fudge cake. It's just chocolate. Can't chocolate be enough, sometimes?

Don't get me wrong—I do

love a complex mix of flavors. But sometimes simple can be just as—if not more—satisfying. Give the recipe a try and see if you don't agree.

FRENCH CHOCOLATE CAKE

½ cup plus 2 tablespoons granulated white sugar, divided
10 ounces good-quality semisweet chocolate
¾ cup unsalted butter, room temperature, wrapper reserved
2 teaspoons vanilla extract or vanilla bean paste
5 eggs, separated
¼ cup sifted all-purpose flour
½ teaspoon sea salt
2 tablespoons confectioners' sugar
Splash of lemon juice

Preheat oven to 325°F. Line the base of a 9-inch springform pan with parchment paper. Use the butter wrapper to grease the paper and sides of the pan.

Reserve 3 tablespoons of the sugar. In a medium-sized, heavy-bottomed saucepan, melt the chocolate, butter, and ½ cup sugar together. Watch the chocolate carefully and stir constantly to prevent the chocolate from burning. Once the butter and chocolate have melted and the sugar has dissolved, remove the pan from the heat and stir in the vanilla. Set aside to cool.

Once the chocolate mixture cools to body temperature, whisk the egg yolks into the chocolate, one at a time, mixing thoroughly each time.

To add the flour, sprinkle over the top of the mixture before stirring it in.

Dampen a paper towel or cheesecloth with lemon juice. Wipe the juice around the inside of a large mixing bowl to remove any remnants of grease. When dry, beat egg whites until foamy.

Add salt to the egg whites and beat until stiff peaks form. Add reserved sugar and beat until whites become glossy. Fold ⅓ of the egg whites into the chocolate mixture, before carefully folding in the remaining whites. Pour batter into the prepared tin.

Bake until the cake has risen and a tester inserted into the center of the cake comes out clean—about 45 minutes to 1 hour. Check the cake after 30 minutes: If the cake appears to rise unevenly, rotate. If the cake starts to crack or brown too quickly, place a piece of foil over the top.

Transfer the cake to a wire cooling rack, and run a knife along the edge of the cake. Carefully remove the sides and base of the springform tin.

Serve warm or at room temperature, dusted with powdered sugar and sweetened whipped cream.

A week after the family exploration of the trunk, I sat back and admired the first part of the article about Grand-mère. There was more to come, but what I had was beautiful—lovely photos, truths about how I felt about food—and I couldn't be prouder.

As much as I admired my handiwork, my neck cracked when turned and my limbs felt stiff. I stretched my muscles before noticing everyone else had cleared out of the office for the weekend.

I drove home, thinking over my next task.

After nearly two weeks of living in my new place, I decided I'd had enough and fished Clementine Grey's card from my purse once I got inside.

I hesitated before dialing.

It felt awkward, calling a near stranger like that. Asking someone to be your roommate—it made me feel eight years old all over again, asking someone to be my friend.

But it was fair and it was logical, so I straightened my spine and dialed.

I didn't expect her to answer but was pleasantly surprised when she did.

"So, listen," I said, after completing the usual phone-call pleasantries. "I've moved into my grandmother's old apartment, and I could use a roommate. I figured since the commute would be just as useful to you once the restaurant opens, I'd ask you first."

"You're...asking me to room with you?" Clementine cleared her throat. "Um, how much is the rent?"

"Nico and I are leasing the building from my mom," I said. "Part of the reason I'm living here is because I need to keep living costs down. Let's say two hundred dollars in rent, plus utilities and all that."

"Okay, wait," she said. "Did you say two hundred dollars?"

"I did."

"And," she said, her voice sounding oddly wobbly, "you're talking about Mireille's apartment over the patisserie?"

"I am," I said, trying to gauge her response.

"Um, yeah," she said, sounding distinctly watery. "Sorry. I...I mean, sure. I'll take it. If you're sure."

"Clementine, are you...are you okay?" I asked, pretty sure I heard something that sounded a lot like muffled sobbing on the other end of the line.

"I can't believe—I mean—you have no idea..." She paused and caught her breath. "I can't make my rent at my apartment, and I was going to have to sleep on a friend's couch or move back in with my parents, and I *cannot* move back in with my parents, and you just called and offered me a place with rent I can afford that's not a health hazard. And I think I'm more stressed than usual because I'm not usually this emotional," she finished, the last word catching. "Sorry."

"No, I'm sorry," I said firmly. "I should have called you a week ago, but I put it off. That was stupid. Listen, there's still stuff in the bedroom—Grand-mère's stuff—but there's a path to the bed. I'll leave a key for you under the blue flowerpot; you can move in anytime you need to. Today, if you want. Just whenever."

Four hours later, I had a new roommate. Clementine had packed her things, minimal as they were, and moved into the back bedroom.

While she set up her room, I decided the wisest thing to do was to make room for her in the kitchen. I cleared out three deep drawers and made space in the pantry.

"Oh good," she said when she saw me clear space next to the oven. In her arms she held a box full of pastry tools. "Thank you again."

"You can stop thanking me. You're good."

Clementine opened her mouth, then closed it. "Cool. I love this kitchen. I used to help Mireille test recipes in here." She set her box down and began to lay out her tools before organizing them into drawers. "Who's taking care of Gigi these days?"

"My sister."

Clementine lifted an eyebrow. "I met her once. Is she a dog person?"

"I don't believe I'd categorize her as such, no," I answered diplomatically. "But her daughter is, and I think her husband is kind to small furry beings, so I think Gigi will be okay."

"You never asked me what I'm like to live with," Clementine said. "Are you sure you're not going to regret this?"

"Pretty sure." I hoisted myself into a seated position on the kitchen counter. "You didn't ask about me either. I'm not a particularly early riser, but not very late to bed either. I don't like lots of noise, but I don't like too much quiet. If I make a mess, it's usually in the kitchen. My family will probably stop by at awkward times, so I don't suggest spending a great deal of time in a state of undress. I'm not very adventurous. I only drink socially, and even then not to excess."

"It's expensive to be a drunk these days," Clementine observed.

"Agreed. That's all I can think of. I don't have any particular pet peeves, but if I develop any, I will attempt to communicate them in a sensitive, civil manner." I moved to the stove. "Would you like some tea?"

"Sure." Clementine closed a drawer and opened a new one. "I tend to get up early, because if I don't, I'll have a headache for two weeks once I'm on a pastry schedule. I'm very good at being quiet in the morning. Since I'm up early, I don't tend to stay up late, but I'm usually so tired that your whole family could come over for a canasta and tap-dance party and I'd never notice. My bedroom tends to be a mess, but I make sure the door will always close. I get grossed out by dirty bathrooms. If I'm bored, I hate-watch the Food Network."

I couldn't help but laugh. "Fair enough."

"Another thing—do not shorten my name. My name isn't Clem, Clemmy, or Tiny; it's Clementine, and if you feel compelled to give me a nickname, I can suggest the names of several respected therapists."

"Fine," I said, "as long as you never call me 'Julie.' I'm Juliette, Etta, or Jules."

"You're just not a Julie?"

"Nope."

"Deal."

I reached for a kitchen towel. "How is work going?"

Clementine wrinkled her nose. "I'm doing some freelance pastry work for a few local caterers, but I'm not getting the hours I need. I have lots of first interviews but not a lot of second interviews, which drives me crazy because I know I'm better than the yahoos they're hiring who churn out molten chocolate cake after molten chocolate cake. I'll be relieved when the restaurant is open and I can focus more on pastry and less on promising to make molten cakes for catering gigs."

"They do sell—those chocolate cakes."

She lifted a shoulder. "A monkey could make one."

"That is a viral YouTube video I would enjoy watching." I tilted my head. "I'm working on a new piece for the paper and my regular column on top of it. If you want to help me test recipes, you're more than welcome."

"Do you have a focus?"

"The first is a piece about Grand-mère, so any memories you have of working with her would be great. The second is pulling together entertaining menus. I have to do a demo of one on *Portland Sunrise* next week."

"That's cool."

I made a noncommittal noise and moved the hot water off the burner. "This is fun. It's nice to have company. What kind of tea do you want?"

"Rooibos, if you've got it."

"Yes, I do." I dropped one sachet each into two large coffee mugs.

Clementine wrapped her arms around herself. "Does it feel weird being here? Since your grandma died? Because I gotta tell you, I keep waiting for her to walk around a corner."

I paused, midpour. "Me too." I looked away and collected myself, and had a bright smile a short second later. "But I think she'd get a kick out of the fact that we'll be living here together."

Clementine took her mug and clinked it with mine. "Hear, hear."

I checked my watch. "Oh, wow. I've got to run and meet with Nico about the restaurant. Here's a key," I said, handing it over. "Help yourself to whatever you find in the fridge."

"Thanks. I will."

"Right. Excellent." I gathered my keys from the kitchen counter and took off in search of my purse. "See you later!" I called, feeling glad in my heart that when it came to my apartment, I was no longer alone.

I woke up Saturday morning to wonderful, amazing smells. When I emerged from my bedroom, I found Clementine in the kitchen next to a plate of freshly baked pain au chocolat and a carafe of coffee.

"Don't expect this every morning," she said, "but consider this a thank-you. For letting me move in."

"You'd be welcome in any case," I said, "but extra welcome in this case." I reached for a croissant and took a large bite. "Oh my goodness," I said once I'd swallowed. "That's the best chocolate croissant I've ever had."

"It should be," she said with a smirk. "Your grandmother rapped my knuckles with a whisk if I overworked the dough."

"She would." I took another bite. "What time did you get up this morning?"

"Four, as usual."

"I didn't hear you at all."

"Good. I also tried to clean up some. I noticed you had some bakeware on that counter that I figured you were keeping there for a reason."

I looked to where she pointed. "Oh yeah. That's Sophie's. She brought it over last week, and I need to run it back to her." Another bite. "Maybe we need to have these at the restaurant for dessert. A kind of breakfast-for-dinner thing."

"No."

"No?"

"I make good desserts, and serving pain au chocolat during the dessert course is like serving a Danish." Clementine tucked a piece of hair behind her ear, showing off a series of silver hoops. "Anyway, why aren't you a chef your-self? Obviously you can cook. What made you join the enemy and become a food critic?"

I laughed. "First off, I don't think of myself as a food critic, rather a food writer. I went to culinary school, but I knew going in that the lifestyle wasn't for me. Some people—people like Nico, like my dad—thrive on it, but," I said, shrugging, "not me, I guess. But I really love writing about food. The way I see it, you can spend hours—days, even—preparing a meal. You eat, you enjoy, but ultimately it's gone and you're left with the memories. I like to write about food to preserve it, to remember the experience. I think that writing about a meal makes it last forever."

"Fair enough," Clementine said.

"Maybe one day we'll serve brunch. Or start a catering company like D'Alisa & Elle. I'm just saying these croissants need to see the light of day." I brushed a crumb from my lips. "I wouldn't want you to lose your touch."

Clementine rolled her eyes. "Like that could happen."

After a leisurely breakfast, I decided not to put off the trip to Sophie's. My old-est sister answered the door, looking more frazzled than usual. I resisted the urge to hold the baking dish like a shield and chose to smile warmly instead.

"Oh, thanks for bringing that. Come on in," she said, using her foot to keep Gigi from making a break for it.

"No problem," I said, bending over to pet Gigi as she jumped by my feet.

I wouldn't have termed myself a dog person, by any means, but even I could tell Gigi didn't seem quite right. She hadn't been groomed recently—Grand-mère had been meticulous about having her trimmed every few weeks. She sat at my feet and wagged her tail, looking me directly in the eyes with an expression that could only be described as begging.

"So," I said, trying to be casual, "how are things going with the dog?"

Sophie rolled her eyes. "She's getting into everything. I just don't have time for it. I'll take your jacket. Do you want something to drink? Coffee? Tea?"

"Tea sounds nice. Is Chloé enjoying having a dog in the house?" I asked, testing the waters.

"Oh sure. But will she walk the dog? No. I'm thinking of going back to work soon, and I don't know what to do with the dog all day. Though," she said, filling the teakettle with water, "I don't even know what to do with it all day as it is."

"Mmm," I said, my mind whirling. Gigi had followed me and stood watch at my feet, again with the begging expression. I patted my lap.

Without hesitation, she jumped up, climbed into my arms, and rested her head on my shoulder.

"Wow," Sophie said. "I've never seen her do that."

I bit my lip and patted Gigi awkwardly on the back.

I don't need a dog, I thought. *The last thing I need is an animal underfoot when I'm testing recipes.*

Despite my thoughts, the words came quickly before I could talk myself out of them. "Do you want me to take her?"

"Really? Would you?" Sophie's face eased. "That would be wonderful."

She wasted no time in gathering up Gigi's belongings and placing them in a pile by the door. She poured tea for both us of, which we drank rather quickly.

I think she wanted me—and the dog—out of the house before I changed my mind.

Sophie even helped me carry everything back to my car.

In my head, I knew this was a terrible idea. I'd never had a dog before; I didn't have the first idea of what I was doing.

But as I drove away with Gigi curled up in the passenger's seat, staring at me with her huge brown eyes, I knew I'd done the right thing.

Even if it was crazy.

16

If you're afraid of butter, use cream.

—Julia Child

Y ou brought her!" Clementine cried out, clapping, when I walked inside with Gigi in tow.

"I have no idea what I'm doing with a dog," I said. "I can't deal with dog hairs finding their way into the custard."

Clementine shook her head as she bent over to pet Gigi. "Bichon frises don't shed. That was one thing your grandmother liked about them."

"Where did she, you know, have the dog do her business?"

"You mean pee?"

I lifted an eyebrow. "You know I do."

"I was just giving you a hard time. No, Mireille would take Gigi on walks, sometimes, but if she didn't want to go downstairs, she'd send the dog on the patio. Had a special patch out there."

"I think I remember that. I guess I wasn't paying attention."

"What were they feeding you?" Clementine asked the dog, who by this time had all four paws in the air and not a care in the world. "Mireille had her on good quality kibble. Her coat had more luster than this. But that's all right. We'll fix it."

"You know how?"

"I love dogs. My aunt and uncle raise whippets out in Gresham. They do the show circuit, the whole nine yards."

I sat down on the floor and crossed my legs. Gigi left Clementine to sit in my lap.

"Huh." I gave Gigi a tentative pat. "I guess I'll be learning."

I rose early Sunday morning, took Gigi out, and dressed for a cool spring day. The night before, Gigi had slept at the foot of my bed—the only night within recent memory when I'd slept soundly, only waking once when Gigi found a rabbit in her sleep. She consented to recline in her kennel while I attended church, though she seemed delighted and ready to play when I returned.

My trip to the antique shop with Chloé had served as an important reminder that there really were people who knew old things. So I could either wonder about the items in the tin, or I could show them to a dealer and find out what I could.

Not that I was at all interested in selling them—I only wanted to know their secrets.

The week before, I'd called and made an appointment for myself at Maloy's Jewelry Workshop in downtown, a shop that specialized in heirloom and estate pieces.

On Tuesday, I wrapped the cuff links and ring in tissue paper and sealed them in a Ziploc baggie before placing them in my purse.

I left Gigi with Clementine, who was busy testing a custard recipe.

At Maloy's, I rang the bell for entry.

A woman, who introduced herself as Marla, opened the door and took me to a back room where I showed her the pieces.

Marla examined the ring with a loop before letting out a long, low whistle. "This is a Van Cleef & Arpels piece," she said, handing me a magnifying glass.

"Look at the engraving inside the band—VCA and a serial number. I can contact my rep and see if I can get a more specific date. It looks like it's from the early forties to me." She sat back and studied them. "To be honest they're… well, I've only seem a few VCA pieces come through here, and none of them this…simple."

"It's okay," I said, suppressing a smile.

"This ring is more likely to be a custom piece, something designed for a friend of an employee on a budget. It's of the highest quality, of course. But most VCA are statement pieces. They designed coronets and tiaras for royalty, after all."

I nodded. I could see Google searches in my future.

Marla moved on to the cuff links. "Now these…these are quite cunning. There's also a VCA engraving on the side, here—" She handed me a magnifying glass so I could look myself.

In the end, Marla quoted me an appraisal value that made me blink. "It's because they're Van Cleef & Arpels pieces," she said. "Very high quality—the diamonds may be small, but they're flawless. I'll give my rep a call today. Let's see if we can't find out more about these pieces."

I thanked her, wrapped up the ring and cuff links, and set off for home.

Dear Neil,

Guess what? I now have a dog. And a roommate. And painters have finished with the walls in the restaurant, which is a load off my mind.

My new roommate is Clementine. She's also our pastry chef at the restaurant. I like her (which is good, since we're now sharing living space). Because of Clementine, we now keep a composting bin on our kitchen counter (the lid is fitted with a carbon filter, thankfully) and donate our collected rubbish to an urban gardening project. She also changed out most of the cleaning products for more eco-friendly solutions. But since that means she's the one doing some of the cleaning, I'm not about to complain.

The dog was my grandmother's, and she was at my parents' and then at my sister's, which wasn't so great for my sister or the dog, so now she's with me.

Do you have a dog? I don't have the faintest idea what I'm doing. I let her sleep on my bed last night—is that kosher? Lady slept on the bed in *Lady and the Tramp,* so it can't be that bad, right? (Though come to think of it, they also gave Lady a bit of doughnut dipped in coffee, and even I know that's not dog kosher. Oh well...)

The restaurant's going fine. There are so many things to keep track of that it can be overwhelming sometimes. And tomorrow's my appearance on *Portland Sunrise*...

So your trip out—do you need me to pick up you up at the airport?

J

Dear Juliette,

You'll have to let me know how your time goes on *Portland Sunrise*! I'll be praying for you.

Thanks for the airport offer. I'm getting in late, and I'll be renting a car. Much appreciated, though.

Yes, we had a dog in the house throughout my growing-up years. I wish I could have a dog here, but with the hours right now, it wouldn't see enough of me for me to not feel guilty.

As far as having a dog on your bed, there's no harm there as long as you don't mind. *Lady and the Tramp* is a good place to check in. Except for the fact that they didn't have a securely fenced yard. Also, feeding a dog doughnuts is a bad idea. (Dogs don't need wheat—their digestive tracts aren't designed for grains.) So maybe Disney's not the best place to pick up pet-ownership tips.

Work's been crazy. I'm working on publishing a paper with a journal, and I want to get it out before flying west. Will it happen? I don't know.

Given the choice, I'd fast-forward to that flight. And I really don't like flying.

Looking forward to seeing you.

Neil

17

People who love to eat are always the best people.

—JULIA CHILD

*T*here was only a little sun out when I arrived at the *Portland Sunrise* studio. Too little. If I'd left the apartment when I'd planned, there would have been even less, but as it was, I was fifteen minutes late with no sign of a parking place and with a gnawing panic in the pit of my stomach.

I'd grown up in Portland—I was a seasoned parker of cars in impossible spaces. But that morning I found myself parking six blocks away and walking uphill in shoes I'd thought were cute but now seemed ill advised.

Three days before, I'd received a call from a production staffer letting me know what time they wanted me there (early), what not to wear (red), and what kind of necklace to choose if I wore one (large).

I dressed for the day in a vintage-looking emerald-green dress from Anthropologie, pairing it with a pearl-and-wire collar necklace I'd picked up at a shop in the Alberta Arts District. My shoes—which would never show up on camera unless I propped my feet up on the kitchen counter—were brown, piped at the edges with bright yellow, and rubbing awkwardly at the bridge of my feet with every step. Hill-hiking shoes they weren't. I could have worn Converse sneakers and not a single viewer would have been the wiser.

Once I made it inside the building, a harried-looking production assistant showed me to the studio kitchen, where we'd film the segment. "It's live, of course," she said. "But if something goes wrong, just roll with it. Our viewers love it—makes them feel like they're watching a blooper reel live."

"Oh," I said.

"Just whatever you do, don't look at the camera."

I nodded with a fake authority. "Sure."

It was a nice kitchen space, though small and clearly not designed for actual cooking. The producer and I had gone back and forth over what kind of demonstration I would do—it would be a short segment, no longer than seven minutes. With Memorial Day looming, we finally settled on hand pies, perfect for picnics and easy outdoor entertaining.

Today's hand pies were rhubarb with mascarpone, and strawberry with basil. Both were special in their own way, each tasting like summer.

I'd brought my own pie pastry, not trusting whichever journalism student-turned-intern got stuck with the task to make a sufficiently elastic dough for my needs. I set my dough on the counter to reach room temperature before following the production assistant to the greenroom.

The greenroom, where visiting talent waited before their turn on the air, was eclectically shabby. The couch was covered in orange-print fabric that looked to be about forty years old. The walls were covered in framed concert posters featuring musicians such as Paul Anka, Brandi Carlile, and the Decemberists, and a signed photo of Weird Al.

In addition to the wall art, there were several vases of dusty, eclectic silk flowers and a pot of equally attended succulents.

I touched up my lipstick before taking a seat on the couch, away from the mirror. Maybe it worked for starlets, but the last thing I needed was to be staring at my own face.

Sometime later, a knock sounded at the door—I'd been summoned. I followed the production assistant to the set, where I met the producer, the director, and the hosts.

The next fifteen minutes passed in a strange, out-of-body blur. After being transfixed by the curled glory that was Waverly Harper's hair and the blinding whiteness of Dean Jessup's teeth, I answered their questions while trying to ignore the hulking black monster that was the studio camera.

How did anyone not stare directly into that thing? It was like facing a bear and looking away.

Prompted by Waverly's and Dean's questions, I launched into my spiel on hand pies, how delicious and simple they were to prepare and serve.

I demonstrated how to make dough and then rolled out my prepared dough before showing them how to assemble the hand pies.

Waverly and Dean asked me questions, which I knew logically that I'd answered, though I couldn't remember a word I'd said. My hands shook as I worked the dough. I reminded myself to smile because I knew that I wasn't and that smiling was probably the right thing to do.

As I moved and talked and worked, my stomach churned uncomfortably. I could barely look at the food. I placed the finished pies in the "oven" and retrieved the completed ones for the hosts to eat with me.

Eat. I had to eat. Could I?

If Grand-mère could move to America as a widow and successfully run a pastry shop on her own, I could eat pie on local morning television. I squared my shoulders and took a bite while Waverly and Dean happily munched away.

The pie tasted like sand to me, absorbing the remaining moisture from my mouth. "The fruit is bright and pairs so well with the buttery pastry," I croaked.

And then it came to an end. Waverly and Dean thanked me before turning to the camera—the hulking menace—and saying something about... something. I wasn't even listening.

The director cut to commercial. Waverly complimented my necklace, Dean shook my hand, and I was whisked away from the set by yet another production assistant.

After a ten-minute walk, I was safely back inside my car, a depleted husk of a human being.

And I still had to go to work.

I stopped back by home just long enough to change my shoes and then left for the office.

Marti whooped when she saw me. "It was perfect!" she said, wrapping her short arms around me in a hug. "Wouldn't have changed a thing. You were so natural. And your column? The Internet traffic has tripled. Good work!"

I thanked her and continued to my desk.

"You made it!" Linn cried when she saw me. "How did it go?"

"I still think I might throw up," I said as I sank into my chair.

"We all watched from the break room—you looked great, you sounded great. Very natural."

"I don't know how," I replied, my voice flat. "I was terrified."

Linn nodded sagely. "Well, it didn't come through that way, and you haven't thrown up so far. That's the important part."

I wrinkled my nose. "I guess."

"Are you going to do it again?"

"Good heavens, I hope not," I told her, before opening my latest article and digging into the familiarity of work.

My phone started ringing the second I started my lunch break. "You were wonderful," my mother said, sounding happier than I'd heard her for weeks. "Your dress looked wonderful on camera, so much better than that Waverly woman. And your pastry looked perfect—I'm so proud of you. Your grandmother would have been too."

My heart squeezed. "Thanks, Mom."

"Those hand pies looked really good," Sophie said when she called moments later. "I'm glad you told that Dean guy that premade dough is a bad idea. All those additives and stabilizers. Did you have fun?"

"It was an experience," I told her.

Alex sent me a congratulatory text. Chloé called after she'd watched the segment on the DVR, squealing over the experience of seeing me on TV. My dad called from the restaurant after the lunch shift ended, telling me how proud he was and how authoritative I sounded.

Caterina sent me an e-mail ranting about how long it was taking the studio to upload the day's episode onto the Internet.

I responded to each conversation and missive as graciously as I could; I didn't have the heart to tell them that it had been the worst morning of my life within recent memory. By the end of the day, the video clip had been posted on the front page of the food section's website. Lots of clicks, lots of comments, and all I wanted was to go home and go to bed.

Instead, I left work an hour early to supervise the workers installing the range for the new restaurant. Though I took my laptop, I still didn't get the work done that I wanted to, so I had to use the late-night hours to complete my latest column.

The following Monday, Nico, Adrian, Clementine, and I gathered in the newly refurbished kitchen to begin work on the menu.

Nico and Adrian brought the groceries, bags and bags of supplies, every food group represented. Clementine parsed through the goods, setting aside the eggs, butter, fruits, and vanilla beans, dipping into her own stash of Valrhona chocolate.

"Saw your segment on *Portland Sunrise*," Adrian said. "You looked good."

"Thanks," I replied as I organized dry goods on shelves.

"I was sorry to hear about your mom and her cancer," he continued. "How is she?"

"Hanging in there, doing treatments," I answered. "She's a strong lady."

"I'm praying," he said, before getting to work with the ingredients.

I wondered later what he'd meant. Was he a man of faith, a believer? Or was he the sort of person who threw out spiritual-sounding platitudes? Only time would tell, though I reasoned that if I really wanted to know, I could ask Nico.

While Nico, Adrian, and Clementine worked, I busied myself with the front of the house. Alex had delivered the chairs from D'Alisa & Elle the day before, and I spent the next half hour dragging tables around and arranging the chairs around them.

Strains of friendly banter floated toward the front; I smiled. It would be a happy kitchen, the kind where everyone competed a little but gave a lot, where the camaraderie created strong friendships and better food. The strains of Barcelona, R.E.M., Caro Emerald, and Mumford & Sons provided the soundtrack to the work.

I ached to be there, in the midst of it. To be working with my hands, tasting, choosing.

But my job was to make the whole thing work, to make sure the front of the house complemented the food, to make sure that the whole thing ran smoothly. And anyway, my place was at the newspaper.

Wasn't it?

~ STRAWBERRY AND BASIL HAND PIES ~

For the crust:

2 cups all-purpose flour

$1/2$ cup whole-wheat pastry flour

1 teaspoon baking powder

1 teaspoon fine sea salt

1 tablespoon powdered sugar

1 cup unsalted butter, sliced and chilled

1 egg, lightly beaten and chilled

3 to 5 tablespoons ice water

For the filling:

3 cups fresh strawberries, preferably small and organic,
    hulled and sliced

1^1/$_2$ tablespoons sugar

1 tablespoon cornstarch

1^1/$_2$ tablespoons honey, more if the berries are on the firm side

^{1}/$_2$ teaspoon basil leaves, minced

^{1}/$_2$ teaspoon lemon zest

Squeeze of lemon juice

After assembling:

1 to 2 eggs, beaten

Sparkling or demerara sugar

To make the pastry:

Whisk the dry ingredients for the crust together in a medium-sized mixing bowl.

Add the chilled slices of butter and work into the dry ingredients with a pastry cutter (or use a food processor). Cut the butter in, or pulse, until the mixture looks like small peas.

Add the egg and mix with the pastry cutter. Add the ice water a tablespoon at a time, cutting and scraping until a dough forms. The dough should feel just a little tackier than a standard pie dough.

Shape the dough into two equal disks, wrap tightly with plastic wrap, and allow the dough to rest in the refrigerator for 1 to 2 hours.

To make the filling:

Place all the filling ingredients, save the basil, in a large saucepan—an enameled dutch oven is perfect for this—and give everything a good stir.

Cook over medium heat, stirring constantly, until the sugar

melts, the berries soften, and the juices have thickened—about 5 to 8 minutes.

Remove from the heat and sprinkle the basil over the top. Stir and then cover, and allow to cool. If you're going to assemble the pies much later, refrigerate the mixture.

Assemble the pies:

Preheat oven to 375°F. Line two baking sheets with parchment paper.

Place a small handful of flour on a pastry cloth and spread it around. Working with one pastry disk at a time, dust the top and bottom with a bit of flour to prevent sticking.

Roll the dough out with a rolling pin in single-direction strokes (center to back, lift, center to back, rather than back and forth over the dough) until the dough is about $1/8$-inch thick.

With a sharp paring knife, cut dough into circles about 6 inches in diameter. You can use a teacup saucer as a guide, but just know that they might come out smaller, depending on the saucer. If you have enough dough, roll your scraps together for another circle. (If not, brush the scraps with butter, dust with cinnamon-sugar, and bake separately from the pies to make piecrust cookies.)

Repeat with the second disk of dough. In a small bowl, beat the egg for the egg wash.

Spoon about $1^1/2$ tablespoons filling into the rounds—you don't want to overfill. Dip your finger—or a pastry brush—into the egg wash, and brush the egg around the edge. Carefully fold the pie closed into a half-moon shape, running your finger over the edge to seal it shut. Crimp the edge with a fork, and then use the fork to poke a few holes in the top to vent.

Coat the pie all over with the egg wash, and place on the baking sheet. Sprinkle with sugar. (You could also sprinkle a little coarse sea salt, if you wanted.)

Bake for 20 to 25 minutes, rotating the baking sheets halfway. Serve warm or at room temperature.

Makes about 12 pies.

18

You have to be a romantic to invest yourself, your
money, and your time in cheese.

—ANTHONY BOURDAIN

*B*etween all my work at the newspaper and work at the restaurant,
the weeks flew by. The producer at *Portland Sunrise* called to
thank me for my appearance and asked if we could schedule another
appearance.

The date she asked for turned out to be the Friday when Neil would be in
town.

I couldn't turn it down—with all the publicity from the appearance bol-
stering my column and the rest of the department, Marti would be livid if I
pleaded anxiety and backed out.

My nerves were not calm when the producer informed me that the Friday
episodes were filmed before a live audience. But I agreed to the appearance on
the condition that I could procure an audience ticket for Neil.

Maybe he wouldn't use it. Maybe we wouldn't hit it off. As his visit approached, so did my apprehension. What if he didn't like me? What if I didn't
like him?

What would I do if we didn't like each other in real life? Because the uncomfortable reality remained: I had grown very attached to the version of Neil
who arrived in my e-mail inbox.

I wanted to go shopping, wanted to find something new that I felt fabu-
lous in, but time I used shopping would have been time not working, and I

intended to have as much writing saved up as possible to maximize my time with Neil.

Instead, I searched my closet for a navy swiss-dotted sundress and paired it with one of Grand-mère's cotton cardigans, a raspberry-hued number with beading at the neck. The sleeves were too short, but I figured folding them up would make them three-quarter length enough to pass muster. I also found a set of beaded hair combs the same shade as the sweater and set those aside to use.

The Wednesday he flew in, he sent me a text.

Just landed! Bought an umbrella at the airport. Looking forward
to seeing you :-)

My fingers shook slightly as I texted a reply.

Glad your flight landed safely! Sorry about the umbrella—it does
rain in Tennessee, doesn't it?

See you Thursday!

When Thursday rolled around, I was undeniably jittery. At around T minus four hours, Clementine fixed me with her gaze.

"Okay, what is going on?"

I stopped mid–nail polish swipe. "Nothing. Just needed a fresh coat."

Clementine sat down beside me. "Uh-huh. So you finally agreed to go out with Adrian?"

"No! And what do you mean, *finally*? He's never actually asked."

"Probably because you've worked very hard to make sure he knows you're not interested."

I straightened my shoulders. "It has been a lot of work, thank you."

"You could stop that work and just go out with him."

"No." I shook my head hard. "Not happening."

"So if it's not Adrian, who is it?"

"Just a guy."

"Just a guy," Clementine repeated dubiously.

"Yup."

"Just a guy you met…"

I averted my eyes.

Clementine narrowed hers and leaned in closer.

I swatted her away. "What are you doing?"

Clementine leaned still closer, until her nose was a thumb's width from my own.

"Fine!" I squirmed away. "I met him on the Internet."

"Huh, it works then."

"I guess."

"I was referring to the nose trick—my mom did that when I was a teenager and she wanted to get me to talk. I never knew if it was the trick or just *her* that got me to crack."

"It works, because that was really disturbing."

"Thanks." Clementine shoved a length of her dark brown hair over her ear. "So. You met a guy online? Cool. You're sure he's not an ax murderer and all that?"

"I should probably check that before the date, shouldn't I?" I said, finishing off the nail polish on my right hand. "You think the FBI has a background-check app I could download?"

Clementine pulled her phone from her pocket. "I could find out."

I couldn't stop my grin. "He's kind of great, though. Funny. Smart. Good looking, from what I can tell."

"Where's he from?"

"He's living in Memphis, currently," I said, aware that my nose seemed to wrinkle of its own volition.

"Have you been to the South?"

"Not really. Texas, once."

Clementine lifted her eyebrows. "It's a whole 'nother world down there. Different from Texas. Very, very different from Portland. The whole Pacific Northwest, for that matter."

"Lots of places are different from the Pacific Northwest. France is different. I like France."

"The South is its own brand of different. And there are parts of the South that don't really like France."

"That's probably true."

Clementine gave a knowing smile. "I'm sure he's nice, and I'm sure you'll have a good time tonight."

"You think?"

"I do. And it's mainly because of the nail polish."

I swatted her arm—carefully, so as not to smudge the varnish—as we laughed together.

Twilight hung over the city, but I couldn't convince myself to get out of the car, not yet. What if I didn't like him? My heart clutched at the thought.

After a deep breath and a Cambridge & Thames lemon drop, I adjusted my hair combs, grabbed my purse, and climbed out of the car. I walked inside and scanned the room—busy, even for a Thursday—but didn't see anyone who looked like Neil's photo. After a moment passed and he didn't turn a corner holding, say, a red rose, I approached the maître d's podium. "I'm meeting someone," I said, hoping against hope not to be recognized.

The maître d's expression remained impassive. He consulted a hidden sheet of paper. "Are you Juliette, to meet with Neil?"

"Yes."

The maître d' gave a vague smile. "One moment."

My heart dropped.

I could have scripted the following minutes; it had happened often enough over the years. The maître d' made a phone call; hushed words were exchanged. From my vantage point in the foyer, I could see two members of the waitstaff emerge from the kitchen. They sought out a man, a nice-looking man with ginger hair, seated near the kitchen doors, and through the pantomime gesturing and broad smiles, I could tell that Neil was being offered a different table, a better table.

A table out of my personal visual range, but I didn't need to be able to see to know what was happening.

Thirty seconds later, the maître d' sought me out, accompanied by waiter number one. "Mr. McLaren is here," he said with a glowing smile, as if Neil hadn't been there earlier, had slipped out the back for a smoke and recently returned. "And this is Kurt. He'll be taking care of you this evening."

I followed Kurt to the new, improved table. Neil—it had to be Neil— stood when he saw us approach. As I walked toward him, I took him in—he was tall, even taller than I thought. There were laugh lines by his eyes, and his ginger hair caught the light and turned gold.

I couldn't help but smile as I realized he was looking at me the same way, taking me in.

"Hi," he said once I stood in front of him.

"Hi back," I said, grinning like an idiot.

Our waiter babbled about how he was going to take great care of us and would return shortly to take our drink order, unless we knew what we wanted now, but if we needed time to decide, that would be fine too, and that he would be back, like he said, shortly.

Neither of us spared him a glance.

"Friendly staff," Neil said, a twinkle in his eye. "I'm not naive enough to think they care about impressing me."

"They should, you know," I said teasingly, sounding more authentically flirtatious than I'd ever managed before. "I've heard you're a seriously tough critic."

"You've heard, have you? Well, you're right. I'm very particular about my macaroni and cheese."

I grinned. "It's good to see you."

"You look even better in real life than you do in my inbox."

My flirtatious bravado wavered. I wanted to tell him I felt the same, but I smiled instead and unrolled my silverware, draping the napkin over my lap.

The table came complete with a candle, which didn't look like it had been burning all night, and a plate of fresh bread near a saucer of olive oil and vinegar.

So much for anonymity.

"You know what I like about this place," I said, reaching for the bread, "is that they use such high quality oil and vinegar for dipping. The oil's from this tiny town in Sicily—much spicier, much greener than oils you'll find here. They don't make oil like this in the States."

"Really?" he said, and for a horrible split second, I wondered if I should have just shut up about the stupid green olive oil.

"I wonder if it's the soil profile or the processing," he continued, and I felt my entire body relax. "Probably both. I know they talk about terroir and all of that, a geographic location's soil and microclimate, and the bacteria and micro-organisms specific to that region. Of course," he said, "I can get more excited about the bacteria end of things. But I think it's cool how it can mean that stuff tastes better."

A goofy smile threatened to stretch off my face. "I think so too," I said.

19

Cooking is like love. It should be entered into with
abandon or not at all.

—Harriet Van Horne

The restaurant did its best to impress us, bringing course after course
of beautifully plated dishes out for our enjoyment, one of them
"compliments of the chef."

Neither of us paid much attention.

We'd talked about his research, about the paper he was working to pub-
lish, and about his colleagues at Oregon Health and Science University—
OHSU to the locals. He asked after my restaurant, how Gigi was adjusting to
life back at the apartment, and about my appearance on *Portland Sunrise.*

"You were so nervous I was concerned for you," Neil said. "But you looked
so relaxed and natural, and you sounded so knowledgeable. I'm sure it's because
you *are* knowledgeable," he hastened to add. "I was glad it turned out so well."

I rested my forehead in my hand. "I don't understand, not for the life of
me. I was so nervous, and I barely remember what happened when the camera
was rolling."

"Really?"

"I keep hearing it was great, and either my loved ones are the world's nicest
liars, or somehow me being terrified makes for quality television. I don't get it."

Neil clasped my hand. "But you made it."

I couldn't help but smile at him. "Just barely, yes. And I'm going to be doing it again tomorrow. I don't know what your schedule is, but I got you an audience ticket, if you want to come."

"Of course I want to come. It's first thing in the morning, isn't it?"

"It is. And no pressure, if you have other things…"

"I'll be there. How's your other piece coming? The one about your grandmother and the chocolate cake?"

"It's coming. I was hoping for a little more information about her early life, though at some point I'll lose the timeliness factor and I'll just have to write with the facts at hand."

"Makes sense." Neil sipped his water. "My grandmother had a chocolate pudding cake that I remember. You inspired me to try making it for myself."

I leaned forward. "Yeah?"

"She made it all the time for my dad when he was a kid. Made it every night for six weeks, just so she'd be sure that she'd got the recipe down."

"I love it."

"When she moved on—I think it was to custard or something—my aunt said, 'Thank goodness you're off that kick.' That's how the story goes, at least."

I laughed. "It's a good story. How did your cake come out?"

"Good. Tasted like I remembered. Maybe a little crispy around the edges, but still gooey."

"I'll bet it was good," I said, choosing not to suggest checking on a cake when its aroma becomes apparent.

"I thought so. Tell me how the restaurant's shaping up."

I tilted my head, considering. "Would you…would you want to come see it?"

He did. So we left—the check having been paid long before—and drove our separate cars to the patisserie.

He parked on the street while I pulled my car into the hidden back space. "One of your front headlights is out," he said, once we could see each other's faces again.

"Yeah?"

"I can fix it for you. It's probably just the bulb."

"Yeah?"

"Yeah."

"Okay," I said, ducking my head to hide a pleased smile, using key selection as my cover. We used the back entrance, mainly because that's where all the light switches were located.

He followed behind me in the dark and waited patiently as I flipped each dining room light switch.

"This is incredible," he said, taking it in.

I couldn't disagree.

The floors that I'd had stripped and stained myself over two long weekends, the fresh oyster-gray paint that lent the room its sophisticated air. The oriental rugs I'd purchased mainly because they came with a perfectly worn-in patina, but had not yet been destroyed. The vintage light fixtures over the tables.

And the chairs—oh, the chairs. The ones Nico and I had argued over endlessly. They were my biggest expenses, even though I'd used Dad's chairs, but having them restored with leather made the room look so cozy and perfect, like you could sink into one and sit and eat forever, without a care in the world.

Neil knew all of this, of course, because I'd told him in one e-mail or another. In many ways he'd wrestled alongside me as the various pieces came together.

This was his first time seeing it, though, and I couldn't help but take pride in his reaction.

"You did good," he said at last.

"Thanks," I said, rubbing my arms. "The last detail I'm working on is some fused-glass accent pieces for the tables. But the wiring has been cleared, and the inspector's coming next week."

"Have y'all set an opening date?"

"We're aiming for early September. I'll be meeting with vendors, tasting wines, that sort of thing, until then. We'll have a seasonal menu, but I want to make sure we've got some classics down before we open."

I looked up at him to see him staring down at me, intently. "What?"

He shrugged. "I like hearing you talk about the restaurant."

"Yeah?"

"Yeah."

I looked up into his warm brown eyes. "I had fun tonight."

"Me too," he said, smiling down at me.

Our gaze held. I knew deep inside, in that moment, that I wanted him to kiss me. I craved his kiss like I craved the first sunshine of the year, like a hot shower on a snowy day, like cold milk with chocolate cake.

Did he feel the same? I thought so. We stood there, kept company by eight tables, sixteen chairs, and some charmingly worn rugs, simply gazing at each other. My gaze flickered to his lips, surrounded but certainly not buried in his well-trimmed beard. I wanted to touch him, but my hands, my arms, seemed frozen.

His eyes studied my face. I couldn't tell what he was thinking, feeling, but I thought I read desire in his gaze.

I tipped my head back.

He smiled.

"I'll see you tomorrow?" he asked.

Tomorrow? I could barely think about tomorrow. "I, um, sure," I said, which was the slightly cooler way of saying yes, absolutely.

"You live upstairs, right?" His eyes drifted upward.

I couldn't seem to catch my breath. "Yes."

"What time do you need to leave?"

"Seven," I said, my voice laced with apology.

"That's fine. You can introduce me to Gigi."

I nodded stupidly. "Sure."

"It's a date," he said, the last syllable of his sentence disappearing into a yawn. His hand flew to his mouth. "I am so sorry."

"Don't be," I said, instantly regretful. "Jet lag—what time is it for you?"

"Late enough," he hedged. "Seven tomorrow?"

"Seven tomorrow," I repeated. "I'll walk you out."

I switched off the lights, slowly and regretfully.

I didn't sleep much that night.

Did he not want to kiss me?

Was it too early?

Was I too obvious?

I tried tossing, and when that didn't work, I gave up and tried turning. Neil would be over at seven the next morning, and like as not, I'd wind up with the biggest bags under my eyes.

He did seem to like me, didn't he? I racked my memory for signs of disappointment. Nothing. Nothing that I'd noticed, at any rate.

I flopped over again and considered my options. I could get up, but I might wake up Clementine. Gigi was already snuffling her sleepy displeasure at my inability to hold still and leave her headrest—my left calf—in one place.

Since movement was out of the question, I reached for my phone and typed a quick e-mail to my sister Cat.

From: Me, j.dalisa@netmail.com
To: Caterina, cdesanto@beneculinary.com

I know I should know this, but how do you know when a guy
really likes you?

J

Moments later, my phone buzzed in my hand.

From: Caterina, cdesanto@beneculinary.com
To: Me, j.dalisa@netmail.com

A grown guy? The short ones pull your hair. The big ones—if they're actually grownups—will give you incontrovertible proof. He'll ask you out. He'll propose. He'll give you flowers—that kind of thing.

Lucky for you, I'm awake because your nephews refuse to sleep. What would you do without me?

And why are you asking????

C

I hesitated, considered my words, and typed out my reply.

From: Me, j.dalisa@netmail.com
To: Caterina, cdesanto@beneculinary.com

Um…can I explain later? Hope the boys go to sleep soon.

J

Another buzz.

From: Caterina, cdesanto@beneculinary.com
To: Me, j.dalisa@netmail.com

Just promise me it's not that guy Nico keeps nattering on about. He sounds like he could be related to us, and TRUST ME THAT IS NOT WHAT I NEED IN A BROTHER-IN-LAW, THANK YOU VERY MUCH.

I snorted, waking up poor Gigi.

From: Me, j.dalisa@netmail.com
To: Caterina, cdesanto@beneculinary.com

Different guy. Put your caps away.

Moments later, more buzzing. I rolled back, settling in for what was likely to be a lengthy e-mail exchange with my sister.

From: Caterina, cdesanto@beneculinary.com
To: Me, j.dalisa@netmail.com

Sorry. I'm just really tired and I have to teach twenty-five students tomorrow while using sharp objects, and Damian's out of town. Want to come over and baby-sit? Tonight? There's got to be a red-eye flight... Chicago is supereasy to get to...

From: Me, j.dalisa@netmail.com
To: Caterina, cdesanto@beneculinary.com

I would, but I've got another morning television appearance, and I'll be puffy as it is. And the guy is coming along in the audience.

From: Caterina, cdesanto@beneculinary.com
To: Me, j.dalisa@netmail.com

!!!!!

Call me tomorrow? Or whenever you have time. Sleep soundly, baby sis.

From: Me, j.dalisa@netmail.com
To: Caterina, cdesanto@beneculinary.com

DO NOT TELL MOM. OR ANYBODY. NOT EVEN DAMIAN. OR
THE BOYS.

From: Caterina, cdesanto@beneculinary.com
To: Me, j.dalisa@netmail.com

HAHAHAHA no. Of course not. I REMEMBER HOW IT WAS. Not
a word from me. I'll even change my e-mail password for extra
security. So if you don't hear from me, it's because I forgot the
new password.

SERIOUSLY.

Gosh, I love capital letters.

From: Me, j.dalisa@netmail.com
To: Caterina, cdesanto@beneculinary.com

I noticed. Good night!

Fine. If Cat felt confident in my personal state of affairs, I had to stop worrying. And to Gigi's immense relief, I finally fell back to sleep.

I woke up well before dawn on Friday. Gigi lay at my feet, nestled against my legs with her paws gently aloft.

Clementine had a pastry job and had left earlier in the morning. Gigi and I moved through our morning routine, with Gigi performing her morning kibble dance, followed by a nap on my bathrobe while I showered.

For this appearance, I started with my most comfortable ballet flats—a pair in bronze leather—and worked up. I picked a white pencil skirt and paired it with a sapphire-colored blouse with a wide V neck and tiny cap sleeves.

Since I had woken up so early, I had plenty of time to primp myself into a state of casual perfection and even take Gigi out for a morning stroll.

I ate a quick bite—a scone and espresso—and tossed a ball for Gigi while I mentally prepared myself for the day. I pulled out the crepe pans and spreaders I would use for my segment and stashed them in a tote bag, wrapped in a wrinkled tablecloth.

When I heard the knock at the door, I'd almost begun to relax.

I swung the door open wearing my brightest smile.

Neil stood on my front porch, dressed in khakis and a striped polo and holding a bouquet of…

"For you," he said, handing me the ribbon-wrapped bouquet of…

"Spoons! I love them," I said, taking a closer look. The wooden mixing spoons—the ends of each painted a different bright hue—were tied with a wide grosgrain ribbon. "Thank you, Neil!"

"They reminded me of you," he said, his hands placed bashfully in his pockets. "I figured that flowers wilt, but spoons…"

"They're perfect." I gestured him inside. "I need to grab my purse and my crepe supplies. Come meet Gigi!"

Gigi had waited through the whole exchange on her blanket by the fireplace. We had been working on her door manners, and while her short tail threatened to launch her forward, she managed to stay put. "Okay, Gigi," I told her, and she rocketed toward Neil. A bounce in the air and she settled into an impatient sit while Neil stooped to pet her.

After Gigi received several pets and Neil quite a lot of hand licking, I carried her to her kennel. Then I retrieved my purse. "I'm ready."

"How are we on time?"

"Early," I admitted. It was a nice change of pace.

"Then I'll take care of this," he said, fishing in his pocket. He held out a small, shiny bulb.

"You found one!"

"I did. It'll just take me a couple minutes."

I followed him out, locking the door behind. True enough, he removed the clips to the headlight, removed the old bulb, and spun the new one into place. Once the cover was back in place, he started up the car and turned on the lights. "How's that?"

"Bright and shiny," I said. "Thank you."

We drove to the studio together, with me keeping a running monologue about the buildings we were passing, the shops and restaurants and ways that things had changed over the years. I knew I was rambling, but in this moment it kept my panic down to a manageable level.

Once we arrived, the countdown began much the way it had before, only this time Neil was escorted to the audience area while I continued to the green-room alone.

Today's segment would pull from the column that started it all—crepes. I brought three pans so that Waverly and Dean could give it a go, if they wanted to. I brought premade batter that I'd prepared the night before. The batter had separated, but a short stir would fix it easily enough. I put the batter into the small fridge on set, and set the pans to the right of the range.

I sat in the greenroom, half wishing Neil could have been there with me, half glad he couldn't see how green I looked as I waited.

After a thousand years had passed, the production assistant knocked on the door and escorted me to the studio kitchen. I pasted a huge, stupid smile on my face and greeted the hosts.

If talking and walking and functioning in front of a camera had made me nervous before, the studio audience made it ten times worse. From the corner of my eye, I was fairly certain there weren't more than fifty or sixty people there, but it was still fifty or sixty more people than I was used to.

With Waverly's prompting, I began my demo, heating the crepe pans and melting the clarified butter. I reached for my bowl of batter in the refrigerator and...

It wasn't there.

I looked to Dean, I looked to Waverly, and both smiled at me in pleasant anticipation. What did they expect me to cook with? "The batter has wandered off," I said, keeping my voice light while the blood left my face.

The audience tittered as three of us looked around, double-checking the refrigerator and cupboards, but the batter remained MIA. Two production assistants and three very young interns scurried backstage, as Waverly asked me questions about batter preparation and the reasons behind letting the batter settle before cooking.

The director signaled with his hand. Crepe batter or not, we had four minutes left.

"If only we had food in this kitchen," Dean said, "we might be able to make more batter."

I had thought of that. But while they had some flour, there were no eggs, and the milk looked past due. I thought fast. "Do you have some paper towels?" I said. "We can make some paper towel crepes and show the audience how to fold them."

Waverly and Dean brightened. "We've got lots of paper," said Waverly, and sure enough a youth appeared with a roll of towels and three pairs of scissors.

So we cut wonky circles from the towels and carried on, filling the paper circles as if they were edible. I demonstrated three different crepe-assembling techniques and dusted powdered sugar over the top.

At the end, I used my fork to pull a bit of filling from the center of my paper roll and taste the filling combination, despite my roiling stomach. "It's sweet and tangy," I said of the lemon curd, basil, and mascarpone blend. "And it would be even better inside a real crepe."

Waverly and Dean laughed heartily, and I pretended to join in.

Once the director yelled for a cut to commercial, I exhaled so deeply I expected my legs to go out. I collected my crepe supplies, washed my pans beneath cool water until they were safe to transport, and then retreated to the greenroom.

When I was safe inside the greenroom, I made a beeline for the ugly floral couch and immediately placed my head between my legs.

A soft knock sounded at the door.

I stood to answer, even though my stomach protested.

Neil stood in the hallway. "I bribed one of the interns to help me find you. And she said they found your bowl. Apparently, one of the other interns saw it in the fridge and thought because it was separated that it was from a previous segment and went bad."

"Oh," was all I could say, because at that moment my stomach decided to stage its own protest. I made it to the trash can, hair in hand, just in time.

As my breakfast deposited itself into the trash-can liner, I vaguely registered Neil's hand on my back, another on my hair.

When it was over, I spat to get the taste out of my mouth. My eyes burned. "I'm so embarrassed."

"Do you want a mint?" he asked, reaching into his pocket.

I nodded without meeting his eyes.

"Sit back down," he said. "Feel better?"

How to answer that? I'd just thrown up in front of a man—whom I had hoped to impress—on what was effectively our second date.

And yet my stomach rested contentedly, having ended its battle to retain its contents.

"Would you mind driving me home?" I asked instead.

"Of course not."

I didn't move. Neil paused and then sat down in front of me.

He placed a hand on my knee. "I'm just going to say this—you don't enjoy any of this television business, do you?"

I shook my head miserably. "I hate it."

"And your boss wants you to continue."

"She loves it."

"And you feel overextended, balancing your job with the restaurant."

I nodded. It was all true.

"So, do you think it's time to reevaluate?"

I let his words sit in my head for a moment—evaluating them, turning them in my head, examining them from all angles.

"I have to quit my job, don't I?" I said as the realization set in.

Neil shrugged. "That's your call. But if your job depends on you doing this"—he waved his hand—"and if you hate it so much it makes you sick to your stomach, it may be that moving on to something new could be the wisest."

"Puking is bad," I said.

Neil's lips formed a thin smile. "I agree. And it's not good for your esophagus or your tooth enamel."

"Sage words." I considered the possibilities. "Maybe if I talk to Marti, tell her how...difficult it is, maybe she'd reconsider. You know the funny thing? My coworker Linn? She's great at this stuff. Stick her in front of an audience and she comes alive. I'm only here because I told another coworker to make chili and corn bread for a dinner party."

"You're also talented," Neil pointed out. "And natural, even if it doesn't feel like it."

I shook my head. "It doesn't, and I have no idea why the fact that I'm wigging out isn't blindingly obvious on camera."

"Everyone has a strange superpower, I suppose."

"Yeah? What's yours?"

"I'm good at finding north."

"So you're like a human compass?"

"Often, yes."

"Good for you." I looked around. "Can we leave?"

Neil chuckled. "Feeling better?"

"Ready to be done." I pressed my hands to my eyes. "The intern really thought the batter had gone bad because it had separated?"

"That's the story."

I shook my head. "I tell you. Kids these days."

Neil grinned. "Let's get you out of here."

20

Eating, and hospitality in general, is a communion,
and any meal worth attending by yourself is improved
by the multiples of those with whom it is shared.

—JESSE BROWNER

*E*arlier, I'd planned on going in to work after filming, but just walking to the car, I still felt unsteady on my feet. Once I settled in the car, I reached for my phone to call Marti.

"Great work today," Marti said. "Quick thinking with those paper towels."

"Thanks," I said. "Listen—I'm wiped out. Mind if I call it a day?"

After she agreed, I thanked her and hung up. There would be a longer conversation later, but I wasn't about to have it over the phone.

"That's that," I said to Neil. "As far as today goes, I don't have plans." I bit my lip. "Though I might be hungry."

"Already?"

"Consider that I eat for a living."

Neil laughed. "Just tell me where to go."

We left the parking lot, Neil behind the wheel, and landed at Mother's Bistro & Bar for brunch/elevenses. As we enjoyed our meals, we never found ourselves at a loss for conversation. My restaurant, his research, our families, our cars, our careers—we jumped from one topic to another as easily as a stone skipping a lake.

We were just finishing our coffee when my phone rang. I picked it up to silence it, but the number gave me pause. "Just one moment," I told Neil, who nodded with understanding. "This is Juliette," I said, my heart beating a little faster.

"Juliette," the voice said, "this is Marla at Maloy's. I wanted you to know I heard back from my contact at Van Cleef & Arpels."

"Yes?" I said, rummaging in my purse for a pen and my miniature notebook.

"Both the ring and the cuff links were made by an S. Roussard. The ring was commissioned by a Monsieur G. Roussard, the cuff links by Madame Roussard."

"So S. Roussard was the employee," I said, "making pieces for family members? Like we were talking about?"

I found the notebook but no pen. I scowled. But Neil had been paying attention and quickly pulled a ballpoint from his jacket pocket. I beamed at him and began to scribble.

"It appears to be possible. The ring was commissioned in May of 1938, the cuff links in September of '42."

"But they don't have the first names in the database?" I asked. I could do a lot with first names.

"I'm sorry. They didn't seem to."

I shrugged, thanked Marla, and hung up. Before I tucked my phone away, I noticed I had two missed calls and a text from Linn.

She wanted to hear about my paper-towel escapades, no doubt. I'd call her later. For now, I focused on my new discovery. "Huh." I stared at the scribble in my notebook before looking up at Neil. "Thanks for the pen."

"Anytime."

"That was the lady from the jewelry store, following up on the pieces I had appraised. They turned out to be Van Cleef & Arpels—did I tell you that?"

"I don't remember. Go on."

"Well, think Tiffany, but older, more prestigious, and French."

"Got it."

"So now I've got a first initial and a surname. Might get somewhere with a Google search, maybe not…"

Neil smiled. "But you're curious."

"I am."

"Then come on," he said, reaching for his wallet. "Let's get out of here."

I spent the drive back to my apartment telling Neil that we didn't have to go back to my apartment.

"It's a beautiful day," I argued. "The sun's out. The mountain's out. Are you sure you don't want to see more of the city?"

"Yup," he answered simply.

By the time we walked inside, I realized what a gift he'd given me. For the first time since my strange discovery, I could share my findings as a whole.

I decided to leave Gigi in her kennel, but gave her a rawhide twist to encourage good behavior.

She didn't seem to mind.

I caught up with Neil in the kitchen. "This is the prep table where it all started," I said, opening the side drawer. The cookbook lay inside, wrapped in a tea towel for protection; I'd kept the photo tucked between the pages. "Here it is," I said, handing the photo to him.

"Look at that." He examined the photo, holding it close to his face. "And you found it because you were taking the cookbook to work?"

"It was pasted inside the dust jacket. It probably doesn't mean much to you. Here—I'll show you a picture of my brother."

After scrolling through a few photos on my phone, I found a somewhat recent shot, taken at a family dinner while Caterina was in town.

"You look pretty," he said.

"Thanks, but you're supposed to be looking at my brother. See the resemblance?"

"It's certainly striking."

"Hold on—" I pulled up Cat's Facebook page and scrolled until I found her wedding photos. "See?"

"Nice dress."

I felt my face flush. Luckily for me, Cat had chosen flattering bridesmaid dresses. "You're good for my ego."

"I'm glad. Looking at these photos… I went into immunology rather than genetics," he said, comparing Nico's photos with the antique photo, "but it would be unlikely for them to not be related. They both have cleft chins, the shape of the eyes—it's almost uncanny."

"Agreed." I reassembled the book, rewrapped it, and put it away. "The trunk is in my bedroom," I said, leading him inside.

I was grateful I'd left things so tidy for once.

I lifted the trunk lid and showed Neil the hidden compartment.

He chuckled. "That's really cool, you know."

For the first time, I got to see the trunk through someone else's eyes, from a viewpoint not clouded by family drama. "It is cool, I guess. Secrets in a trunk? It's like something from a schoolgirl novel."

"And that's where you found the jewelry?"

"Yes. Though right now I've got it under my bed since my niece has a fascination with the trunk."

"Clever."

"It was that or my sock drawer," I said, reaching under the bed for the tin. "This is the box I found inside the compartment."

I opened the box and laid out the contents. The hanky in particular caught my eye. "That's one tiny mystery solved—I found out today that the purchaser of the engagement ring was a Monsieur G. Roussard." I held up the handkerchief and pointed at the initials. "I can assume G. Roussard is 'GR.'"

"What are these?" Neil asked, fingering the cuff links. "I mean, I know they're cuff links, but—"

"One's a whisk, and one's a pastry cutter. I think Monsieur Roussard was a baker and his wife gave him the cuff links. What I want to know is—was my grandmother his wife? Well," I said, "there are several other things I'd like to know. But that one's a start."

"It's too bad the hair sample is a cutting. If you had some roots, you might be able to perform some tests."

"That would have been nice. If only it were fashionable," I said dryly, "to yank your hair out instead of cut it for loved ones."

"I'm just saying—a little DNA and you'd have some concrete answers. Though it would be a small miracle for the hair follicles to survive this long undamaged. Now, if there were any dried blood spots"—Neil opened the hand-kerchief and examined it—"from cutting himself shaving, for instance…"

Our eyes zeroed in on the stain at the same time.

"Does that look like—"

"Yes, it does," Neil said, casting a critical eye over the spot.

It wasn't large, by any means—no more than a few millimeters in each direction. It did look very much like the kind of stain that might have been left after a shaving nick or small scrape.

"I wonder if Grand-mère knew about it. She was so particular about laundry and cleanliness… So, is there enough?"

"Enough to run a genetic test? Maybe, but only if it's not been washed. Laundering would likely remove the white blood cells, and those are the ones that actually carry DNA. If they were present, you certainly wouldn't be able to get the information you'd otherwise get from, say, fresh blood or bone, but enough to prove a relation? Maybe. But that's a lot of ifs."

"That sounds like a crazy long shot."

He gave a wry smile. "Most likely. Sorry—I'm a doctor. I can't offer too many absolutes."

"I understand. Do you know what that would mean, though? I'd know. I'd know for sure that we were related. That our grandfather wasn't actually our grandfather."

"Do you want to know for sure?"

"Yes," I said finally.

"Maybe your grandmother kept it because of the blood. Some people get sentimental over bodily fluids."

I snorted.

"Hey, people do weird things. That's practically the first thing they teach you in medical school."

"I believe it."

We smiled at each other, and suddenly I was reminded of the fact that, first, Neil had a killer smile, and second, we were sitting on my bedroom floor, only inches apart.

Smiling at each other like idiots.

"Thank you," I said. "You have no idea how much it means to me to finally show somebody this stuff, to talk about it."

"My pleasure."

"So," I said, folding my hands around my knees, "what do you want to do next?"

Instead of answering, Neil leaned forward, swept my hair from my face and tucked it behind my ear. He leaned in, searching my face.

His eyes held mine. I couldn't look away.

I sighed as his hand slipped behind my head, into my hair. In a single smooth motion, he gently pulled me close.

Our lips touched.

I thought of Éric, but only for the tiniest moment. Neil's caress was gentle and sweet, giving me the opportunity to end it if I wanted to.

I didn't. I deepened the kiss, my free hand finding his back, his neck, his ginger hair.

He kissed me back with the same enthusiasm, his other hand running down my arm, our fingers twining.

The kiss ended naturally, once we were both breathless.

I wanted to hug him. I wanted to cry.

I didn't want him to ever leave.

After what I decided was possibly the Best First Kiss Ever, we left the apartment to go to Powell's City of Books, with plans for lunch afterward.

But now that the kissing barrier had been broken, we walked down the exterior apartment stairs, hand in hand, fingers laced together.

Which was how Adrian saw us, at the bottom of the stairs.

"Hi," I said, my face flushing a bright pomegranate red.

"Hey," he said, taking in the scene.

There was plenty to take in, I supposed. Neil and I, hand in hand, my lips swollen from our recent kiss.

"I brought the tax forms," Adrian said. Sure enough, he had several pieces of paper in his hand, folded once down the center.

I cleared my throat. "Oh. Good."

My mind whirled. I knew I should probably take the forms. But what to do with them? The responsible thing would be to take them to the filing cabinet in my office, but that would mean—most likely—letting go of Neil's hand.

I didn't want to let go of Neil's hand.

"You look like you're going out," said Adrian, which I figured was true in more than one sense.

"Yes," I answered, confirming both interpretations.

"Want me to drop them in the mail slot?"

"That would be perfect," I said, nodding like a bobblehead doll.

Adrian didn't move.

"I...uh... Neil, this is Adrian. Adrian," I said, my hand flailing between the two, "this is Neil. Neil is my...friend." I winced at my word choice but carried on. "Adrian's the sous-chef for the new restaurant."

"Good to meet you." Neil extended his right hand, while hanging on to my hand with his left.

Adrian shook it with a shadow of his familiar bravado.

"We're off to Powell's," I said, my voice awkwardly bright. "See you later."

"Later," Adrian echoed, chin lifted.

We got in the car and drove away. Once we were about a block away, I scrunched up my face and exhaled. "That...was not ideal."

"Adrian? Why?"

"He's my brother's new best friend. And I can't imagine—," I started to say, but stopped. Stopped because my phone had already started to ring.

"You don't have to answer that," Neil pointed out. "Not if you think it's your brother."

"No," I agreed. "But the phone is only the beginning."

With my phone turned off—all the way off, not just to vibrate—we finished out the drive to Powell's on Burnside. We wandered through the floors and explored the nooks and crannies of the gigantic bookstore. Neil found a novel and I found a cookbook, which he insisted on paying for.

"So you remember the weekend," he said, patting the cookbook.

I lifted an eyebrow. "Trust me," I said. "I'll remember."

"If you're interested," he said as we walked back outside, "I'm giving a lecture tomorrow. It's not a big deal..."

"I'm still impressed."

"If you'd like to come, you're very welcome. I can reserve a space for you."

"I'd love to," I said. "What's the topic?"

"Genetic engineering and bacterial drug resistance."

I gave a sage nod. "You know, I was just wondering about that."

"I thought so," he said, eyes twinkling. "That's why I asked."

"Seriously"—I beamed up at him—"I'd love to."

We said good-bye at the end of the day with the kind of reluctance usually reserved for small children leaving Disneyland.

"I'll pick you up in the morning," he said, pulling me close for another
breathless kiss.

I squeezed his hand just before releasing it and going inside, our romantic
lingering cut short by a fresh sprinkling of rain.

"Morning?"

"Morning," he promised before walking away.

I sighed and let myself into the apartment. Chilled, I shed my jacket but
left my scarf on, then set to work making myself a mug of cocoa.

As I stirred the milk on the stove, I switched my phone back on.

Granted, I'd turned it on briefly earlier to verify that Clementine would be
able to puppy-sit Gigi for the rest of the day. By then I had a small collection of
voice mails and text messages that I'd studiously ignored.

And now? I lifted my phone to listen to my voice mails.

Of which I had nine.

Five from Nico, which wasn't any surprise.

Two from Cat.

One from Sophie.

And…one from my mom.

Asking if Neil wanted to come for Sunday-night dinner.

~ SEA SALT HOT CHOCOLATE ~

1 cup whole milk
1 small cinnamon stick
3 ounces semisweet chocolate, divided
Whipped cream, for serving
Sea salt—fleur de sel, if you have it, to taste

Set aside about $^1/_2$ ounce of chocolate for garnish. Shave it, grate it, whatever floats your boat.

Heat milk in a small saucepan, stirring constantly.

Add chocolate, stir until melted and blended, and the milk is frothy. Taste, add salt to taste.

Serve immediately with whipped cream and reserved chocolate on top.

21

It is a true saying that a man must eat a peck of salt
with his friend before he knows him.

—MIGUEL DE CERVANTES

*I*n a panic, I called Cat.

"You are so lucky I'm awake," she said when she picked up. "The
boys are sick and not inclined to sleep, and not inclined to let me sleep either.
Just so you know, Jules, if you'd woken me up, you'd be so dead to me."

I closed myself in my room and unzipped my boots. "Nico is freaking
out."

"Caught that."

"Everyone knows."

"Figured as much."

I released a pent-up breath. "You have to tell me what to do."

"Honey, I moved to Chicago—that's what I did."

"Mom invited him to Sunday-night dinner."

"She's good, that one," Cat acknowledged. "So, is he sticking around until
Sunday?"

"He's scheduled to leave that morning," I said, scanning my room for
projects. I could put away clothes—the morning's attempt at dressing had
wreaked its havoc. I smushed the phone between my ear and my shoulder and
began to throw garments into piles.

"So what are you worrying about?"

"Aside from the rest of the crazy?"

"How did Nico find out, anyway?" Cat asked.

I folded a pair of jeans. "Adrian."

"That's Nico's new best friend, right?"

"Right."

"Always makes me think of *Rocky*. Anyway—why did it matter enough for him to tell Nico?"

"There's a vibe," I said, tossing two blouses to the end of the bed.

"A boy-girl kind of vibe?"

"Yup."

"And nothing's come of it—you're just vibing each other?"

"Dating a coworker is bad news. And he's enough like Nico that it would be a terrible idea. I don't take him seriously."

"Well, boo on him for outing you."

"I miss you."

"I miss you too. Did you at least have a good second date?"

I couldn't stop my smile. "After a fashion? Yeah."

"Cool. I won't ask, because if I did, I'd be the biggest hypocrite, but I'm glad it was good. So—other than everyone being in your business, is there a reason you wouldn't want him at a family dinner?"

"No. Yes. He's wonderful, but he's different."

"'Different' as in he wears capes publicly, or 'different' as in…"

The bed squished beneath me as I sat down. "I don't know. I guess he's not the epicurean, big-personality guy that I think everyone's pictured me with."

"Whatever. You're the one dating him."

I lowered my voice. "I don't want him to be the next Nelson."

"Okay…" She paused in thought. "Nelson's not actually that bad."

"He's boring."

"Not to another CPA he's not. And he's good-natured. Sophie wanted stability, and that's what she got. He's a good dad to Chloé. You could do worse than someone like Nelson, if it was a guy you really liked."

"I guess that's true."

"You could always invite him to dinner, you know, so he knows the offer's out there. See what he does with it."

"What if they scare him away?"

"If that's the case," she said, "he doesn't deserve you. Also—know that when Nico called, I acted totally shocked. He didn't hear anything from me."

"Thanks for that."

"Anytime."

"I might skip Sunday-night dinner just to spite everyone."

"Go for it," Cat said. "A little rebellion is good for the soul."

Neil picked me up at eleven the next morning, already dressed in a suit for his presentation.

"You look great," I said, taking in his ensemble. Not many men owned a day suit, but the caramel color looked wonderful with his ginger hair.

"You look better," he said, offering his arm as we walked out the door.

"Glad you like it. I haven't dressed for a medical lecture for a little while."

"Ah," he said. "Just a little while?"

"More like ever." I grinned up at him cheekily. I had to admit I felt pretty sharp. I'd donned a white sheath dress and paired it with my black boots, a black blazer, and a cobalt-blue necklace.

We walked to the car arm in arm.

"I had a thought," Neil said once we were en route. "I don't want to leave on Sunday."

"No?"

"No. And I've got plenty of vacation time built up. How would you feel about it if I flew out early Tuesday instead? Then we'd have some time Monday evening, maybe meet for lunch in between, if you can get away."

Tuesday. I froze.

"If you'd rather I didn't, that's okay," he said, eying my face nervously even as he negotiated traffic.

"No, I *want* to see you," I said, sounding more panicked than pleased. "It's just that, um—"

"Don't worry about it. Forget I asked."

"My mom invited you to Sunday-night dinner," I blurted.

"What?"

"Sunday-night dinner. Most of my family has dinner together every Sunday. Sunday because that's the day the restaurant's closed. Adrian saw us together yesterday, and he told my brother, and now everyone in my family knows about you, and my mom invited you to dinner."

"That's kind of her," Neil said.

"Yes," I said, "kind. Or recon with food."

"And?"

"And what?"

"There are a lot more thoughts in your head. I can see them on your face."

I crossed my arms and schooled my features. "You're supposed to be watching the road."

He pointed forward. "Stoplight."

"Whatever."

"It's up to you. I'd be happy to meet your parents."

"Oh no, it wouldn't just be my parents. It would be my brothers, and my sister and her spouse, and my niece, and it's basically a room full of multilingual people eating food and bossing you around and getting in your business."

"I can handle myself."

Ungraciously, the first thought in my mind was a retort about him spending his days with petri dishes. But I caught a hold of myself. If he liked me, maybe he wouldn't be totally overwhelmed by my family.

Maybe?

"It's up to you," I said finally. "They're a lot. Have you seen *My Big Fat*

Greek Wedding? Dinner with my family is like that, but not Greek and with smaller hair."

"I think I saw that movie at some point."

I squinted at him. "You'd remember if you had."

"This may surprise you," he said dryly, "but I don't watch a lot of chick flicks."

"I hate that term," I said, looking out the window, "but that's an argument for another day. Are you in or out?"

"I'm in."

"Fine," I said.

I spent the rest of the drive trying to decide how to tell my mother I *would* bring a guest on Sunday.

Neil would give his lecture at the OHSU's Old Library Auditorium. I gave him a parting kiss on the cheek before we entered, and I allowed the event's coordinators to sweep him away. An assistant gave me a paper program and showed me to a seat in the front row. While I waited, I examined the program.

"Phagocytes in Opportunistic Mycoses," it read. Before I could fully wrap my head around what that could possibly mean, another man in a suit—not as nice as Neil's—stood at the podium to greet everyone and announce Neil.

I could see Neil standing to the side. In his suit, in the setting, he seemed almost a different person. Self-assured, certainly. He was calm and collected, his features composed.

Seeing him so serious, I found myself wanting to make silly faces at him. But there were still other people up front with him, so I bided my time.

Neil made a few opening remarks, thanked the gentleman who introduced him, and settled in for his lecture. While my science background wasn't bad—I had to be conversant in the chemistry of baking and the biology of roasting meats, after all—so much of what he said was completely and utterly over my head. At least the slides were pretty and colorful in their own way, even if they were the interior of some sort of cells.

Ten minutes later, Neil was alone at the podium, without even an assistant waiting in the wings to give him bottled water.

So I waited.

I waited until his eyes landed on me. His eyes crinkled at the corners, and his mouth turned up into the gentlest smile.

I had him.

Holding his gaze, I turned my lower lip down into an exaggerated pout and slid my tongue up until it covered my upper lip. He wanted to laugh. I could tell. But instead, he paused for the briefest instant—which sounded dramatic and professional—and flashed an irresistible grin.

Ha.

My eyes slid from left to right, checking the attendees seated next to me. Both were scribbling notes, absorbed with Neil's material.

And nobody was the wiser.

I stayed at Neil's side during the following reception. Neil introduced me to people whose names I immediately forgot. I made charming conversation but mostly smiled and nodded silently. All in all, I felt very much like a political wife.

Another ten minutes and my wrist would start to pivot my hand into the royal wave.

Thankfully, we left nine minutes later, almost as if Neil knew I wouldn't be able to behave for much longer.

"You were amazing," I said, as we walked to his rental car.

He gave me a sideways look. "Nice faces there."

"I just wanted you to connect with your audience," I said with an innocent shrug. "And it was only one face. Don't exaggerate your data."

"Mmm. I wouldn't want to do that," he said, his hand finding its way onto the small of my back.

"So, are you sure you're still up for dinner tomorrow?"

"I am."

"I should call my mom and let her know. I was also going to ask if you would like to come to church with me tomorrow."

"Of course."

"Great," I said, trying to quell the butterflies that decided to take flight. Dinner with the family, going to church together—I couldn't get ahead of myself. Instead, I smiled and made a conscious choice to focus on the present.

At church the following morning, I chose the service my family didn't attend and sat in the back rather than the seventh row, right-hand side.

"Is everything okay?" Neil asked after we'd shaken the hands of everyone in the general vicinity.

"Yes. Of course. Why wouldn't it be?"

"You seem a little...twitchy."

"Twitchy?"

"Like a bunny rabbit."

"Bunny rabbit?" I repeated, incredulous. "Who says 'bunny rabbit'?"

Neil took his seat and crossed his arms. "I guess I do."

"It's just...my family and I usually come to the later service. It's restaurant business," I explained. "Most everyone tends to work late on Saturday nights."

"And we're here at the early service to avoid them."

"Not avoid," I said, trying not to feel defensive. Trouble was, I couldn't think of a better word for it. "Just...temporarily evade them."

"That sounds a lot like avoidance," Neil replied dryly.

"You're going to meet them tonight," I said.

"You're worried."

"I am not."

Somehow, I got through the rest of the service without looking over my shoulder. I even managed to take sentient sermon notes. "Want to see if there are any good cookies out?" I asked afterward.

Neil searched my face for signs of stress—or maybe mental illness—before giving his assent. We threaded our way through the crowd and into the foyer where two eight-foot tables stood laden with baked goods.

"People bring things voluntarily," I explained, picking up a paper cocktail napkin. "Some weeks it can be a little thin, but—"

My words stopped when my eyes landed on a familiar platter and an unmistakable pile of cookies. "Oh no."

"What?"

"Those." I pointed. "Those there."

"They look like cookies."

"My mother made them. Which means—"

"Do I smell bad?"

I turned to face Neil. "What?"

"Do I have terrible people skills?"

Where was this going? "No..."

"You find me interesting company."

"You know I do."

He rested his hands on my shoulders. "So is there anything you need to tell me about your family? about me?"

I stepped away from the table, into a corner behind a pillar. "They're intense."

"I've encountered intense people."

"They have no sense of boundaries."

Neil shook his head at me ruefully. "I'm from the South."

"I'm just saying they're loud and they have expectations."

"I see." Neil took a half step back. "Expectations of me? Or of you?"

I looked away. "Both, probably."

"I don't have to go, Juliette."

My stomach twisted into a series of unpleasant knots.

I wanted to keep Neil to myself. I wanted him to be my little secret. Was that the adult thing to want?

Probably not. I forced a smile. "It'll be fine."

Neil studied my face, clearly unsure as to whether he believed me or not. I couldn't blame him.

I forced my shoulders to relax, stepped back to the cookie table, and reached for a polenta cookie. "You really should try one," I said, trying to sound breezy and relaxed, even though I felt anything but.

Neil tucked a piece of hair behind my ear. "I'm sure they're wonderful."

LEMON-SCENTED ITALIAN POLENTA COOKIES

$1^3/_4$ cups all-purpose flour

1 cup dry polenta or yellow cornmeal

$1/_2$ teaspoon sea salt

1 cup (2 sticks) unsalted butter, softened

1 cup plus 2 tablespoons sugar

1 tablespoon lemon zest

1 large egg, plus 1 large egg yolk

1 teaspoon vanilla

$1/_2$ teaspoon lemon extract (optional)

Sparkling or raw sugar, to finish

Preheat oven to 350°F. Line a baking sheet with parchment paper.

Mix dry ingredients together in a medium bowl.

Beat butter and sugar together with an electric mixer until pale and fluffy and pretty; add lemon zest.

Add the egg, beat for 10 to 20 seconds, and then add the yolk and continue to beat for another 10 to 20 seconds. Add vanilla and lemon extract (if using).

In small portions with the mixer running, add the flour mixture. Continue to beat until just combined.

If the dough feels too dry to the touch, add a tablespoon or two of milk to the mixture. Prep a pastry bag with a large-sized star tip. Scoop dough into the pastry bag and pipe onto prepared cookie sheets into curly S shapes, spacing the cookies about 1 to 2 inches from one another. Sprinkle with sparkling sugar.

Bake 15 to 18 minutes or until edges are golden and cookies are fragrant. Allow to cool before eating.

Makes about 36 cookies.

Note: If you don't have pastry bags or tips, you can substitute gallon-sized Ziploc bags and cut a hole in one corner. Also, the cookies can be made simply as drop cookies.

22

Food is our common ground, a universal experience.

—James Beard

*T*ell me about your siblings," Neil suggested as he drove the two of us to Sunday dinner. "Which ones will be there?"

"Almost all," I said, rolling my eyes. "Caterina's in Chicago with her husband and little boys; otherwise she'd be in the kitchen trying to boss my dad and elbow Nico out of the way. She's great. She goes by Cat, and half of the time, she tells people she was named for Cat in *Breakfast at Tiffany's*."

"So she's funny."

"She is. She's the sibling second-closest in age, six years older than me. Sophie's the oldest. She and Cat couldn't be more different. Sophie's very cautious and conservative, whereas Cat's more free-spirited. Sophie is married to Nelson—the CPA—and their daughter is Chloé. Chloé is twelve and awesome. Really a good kid. Nico is a lot like Cat, and they tend to fuss at each other because of it. He's a big personality, likes to get his own way. Alex is more studious. He and his wife divorced six months ago, so that's been rough." I peered out the window as we crossed Morrison Bridge. "And then there's me."

"The baby of the family."

I made a face at him. "I hate that term."

"Sorry."

"Being the youngest of five is a heavy mantle to wear sometimes." I brushed my hair from my face.

One of these days, I needed to invest in a good hair spray.

For the occasion, I'd dressed in very careful layers. I wore a pencil skirt with a sleeveless chiffon shell, a cardigan, and a scarf.

If I got warm—or very, very nervous—I could shed layers before sweat started to become a problem.

Hopefully.

When we pulled up to the house, I noted with no little horror that each sibling's car was parked nearby.

Clearly, everyone was inside, lying in wait.

"Mmm," I said mildly, trying to sound casual. "Looks like the gang's all here."

"Relax," Neil said as we made our way up the walk. "And don't forget I have siblings too."

I didn't have time to process that reminder. Chloé threw open the door. "You're here!" she squealed. "She's here," Chloé repeated over her shoulder.

"Hello, sweetie," I said. Neil chuckled behind me, but I didn't ask why. I was too busy trying to process the tableau of awkward domesticity in front of me.

Sophie sat on the sofa, crocheting, of all things. My father and Alex were engaged in a game of chess, using the board usually reserved for décor.

Maman sat next to Sophie, a slim cookbook in her hands.

Nico had perched himself on the edge of the leather chair, a tower of Jenga blocks in a stack in front of him.

Nelson seemed truly oblivious, his thumbs busy on his cell phone.

Cell phone aside, I felt like I'd just walked into a Jane Austen adaptation.

"Hi, everybody," I said, forcing a smile. "This is Neil."

Neil greeted my mother first, giving her the tub of pure shea butter he'd brought as a hostess gift. I assumed he didn't miss her near-translucent skin, her penciled-in eyebrows, and the contrasting full head of hair she sported, thanks to her wig. He gave her a warm smile and complimented her scarf, which I knew to be an Hermès.

My father stood to shake Neil's hand. A sort of receiving line seemed to form. I watched with a mix of pride and horror as Neil shook each hand graciously, his grip appearing firm.

A momentary silence struck after everyone exchanged greetings and identities, and in that moment, I heard a flush from the hall bath.

My eyes scanned the room. No, everyone was here.

And then my sixth sense tingled.

My eyes swung to Nico, who had the grace to look—just maybe—almost guilty. When Adrian emerged from the bathroom, I wasn't surprised. I could read Nico's face like a book. He didn't like that I'd brought an outsider over, a man so completely separate from the world of cuisine. He brought Adrian to meet the family, thinking I'd come to my senses.

Deep disappointment with my brother flooded my chest.

"We're so blessed to have special guests tonight," my mother said. "Adrian brought some lovely hors d'oeuvre with him."

Sophie and I exchanged glances. Adrian had brought food to *add* to our mother's dinner? And she was happy about it? I'd tried to bring a saffron-spiked dip once and my mother declared that—while it was lovely—it didn't match the balance of the menu that she'd achieved. Cheese, chocolate, and wine were allowed.

Foods requiring assembling or preparation were not. Until now.

No one mentioned this fact, even Nico, who'd had a wilted chard and pancetta dish turned away. No, Nico looked about ready for his victory lap.

Neil and Adrian shook hands. This time, Adrian's shoulders were squared, his chin high, his eyes taking measure of Neil.

To his credit, Neil either didn't notice or did an excellent job pretending, merely shaking his hand without the encounter turning into a chest-beating session.

At least not yet.

I realized as we walked to the dining room that Neil didn't have to do or say anything to Adrian; instead, he merely walked beside me with a gentle hand located at the small of my back.

My father had outdone himself. We started with seared scallops on a bed of kale, moved on to risotto, and continued to osso buco.

"It's veal," my father told Neil in his outdoor voice. "*Osso buco* means 'bone with a hole.' See?" he said, pointing at the round hole at the center of the veal shank. "There's a hole in it."

"It looks delicious," Neil said, nodding. "I've never eaten veal before."

Every head but Nelson's whipped around to stare at Neil.

Neil cleared his throat. "I'm from the South."

"What do you eat in the South?" Dad asked.

"A lot of pig," Neil said, with a discreet wink in my direction. "The main southern food groups include bacon, sausage, pork, ham, and lard."

Sophie's head shook from side to side in horror.

"Also catfish," Neil said, reaching for his utensils, "if you're farther south."

"So where are your people from originally?" Dad asked.

"My dad's family was from Scotland. My mom's people were Norwegian."

"Norwegian," Dad said, rolling the idea around in his head. "And Scottish."

"Have you ever eaten haggis?" Chloé asked Neil.

Neil chuckled. "No, and I have no plans to."

My father nodded as if the haggis abstention comforted him.

"My mom's from Spain," Adrian volunteered. "Great food in Spain."

"Eh, that is true. Some of the great chefs of this era are Spanish chefs." Dad sipped his wine. "The rest of them are Italian."

My mother cleared her throat pointedly. My father splayed his hands. "I cannot help that French cuisine is dying. I didn't come up with the exorbitant taxes for restaurant dining. At least the Italians had the sense to keep Starbucks out of Italy. France practically turned out a welcome mat for"—his face contorted into a grimace—"McDonald's."

My mother took a deep breath. I knew what was coming—twenty or so minutes of debate. "The osso buco is so tender, Dad. What kind of wine did you braise it in?"

"Sangiovese."

My parents still glared at each other, but the dueling pistols had been temporarily avoided.

Neil squeezed my hand. I smiled at him.

"Now, Neil"—Sophie leaned forward, and I caught my breath—"if you're from Tennessee, how exactly did you and Juliette meet?"

"We met online," Neil answered simply.

"Online," Sophie repeated, her eyes narrowing. "You mean, like—Facebook?"

"Something like that," I hedged.

"So it wasn't Facebook," Sophie clarified.

Because she couldn't exist in a world where she didn't know everything. I took a deep breath, doing my best to ignore Adrian's stare. "We met on an online dating site."

Sophie tried, and failed, to stifle a gasp.

"Really?" said Chloé. "That's so cool."

"I have no complaints," said Neil.

"When did you, you know, meet?" Sophie asked.

"Thursday," I said.

Sophie shook her head. "But *online*—when did you meet then?"

"I think it was the end of March," I said.

Neil nodded. "That sounds about right."

Sophie folded her arms. "March? Well, that was quite the secret."

"Not really," I lied, as if the fact hadn't been one part in a towering stack of secrets. "You never asked."

"Seriously, Soph," Alex interjected. "Enough with the twenty questions."

Oh, Alex. I would have to make him cookies.

"Cat's going to flip," Sophie muttered to herself.

"So, Neil," Nico began, "has Juliette told you much about the restaurant we're starting?" Nico's hand drew a circle in the air, one that included himself, Adrian, and me.

"She has. I know she's been working very hard."

"Yes," said Nico.

I raised an eyebrow. Really? I'd thought my hard work had been largely taken for granted.

"Even with all the work ahead of time," Nico continued, "the preopening is the calm before the storm. After the opening, well…"

My father nodded. "It's true. When we first opened D'Alisa & Elle, I barely slept for a year."

"The late nights, the long days…," Nico said, his voice trailing off.

I glared at my brother. "Neil's a doctor. I'm sure he's no stranger to crazy schedules."

"True," he said, turning to Neil. "It is nice that your schedule is so flexible. Will you be able to fly out for the restaurant opening?"

"I'd like to, yes," Neil replied.

"That is excellent," Nico said, but he'd already made his point. "I did not think most doctors were able to have so much time off."

With Neil's schedule in Memphis and my schedule here, when would we ever see each other? The travel, the time, the hours. We had our time now, partly because Neil had needed to come to Oregon for business and partly because he was using his vacation time. What happened when that was used up?

And what about me? Even if I did leave my job at the paper—especially if—I would have to stay close to home, more often than not.

My heart clenched as I realized I was falling for a man I'd never be able to keep.

I made it through the dessert course, but as soon as the last piece of cheese had been shaved off and eaten by Alex, Neil and I left.

On the drive home, I tried to pretend everything was okay.

"Why did you laugh at me when I greeted Chloé?"

"When?"

"When we were at the door."

Neil thought for a moment. "I remember," he said. "You said, 'Hello, sweetie.' I'm a geek," he admitted easily. "It's a *Doctor Who* line—one of the characters always greets the Doctor by saying 'Hello, sweetie.'"

I squeezed his hand. "I think you're a very nice geek."

"Thanks."

"You were wonderful back there."

"Glad you think so."

He didn't pick my brain to find out what I thought my family might have thought, and I was grateful for that.

Because I was certain they thought he was all wrong for me. A nice guy. Kind, funny even. But wrong for me because he lived in Tennessee, worked as a doctor, and would never be able to understand my world.

"I was thinking about that photograph of your grandmother's," Neil said, his eyes on the road.

"Oh?"

"I was thinking about hidden things. You know, you see it in movies."

"True," I said, almost feeling silly for putting so much time and thought into Grand-mère's mystery.

"What never makes sense to me is when people hang on to incriminating objects. Like in *The Da Vinci Code*—you'll never be able to convince me that the right way to hide something is to keep all the clues. So you wouldn't keep things unless they meant a lot or unless you meant to tell someone, someday.

"What I mean, then," he continued, "is to say, the man in the picture was someone I think your grandmother loved very much. And if you're related to him, that must be something special."

"Thanks. Those are good thoughts." I studied his profile. "Can I make you dinner tomorrow?"

He gave a sideways grin I found devastating. "Sure."

His right hand found my left, and I clung tightly.

"I had a great time with you today," Neil said as he walked me to my door.

I smiled up at him, hoping the cover of night would hide my misty eyes. "I could do it every day."

"I agree."

But we couldn't, and there was the crux of it. We were stuck in a game of relocation chicken, and I knew in my gut that neither of us was willing to flinch first.

I hated the distance between our homes. I hated that his life was in Memphis and mine was inextricably in Portland. Neither of us could pick up sticks anytime soon—too many people depended on us.

I pointed up to my apartment windows. "Clementine's home. We should say good-bye down here." Tears stung my eyes. "I am really, *really* going to miss you when you go," I said, then paused to clear my throat. "I know it's just been a short time in person, but—"

He held my face in his hands. "I know," he said, before tilting his face toward mine.

It wasn't a kiss where one person kisses and the other responds. Instead, we kissed each other; I wrapped my arms around his neck as he pulled me closer, his hand on the small of my back.

"I'll see you after work tomorrow?"

I wanted to cry. It wasn't enough.

Neil stroked my cheek. "We'll be fine."

I took his hand between my own. "I'll see you tomorrow?"

"Tomorrow," he echoed in confirmation.

One last kiss and I walked up the stairs to the apartment.

Gigi greeted me at the door. I found Clementine at work in the kitchen, stirring a pot surrounded by panna cotta molds.

"You're back." She checked the pot and removed it from the heat. "Just in time—the first batch is about ready. How did it go?"

In reply, I burst into tears.

PANNA COTTA
FOR THE BROKENHEARTED

1 packet powdered gelatin (about $1^1/_4$ teaspoons)
3 tablespoons cold, filtered water
2 cups heavy cream
$^1/_4$ cup sugar
1 teaspoon vanilla extract or vanilla bean paste
$1^1/_2$ teaspoons orange zest
A few saffron threads
Pinch of sea salt

In a small bowl, add the gelatin to the cold water; allow to set for at least 5 minutes.

Heat the heavy cream and sugar in a saucepan, but do not boil. Stir until the sugar has dissolved. Remove from heat, and add the vanilla, orange zest, saffron, and salt. Taste, and adjust flavorings as necessary.

Add the gelatin and stir until incorporated. Cover and let stand for 10 minutes.

Lightly oil four custard cups with a neutral-tasting oil, such as safflower oil.

With a fine-mesh strainer, strain the warmed cream mixture into a separate bowl.

Divide the mixture into the prepared cups and chill them until firm—at least 4 hours and up to 3 days.

Run a sharp knife around the edge of each panna cotta before unmolding onto a serving plate. Serve chilled, and enjoy them with at least one pair of listening ears.

Note: Panna cotta is traditionally served as a molded dessert, but can also be served out of teacups, jelly jars, stemware, or glass tumblers.

23

All sorrows are less with bread.

—Miguel de Cervantes Saavedra

*C*lementine spent the evening plying me with panna cotta (I ate two), brioche (two slices, buttered with jam), and tiny fresh strawberries (too many to count).

I stopped weeping after the panna cotta, stopped sniffling after the brioche, and stoically considered the situation as I nibbled the strawberries.

"I'll reimburse you for the strawberries," I told Clementine. "Organically grown, locally sourced—they couldn't have been cheap."

Clementine shrugged. "I got them from a farmer friend of mine."

"Still."

"Consider them a gift. So, you're making him dinner tomorrow night? What are you going to make?"

"I was thinking of making fresh pasta. Haven't decided what to do with it yet."

"What about dessert?"

I toyed with the dishcloth on the countertop. "Don't know yet."

"When planning a menu," Clementine suggested, "start with dessert and work backward."

"Spoken like a pastry chef. What do you suggest?"

"I'll think on it."

I splayed my hands. "After all that?"

"The inspiration for a good dessert comes inexplicably and without method." She shrugged. "But don't worry. I always think of something."

I sat up straight. "I'll make him dinner," I said, "and we'll say good-bye, and if I see him again, I'll be glad, but if I don't, we had a wonderful weekend."

"You think you won't see him? He seemed pretty...attached, when we met." She gave me a direct look. "And by 'attached,' I mean he was holding your hand or touching your shoulder or just plain looking at you with cow eyes."

"I don't know what to think. I don't know how this can work."

"To start with, you're both American citizens. That's one insurmountable difficulty you don't have to deal with."

"True." I ate another strawberry. "Because love and the INS do not mix well."

She laughed. "When's he coming over? I can make myself scarce for the night."

"I think I told him sixish. Not too late—he's flying out early the next morning."

"Something tells me he won't mind."

I gave a wan smile. "I appreciate your optimism. I'm spent—thanks for sitting with me."

Clementine patted my shoulder. "Anytime."

After two hours in bed, I'd made no progress sleeping. Gigi didn't seem to mind, simply readjusting her sprawl every time I tossed or turned.

I wanted to talk to someone—my head was too full. I prayed first, hoping a spirit of calm would descend and allow me to drift off.

But the Lord said no.

I considered calling Cat, but I knew she'd been exhausted, and I couldn't bank on her being awake with the boys yet again.

Clementine had already gotten an earful.

As I flipped over one more time, I found myself reaching for my phone and calling the only person I really wanted to talk to.

He answered on the fourth ring.

"Juliette? Is everything okay?"

Neil's voice managed to soothe me and send my heart skittering at the same time. "I can't sleep."

"Oh?"

I chewed on my lip. "I really like you."

"That's good," Neil said easily. "I like you too."

"How could it ever work out, though? I don't...I don't see how this can end well."

Neil sighed. "Is this something you were worrying about before Nico brought it up?"

"Not yet, no."

"I don't mean to sound rude—"

"Sure you do."

"Okay, maybe I do. I was going to say that neither of us is dating Nico. So neither of us needs to worry about whether he thinks it's going to work or not."

I mulled that thought around in my mind. "True. But what if he made a good point?"

"The poet Robert Browning married Elizabeth Barrett even though she was in poor health and likely an opium addict."

"So, which of us in this scenario is Robert and which is Elizabeth?"

His chuckle reverberated through the phone. "My point is that sometimes unlikely relationships can thrive."

"I am shocked you know about Robert and Elizabeth. You didn't strike me as a poetry man."

"I'm a man of many interests." He cleared his throat. "I also attended a lecture on hypokalemic periodic paralysis. The lecturer addressed speculation that Elizabeth Barrett Browning may have suffered from it."

"I see."

"It's a genetic disease."

"It sounds terrible."

"But she and Robert Browning married and had a good life together."

I rested my head on my pillow. "They have a good story."

"Jules, I don't know what kind of future the Lord has in store for us. But I want to find out and enjoy spending as much time getting to know you along the way—even if it's over the phone or over e-mail. I'd rather have an e-mail from you than an in-person date with someone else who lives nearby."

"I like it when you call me 'Jules.'"

"I like it when you call me 'Neil.'"

I snorted. "That makes no sense."

"Sorry. I was asleep five minutes ago. Cut me a little slack."

"Do you have a nickname?"

"None. I have no embarrassing nicknames."

"Liar."

"Maybe. That's a conversation for the middle of another night."

"Fine." I sank deeper into the covers. "Thanks for picking up the phone."

"I always love hearing your voice, Juliette," he said. "Day or night."

"Yeah?"

"Preferably day. But I can make night work too."

I gave a soft laugh. "I'll let you go back to sleep."

"Do you think you'll be able to sleep yourself?"

"I think so," I said after a moment of reflection. "Thanks."

We said good night and hung up. I pulled the covers up to my chin, gave Gigi a chance to resettle, and slept until morning.

The morning began bright and sunny. I dressed quickly, walked Gigi, and found Clementine in her natural habitat.

"Mmm—babkas. Those look amazing," I said, closing my eyes as I took in the scent.

Clementine wiped a floury hand on her apron. "They're not rising the way I want them too. I think there's a weather shift coming."

"Any inspiration for dessert tonight? I'm going to meet Neil for lunch, I think, and then do a bit of light grocery shopping."

"What are you making?"

"Fresh pasta carbonara with leeks and lemon," I said, "with broccolini on the side."

Clementine's eyes rolled to the tin-tiled ceiling as she thought. "Ordinarily I'd say a sorbet, to offset the heaviness of the egg yolks. But you're feeding a man."

"True."

"And it's a romantic dinner. I think chocolate."

"How about my grandmother's chocolate cake? Her famous one?"

"Perfect." Clementine's expression softened. "Mireille would have liked that."

I waved good-bye to her and Gigi as I left for work.

Today, I would have to talk to Marti. Maybe we could make it work, she and I. If I stayed at the paper, only staying with the restaurant long enough to get it launched, then maybe my schedule would be manageable enough to figure out a trip to Memphis to see Neil.

Maybe we could make it work.

The tenor of the building that morning seemed...off. More scurrying than usual, but somehow fewer people scurrying.

Had something happened that I hadn't read about? Were a lot of people reporting on scene? I'd find out soon enough.

I set my things down on my desk and leaned over to check in with Linn.

Except she wasn't there.

And her space was clear. Everything was gone—her books, her photos, her computer.

She'd texted me Friday. Why, oh why, hadn't I remembered to call her back?

I strode away from my desk, away and into the emptiest hallway as I dialed her cell number and listened to it ring.

"It's about time I heard from you," she said when she picked up.

"Are you okay? Your stuff's gone. What happened?"

"Budget cuts. Marti sacked me."

"What?"

"Newspaper shrinkage and all that. I shouldn't be surprised. Sam got let go too. He had quite the *Jerry Maguire* moment; it's too bad you missed it."

"Linn, I'm so sorry. I'm so, so sorry."

Her voice softened. "It's not your fault."

"Well, I may well be next. Marti wants to see me this morning."

Linn gave a bitter laugh. "You? The golden girl? That bit with the paper towels—Marti ate it up."

"That was the worst."

"I'm sure your job is plenty secure. You're generating a lot of Internet traffic and ad revenue."

"I'll talk to Marti. There's got to be something you can do."

"It's over, Jules. I'll become a food blogger like the rest of the out-of-work food journalists. I'll write scorching Yelp reviews. You just wait. It'll be—"

"Terrible," I finished for her.

"Hope may not be warranted at this point. I'll make it work. Have your meeting. I don't envy you the extra work you'll pick up."

"I'll call you later," I promised. I shoved my phone in my pocket and strode to Marti's office.

"There you are!" she said, eyes bright. "You were so great last Friday. Quick thinking! Everyone loved it."

"I'm glad," I said, as I sank into the chair opposite Marti's desk.

"I don't know if you checked your work e-mail or not while you were out, but corporate cut our staff on Friday," Marti said, "and that included cutting reporters. Food reporting is essential to the community, to our culture. I fought for the department as much as I could, but in the end I had to let Linn and Sam go."

"Linn does so much," I said. "Isn't there anything that could be done to be able to retain her?"

"I've got enough funds for myself, one additional reporter, and a freelancing fund. Times are tough. There's a lot of restructuring. People consume their news differently, and our job is to figure out how to make ends meet as we adjust." She shrugged. "In other news, I had a long conversation with Susan Piecely, the producer at *Portland Sunrise*. She'd like you to do a segment once a week. You're a hit, Juliette."

"I wish I could," I said, with as much confidence as I could scrape from the depths of myself. "But you need Linn. She's so much better at the spontaneous thing, so great in front of people—and she loves it."

"You don't?"

"No." I shook my head vigorously. "After two tries, I can say no, no I don't. I've been busy with my brother's new restaurant, and we've talked about that. But I'm feeling stretched thin, and I hate not giving one hundred percent of myself either here or there. So, please, cut me. Let Linn come back. She's your girl."

"You really don't want it." Marti sounded stunned. "This could be big, you know."

"I threw up after the crepe debacle. I don't want it."

"If you go, you'll have to leave today. I can't afford to keep you in-office two weeks, but you'll have medical through the end of the month."

The idea of life without work benefits should have made me nervous, but it didn't. Instead, I felt relieved. "That's fine."

Marti folded her arms against her chest. "I won't say I'm not disappointed."

"It's time, I think, for something new."

"I'm coming to eat at your place once it's open. You know that."

I smiled. "Looking forward to it."

And that was it. I'd quit my job.

I walked back to my desk and packed up my things, which didn't take long. I paused just long enough to text Linn.

I took care of it.

Once I was back at my car, I called Neil. "I did it," I said. "I quit my job." I explained about the budget cuts and the *Portland Sunrise* producer and Linn.

"So you're a hero," he said.

"Just setting things to how they should be. Linn was always better suited to what I was doing anyway."

"Feel good?"

I breathed in and then out. "Yes. It's strange to have that chapter closed, but it's a good thing."

We said our good-byes, and I left to go grocery shopping. At Trader Joe's I picked up wine, Marcona almonds, eggs, and a whimsical bundle of fresh flowers for the table. At City Market, I purchased bacon, a bundle of leeks, and a beautiful organic lemon.

Back at home, I organized my kitchen workspace and set to work. I scooped out my flour blend—I preferred two parts semolina to one part all-purpose white—on a pastry cloth and made a deep, round well in the center before cracking the eggs into it.

Even though I'd grown up next to my father, sister, and brothers making pasta by hand, there was always something dangerous to me about placing a mound of flour on the countertop and then cracking eggs into it—as if I were about to make one big mess even worse. But I loved the magic that happened as I worked the eggs into the flour, kneading them together and watching as smooth, elastic dough began to take shape.

After the dough finished resting, I rolled it into long tubes and sliced it, and then formed it into orecchiette with my fingers.

The word *orecchiette* means "little ears" in Italian, but to me the pasta often looked like tiny cupped hands—hands to hold sauce, hold flavor, hold love.

My mind wandered as I repeated the motion over and over, rolling each piece of dough with my fingers until it reached the shape I wanted. I thought about Neil. I thought about how much I'd learned about him, about how much I'd come to care for him in the short time we'd spent together.

I tried not to think about how much I would miss him, and failed miserably. My heart ached, and I quickly learned I had to improve my mood lest my orecchiette become flattened.

So instead of thinking of Neil leaving, I thought about our dinner and how the food that I created with my hands had the power to bind us together in a shared experience.

When I'd formed the last little ear, I set the lot of them aside on a baking sheet to dry.

I prepped the rest of the dinner ingredients and set the chocolate cake to bake before stopping to primp.

My mother always looked tidy and fashionable even if she'd been cooking all day, but my clothes were covered in little bits of food debris, even though I'd been wearing an apron.

I slipped into an easy black knit dress with a scooped neckline and full skirt. Around my waist I fastened a ballet-pink leather belt and slipped my feet into ballet flats just a shade pinker. The look was sophisticated and romantic.

My hair had grown wavy from the day's humidity, and I let it stay that way. I dusted a bit of gray eye shadow on my lids, lined my eyes with black liquid eyeliner, and finished my face with some pink blush and lip gloss.

I studied myself in the mirror.

Tonight, I would relax. I would enjoy my time with Neil. I wouldn't worry about the future, about our relationship, about my family, about my job. About life.

I looked deeply into the reflection of my own eyes.

Who was I kidding?

There were so many butterflies in my stomach I feared I might fly away.

Pasta Carbonara
with Leeks and Lemon

For a recipe like this with so few ingredients, it's important to use good quality ingredients. Use very fresh organic eggs if you can find them. Be sure to set them out ahead of time to reach room temperature, or set them in a bowl of warm water.

While many Italian American recipes include cream in the sauce, the authentic Italian version skips the cream and relies on the egg for the sauce. I like the leeks, lemon, and parsley for this version because they lighten up the dish and add a fresh twist. Broccolini would be nice in it as well.

A note on leeks: They can come very dirty and also be tricky to clean. I like to soak them in a sink full of water to loosen up debris. Afterward, I slice off the root end, slice off the dark green ends (keep an eye out for lighter green bits in the center—you can use those), slice them in half lengthwise, and run them under a faucet to get rid of any residual dirt.

Coarse salt and ground pepper
7 slices bacon, cut on the diagonal into $1/2$-inch-wide pieces
3 leeks (white and light green parts only), halved and sliced thin
$3/4$ pound orecchiette
2 eggs at room temperature
$1/3$ cup grated parmesan cheese, plus more for the table
$1^1/2$ tablespoons finely grated lemon zest
1 tablespoon fresh lemon juice
$2/3$ cup fresh parsley leaves, coarsely chopped

Set a large pot of water to boil with a handful of sea salt.

In a medium bowl, whisk together eggs, parmesan cheese, lemon zest, and lemon juice.

Cook bacon in a large skillet, over medium heat for about 7 minutes, until they're just this side of crisp. (If the bacon is too crisp, it won't blend as well into the sauce.) Allow bacon to drain on paper towels, and pour off all but 2 tablespoons of bacon drippings. Pepper the leeks generously and sauté them until golden and soft, about 10 minutes.

Set pasta to boil and cook until just al dente. If using dried pasta, refer to the packaged instructions. If using fresh pasta, it will be done in 2 or 3 minutes.

Slowly pour $1/4$ cup pasta water into egg mixture while stirring briskly with a whisk to temper the eggs.

Drain pasta and pour all ingredients into the skillet. Add parsley. Add additional cheese to taste. Serve immediately.

24

What I love about cooking is that after a hard day, there is something comforting about the fact that if you melt butter and add flour and then hot stock, *it will get thick*! It's a sure thing! It's a sure thing in a world where nothing is sure; it has a mathematical certainty in a world where those of us who long for some kind of certainty are forced to settle for crossword puzzles.

—NORA EPHRON

Because the pasta wouldn't keep well, I refrained from doing any of the actual cooking until Neil arrived. The pasta pot simmered rather than boiled, and the bowl of whisked eggs waited. The cake was done. I'd toasted the almonds and tossed them with olive oil, salt, and herbs. The broccolini waited to be placed under the broiler. The wine chilled in the fridge.

Everything was ready. All I needed was Neil himself.

I straightened the kitchen. Rearranged the place settings at the table. Moved the throw pillows on the slipper chair to the settee and back. Fanned out the coffee-table books so they unfurled clockwise, rather than counterclockwise.

Neil called ten minutes later.

"There's a giant traffic snarl on I-5," he said. "I'm so sorry I'm late."

"That's all right," I said, clutching the phone with one hand and adding water to a flowerpot with the other. "Do you have a time estimate? I can have dinner going so it's ready when you arrive."

"It looks bad," Neil said. "I couldn't begin to guess when I'm getting out of here."

"Oh." My chest tightened. "What exit is next? What if I met you somewhere?"

"I'm on the on-ramp to one of the bridges, so I don't think I'll have any options anytime soon. Don't worry. Just hold on tight, and I'll be there as soon as I can."

I sighed as I hung up. But rather than stay and twiddle my toes, I refrigerated the eggs, grabbed Gigi's leash, and took her for a brisk jaunt around the neighborhood. If my face glowed a little, well, at least it made my makeup blend a little better. Or something.

Still nothing from Neil.

I prayed that the Lord would choose to encourage the traffic into motion.

My stomach rumbled.

Resignedly, I retrieved a tub of hummus and some baby carrots from the fridge and dug in. I found myself sagging against the countertop in exhaustion. I'd been so busy preparing everything that I'd worn myself out. Without the adrenaline rush that Neil would have brought with him the second he'd stepped through the door, I felt my muscles complain and my spirit droop.

I needed a nap. Just a short nap and I would perk up like daisies in fresh water. With that thought in mind, I curled up on the couch, rested my head on a throw pillow, and draped the knit throw over myself. Gigi seemed to agree with my plan and jumped up immediately, settling with her head resting on my ankles.

I awoke to a stream of drool sliding from the left corner of my mouth and a man's finger tracing a line down my cheekbone. My eyes flew open, and I saw Neil smiling into them. "Hi."

"Hi," I said, wiping my chin self-consciously.

"The door was unlocked. You're cute when you're sleeping."

My eyes squeezed shut. "I'm so embarrassed," I said, holding my hand over my face. Come to think of it, my mascara had probably smudged onto my cheek.

"Don't be. I'm the one that showed up"—he checked his watch—"more than an hour late. There were four cars and a police cruiser in a wreck."

"No wonder."

Neil shrugged. "I'm from Memphis, where most drivers don't realize they're mortal. Car crashes happen; I'm used to it. Just glad to be here."

I sat forward and straightened my spine. "So, dinner. Are you hungry?"

"Starved," he said, but he seemed less interested in food than in staring at my lips.

I tilted my face toward his, smiling as he brushed a kiss against my mouth. "You taste like...orange," I murmured.

"Orange candies," he whispered into my ear as he stroked my neck. "They were all I had in the car."

I snorted. "Okay. I'm making you dinner. And for starters," I said, picking up the plate I'd put on the coffee table, "would you like some almonds?"

"That was an amazing dinner," Neil said afterward as he ran his fingers through my hair.

I smiled as I leaned against his chest. "Glad you liked it."

The two of us had polished off an impressive amount of dinner. Neil ate his chocolate cake with enthusiasm; half of mine lingered on the plate near an unfinished glass of wine.

"I've had a wonderful trip," he said. "You should know I thought very highly of you before I came. But now—"

My head rose and fell against Neil's chest as he sighed.

"Now?" I prompted.

"I don't want to leave you."

"I have a trip to Europe planned soon," I said, holding his hand in mine. "Maybe afterward—maybe I could visit you in Memphis?"

His hand squeezed mine. "I would like that. When are you leaving for Europe?"

"Third week of June. I'll be in Provence, in Montagnac first. Paris for a little while, and then Italy for my nonno's birthday party." I paused, turning to look into Neil's eyes. "I want to talk to my great aunt," I said. "I want to find out if she remembers anything that could explain the photo or the things I found in the trunk."

"Really?"

I nodded. "My *grand-tante* Cécile. Younger sister, which you probably guessed. I've heard she has Alzheimer's or some sort of dementia, so who knows how much information I'll be able to get." I shrugged. "That sounds heartless. I'm looking forward to seeing her and my French cousins. And they run the family château as a bed-and-breakfast, as well as a honey business. Lavender honey. I'm hoping to use some at the restaurant. Maybe in a dessert and in an entrée as a signature."

"Sounds delicious."

"Thanks. Anyway, I'm looking forward to seeing Grand-tante Cécile— though the story for the family is that I'll also be sourcing some ingredients, visiting vineyards. Which I will, but Nonno and Grand-tante Cécile are my first priority. We'll see," I said. "We'll see what she's able to remember."

Neil massaged the base of my neck. "A lot of dementia patients will remember their youth the longest."

"I've heard the same," I said, leaning into his hand. "I'm hopeful. I'll take the photo with me."

"I'm surprised you're going alone," Neil noted. "I would have thought Nico would have tried to go with you. I imagine he would have been happy to source ingredients."

"He's too busy," I answered.

"He didn't try to get Adrian to go with you?"

I cleared my throat. "He tried."

"Oh?"

"I reassured my brother that my palate is quite reliable."

We were both quiet, allowing us to hear the full range of Gigi's snores.

"Your family likes him."

"They do."

Another pause. "Do you?"

"He's not my type," I answered honestly.

"What is your type?" The words were whispered near my ear.

I shivered.

"Oh, you know," I tried to say airily, but sounded hopelessly out of breath. "Clever. Educated. Gives talks on bacteria."

Neil gave a soft chuckle. "Oh yeah?"

"My parents have a restaurant marriage," I continued, more seriously. "I decided a long time ago it wasn't for me."

"A restaurant marriage?"

"Their lives revolve around D'Alisa & Elle. And it works for them, the kind of partnership that they have, and they enjoy working together. Well," I shrugged. "I take that back. They fight—a lot—and they always have, but they make up every time." I cleared my throat. "There's a reason, you know, that I have four siblings."

"I did notice it was a large family."

I shrugged. "They were never much for family planning. My mother told me as much once, which was…awkward. All that to say, the restaurant is like a third person in their marriage. And that life, it's not for me." I looked away. "I once…I once dated a chef. Well, a sous-chef. He was Nico's last sous. He and Nico were like brothers, even more than Nico and Adrian are now. And…we dated."

"You don't have to tell me your dating history, if you don't want to," Neil said, putting a gentle hand on my arm. "At least not tonight."

"No, it's okay." I took a deep breath. "His name was Éric. I was young, really young. Not that young," I qualified when I saw his face. "I was out of college, but just barely. He was older, a wonderful cook. Mostly, he fed me. Anyway, we were together for a year before we had a terrible argument and he quit the restaurant. Left town. Nico was devastated. And"—I moved a stray piece of hair from my face—"his restaurant began to fail shortly after."

"You never told Nico," Neil guessed. "And you feel guilty."

"Maybe."

Neil tilted his head.

"Okay, yes, I have often felt guilty about Éric leaving. And I never told anyone about our relationship."

"That's a long time to keep that kind of secret."

I gave him a slanted look. "I'm very good. And the last thing I wanted was my entire family nose-deep in my business, because that's what would have happened."

Neil gave a wry smile. "I believe that. I would worry that you're participating with the restaurant out of guilt," Neil said, "but I can tell you love it."

"I do," I agreed. "I don't know that I'll do it forever, but I'm very happy right now. But the point of my sharing the story is that I learned to never date my brother's sous-chef."

"You know, I think Confucius said something about that."

I gave his arm a soft punch. "You're funny."

"It's the pasta."

"Pasta makes you funny?"

"It's the refined carbohydrates."

"I see." I wrapped my arms around my torso. "Well, you asked me my type. And the truest answer is 'not my brother's sous-chef.'"

"He probably won't be your brother's sous-chef forever."

"Even if he weren't, he's too"—I wrinkled my nose—"smarmy. Like, I'm not sure he washes his socks regularly or not."

"That is often a failing among many men," Neil observed. "And some women. My sister only washes her clothes quarterly."

"What? How does she—"

"I believe she just goes out and buys more underwear. And socks."

I stared at him in disbelief. "That's crazy."

He shrugged. "Don't look at me like that. Those are the facts—I just report them. But I appreciate your being honest with me. In the spirit of truth, you should know I was engaged, three years ago."

"Oh?"

"Meredith and I had been dating for a couple years. I never dated much, so my parents were happy. But I was finishing my doctorate…"

"You were busy."

"I was busy," he agreed, "but in all fairness, it was more than that."

Neil took my hand, rubbing my fingers and knuckles methodically. "When I was eleven years old, my best friend, Felicia, was diagnosed with spinocerebellar ataxia. It's a genetic disease, and some forms of it are less severe. Felicia's wasn't."

"I'm so sorry. I can't—can't even imagine."

"Felicia and I had grown up together—her family lived two doors down. In all reality, she'd begun to present symptoms the year before, but her parents thought it was typical adolescent clumsiness.

"Spinocerebellar ataxia," he explained, "is degenerative, and it was very severe in Felicia's case. She went from being a normal bike-riding, tree-climbing kid to a girl who had difficulty walking, all within the space of a year. Diagnosing it—there were lots of tests, I remember that. I remember spending an entire Saturday with her watching movies after her spinal tap. We watched *Big*. And *Star Wars.*"

He sipped from his water glass. "Fee lost her motor coordination. Her eyes," he said, pointing at his own, "would move back and forth sporadically. Some of the kids at school were very kind. Others weren't. Her parents pulled her out. But we still spent most afternoons together. And then one day—"

I watched as Neil's face became very still.

"It's okay," he said, his hold tightening and then relaxing around my hand as he exhaled. "Fee had an accident the summer before ninth grade. There was a tree house in the backyard. It was our clubhouse when we were younger. Felicia must have decided to climb up by herself."

I felt the blood drain from my face. "Oh, Neil..."

"She fell," he said. "And as far as anyone would tell me, she died instantly."

Tears swelled in my eyes. "I'm so sorry."

"I knew she was a believer"—his voice became husky—"and I knew she had a better, more perfect body in heaven. But I was a kid. I'd never lost anyone before, and I took it hard. I don't remember much about my freshman year of high school. For those four years, I buried myself in academics. In college, I started to make real friends again, and I found myself studying genetics. To understand."

He shrugged. "I veered from genetics to immunology after a while. But what I learned after Meredith broke off the engagement was that I was still struggling to connect with people on an emotional level." He cleared his throat. "I couldn't be the fiancé that Meredith needed me to be, and after all that time, she gave up on me spontaneously becoming the emotionally involved man that she wanted me to be. After we broke up, I did what southerners tend not to do, which is admit I had real problems, and I went to see a therapist."

"That was brave," I said.

"I did the work—saw my therapist once a week for two years. Learned about emotions and how to have them." He squeezed my hand. "After that, I decided I was ready move on. And I met you."

"Wow." I found myself leaning against his chest again. "I'm glad we met," I said.

"Me too." He pressed a kiss to the top of my head. "And I've had just enough therapy to feel miserable about leaving here."

I thought about how similar the scene felt to the time when Éric cooked for me, before we argued, before he left.

"I have to be honest," I said. "I'm not sure I'm cut out for long-distance relationships."

"Have you ever been in one?"

"No," I admitted. "But I hate the fact that you're leaving."

"What made you cast your dating net as far as Tennessee?" Neil asked. "I'm curious."

"Oh, I don't know. Sheer desperation? What about you?"

Neil's shoulders shook as he laughed. "Oh, probably the same."

"And now—what's to become of us?" I droned, both intoning and paraphrasing a distraught Eliza Doolittle.

"We'll write letters," Neil said calmly. "We'll fly on airplanes. We'll talk on the phone. We'll get to know each other now and make big decisions later."

"You're so sensible. I'm hungry."

"You can finish your dessert."

"True." I sat up and reached for the plate.

"I should probably go soon," Neil said. "Though I don't want to. My flight's an early one."

"You don't want to pull an all-nighter?"

He shook his head ruefully. "I'm not twenty-four anymore. If I wanted to be awake in the middle of the night, I would have chosen emergency medicine."

"So you chose research for the sleep? That sounds sensible." I sighed. "I'd send you with snacks for the plane if I knew they wouldn't be confiscated."

"I'll be fine." He squeezed my hand. "Let me help you with the dishes."

We both stood, and I gave him a teasing bump of the hip. "I already told you I liked you. Don't you think dish duty is laying it on a little thick?"

"My mother raised me to be a gentleman," he said, his accent comically pronounced.

The dishes weren't much since I'd tidied most of the cookware while waiting for him to arrive. We loaded the dishwasher and hand-washed the pots and pans.

"You're making yourself indispensable," I said. "It's only going to make this harder."

Neil gave the counter a final swipe with a dishcloth. "Would you rather I stop?"

"No."

"I'm done anyway." He put the cloth down, faced me, and encircled my waist with his hands.

I leaned into the kiss. Neil held me tight, a hand on my waist, the other cupping my cheek. I tasted salt and knew that at least one tear had escaped.

Neil pulled away and dried my eyes, wiping the tear from my face tenderly. "No crying," he said gently. "Do you want to pray?"

"Sure," I said. And we spent a few quiet moments asking the Lord for his guidance, for patience, for peace.

At the end, I simply hugged him and let his shirt absorb any wetness. He stroked my hair, whispering soothing southern endearments into my ear.

Several such embraces later, Neil walked out my front door.

I retreated to my bed, shoulders shaking with sobs. I prayed for peace, but I couldn't pretend I wasn't devastated.

25

The tradition of Italian cooking is that of the matri-
arch. This is the cooking of grandma. She didn't waste
time thinking too much about the celery. She got the
best celery she could and then she dealt with it.

—MARIO BATALI

I watched as my mom settled into her chair, like a queen settling into
a throne, and allowed the chemo drip to be set up around her.

Sophie had been banned from the clinic the week before; she had bullied
one of the nurses to tears. We had already scheduled the session to coordinate
with my lunch schedule that Tuesday, without knowing that my lunch schedule was about to get more flexible.

But I was glad to be there, keeping Mom company as she allowed the
poison to drip into her veins, making her both more and less sick as the days
wore on.

This also meant that she had me all to herself for an extended period of
time, and she meant to be resourceful with her allotment.

"We will talk about your leaving your job, but first tell me about this man
Neil, *ma biche*," she said. "He seemed very fond of you."

"He's a good man, Maman. He's on the plane home now."

She patted my hand. "You never enjoyed absences."

"No."

"But what is he like, this Neil?"

"He's kind and smart. Very smart. And he...he sees people, really notices them, gets them. He sees me. And Gigi likes him," I added.

"Bah." She waved a hand. "Gigi likes everyone."

"Not Sophie so much."

"True. But then, it was mutual, *non?*"

"How did you decide you wanted to be with Papa?"

She gave an unladylike snort. "I think the women in our family tend to fall in love with very strange men."

"Caterina and Damian are a natural fit," I said.

"She got that from her father's side of the family. Or a fluke—*je ne sais pas.* Sophie chose Nelson"—she shrugged—"and you have your Neil. And I have your father—oh how we argued when we first met!"

"Different than now?"

She considered this. "About the same. But I was not used to it, *naturellement.* At home, all the boys agreed with me because I was beautiful. *Mais oui—c'est vrai.* I was beautiful, and I met your father on the plane to America. And he argued with me the whole flight."

"Are you sure you weren't arguing with him?"

"Quite sure."

"Ah." I restrained a smile.

"I left France to work in America, and I fell in love with an Italian in the process. My papa was not happy, not at all. Maman made him come and visit and meet your father. I would have married him either way, of course. But it was nice for my papa to come and pretend to be pleased."

"But Grand-père came around, didn't he?"

"Eh," she said with a shrug. "He liked that your father made me happy."

"When you weren't arguing."

"Oh, even then," she said, her eyes twinkling.

"So when you say the women in our family—did Grand-mère fall in love with a man her family disapproved of?"

"She told me once there was a man before my father, a man she loved very much. I was in my twenties and wanted to know more, but she had her secrets. I assume her family did not approve—they were very proper. But she was happy, I think, in the end."

"You're not sure?"

"Who can know? And you"—she slid a glance at me—"had your Éric."

My mouth fell open. "How—"

"How did I know?" She threw me a reproachful look. *"Ma biche,* I am your mother. I know everything."

"Does Nico—"

"Your brother has many talents, but observation has never been one of them. Not subtlety either. If he knew, we would know."

I relaxed, but only a little. "I suppose that's true."

"Éric is doing well at his restaurant," she said gently.

"So he did open one?"

Her brows furrowed. "I thought all you young people kept track of one another on the Google."

I opened my mouth and closed it. "Um…sometimes. But I didn't, not with Éric. I…I couldn't."

"He opened a Moroccan fusion restaurant in Seattle."

"Oh."

"Tahmira, it is called. It's small, but doing well."

"I'm glad. I'm really, really glad."

She patted my cheek. "He wasn't going to stay at Nico's restaurant forever. I am sorry that he broke your heart, though."

"He didn't break my heart, Mom."

"Non?"

I shrugged. "Maybe. At least at the time it seemed worse that Nico's restaurant closed."

"Nico learned things from L'uccello Blu, things he needed to learn. Any experience that ends in knowledge is not a waste. And now he has the new restaurant, and you have your Neil."

A smile stretched across my face at the thought. *My Neil.* He and I had been texting before his flight from Portland to Atlanta; I hoped to hear from him before he made his connection to Memphis.

I missed him terribly.

"Did Grand-mère ever tell you anything else about her sweetheart?"

Maman thought for a moment. "I remember thinking they must have cooked together. I know there was one of her cooking instructors she was very close to. I don't know if it was the same man or not."

I ventured another question. "Did she say a name?"

Another moment of reflection. "I do not remember a name. But she spoke of him fondly. Why the interest?"

"It's romantic, don't you think?"

"Good girl. You take after the French side. Italians are so bad at secrets affairs. Bad at secrets altogether—they're terribly indiscreet."

"The Mafia seemed to figure it out well enough for a while."

She glared at me. "If they were so good at keeping secrets, they wouldn't have had to kill people."

I conceded the point.

"And the newspaper?" she continued. "You are glad to be done?"

"I am…I think. It was time."

She shook her head. "You looked so elegant on television."

"Thank you. I felt sick the whole time."

"Oh, I could tell." She patted my hand. "Will you be happy at Nico's restaurant?"

"I hope so," I said, and I meant it.

Dear Juliette,

Thank you for a wonderful time in Portland. It's early in the morning and I know you're asleep, but I wanted to write to you since I couldn't pick up the phone (at least not without waking you up).

I'm home, but it feels even less like home than ever. I miss you. I miss your smile and the way you held my hand. I miss talking to you.

(I miss kissing you too, but is it ungentlemanly to say so?)

Sorry if that sounds weird and mushy. I'm not great at romance, unless it involves introducing one strain of bacteria to another. That, I'm good at (though it's been a while, so I might be rusty).

I wish I had more to say, but after a day of flying, I came home, watched a few recorded episodes of *Top Gear,* and went to bed. At the office, I will be expected to be able to string sentences together—or at least socially correct greetings. (Though in truth, people often have very low expectations toward the social abilities of doctors. The show *ER* perpetuated that, unfortunately.)

Do you have time to chat tonight—eight your time? I look forward to hearing your voice.

Neil

Dear Neil,

Thank you for such a lovely note—certainly worth waking up for. I miss kissing you too—is that unladylike? Probably. But it's true. I also miss cooking with you, walking with you, getting to see you face to face. As much as I love your words, I love your presence most of all.

As far as long-distance relationships go—well, there are moments when I don't know what I was thinking. Those are the same moments when I feel so desperately thankful for meeting you, for having you in my life. But can I say/write something cynical? Here's my observation about long-distance relationships—they're basically an interpersonal game of chicken.

Granted, I don't say this from personal experience, but do you see what I mean? You keep driving, driving, and driving until someone flinches. And either you flinch right, and someone moves and you're together. Or you flinch left and someone calls it quits.

Where does that leave us? I really don't know. Do we ease up on the gas? Do I stop using driving metaphors???

To be fair, the driving metaphors are possibly your fault. I found myself watching some *Top Gear* on Netflix. I laughed and enjoyed it, just as much as you said I would. So am I a true "petrolhead" because I drive an Alfa Romeo? You tell me. That car spends so much time falling apart that I have no idea how it could be true, but if the experts say so...

As much as I want to hear your voice, I invited Linn and Clementine (my roommate, whom you met) over for a movie tonight to distract me from my sorrow. Can we chat earlier, maybe? Linn's headed over between 6:30 and 7. Is 8 your time possible? Can we just switch the time zones?

(A last thought—if anything, *Grey's Anatomy* may have convinced America that doctors are in fact rather verbose. Do you think the two shows have canceled each other out?)

Juliette

Dear Juliette,

Chat tomorrow? I'll let you enjoy your night with your friends.
Just don't be too sorrowful—everything's going to be okay.

Neil

I had a wonderful time that night with Clementine and Linn.

Linn arrived glowing with the reality of her newly reinstated job. "I don't have to blog!" she said. "I can't even imagine explaining the point of that to my mother."

Clementine made Bavarian sugar cookies, and then we watched *Stranger than Fiction*. After the movie, we sat around and chatted, feet up on the furniture, plates and glasses everywhere. Gigi lay asleep on the floor, having long given up on the prospect of a proper tug-of-war session.

When there was a break in conversation, I told Linn about Neil, and we all giggled together even as I wished he was nearer.

Clementine told stories about working for Grand-mère, and Linn caught me up on the last twenty-four hours of office gossip.

Around nine o'clock, my phone dinged with a text from Neil.

Thinking about you. Hope you're not too sorrowful.

Chat with you tomorrow—have a good night, Jules :-)

I smiled and texted him back.

Not too sorrowful. Having a lovely time eating cookies, actually.
By the time you see me next, I'll look even more like Nigella
Lawson.

Another ding.

Googled Nigella Lawson. Not concerned.

I giggled and put the phone down again; when I looked up, I found Linn and Clementine staring at me.

"Don't worry about us," Clementine drawled. "We're still here. Watching you text your boyfriend."

I blushed at the word but couldn't argue. "Sorry."

"Don't be. I was a second away from texting my husband anyway," Linn said.

Clementine shook her head. "You ladies and your relationships," she said.

I didn't say anything. If Nico was smart at all, Clementine wouldn't be single for long.

~ BAVARIAN SUGAR COOKIES ~

Here's the thing—there's not exactly any such cookie as a Bavarian sugar cookie. But it's such a charming part of the movie that I've gone along with it—we'll consider them Bavarian inspired. In any case, these cookies are more flavorful than most sugar cookies you'll get your hands on.

For the cookies:

$1/2$ cup unsalted butter (pasture butter is nice if you can get your hands on it)

1 cup sugar

1 egg

1 tablespoon cream

1 teaspoon vanilla extract or vanilla bean paste

2 cups flour

1 teaspoon baking powder

$^1/_2$ teaspoon sea salt

For the icing:

1 pound powdered sugar

$^1/_4$ cup salted butter

1 teaspoon vanilla extract

Enough cream to reach desired consistency

Sift flour, baking powder, and salt together.

Cream butter with sugar for 5 minutes, until butter is pale and fluffy. With the mixer running on medium speed, add egg, cream, and vanilla.

Add flour mixture slowly, blending until fully incorporated.

Allow dough to chill overnight.

Preheat oven to 350°F. Roll dough out a little at a time on a lightly floured pastry cloth. With cookie cutters, cut dough into shapes. Bake on a parchment paper–lined baking sheet for 5 minutes or until the edges just become golden.

For the frosting, beat butter until fluffy. Add the sugar in small amounts, and use the cream to adjust the texture as necessary.

Frost with a wide spatula once the cookies are cool. Once the frosting has set, store cookies between sheets of waxed paper.

Makes about 36 cookies.

26

You can never have enough garlic. With enough garlic,
you can eat *The New York Times.*

—MORLEY SAFER

*W*eeks passed. Preparations for the restaurant took over my life, but
by now, though, I was hooked. As every piece of the restaurant
fell into place, I felt my excitement grow.

The night of the trial dinner, I made time over lunch to tap out an e-mail
to Neil—there would be no time at all for the rest of the night, but I couldn't
not write.

Dear Neil,

Here's the thing—I really like writing to you. Is that okay? Don't
get me wrong, I enjoy hearing your voice and seeing you in
person, but there's something about being able to write to you
and receive an e-mail in return. I guess I'm addicted to your
words.

I hope you don't mind.

Lately I've been driving out to several of the farms and wineries
in Donald, Brooks, Newberg, Canby, and Wilsonville in my "free
time." I chat with farmers, I sample produce, I discuss farming
techniques. The relationship is important. (Come to think of it, I

should stage a photoshoot with Nico and a few of the farmers for the restaurant entryway. Call it smart PR.)

I take Gigi with me when I go. She stays in the car and presses her nose to the window. (I've got the window nose prints to prove it!) I swear, I can practically see the visions of sheep chasing dance in her head, though she wouldn't turn down a chance to run through the strawberry fields with the wind blowing through her ears.

I mean—who would?

Hope you're well and settled into your regular schedule—I'm terrible at getting over jet lag. Jet lag and daylight savings. Missing you very much, to the point that I'm wondering if maybe that statement should go without saying, lest I sound overly repetitive. It's still true, though.

Yours, Juliette

Frank Burrows, Linn, my parents, and I waited at the long table in the dining room. While I couldn't speak for my compatriots, I was hungry—and I hoped the rest of them were too because a lot of food was about to emerge from the kitchen. Knowing that Nico and Adrian would be busy plating in the kitchen, I'd hired Chloé for the evening to carry a tray back and forth. Earlier, we'd practiced the art of carrying a tray with three plates until she wielded it like a pro. Nico would write down what each item contained, and Chloé would read off the list.

For the occasion, she'd decided to wear all black with an apron tied around her waist.

I had a hunch that, at some point, she would ask for a tip.

A mix of Over the Rhine, Norah Jones, and Iron and Wine played in the background. The five of us settled into our seats.

Over the next two hours, we sampled from cheese plates, charcuterie platters, salads, roasted vegetables, tarts, and two risottos.

I knew we were nowhere near done, but I was glad I'd worn a stretchy, forgiving dress.

Next came the pastas, spring vegetables tossed with prawns and cavatappi, a beautiful macaroni and cheese, and a lasagna with duck ragù.

It didn't end there—Chloé began to bring out the meats—a beautiful pork loin in a hazelnut cream sauce, a charming piece of bone-in chicken breast coated in cornflakes, a peppery filet mignon, and a generous slice of meat loaf with a tangy glaze. My favorite was the duck in marionberry sauce—the skin had been rubbed with an intoxicating blend of spices, the meat finished with a sweet, tangy sauce. It tasted like summer and Oregon all at once. We planned to open in mid-August, so the duck with fresh berries would be a perfect item for the opening menu.

While I took measured bites from most of the plates, I kept the duck near and continued to enjoy the complex flavors offered by the spices and berry.

Next came the desserts, which Clementine brought out herself.

She presented miniatures of her pastry offerings—a two-bite strawberry shortcake with rose liqueur-spiked whipped cream, a peach-and-brown-sugar bread pudding served on the end of a spoon, a dark chocolate torte with a hint of cinnamon, and a trio of melon ball–sized scoops of gelato. The results were perfect—we were able to taste each one without being overwhelmed after so much food.

When Nico, Adrian, and Clementine emerged from the kitchen, flushed from work and looking proud, we gave our hearty applause.

"Well done," said Frank, giving his stomach a pat. "That was some exceptional food."

"My favorite was the lasagna with the duck ragù." My father kissed his fingers. "If you have more, I will take it home with me to study."

Nico preened.

My mother nodded. Her color seemed better today, and her eyes glowed. "I loved the desserts in miniature. It might be a lovely option, to offer both a full-size and a miniature of each one."

"Or simply order a platter of bites," I suggested. "Obviously, timing is everything. The bread pudding is delicious when it's still hot and moist. If it cooled and became chewy—no one wants that."

"And that would be harder for a busy service. Maybe other desserts would lend themselves better to being miniature, be more forgiving," said Maman. "I loved the strawberry shortcake."

Clementine blushed with pleasure, a fact that didn't escape Nico's notice.

"I have to say," I said, trailing my fork around the marionberry sauce on the duck plate, "that I will be dreaming about that duck for some time to come. The spices—I got coriander, ginger, cinnamon. Some cumin, I'm sure. And smoked paprika? I'm sure there were more, but it was very, very good."

"That one was mine," Adrian said. "But I thought it would be perfect for the opening, and your brother agreed."

I tried not to let my shock show. "It was very good."

In my head, Adrian was like a character in a book, and a flat one at that. But the duck—the duck was special.

The duck made him more complicated than I'd anticipated.

Once the tasting dinner ended, Chloé headed upstairs to play with Gigi, and the rest of us huddled around the table to finalize the opening menu.

I stayed downstairs to tidy the dining room before going back upstairs. Clementine left for a catering gig, and I settled in for a late quiet night.

After a while the clanging downstairs died down, and I figured that Nico and Adrian had finally finished cleaning the kitchen. I wasn't surprised to hear footfalls on the steps outside or the knock on the apartment door.

What did surprise me was the person on the other side of the door.

"Oh," I said, startled. "Hi, Adrian."

"Hey, Juliette," he said, far less confident and suave than usual. "Mind if I come in for a moment?"

I hesitated, as any sane single girl would. But after a moment, I realized that if Adrian had harmful intentions, Nico's revenge would be swift.

And would also likely involve a *Godfather*-esque utilization of an ice pick. Ice pick in mind, I swung the door open. "Sure."

"Thanks." He peered around. "Haven't been up here since you moved in. It looks good."

"I like it. Can I, um, offer you some water?"

"Yeah," he said, clearing his throat. "Water would be great."

I nodded and headed to the kitchen where I filled a glass with water. When I turned around, I found he'd followed me in.

"Nice kitchen," he said, taking in the counter space and vintage fixtures. "Your gran knew what she was doing."

"She did." I handed him the glass. This clearly had to be about something, but I wasn't going to ask.

Better to watch him suffer.

Adrian drank half of the glass before shifting it from his right hand to his left, and back again.

"I hope you're happy with…Neil," he said, his voice soft. "I, well, I like you. I did the first time I met you. But Neil seems like a good guy, and with the restaurant and everything, well, I just hoped we could be friends."

"Of course," I said, mainly because it seemed like the right thing to say.

"Good." He took another long drink of water. "I just— I'm sorry I told Nico about Neil. I figured out later I totally let the cat out of the bag."

"True. But no harm done in the end. Neil had to meet everyone at some point anyway."

"Your family's cool. I'm sorry about your mom."

"She's a tough lady." I looked around the kitchen. "Normally I'd offer you something to eat, but…"

I watched as Adrian turned a gentle shade of mint. "No. I couldn't eat anything. Probably won't eat again for a week."

"You'll make the busboy do the tasting for you?"

"Something like that." His mouth quirked to the side.

I decided not to notice how shapely his lips were.

"Thanks for stopping by," I said, bringing the visit to an end. "And thanks for being a part of the restaurant."

"You're welcome," he said.

I walked him to the door and waved good-bye, stopping myself from wondering what might otherwise have been.

To distract myself, I made a pot of tea and settled in the living room with my steaming mug and stacks of papers.

But instead of organizing, I found my thoughts drifting from Adrian to Neil to Grand-mère.

I planned on trying to figure out more about Grand-mère's past while I was in France, but more and more the whole idea made my stomach churn.

I didn't understand how she and I could have been so close and yet she kept such a huge secret from me, from the family. Sure, maybe the man in the photo was just a sweetheart. But my gut told me that this man was special, that he meant something more to her than just a fleeting sweet memory.

And if that was the case, why keep it such a closely guarded secret?

The way I saw it, people kept secrets to protect themselves or to protect others. So who had Grand-mère been protecting? Because she certainly hadn't

meant for me to find what I'd found. The clues I'd found—if they were clues—
were small and almost innocuous, and yet my intuition told me they meant
something.

This was no *Da Vinci Code* or *National Treasure*. I wasn't following a trail
of carefully crafted artifacts toward an abstruse yet correct conclusion. All I had
were bits and pieces, mismatched ones at that.

And not one of them was property of the Vatican or the Library of Congress, so their accuracy was clearly up for discussion.

If I admitted it to myself, I could recognize feeling hurt that Grand-mère
had kept her secrets from me and from my family. Why wouldn't she have
trusted us? Why didn't she trust us to love her, past included?

Once again, I weighed my options and considered telling Maman about
what I'd found.

Except…what I'd found was still so thin, so circumstantial. I remembered
the difficult months after she passed, the dark circles beneath my mother's eyes.
Some people were prepared to deal with the loss of a parent, but my mother
wasn't one of them.

Until I knew—truly knew—I decided to keep my findings to myself.

Dear Juliette,

In fact, I've been wanting to run through a strawberry field with
the wind in my ears for some time. I keep trying to work it into my
schedule, but without success. I encourage Gigi to live the dream.

I enjoy reading about your adventures in farming. Did I ever tell
you that my grandfather was a farmer? He and my grandmother
ran a peach orchard in—of all strange places for a peach
orchard—Georgia. He loved his trees and supplied several of the
best restaurants in Atlanta.

I don't believe the chefs wanted to take pictures of him, though. He lived in his overalls.

Life here in Tennessee has returned to a kind of normal, but with the difference that you now make in the way that I see the world. Now you're not just an idea, but a flesh-and-blood woman. I felt I knew you fair to middling before, but now—now you're both more real and more mysterious.

Does that make sense? Or are these just the ramblings of a man who's smitten? You tell me.

I hope you enjoyed your tasting dinner. Myself, I went out to a new Italian restaurant with some work colleagues. Italian food is second to barbecue in Memphis—there's even an Italian food festival in the spring. Anyway, the restaurant was good, but I definitely found myself wondering what your take on it would be.

The food scene in Memphis is growing—at least that's what my knowledgeable friends tell me. All I know is there are enough pork barbecue joints, scenting the air with their smoking drums, that I don't know how Jews around here keep kosher.

Just so you know, I'm missing you too. So it's okay to say it. If we're going to be miserable, may as well do it together, I suppose :-)

Neil

Dear Neil,

It's late and you're sleeping, and I wish I could pick up the phone and wake you up, but you probably wouldn't appreciate that much.

At least I wouldn't. A lot of people talk about having friends they can call in the middle of the night, and I always hear/read that and think about how I would throw a fit if someone called me at 3 a.m. True, that makes me a tiny bit of a hypocrite, since I did that to you. And to my sister Cat a little while ago. (There was this guy I met online and I had to talk about him with my sister. YOU KNOW.) But at least with her, there's a 50/50 shot that she's awake around the clock, since she's got twin boys who don't sleep much.

The tasting went well. We got the menu down to ten items. Nico argued for more, but training kitchen staff to make a ten-item menu quickly and reliably is a lot easier than with a twenty-item menu.

Among the dishes that I love are a wonderful duck dish and a creamy macaroni and cheese dish with chipotle that I think you'd like. Technically, it's made with penne, which I like better because it stands up to a thick cheese sauce. If you were here, I'd make it for you. I don't think it would freeze well—otherwise I'd consider shipping it to you on dry ice.

You hadn't told me your grandfather was a peach farmer! I love it. What was that like? What did the orchard smell like? I'll admit I almost dated a man who grew up in an orange grove, mainly because I was romanced by the idea of the orange grove. Is the orchard still in your family?

How are your experiments going? I saw some beaker, petri dish, and test tube-like glassware in the new Anthropologie catalog, and I thought of you. Before you ask, the glassware was all colored on the bottom in jewel tones. So if you feel your equipment needs a colorful update, you know where to look.

That said, I think your work is fascinating. I admit I don't understand it as much as I wish I did, but I think the fact that you do and you're using it to help people is quite wonderful. Isn't it cool that God gave us such uniquely gifted brains?

I hope you're sleeping well. Let's talk tomorrow—I miss your voice.

All the best,

Jules

Chipotle-Spiced Penne and Cheese

For the sauce:

4 tablespoons unsalted butter

2 cloves garlic, peeled and crushed

$2/3$ cup plus 1 tablespoon flour

3 cups whole milk

14 ounces sharp white cheddar

2 ounces monterey jack cheese

1 teaspoon sea salt

$1/2$ teaspoon chipotle powder (see note)

For the pasta:

12 ounces penne

2 ounces cheddar

1 ounce monterey jack for the top

For the panko crumb topping:

$3/4$ cup panko crumbs

$1/4$ cup minced parsley

2 to 3 tablespoons salted butter (or add salt to unsalted butter)

$1/4$ teaspoon chipotle powder

Preheat oven to 350°F. In a large saucepan, add butter and crushed garlic, sautéing the garlic as the butter melts, scenting the butter. Remove the garlic with a slotted spoon. Add the flour and whisk until smooth, about 2 minutes. Pour in the milk, and cook until thickened and mixture coats a spoon, about 10 minutes. Remove from heat, add cheeses and chipotle powder. Stir until cheese melts. Salt and pepper to taste.

In a separate pot of salted boiling water, cook pasta for 2 minutes less than the package's recommendation, about 7 minutes. Rinse and drain the penne, and add pasta to cheese sauce. Stir to combine, and do not panic when there seems to be twice as much sauce as necessary. (The sauce will absorb into the pasta.)

Transfer into a 9-by-13-inch baking dish, and sprinkle top with cheeses.

To make the panko topping, melt butter in a glass measuring cup in a microwave. Add crumbs, parsley, and chipotle powder. Stir to combine—mixture should have some cling but not be too wet. Add additional butter or crumbs as necessary. Sprinkle mixture over the pasta.

Bake uncovered 25 minutes, and let stand 5 minutes. Serve warm with a salad of young greens.

Note: The spice is easily adjustable. Add more chipotle for the adventurous; decrease for younger diners.

27

Enchant, stay beautiful and graceful, but do this, eat
well. Bring the same consideration to the preparation
of your food as you devote to your appearance. Let
your dinner be a poem, like your dress.

—Charles Pierre Monselet

For a tiny moment, I considered feeling guilty about using Clementine in my plot for revenge. I considered and then dismissed my
reservations; the fact of the matter was that my brother was clearly drawn to the
petite pastry chef. He needed a shove, my brother.

And me? I was happy to provide that shove.

"I was just thinking," I mentioned to Clementine late Friday night, in the
most causal tone I could muster, "would you like to come to this week's dinner
with me?"

"Well…"

"My dad's cooking is not to be missed."

"It wouldn't be awkward? I hate to intrude."

"Not at all. Guests come all the time."

Clementine shrugged. "Sure. Sunday night?"

"Sunday night."

"Good." I gave my bravest smile. "I'm off to bed, then. And I think I'll take
Gigi with me."

"Oh, she'll hate that." Clementine nodded toward Gigi, who was already
halfway down the hall to my room, tail wagging in anticipation of pillows and
blankets at her disposal.

"Is there anything I should bring tomorrow?" Clementine asked on Saturday morning, as we both prepared for the day.

"My mom is a sucker for a good hostess gift," I answered, toothbrush in mouth. "I can give you a few ideas, if you're in need."

"I found a couple antique handkerchiefs at a flea market the other day." She squeezed toothpaste onto her own toothbrush. "I don't have specific plans for them—thought your mom might like them."

"That sounds perfect." I spat into the sink. "I'm impressed."

Clementine shrugged. "Your gran would have liked them, and she mentioned your mom's good taste a few times."

She was right—my mother did enjoy the handkerchiefs, though not nearly as much as I enjoyed Nico's expression when he saw Clementine on Sunday.

Nico's eyes were wide, his jaw slack. Best of all, he couldn't speak—a first, since the tender age of nineteen months.

Clementine, of course, was so focused on my mother and meeting the rest of the family that she either didn't notice Nico or ignored him altogether.

For dinner, my father had prepared a robust pot of cioppino, serving it with a green salad and miniature baguettes of bread.

It was a simple meal, but the shadows beneath my parents' eyes were their own explanation. My heart ached. I knew that all of us were pitching in—Alex with maintenance around the house, Sophie with coordinating doctors' visits and treatments, Nico with food, and Caterina—Caterina sent care packages full of silly novels, loose-leaf tea, and scented candles.

As the last born, I was the official pinch-hitter, filling in where needed. Sure, I felt like the fifth wheel, but that was part of the gig as a fifth child.

We sat down at the dinner table, and to my dismay Sophie practically elbowed her way to the seat on my right, while Clementine took the chair to my left.

Nico, I noted, was at the opposite end of the table. Not that it stopped him from staring at her. At some point, I needed to have words with my brother. He had to stop acting like a thirteen-year-old boy.

Within moments, it became clear Sophie was on a mission. "You must go and get genetically tested," she said, leaning toward me. "I finally went two weeks ago."

"Oh." I draped my napkin in my lap. "So…what precipitated that idea?"

"Mom's cancer, of course. Ovarian cancer often has a genetic component, and I wanted to find out if I had any of the markers."

"Makes sense," I said.

"Well, apparently, I am a carrier. I'm going to have Chloé tested too. It doesn't mean we'll get it, just that we could, you know?"

"Right," I said. It was a depressing enough thought and not what I would have considered dinner conversation, but Sophie would not be deterred.

"I had them run a general test and look for any other diseases, while I was in. Better to know and to be prepared. Do you know what they found? I'm a carrier for Tay-Sachs disease. Can you believe it?"

I shook my head. "I think I've heard of it, but I don't remember what it is."

"It's a genetic disease. It's usually associated with Jews, but according to my reading, it occurs in other small gene pools, like the Acadians. But you should get yourself tested. It's best to know for sure. Now is a good time to be taking lots of antioxidants."

"I will…have to get on that," I said, my mind whirling but not settling as I passed Clementine's soup bowl to my father, who stood at the head of the table, ladle in hand.

The dinner passed easily, with Clementine slipping seamlessly into the conversations that churned across the table. Everyone seemed to adjust to Clementine far more effortlessly than to Neil, but wasn't that to be expected? She was a pastry chef, a breed my family understood. With the exception of Nico—whose inclusion of Adrian was simply bad behavior—I didn't begrudge the uneasiness I'd seen during Neil's visit.

I stole a glance at Nico. He'd moved on from staring at Clementine to conversing more heartily with Nelson than any of us had ever seen, or were likely to see again.

After dinner, at a moment when Clementine was safely out of earshot, I edged over to my older brother and leaned toward his ear. "When are you going to ask her out?"

He stood up straighter. "What?"

"You like her. I think you'd be good together. You should ask her out."

"Why don't you go out with Adrian?"

I rolled my eyes. "First off, he never asked. Second, I'm seeing Neil. And third—and most important—we work together."

"Well, I'll be working with Clementine. Actually, she'll be working *for* me."

"But you like her."

He didn't answer.

"Just think about it," I said, giving his arm a squeeze. "Because if you don't make a move, sooner or later someone else will."

Nico frowned, his gaze never leaving Clementine's animated face.

"She's good here," I said. "Think about it."

"Do you think"—he fiddled with his pockets—"she would?"

"I don't know," I answered honestly. "But I bet if you asked, you'd find out."

When I got home, I took Gigi out, then headed to my room and called Neil.

"How did it go?" he asked.

"Fine," I said, scratching Gigi's chin. "Better than fine, actually—Mom adores Clementine. Nico was absolutely miserable, sat and stared at her the whole time. He tried to talk to her at one point, but got completely tongue-tied."

"Poor guy."

"I have no sympathy for him."

"None?"

"Maybe a little, but it doesn't stick around for very long. I cornered him at the end and told him it was time to ask her out—that was fun. Oh—and I had a fantastically surreal conversation with Sophie. Granted, most of our conversations have their own touches of surrealism. One of these days we'll be talking and my face is going to melt. Anyway, she's gotten herself genetically tested for the ovarian-cancer gene and in the process found she's a carrier for Tay-Sachs disease." I waggled my fingers on the bedspread to get Gigi's attention.

"She's going to have Chloé tested and wants me to get tested as well. I'm honestly not sure what I think about it all."

There was a momentary silence on the line. "Sophie's a carrier for Tay-Sachs?" he asked. I could practically hear him thinking. "And your mom's cancer…" He cleared his throat. "Genetically, I would surmise that one of your genetic contributors includes an Ashkenazi Jew."

"A what? I'm not Jewish, so I'm not up on my lingo."

"An ethnic Jew with origins in central and eastern Europe. Because Jews typically only married other Jews, certain genes are especially prominent generations later. The same is true in other communities begun with small gene pools—the Pennsylvania Dutch, for instance. The Acadians are another. Sorry—am I starting to sound too much like a lecturer?"

"It's interesting," I promised, my mind whirling with possibilities. "Keep going."

"Tay-Sachs does appear within other populations with the same frequency—Acadians, for instance. However, if your sister tested positive for a BRCA1 or BRCA2 mutation—"

"BRCA2, is what Sophie said."

"BRCA2, then—the presence of both of those genes would suggest an Ashkenazi Jew as a genetic source."

My heart began to beat hard within my chest, and the thoughts that had begun to flutter at dinner now settled into clarity. "That was why she never told anyone," I breathed as the pieces clicked together. "He was a Jew. The man in the photo was a Jew. She married Grand-père in 1943, so anything much before then would potentially be in preoccupation France. Mom said there was a man, earlier, that her family didn't approve of, and that would explain it. She was with him—married him even, if that ring from the trunk means anything—and had my mother." Gigi nudged my hand with her nose; I stroked her ears absently. "Something must have happened to him, but they had to have been in love if she kept mementos, wouldn't you think?"

"Makes sense to me."

"And then she married Gilles, my grandfather, and never told a soul. Does that…does that sound crazy?"

"Plenty of crazy things happened during that time period."

"I hate to think she wasn't happy with my grandfather. They grew up together, you know. If only she were still here—I have so many questions to ask her!"

"Didn't you find out the last name of the person who ordered the engagement ring?"

"Roussard. G. Roussard. Not a Jewish name, but plenty of Jews assimilated in France." I thought for a moment. "The jeweler was named S. Roussard. It could have been a family member—there's a long tradition of Jewish craftsmanship in jewelry. It…it could be."

"Do you think your great-aunt in France might know more?"

"Maybe. I mean, I think I'd remember if Sophie or Caterina married someone, had a child, and then remarried. Mom said the family disapproved, so it couldn't have been an entirely secret affair." I chewed on my lower lip. "Come to think of it, the wedding date—the wedding to Gilles—must have been fudged, some, if my mother had a different father. Or my mother's age, a bit."

"Or both. Unless she was still pregnant at the time and married your grandfather quickly."

"True." I pressed my hand to my cheek. "This is nuts, but it feels like the first thing in a long time to have made sense."

"There could be other explanations."

"I know, but something tells me this is the right one. And as far as I know,

my mother has no idea her brother is her half brother and that her dad wasn't
really her dad."

After going so long with very little attention, Gigi sighed and sprawled
across the bed.

"What was their relationship like?" Neil asked.

"Fine, I think. He wasn't a very affectionate man, from what I've heard.
He died before I was born, but Alex and Sophie remember him. They said he
always had candy in his pockets. Wrapped lemon drops."

"So he was kind to children, at least."

"I suppose. I guess I'll find out more when I'm in France." I shifted the
phone to my other ear. "I wished you could have been there at dinner tonight."

"I would have liked to be there with you. Did I tell you I have a new
system?"

"A new system? No."

"Every time I miss you, I make plans for what we'll do when I see you next."

I couldn't stop my grin. "Oh, really?"

"It'll have to be a long trip," he said. "So far I've come up with a lot of
plans."

"We'll work something out." I took a deep breath, knowing I needed to
sleep but not wanting to let go of the sense of peace I felt when I heard his voice.

Neither of us spoke for a long moment.

"I should probably sleep," I said, finally. "And you too, since you're two
hours ahead."

"I know," he said. "I just didn't want to say it."

I gave a soft chuckle. "Sleep well, Neil."

"You too, Juliette. I love you."

My phone intoned the end of the call, but all I heard were the mental
echoes of those last three words.

I prefer butter to margarine, because I trust cows more
than I trust chemists.

—JOAN DYE GUSSOW

*T*he words played themselves over and over in my head—*I love you,
I love you, I love you.* Maybe I'd heard wrong. Maybe he'd said
"dove." Or "glove." Maybe "luck"? Or perhaps "live"? But none of those actually made sense unless he was calling me a dove, which would be oddly abstract
for an immunologist.

Which meant…maybe I'd heard right the first time.

Maybe he loved me. Or maybe it had just slipped out.

The sounds of Clementine in the kitchen started at four in the morning. I
stumbled out three hours later—realizing there was no point in trying to sleep
between my conversation with Neil and the kitchen happenings.

At least the air smelled like sugary perfection.

"You're up early," Clementine said as I rounded the corner into the kitchen.
Gigi raced past me, bounced around Clementine's feet, and bounded toward
the patio door.

I let her out to do her morning business.

"Couldn't sleep," I said, eying the array of assembled cream puffs on the
prep table.

Clementine winced. "Sorry—my fault?"

I shrugged. "I was awakeable."

"Sorry," she repeated. "I woke up inspired."

"That's good." I tilted my head from side to side. "I think I woke up with a crick in my neck."

"Want some tea?" Clementine asked.

"Sure."

I settled on a kitchen stool, watching as Clementine set the kettle of water to boil. "You know, it's funny."

"What is?"

"For years, I found that within my circle of friends, I was always the one who cooked for and took care of everyone. When I was a kid, it was the same—everyone was so busy doing other things that I did things for myself. It feels funny watching someone do something for me."

"It's good practice," Clementine said. "Let someone do something for you for a change."

"Feels weird."

"I promise you can feed me sometime, when you're not packing to go to Europe."

"Fair enough."

Clementine set a tea bag into a mug and poured the water over the leaves. "So what's got you in a twist?"

"Neil."

"Mmm," said Clementine.

I accepted the tea and took a sip. "We might be moving to a different stage of the relationship."

"You're not sure?"

"It's a relationship—is anyone ever sure?"

Clementine conceded the point.

"Anyway, it might be"—I searched for the right word—"shifting. But I'm not sure. And I'm not sure I can ask him to clarify. And I couldn't sleep much because of it." I got up and let Gigi back in. "Do you need a hand with anything? Because I could stand to be distracted."

"I need you to taste things. I've been thinking of a revision to the dessert menu, and this morning it was like everything in my head aligned. I came up with a variation on the molten-chocolate cake that doesn't make me crazy with how brainless it is. You said the theme was date restaurant, man accessible, right?"

"Right."

"So I added the Black Butte Porter—the one from Deschutes Brewery— to the chocolate cake. It makes the flavor a little darker, a little more complex. I wanted to do five or six desserts, with at least three of them seasonal. For the standards, I thought the chocolate cake and an Italian-style cream puff." She nodded toward the cream puffs on the table. "Try one and tell me what you think."

I wasn't awake enough for silverware, so I picked up the cream puff and bit straight into it, forming a small cloud of powdered sugar. "That's so good," I said.

Clementine continued to watch me.

I dove in for a second bite. And then I found it—cherries. Ripe, real cherries in a fruity filling hidden at the center. "Oh my goodness," I said, my mouth full. "That is amazing."

"Glad you think so. I thought it was a clever play on Saint Joseph's Day zeppole—cherries, but not those awful maraschino cherries."

I nodded. "Maraschino cherries are the worst." Another bite. "This cream puff almost tastes like a grown-up doughnut. And I mean that in the best way."

"Oh, I agree. And while cherries will get difficult after a while, we can swap out the fillings seasonally. Maybe a citrus in the winter, that sort of thing. Though I was also thinking about putting some cherries up for the winter, so we'd have some."

"No arguments from me. This is the best breakfast I've had in ages," I said, licking almond-flavored pastry cream from my fingers. "So—what else have you got?"

"I'm working on an updated tiramisu spin. We'll see. It might be too close to the cream puff, with the pastry cream."

"Maybe. Maybe not," I said, considering. "We can let Nico think about that."

"I'll be working on it. But tiramisu is popular and not at all seasonal."

"That's true. You could do a layer of candied hazelnuts on the top. That wouldn't be terrible."

"No, it wouldn't be. I was also thinking of doing a selection of ice creams and a sorbet special every week, during the summer."

"I have full trust. Don't forget about that Nutella mousse you made for Nico and me. That was memorable."

"Have you decided what you're going to do about Neil?"

"Me?" I wiped my mouth with a napkin. "Not at all."

That night Neil and I chatted about our respective days. I kept things breezy and light on purpose. Once again, our conversation ended much the same way. I wished him sweet dreams.

In reply, he said, "You too, Juliette. I love you."

"Wait," I said, before he could hang up. "Do you mean that?"

"That I love you? I suppose I do."

"Are you sure?"

He chuckled. "Pretty sure. G'night, Jules."

From: sandrine@chateaudelabeille.fr

To: j.dalisa@netmail.com

Dearest Juliette,

Maman and I are so very happy to see you in two weeks! Please send me your flight details when you have them. Would you like me to pick you up from the airport, or are you planning to rent a car?

I will have guests at the château during your visit, but we do keep a family wing, where you will have privacy. Do you and Nico still want honey for your restaurant? We just harvested a good batch of honey from our hives. Tell me how much you want and I will make arrangements to have it shipped to you. This harvest in particular has even more lavender tones than the last—I am very pleased.

Maman sends her best. *À bientôt!*

Sandrine

From: j.dalisa@netmail.com
To: sandrine@chateaudelabeille.fr

Lovely to hear from you! I will be landing at Charles de Gaulle on Wednesday, June 18. My plan is to stay for three or four days before moving on to Paris, and then to Italy for my nonno D'Alisa's 90th birthday in Montalcino. I'd be happy to rent a car during my time in France. I was thinking of having a car in France and then returning it in Paris before taking the train to Italy. There are quite a lot of cars to go around with my dad's family, so I'll be covered there—or at least be able to catch a ride.

I'll ask Nico and Clementine how much honey they want and get back to you. I'm starting in on some of our ordering to make sure we get on the farmers' delivery schedules. Excited and nervous as our grand opening day approaches in August!

Love to Grand-tante Cécile!

Juliette

The next two weeks were even more of a flurry of preparations. Nico hired a line cook and a pair of dishwashers. After discussing the subject, we agreed that I would interview for waitstaff once I'd returned from the trip.

My travel plans were finally set in stone; I'd decided to do some sleuthing in France before moving on to Italy. Although my grand-tante Cécile suffered from Alzheimer's, I had hopes she might be able to remember some of her late girlhood, before the war. I also wanted to search in Paris for records relating to G. Roussard and the jeweler S. Roussard. While it was true we lived in the Internet age, I hadn't been able to uncover much from home.

In preparation for the trip, I used a bit of my nest egg to spruce up the holes in my wardrobe and make myself fit for Paris and Rome. I bought a lovely pair of heels on sale at Nordstrom, a navy sundress at Anthropologie, and a black short-sleeved silk blouse at T.J. Maxx. From Grand-mère's bureau I set aside several vintage silk scarves.

Neil and I talked or e-mailed most days. I watched episodes of *Doctor Who*—starting with the Ninth Doctor—as I made meals, and Neil humored me as I mulled the intricacies of the plot lines.

"Just keep watching," he'd say, refusing to let slip a hint, though we both knew I could take to Google in an instant to satisfy my curiosity.

I tidied the apartment and made arrangements for Gigi to attend doggy day care three days per week while Clementine was away from the apartment. The morning before my flight, I packed my suitcase while Nico worked in the kitchen downstairs. I heard a truck engine, followed by raised voices.

Nico's, naturally, rose to the top.

A moment later I heard footfalls on the exterior stairs and a sharp rap at my door.

Nico stood on the other side, fuming.

"Potatoes!" he yelled, invoice in hand.

"Carrots," I said, hands on my hips. "What's this about?"

"You placed an order for twenty-three crates of potatoes to be delivered today. Why would you do that?"

I plucked the invoice from his fingers. It was for an order I'd placed with Haven Farms. I remembered the order, but there was no way I'd intentionally order twenty-three crates of potatoes...

And then it hit me. "Oh. Oh dear..."

I had placed the order. And then I'd gone back and updated it because I'd forgotten the potatoes. In my rush to correct the order, I'd hit both the wrong quantity—twenty-three, rather than two—and the wrong month. Which meant we had more than eleven times the expected number of potatoes, a month before the soft opening, two months before the grand opening.

"What am I going to do with twenty-three crates of potatoes? Potatoes are perishable, Juliette. They stink when they rot. I can't have twenty-three crates of potatoes rotting away in my dining room—that's right, the dining room. They don't even fit in the kitchen. And they won't take them back," Nico added. "I already asked."

"I'm so sorry," I said, arms folded protectively around my torso. "It was a clerical error, and I'm sorry."

"You're distracted. You're distracted with that Neil fellow, and it's twenty-three pounds of potatoes worth of bad business."

"I'm sorry!" I repeated, my voice starting to sound shrill. "I don't know what more you want me to say, but I think it's stupid to bring Neil into this."

Nico pointed at the invoice. "You ordered these the day after he left."

"So?"

"Where are your priorities? If you're going to go moony over a man, this isn't going to work."

"Lots of people have relationships and work in the restaurant business. Mom and Dad did it."

"Mom and Dad worked together. Do you know what the divorce rate is for people who work in the restaurant business?"

"No, do you?" I shot back.

"Neil's going to take you away from what you love. You know that, right?"

My hands balled into fists. I kept a tight rein on my temper, but Nico had really overstepped. "How is this Neil's fault?"

"He's a doctor in Memphis. You think he's going to leave that behind and come here for you? I don't think so. I thought you loved this business."

"I do!" I yelled. "I've always loved it."

"If you marry him, you won't be able to do it. You'll work opposite schedules, and something will have to give. Look at Alex and Stephanie."

"Alex and Stephanie had their own challenges. Neil and I are different."

"Isn't that what everyone tells themselves?"

"Stop it, Nico. You're being a bully."

He sighed. "You're my baby sister. I don't want to see you get hurt. And I don't want to see this restaurant fail."

"I don't think it's going to fail because of a bulk order of potatoes," I evaded, but I understood his point. "I don't want to see this restaurant fail either." I glanced inside, where my packing waited. I had no idea where Gigi had gone off to. "I have to keep getting ready. My flight's tomorrow morning."

I closed the door and returned to my room.

Nico may have been a bully, but that didn't make him wrong.

29

What I say is that, if a man really likes potatoes, he must be a pretty decent sort of fellow.

—A. A. MILNE

*W*here I had been packing neatly and methodically, now I angrily began to throw articles of clothing into my suitcase.

Gigi made a nest on my pillows and watched warily.

Of all the high-handed, condescending arguments I'd ever had with Nico, this had to have been the worst. And the very worst part? The more I thought about it, the more I realized he was right.

Obviously, the potatoes were only a symptom of a deeper problem. And even if I never made another ordering mistake for the rest of my life, the fact remained that Neil and I were living in a dream world.

Our worlds were too divergent and careers too individually all-consuming. If there was a way we could work together, or that one of us worked less, we might be able to make things work—after solving the distance issue.

But all together?

I loved Neil. I knew I did. More than I'd loved Éric, though they were two different men, in different stages of my life. I loved him, but we were still new. Our love hadn't grown deep, coiled roots, not yet.

Did we keep working at it, yanking and cutting on those roots down the road when things didn't work? Or stop now, before things got too messy?

I continued to throw things into my suitcase, things I hadn't intended to pack. I didn't care.

I reached for my phone and looked at the time. Neil was on lunch, if he wasn't working through it. I dialed his number.

"I was just thinking about you," Neil said when he picked up, a smile in his voice.

My eyes squeezed shut. I loved his voice. I loved *him*. But he deserved someone who could be near him, who would be home when he was. Someone who would be around to hear about his day, and not just in a series of text messages, e-mails, and phone calls.

"Hi," I said, my voice wavering.

"What's wrong?" he asked, the smile in his voice gone.

I poured out the story of the potatoes and my argument with Nico.

"That's…the stupidest thing I've ever heard," he said. "You can't tell me there aren't food banks in Portland that could use a cache of potatoes. Your brother needs to grow up."

"He does," I agreed, "but that doesn't make him entirely wrong. I can't afford to make stupid mistakes, not with this restaurant. How is this going to work? We had a wonderful long weekend together. It was amazing. But I keep looking at us, and at the distance, and at our jobs, and I don't see how it can work."

"What do you want, Juliette?"

I frowned. "What do you mean?"

"What do you want in life? You stayed at a job that made you miserable until it made you ill. And now it sounds like you're letting your brother dictate your personal life. Tell me what you want, because I can't figure you out."

I opened my mouth to tell him, but to my horror my mind went blank, and I realized the truth.

At that moment, I had no idea.

"I think we could be good together, Juliette," Neil said when I didn't answer. "But you have to want it too. I'm not going to guilt you into fighting for us or try to convince you of something you won't ever be able to own in your heart."

I could hardly breathe. "I'm sorry, Neil. I'm so, so sorry."

With shaking hands, I hung up.

I sat on the bed and stared out the window.

I'd lost Neil.

For several moments, I tried to wrap my mind around that concept. Around never writing to Neil, never hearing his voice. I wanted to call him back, to tell him we could try again, that if we fought hard enough, we could make a way for ourselves.

But in my head I heard his voice asking me what I wanted, and the silence that followed.

That awful silence.

I tucked Gigi into her kennel, grabbed my purse, and got in my car.

Sophie was working in her yard when I pulled up outside her house, clad in dungarees and a wide, floppy sun hat. She looked ridiculous, but so content that I envied her.

She set her trowel aside when she saw me. "Juliette," she said, her smile fading when she took in the puffy redness of my eyes. "What happened?"

"I know we don't always see eye to eye," I said, "and we don't always understand each other. But I've had a rotten morning, and I need my sister."

Without question, Sophie stood and enfolded me in a powerful hug. "Come inside," she said. "Come tell me all about it."

30

Context and memory play powerful roles in all the
truly great meals in one's life.

—ANTHONY BOURDAIN

After several years of post-9/11 travel, I considered myself profi-
cient at getting through airport security quickly—no belt, ballet flats, no jewelry with metal. I was in and out quickly; in truth, the flight
from Portland to Sea-Tac lasted nearly as long.

I maneuvered my way from arrivals to departures to board my interna-
tional flight, only to find that my flight was delayed.

Very delayed.

The woman at the desk said something about flight checks and mechani-
cal concerns and a weather system somewhere over the Atlantic, and, all in all,
the plane wouldn't be ready to board for five hours.

I spent five minutes sitting in the gate, staring out the window.

After five minutes, my mind began to wander. I was in Seattle, after all. I
could go out. Leave the airport. Get a bite while not surrounded by people
clutching their carry-ons.

I found myself boarding the light rail and watching the scenery change
from airport industrial to Seattle urban, before I disembarked at Beacon Hill.

As the scenery sped by, my last conversation with Neil echoed through my
mind. The words I'd used, the words I'd heard—the hurt in his voice.

There were no new e-mails; I ached at the idea of never hearing from him
again, reading his perspective on the world. I hated the idea of him hurting—

and of him thinking poorly of me. His good opinion meant a lot to me, but I couldn't imagine I had retained it in any way.

And yet—I couldn't see a way out of it.

That was the part that hurt the most.

The weather was good, and I was glad for my comfortable flats as I traveled down the sidewalks, walking, searching. And then I found it—Tahmira.

Éric's restaurant.

From the outside, it was beautiful. Small, but with elegant lines and old paned-glass windows. The outside was painted a grassy kelly-green, with navy trim. The door was natural wood, burnished with the patina of time. And, I supposed, no small amount of rainfall.

I checked my watch. They served lunch until 2 p.m., and it was...1:50. I walked through the door anyway.

The waitress saw me, waved, and pointed at a table by the window. "I'll be right with you," she said cheerily, as if I hadn't shown up at the tail end of her shift.

After a short moment, she brought me a glass of water with a slice of lime, followed by a menu. The menu—it was pure Éric. I saw his flair for juxtaposed ingredients, for layered flavors, for breathing fresh life into traditional cuisine.

I would have known it was his restaurant, solely from the menu. It contained his signature dishes, in particular the ones he made for me that chilly, rainy night so long ago. When the waitress returned, I heard myself ordering that meal all over again, pairing it with a glass of iced Moroccan mint tea.

As I ate and drank, so many memories came flooding back. Happy memories. Bittersweet memories. The restaurant cleared out, the waitress made herself scarce, and I enjoyed my meal in peace.

"Of all the gin joints," said a warm male voice. "It's good to see you, Juliette."

I looked up, both surprised and, somehow, not. "Hello, Éric," I said, my heart too full to say much of anything else.

He was older, of course. His skin was still the dusky tan I remembered, and he wore his hair in the same ponytail, but now the lines on his face were deeper and his dark hair sported streaks of gray. In his hand he cradled an oversized coffee mug. I watched as he took the seat opposite mine and sank into the chair.

"Busy lunch crowd today," he said, setting his coffee on the tabletop. "Almost fifty covers."

"That's a lot for a space like this."

"You haven't even seen my kitchen! It's like a galley in there. But the crowd thinned out, and then Salima came and brought your order in…"

"My flight was delayed; I thought I'd stop in. Ordinarily I wouldn't come in so late."

Éric smiled at me, and just like that, we slipped into the easy shorthand of shared history.

"Don't worry—I've dined with you enough to know that to be true." He gave me a once-over. "You look good."

"You too." And he did. Despite the signs of age, he was just as handsome as ever, even if he was a little rounder around the edges than I'd remembered. "How have you been?"

"Good. This place is still turning a profit, even with the economy the way it is. I like Seattle." He shrugged. "I've thought about you, over the years."

"Oh?"

"You, L'uccello Blu. I should never have left the way I did."

"We were both to blame."

"I was the one who did the leaving. Looking back, I know you were trying to protect Nico. I was sorry to hear L'uccello Blu closed. How is Nico?"

"Starting a new place. He's letting me help this time."

"Letting you?" Éric snorted. "He should be so lucky."

"You're sweet."

"I've never met anyone who had a knack for the business, for the food, like you did. Or do, I guess."

"Thanks."

"I read a couple of your pieces when you first started at that local rag of yours. They were good. Though I never would have figured you for morning television."

I groaned. "You saw that?"

"Beauty of the Internet."

"I knew it would be a disaster. No one would believe me."

He folded his hands. "Tell me about your new place."

"We're leasing my grand-mère's patisserie space from my mother."

"That patisserie? Of course. She was good, your gran. Did she pass on?"

"She did, in January. Well, I quit my job at the paper and now I'm living in the upstairs apartment with our pastry chef, and we're opening a restaurant in the old patisserie space. It's coming together."

"I was about to ask if you were seeing someone. So, the pastry chef, huh?"

"Wait, what?" I rewound my words in my head. "Oh goodness, no. And Clementine would be insulted that you assumed she was a man. Seriously. If she were here, I'd tell you to duck."

Éric barked a laugh. "Sorry. I never saw you as live-in-boyfriend type, but some people change, you know?"

"Not me, at least not that much."

"So Nico's got a female pastry chef in his kitchen?"

"He does."

"Are they dating?"

"Not yet. And to answer your question, I was sort of seeing someone recently, but it, um…" In the safety of Éric's presence, tears threatened to fall. I blinked them back. "It didn't work out," I said at last.

"I'm sorry to hear that," he said. I didn't doubt that he saw the tears.

"Things don't always work out." I pasted a bright smile on my face. "Plenty to keep me busy at the restaurant, though."

"Don't I know it." Éric ran a hand over his hair.

"How about you? Are you seeing someone?"

"Oh, you know. Got married a few years ago. She left. Restaurant business is hard on relationships. I thought we were fine—we were never in the same room long enough to have a fight. Turns out that doesn't work."

"I'm so sorry."

"It is what it is. That's life." He waved a hand. "You know, all those things you say when things don't turn out the way you want."

I lifted my iced tea. "Hear, hear."

He clinked my glass with his coffee mug. "We were good together, you and I."

I snorted. "We can't get too nostalgic—it would never have lasted."

"But we had fun, right?"

"I ate well."

"Then it was a success. You were so much fun to eat with. Fearless."

I flushed at the compliment. "I was so young."

"Did you ever tell Nico?"

"About us?" I shook my head, feeling that uncomfortable yet familiar twinge of guilt in my heart. "No. I always felt guilty," I admitted. "Like I ran you off, and then the restaurant closed, and I ruined everything."

"Oh, Etta. I wasn't going to stick around forever. Nico knew that. And that restaurant? Well, there were all kinds of ordering problems, staff problems."

I told Éric about my potato-ordering gaffe. He threw back his head and laughed, a sound at once both rich and familiar. "Easy mistake. It could happen to anyone. Potatoes, huh? Well, Nico's one to talk. Back at L'ucello Blu, he was hemorrhaging money and he wasn't listening to anyone. Not you, not me, not your dad, no one. Three accountants told him to stop serving lunch, and his response was to hire a kid to stand outside with a sign, as if we were Little Caesars. When I was there, we stayed afloat because we were so busy, but I've been around. You can't keep a business going like that forever. When I left— look, I'm sure it didn't help, and I wish I'd stuck around to find Nico a good replacement. To say good-bye. But me being there wouldn't have stopped the inevitable from happening. It's not my fault," Éric said, "and it's not yours."

I felt tears sting my eyes. "Thanks."

"It's the truth."

I swiped at a stray drop of moisture with my napkin. "My mom basically said as much, but…I don't know." I gave a watery chuckle. "She knew. About us."

"Not a lot ever got past her."

"And still doesn't." I shook my head. "She's got cancer right now."

Éric grimaced. "I'm sorry to hear that."

"She's fighting it. And she's strong. I worry, though."

"Tell me about this trip you're on."

I balled the used napkin in my hands. "My nonno's celebrating his ninetieth birthday in Tuscany."

Éric gave a rueful smile. "Of course he is. Why can't anyone in your family live in Nebraska?"

I grinned at him as we fell back into our old camaraderie. "My first leg of the trip is to see my mother's family in Montagnac."

"It's a wonder more people don't hate you."

I threw a napkin at him. "I'm only going in the first place because my parents couldn't make it, because of my mom's cancer."

"Still sorry about that. Are you going to go to Paris?"

"I am."

He leaned back and propped his hands behind his head. "You should go to Timgad. Moroccan cuisine—pricey, but very, very good. I would take you there, but…"

A long moment. I knew, looking into Éric's eyes, that all the old chemistry was still very much there. But I was in Portland, he was in Seattle, and for a guy like him, the restaurant would be his wife. I could only ever aspire to being a mistress, with or without a ring.

"Another lifetime," I said.

Éric gave a slow smile, tinged with sadness. "Agreed."

"I should be getting back to the airport."

"Wouldn't want you to miss your flight."

"I've enjoyed this, catching up," I said.

"Stay in touch. I want to know how your new restaurant goes. First hand," he added as he stood. "Not just from Google."

I hoisted my travel-heavy purse onto my shoulder. "Where would we be without Google?"

"Oh, who knows?"

I reached out my arms and we hugged. I marveled how he felt both familiar and alien all at once.

He kissed my cheek and stepped back, looking into my eyes. "Take care, Juliette."

"You too, Éric."

A wave, a glance over the shoulder, and I left Éric and his Tahmira behind.

~ MOROCCAN MINT TEA FOR TWO ~

2 cups boiling water
1 tablespoon loose-leaf Chinese green tea
8 fresh mint sprigs
1 tablespoon sugar

Place the tea and mint leaves in a heatproof measuring cup or bowl with a spout. Pour water over the leaves; cover and steep for 3 minutes. Strain tea and mint mixture through a fine sieve into a second heatproof measuring cup or bowl. Discard tea and mint leaves.

Add sugar and stir until thoroughly dissolved. Chill and serve over ice with additional mint leaves for garnish.

31

Love doesn't just sit there, like a stone; it has to be made, like bread, remade all the time, made new.

—Ursula K. Le Guin

I had a lot of time to think on the plane. Ten hours and fifty-five minutes, to be exact. With Ellie Holcomb's sweet music piped into my ears via earbuds, I stared out the window and tried to process the last twenty-four hours. And while I was at it, there seemed to be good reason to take stock of more than the last three months.

The truth was, I'd made a truly epic mess of my life.

Sure, I wasn't in prison or anything. But somehow I'd let guilt and perceived expectations dictate my life. When I hadn't gotten what I'd wanted—Éric and a career in a restaurant kitchen—I'd let myself fall into my life choices, rather than make them myself.

I'd allowed my guilt to keep me from being honest with Nico, and honest with myself. I'd allowed my fear to keep me from a healthy relationship with Neil.

Deep shame washed over me.

This wasn't who I wanted to be. It wasn't who God wanted me to be, but I'd been so busy feeling some strange combination of frightened and responsible that I'd stopped listening to him. Instead, I'd let the strong tide that was my family and Marti carry me along.

I thought of Grand-mère and her table. I remembered what I'd told Nico about it, those months ago.

She willed the table to me.

Had it been intentional? Had she left her secrets behind, loosely hidden, for me to find? I'd never know, of course, at least not in this lifetime. But in my gut I knew that Grand-mère's secret story held wisdom that was meant for me.

Was that why I'd chosen not to tell my family? Maybe it wasn't really to protect my mother. Maybe it was because I knew I needed to discover grand-mère's story and to hold its truth close to my heart before sharing it with others.

I landed at Charles de Gaulle airport at 11:25 in the morning, around the time that Parisian minds begin to turn to lunch. I picked up my little rental car—a sunny little Fiat—and called Sandrine to check in.

Rather than make the six and a half-hour drive fresh off the plane, I told her I planned to get a hotel room, stay the night in Paris, and leave in the morning after a fortifying night's sleep.

Sandrine agreed wholeheartedly, offering to call a friend of hers with a hotel in the 4th arrondissement to see if she had room for me, before recommending a handful of restaurants, shops, and markets to visit before heading her way.

First, I would attend to lunch. I negotiated my way southwest on the A3 toward the 4th, just in case Sandrine's lead did pay off. Once I'd reached the 4th, I pulled off onto the side streets, parked, and walked until I found something that appealed for lunch.

Sandrine called me back while I was, admittedly, plowing through my second buckwheat crepe. "My friend had no room, but *her* friend, across the street did. So go to le Petit Hôtel, ask for Inès, and tell her Léa sent you."

I agreed, but not before eating a dessert crepe and walking down the street.

I did spare a moment to stop at a spice shop for a couple of items to add to my pantry collection.

Somehow, walking down the street in Paris made me feel as though I understood Grand-mère just a little better. I imagined her as a young woman, attending culinary school, away from the family château for the first time and loving her taste of freedom.

The funny thing was, I came from a long line of women who wrote their own stories. Grand-mère attended pastry school. My mother left France to go to America and married an Italian in the process.

And then there was my father, who left his brothers in Italy to open a restaurant of his own in the Pacific Northwest.

Why was I so afraid of forging my own path?

Le Petit Hôtel turned out to be only a short distance away, but I reparked my car all the same. Inès greeted me with enthusiastic kisses on the cheek, welcoming me to Paris, wishing me all the best in Montagnac, and inviting me to stay with her upon my return.

"If you bring me some of Sandrine's honey, I will discount your room. Léa has lorded that honey over me for too long!"

I finally conceded to my travel weariness and napped in my hotel room. Upon waking, I showered off the travel grime I'd accumulated over the last twenty-four hours.

Looking out the window, I could see Parisians walking home from work. They wouldn't consider dinner for at least another two hours—it was only six o'clock, after all. I ticked back the hours.

Around nine. Nico would be awake, so I called.

"How's France?" he asked, sounding almost casual enough to make me think he'd forgotten that we'd parted in anger.

"French," I answered. "We need to talk."

Nico yawned. "I haven't had any coffee yet."

I rolled my eyes. "Too bad. Here's the thing. Mom and Dad met on an airplane. While emigrating from separate countries. It was crazy, and Mom's dad hated it. But they loved each other, and they made it work."

"Jules—"

"You're my brother," I said gently. "And I love you. But I have to make my own choices and choose my own mistakes, and I need you to respect that. I'm not asking you to agree; I'm asking you to give me room to figure myself out. As it happens, I think I'm more of a late bloomer than I ever realized.

"Secondly," I continued, "you should know that Éric and I dated for a year when he was your sous-chef."

I stayed silent for a moment to allow Nico time to absorb that tidbit.

"I felt guilty for a long time because we broke up...and he left. I felt like it was my fault that L'uccello Blu failed—"

"No, Jules," Nico interrupted. "It wasn't your fault."

"I'm still processing that. I saw Éric in Seattle, between flights."

"How is he?"

"Good. He wanted to know if you were dating your female pastry chef."

Nico snorted. "You're making that up."

"I swear on my signed edition of *The French Laundry Cookbook* I did not."

"I should go visit him."

"He'd like that. Thirdly, I might go off and move away. Maybe to Memphis, although Neil and I broke up. Maybe somewhere else. I might even move to Paris. I need you to be okay with the fact that I might leave."

Nico sighed. "What would I do without you?"

"For the love of all that is holy, how many times do I have to tell you to take Clementine out on a date?"

"You're really stuck on that," he said dryly.

"I am."

"You're stubborn."

"So are you," I answered lightly. "Are we okay?"

He sighed. "You really liked that Neil guy?"

"He was the one who suggested I reevaluate my work life, when my work life was causing me to vomit in the greenroom at the *Portland Sunrise* studio."

"Huh? All right, then."

"We're okay?" I repeated.

"You're my sister, Jules. We're always okay. You stay safe over there."

I drove south to Montagnac the next morning. I took in the house, surrounded by oaks down the drive and fields of lavender all around. Château de L'Abeille, where my grandmother had grown up.

The sound of the bees filled my ears the second I stepped out of the car. It was the sound of pollination, of new life, of change. I loved it.

A woman stepped out from the front door and waved at me with a dishtowel in hand. She looked a lot like Sophie, with her fine blond hair and pale eyes.

"*Bonjour, Juliette! Ça va?*" Sandrine wrapped me in a hug, complete with double kisses. "How was your drive? How was the room at Inès's hotel? The jet lag—do you need coffee? Come, come inside. Welcome to Château de L'Abeille. We are so excited to have you, Maman and me."

"I am so glad to be here." I looked all around, taking in the views. "I forget how beautiful it is."

"Yes, it is beautiful, *non?*" Sandrine agreed, looking around with her hands on her hips, the picture of a satisfied proprietress. "You were quite small when you were here last."

"I'm happy to pay for a room," I said as we walked inside together. "I know this is peak season for you."

"*Non non, jamais.* There is plenty of room in the family wing. There is room—you will see. The farm makes enough money that we don't have to use the entire château as an inn to make ends meet. Also, I am a very good cook. So I never allow more than six guests at a time. I charge a great deal for my cooking," Sandrine stated, with a dramatic amount of eyebrow waggling, "and nobody complains. *Bon.* I will take you to your room, and then you must see Maman. She will be glad to see you. Hearing of Mireille's death saddened her, *naturellement.*"

"I would love to ask her questions about my grandmother," I said, clutching my suitcase. "About her youth."

"*Oui oui.* You must know that she has *la maladie d'Alzheimer.* How do you say it? The Alzheimer's disease. Some days are good, but other days she thinks I'm the new kitchen maid." Sandrine shook her head. "I am lucky she was always kind to the kitchen maids."

"I'm so sorry."

Sandrine lifted her shoulder in a very French shrug. "*C'est la vie. Voilà—* here are the family rooms. The toilet and bath are down the hall." We stopped at the first room, finished with yellow toile wallpaper and accented with a vase full of lavender buds.

"It's lovely," I said, wheeling my suitcase inside.

Once I was situated, Sandrine took me to see Grand-tante Cécile.

"*Coucou,*" Sandrine called as she rapped on the door with her knuckle. "*Maman! Juliette est arrivée, la petite-fille de ta soeur, Mireille.*"

I looked over Sandrine's shoulder at Cécile. She held court in her sitting room, which overlooked the lavender fields from south-facing windows. When Grand-tante Cécile turned, she took my breath away. Her resemblance to Grand-mère was undeniable. Cécile's hair was soft and downy white. Though her face was wrinkled, her delicate bone structure still showed through.

The genes in my family certainly ran strong—which was, of course, one of the reasons I was there. If I was lucky, Cécile might remember.

"She and my father spoke English together," Sandrine said as we entered the room. "So they could say things without me understanding when I was young. Some days she still has English, sometimes not. It is the same with everything. And her hearing—it is best to speak up."

"*Sandrine!*" Grand-tante Cécile's face lit up when she saw us enter the room. "*Entrez, entrez! Asseyez-vous ici avec moi! Venez et partager un morceau de gâteau avec une vieille dame.*"

I smiled. "You're not old," I said. "*Vous êtes très, très jeune, Grand-tante Cécile.* I'm Juliette, Mireille's granddaughter," I continued, testing out her English. To my relief, Cécile nodded.

"Yes—you look just like her." She patted my hand. "So pretty. You have the same eyes."

My eyes had to be the only similarity—I was tall, curvy, and dark, where Mireille had been fair, lithe, and petite. But the eyes, well, I wasn't about to argue.

"*Très bien,*" Sandrine said, clasping her hands to her waist. "I must return to the inn. The kitchenette is just around the corner, if you'd like tea or anything else to eat. *À plus tard.*" She gave a small wave and left.

"I'll be here for a few days," I said, reaching into my bag. "I would love to chat with you about my grand-mère Mireille."

"Ah, Mireille." Cécile shook her head. "Unlucky, that one."

I froze. "Oh?"

"Would you like cake? It's very good, made with lavender and honey from the château. Our eggs, as well. Not everybody can make a perfect cake, but Sandrine can. Your grandmother could also. She could put something in the oven, leave, and we would be sitting and talking. And then all of a sudden, she would jump up"—Cécile raised her hands in the air—"and she would go and take whatever it was out of the oven. It would always be perfect. She was a very good baker."

I gave a bittersweet smile. "Yes, she was."

"Oh, she made Papa so furious when she insisted on going to pastry school in the city. It wasn't done, you know, at least not for a woman of good family. But she was stubborn, and Papa loved her best. So"—Cécile shrugged—"she went. Changed everything—just like Papa said it would." She turned away and looked out the window before sipping her tea.

"I was looking through some of Grand-mère's photos," I said, trying to sound as casual as possible. My heart beat hard inside my chest. "Not all of them are labeled. Do you think you could tell me," I said, pulling the photo from my purse, "who this is?"

Grand-tante Cécile plucked the photo from my hands. "*Oh là là.*" She shook her head. "*C'était si triste.* I have not seen this face for many, many years."

I didn't dare to breathe.

"His name was Gabriel Roussard." She studied the photo. "Your mother—

she was named for him, *naturellement*. Gabriel was…very handsome. To Mireille, he was the sun and the moon." She smiled. "And all the stars in the heavens."

"Were they together? *Des amoureux?*"

"*Oui oui, c'est vrai*—and they were married! Papa was so angry. She never told you?"

"She did not speak much of the past," I said. "But I wondered."

"Such a scandal!" She clucked her tongue.

"Was he my mother's father?"

"Oh yes, of course. Your grand-mère didn't marry Gilles until your mother was nearly two." Cécile shook her head. "Gabriel was a Jew, you know. But you saw—he was handsome. And Mireille adored him. So sad. Unlucky, my sister."

"What happened?"

Cécile sipped her tea and then made a face. "The tea is cold. I will go make more."

I stood up quickly. "I can make it."

"*Non non,*" Cécile insisted. "I will go. You're the guest. I'll be right back."

"*D'accord.*" I sat back down and watched Grand-tante Cécile as she made slow, careful steps down the short hall to the kitchenette.

I was right.

They were married, and Gabriel was my true grandfather. After all this time, to know—I could hardly take it all in.

A moment later the teakettle whistled, and I could hear the clinking of a teapot lid being removed and replaced. Seconds later, Grand-tante Cécile returned. "*Ah, bon. J'ai de la compagnie. Quelle fête pour une vieille dame comme moi.*"

Oh no. "Grand-tante Cécile? It's me. Juliette." I leaned forward. "Mireille's granddaughter, remember?"

"*Très bien, très bien. Vous êtes ainsi belle comme votre grand-mère. Mais, je parle qu'un petit peu d'anglais. Parlez-vous français?*" She smiled a beatific smile.

"Oui," I said, trying not to cry.

Just that quickly, she was gone. I drank the tea and conversed in French, trying to be jovial and light, rather than bitterly disappointed.

After tea, I walked along the edge of the east lavender field. I knew it could be like this, but having it happen broke my heart.

But rather than dwell on the disappointments in life, I listened to the hum of the bees.

Afterward, Sandrine and I discussed the visit. She told me that Cécile's good days were becoming fewer and further between.

Maybe I would get lucky again. I had a few days. And Sandrine told me that Cécile loved a long phone conversation—though she might forget to whom she was speaking halfway through.

I still had so many questions. Did Gabriel have family? Did any of them survive the war? Did I have cousins somewhere, cousins like Sandrine?

I didn't have the answers now. And that didn't mean I *wouldn't* have the answers later, only that I was to wait, to be patient, to listen.

There was a life lesson in there, somewhere.

I sighed.

There were some areas of my life where I could only wait. Others?

I could also take action. Up ahead on the path, I spied a bench, situated at the corner of the field, angled to face the lavender.

Phone in hand, I took a seat. Dialed Neil's number. Listened to it ring and then listened as his recorded voice promised to get back to me within a business day.

I carried on, undeterred.

"Hi, Neil. It's Juliette," I began. "And I'm in France right now. I'm sitting outside the château where Grand-mère grew up, and I'm looking at her lavender. I don't know that it's the same lavender, but it may be clones of the original lavender plants. Sorry. Anyway, I just wanted to call and tell you"—I paused to breathe in—"that you were right." Then I breathed out. "I didn't know what I wanted. Well, I've had some time to think about it, and here's the thing—I really love restaurants. Always have. But I also want you in my life. I don't know that I'll get to have both. But you asked what I wanted, and that's it. I want to work in a restaurant, and I want to be with you. And I hope—"

My phone beeped.

I pressed on. "I hope that maybe you'll forgive me and that we can figure out a way to try again."

Another beep.

"Even if it means me flying out to Memphis. But I want you to know, I have dreams. I haven't figured them all out yet, but I have them."

A third beep. I moved my phone from my ear.

I had an incoming call.

From Neil. With shaking hands, I transferred over. "Hi," I said, my voice wobbly.

"Hi, Juliette." Neil's voice soothed like warm maple syrup. "I've missed you."

"I've missed you too," I told him.

Looking out onto the lavender, I realized I didn't know what our future held, but I couldn't wait to find out.

PROVENÇAL LAVENDER AND HONEY POUND CAKE

For the cake:

1 tablespoon dried culinary lavender buds

3 cups flour

$^1/_2$ teaspoon baking soda

$^1/_2$ teaspoon sea salt

1 cup honey—lavender honey, if you can find it

$^1/_2$ cup sugar

1 cup full-fat yogurt

5 eggs

1 teaspoon vanilla bean paste or vanilla extract

$^1/_2$ cup poppy seeds (optional)

12 tablespoons unsalted butter (1$^1/_2$ sticks), at room temperature

For the glaze:

2 tablespoons honey

$^3/_4$ cup powdered sugar (or enough to reach desired consistency)

1 to 2 tablespoons hot milk

Preheat oven to 350°F. Butter a 10-inch loaf pan; dust with sugar.

In a spice grinder (a dedicated coffee grinder works for this—but don't use it if it's already ground coffee unless you want the cake to taste like coffee, which you don't), grind the lavender together with a tablespoon or so of sugar, and pulse until the lavender is finely ground. Set aside.

In a medium bowl, whisk together the flour, baking soda, and sea salt.

Pour 1 cup honey into a 2-cup glass measuring pitcher. Add 1 cup yogurt, and stir the honey and yogurt together. Set aside.

Separate the eggs into a large metal or glass bowl, placing the yolks in a separate small bowl. Beat the whites with a hand mixer until they form stiff peaks.

In the large bowl of a stand mixer, beat the butter, sugar, and lavender sugar together until pale and fluffy, about 5 minutes. Add the vanilla, and then add the yolks one at a time.

With the mixer running, alternate adding the dry ingredients and the honey-yogurt mixture three times, ending with the honey-yogurt. Fold in the poppy seeds, followed by the egg whites, and pour batter into the prepared loaf pan.

Bake the cake on the center oven rack for 1 hour or until a cake tester comes away clean. Allow the cake to cool on a wire rack for about 10 minutes, and then invert. Cool the cake completely.

For the glaze, heat the milk on the stove or in the microwave, and add to the honey. Beat the liquid ingredients together with the powdered sugar, and drizzle over the cooled cake.

Makes 12 to 16 servings.

Readers Guide

1. As the book opens, Juliette realizes that her life is in a rut. How do you think she got there? Have you ever felt that way?

2. When Juliette finds the photo, her first instinct is to keep it a secret. Why do you think she felt that way? What would you do if you found a clue to a family secret?

3. As time passes, Juliette finds that Neil is the person in her life she can confide in most, despite the fact they've not met in person. Why do you think she shares with him more easily than her friends and family?

4. On the surface, Adrian seems like the kind of guy Juliette is looking for. Why do you think Juliette is not interested?

5. As Mireille's story unfolds, we learn that she was even better at keeping secrets than Juliette. Why do you think she kept her secret? And why did she also keep the evidence?

6. Juliette shares camaraderie with Caterina and conflict with Sophie. Do you think it's easier to get along with people who are more similar to you or more different?

7. When her mother is in crisis, Juliette makes risotto to show love for her. What do you do when your loved ones are going through a difficult season?

8. As her feelings for Neil deepen, Juliette begins to panic. How do you think her relationship with Éric influences her feelings about the relationship?

9. After the tasting dinner, Adrian apologizes to Juliette. Do you think Juliette's opinion of him changed? Did yours?

10. In France, Juliette decides to take charge of her life. Do you think she'll be successful? What parts of the mystery are you most looking forward to discovering in the next book?

Acknowledgments

The year this book was written turned out to be profoundly eventful and difficult. Writing is hard enough, but writing under less than ideal circumstances is its own kind of heroic.

So too—arguably *more* so—is being the agent, editor, friend, and spouse to that author.

My agent, Sandra Bishop, is the kind of agent every writer ought to have in her corner—persistent, patient, tough, and encouraging.

Many thanks to my editor, Shannon Marchese, who brought me to WaterBrook Multnomah. She patiently waited on the manuscript and then helped me turn the story I'd submitted into the story it was meant to be. It is *so much better,* I can't even tell you.

Thank you to my line editor, Susan Tjaden, who was so supportive through the process of finding all the rough spots and making sure they were buffed out.

Thanks to Laura Wright and the copyeditors (good band name, no?). I could not do what you do, but I'm glad you can.

In the past, I've worked with a slew of early readers, but this book I kept very close (partly for practical reasons—it got rewritten a lot). Love and tea to Kara Christensen and Rachel Lulich, whose thoughtful responses and encouragement were so helpful during the writing process.

Thanks and curry to Maureen McQuerry and Stephen Wallenfels for their readings and critique as I shaped that doozy of a first act. Gratitude and molasses cookies to Joanne Bischoff for her encouragement as I wrapped my head around the rewrites. Thanks also to Jania Hatfield, who lent her legal expertise for a plotline that's no longer with us but was still much appreciated. And to my dear friends who will be reading this for the first time once it hits print (and e-book), thank you for your patience and grace.

Thanks and croissants to Carolyn McCready, who generously helped to develop the Mireille plotline.

Love and Tillamook Mudslide to my family for their love, support, and prayers through the submission, contracting, writing, and production process of this project.

Lastly, devotion and crème brûlée to my husband, Danny, who picked up Thai takeout, talked through plot points, and listened to (near) endless waffling as I named and renamed most of the characters. Seven years ago, though, he was the man I met online, the one I stayed up late e-mailing, despite the fact we'd never met in person. He was the man who didn't flinch when I told him I wanted to write books. From inspiration to process, this book wouldn't exist without him.

About the Author

Hillary Manton Lodge is a storyteller at heart. She is the author of *Plain Jayne,* a Carol Award finalist, and *Simply Sara,* an ECPA best-selling book. A graduate of the University of Oregon's School of Journalism, Hillary discovered the world of cuisine during an internship at *Northwest Palate* magazine. In her free time she enjoys experimenting in the kitchen, watching foreign films, and exploring her most recent hometown of Portland, Oregon. She shares her home with her husband, Danny, and their Cavalier King Charles Spaniel, Shiloh.

A Selection from

Reservations for Two

A friendship can weather most things and thrive in
thin soil; but it needs a little mulch of letters and phone
calls and small, silly presents every so often—just to
save it from drying out completely.

—PAM BROWN

*T*he Provençal breeze tousled the ends of my hair as I tried to or-
ganize my thoughts. "I'm beginning to figure out what I want,"
I told Neil, my voice echoing slightly over the cell connection.

"Oh?"

"When you hang up and listen to the message I was leaving, you'll hear all
about it."

Neil chuckled, and I steeled myself. He had the best laugh. If I closed my
eyes, I could see the way his eyes crinkled at the corners, the way his lips turned
upward.

"You want me to hang up?" he asked.

"Nope."

"So why don't you tell me what you want?"

I shrugged and looked out onto the lavender waving in the breeze. "I want
the impossible. I want to love my job, and I want to be with you."

"Cool."

"Cool?" I lifted an eyebrow. "What are you, fifteen?"

Neil sighed. "Sometimes I feel like it. Here's the thing. We talked about this earlier—I have thousands of frequent flyer miles built up."

"Aiming to get your name on the side of a plane?"

"Not yet. I'd rather use them. And I'm at a good place to pause at work. Do you want company?"

"What?"

"I'll fly out there. You want us to be together? So do I, and spending time in Europe doesn't sound so bad."

"It's not a vacation," I told him. "There will be family members and family dinners and people with opinions. And that's just starting with the French family."

"Do you want me to come?"

"Yes, but—"

"Then I'll see you there."

I snorted. "You don't even know where I am."

"I know you're at Château de L'Abeille. I also know how to use Google."

"Well…fine. Be all smart like that."

"I love you, Juliette. I want you to know that."

Joy blossomed inside my heart. "I love you, Neil."

"Guess what?"

"What?"

"I'll see you soon."

I spent the next thirty-six hours expecting to get a phone call, an e-mail, or a carrier pigeon telling me that it wasn't going to work out. That Neil had been delayed, that he'd come to his senses.

Instead, I was setting the table for dinner when I saw a pair of headlights come down the long road toward the château.

"Either that's the German guests who haven't checked in yet," said

Sandrine, watching the window over my shoulder, "or your *copain* has arrived."

We watched together as Neil unfolded from his rental car, a Fiat like mine, and stretched his arms.

"Oh là là." Sandrine pressed a hand to her heart. *"Très beau."*

My heart fluttered and then burst with happiness when Neil spied me through the window, a grin spreading across his face.

I raced out the door and into his arms. "You came!"

"I told you I would." Neil pressed a kiss to my forehead. "All you had to do was ask."

We returned to discover that the table set for three had become a table set for two; Sandrine and Grand-tante Cécile had disappeared. Two candles flickered at the center of the table.

"I think Sandrine feels invested in our having a happy reunion," I remarked dryly.

"I can live with that." Neil tipped my chin upward and placed a gentle kiss at the corner of my mouth.

My fingers wove into his hair as I kissed him back.

We might have stayed like that forever if the sound of Neil's stomach hadn't broken the moment. "Sorry," he said. "I ate a baguette after landing. That was a few hours ago."

"Do you want to eat dinner?"

"It smells really good," Neil admitted sheepishly.

We sat and portioned food onto our plates; Neil poured the wine Sandrine had left open, a rich, full-bodied Bordeaux.

I told Neil about my time with Cécile, how she'd remembered just long enough to tell me about Gabriel Roussard, the man in the photo—Grande-mère's first husband and my grandfather.

"That's incredible."

"And Cécile confirmed that he was a Jew. That's why her family wasn't happy about it." I shrugged. "And then she got up to make tea, and when she came back, it was gone—she was gone, at least, the version of her that remembered her teens."

"It'll come back."

I shot him a wry glance. "I don't want to bank on her Alzheimer's feeling cooperative. She may well not remember, at least not before we leave." I shrugged. "I shouldn't be greedy—I still found out more than I would have on my own. Anything more is gravy."

Neil lifted an eyebrow. "I think I know you pretty well. I don't think you'll be satisfied with just a slice of the story. You won't stop working until you know it all, from the filling to the crust."

"That's very poetic of you."

"Thought you'd like that."

"I'm impressed. And you're right. I'm just…trying to pace myself. Set realistic expectations."

That evening I baked a batch of madeleines for our evening visit with Grand-tante Cécile. Neil and I brought the cookies to her sitting room on a tray, as well as a pot of strong black tea and an appropriate number of cups and saucers.

"Bonjour," said Cécile, putting her paperback novel down when she saw us.

"Bonjour," I echoed back, showing her the tray. "Would you like some tea?"

"Oh yes," she said, and I breathed an internal sigh of relief. Cécile's English came and went along with her memories. If she spoke English, she was more likely to remember.

We made small talk, and I gently reminded her who Neil and I were. After Cécile and I had each enjoyed at least one madeleine and Neil had eaten four, I ventured a question. "Where exactly did Mireille and Gabriel meet?"

"I don't know, *chérie,*" Cécile said, shaking her head sadly. "Mireille kept him a secret from the family for a long time. There might be something about it in the letters, though."

I sat up straight. "Letters?"

"*Naturellement.* Mireille and Gabriel wrote letters after she returned to the château. How else would they continue their attachment?"

"Um…a telephone?"

"Too expensive…calls from Paris. And besides, Papa wouldn't have it. Mail—she pretended to be writing a girlfriend she'd met in the city."

"Letters, then." I pleated my skirt between my fingers and tried my best to sound casual. "Tell me about them."

Cécile's eyes widened. "I knew she was hiding them, but one day I snuck into her bedroom and read them. They were *very* romantic," she said, leaning forward. "Passionate. I was shocked, of course, but not as surprised as everyone else when she returned to the city to marry the man."

Neil squeezed my hand.

"What happened to him?" I asked. In all likelihood, I already knew the answer. "How did he die?"

"Die?" Cécile's face went blank. "Who told you that?"

"Well…" My voice trailed off. Come to think of it, I had no records. I opened my mouth to say as much, but Cécile interrupted.

"I had a letter just last week from Mireille. She's with child, you know, and they just bought the loveliest flat. He's dead? Are you sure?"

"No." I patted her hand. "I must have been mistaken."

"Never speak lightly about such things! And Mireille with child…" She shook her head. "They love each other so much." Grand-tante Cécile leaned forward. "She's quite large with child, you know. She says she's not so far along, but it's not the first time a woman has given birth to a large baby early, *n'est-ce pas?*"

I pursed my lips together to keep from laughing. "True," I said. "So—Mireille and Gabriel are happy?"

"*Très joyeux.*" She shook her head. "My heart longs for a man to look at me the way Gabriel looks at her. Or," she added, her voice coy, "the way this Neil looks at you."

My face turned pink. Neil winked at me.

I tamped down the frustration inside me. Cécile remembered Gabriel for the first time in days, but only half the story.

I crossed my legs together at the ankle and tried to reorganize my mind into a new line of questions. "So, what is Gabriel's occupation?"

"He is a pastry chef. Mireille assured Papa that he is a very important pastry chef, working at Maxim's."

"What is he like?"

"Handsome—*tres beau*. They look well together—he with his dark hair, Mireille with her blond curls."

I smiled. I'd seen a photo of Gabriel; his resemblance to Nico was uncanny. "And they wrote letters. Did Mireille keep them all, you suppose?"

"She kept all the letters I wrote to her in Paris—she showed me. All tied up with a pink silk ribbon. She read them when she was lonely, she told me. I can't imagine she would part with Gabriel's letters."

"Where do you think they might be?"

"The window seat in the garret, of course," Cécile answered without pause. "It's where she kept all her secrets away from Papa." She leaned forward and took another madeleine from the plate. "These are very good. Mireille is such a good baker—I'd know her madeleines anywhere."

"She's very good," I agreed, while a mixture of pride and sadness stirred in my heart.

Neil and I tidied up Cécile's sitting room before we left; Sandrine arrived to assist her mother to bed. We wished them both a good evening and slipped out of Cécile's rooms and toward the rooms my grand-mère had used in her youth.

The garret above Grand-mère's rooms had once been used as servants' quarters, but had since become the storage nook for stray linens, pillows, lamps, and old clothes.

Neither Neil nor I spoke as we picked out a path to the window. The window seat looked just as Cécile had described; I removed the chintz cushion and lifted the seat.

"Oh," I breathed.

Letters. Bundles and bundles of letters.